"Folklore and mythology, as well as man's catastrophic disregard for nature, are the meat of Joseph D'Lacey's horror. But the prime cuts are always compassion and surprise."

Adam Nevill, author of The Ritual

"Joseph D'Lacey is one of our best new horror writers, delivering surprises, intensity, and scares aplenty with each new book. And with every book, he's upping his game."

Tim Lebbon, author of The Heretic Land

"Joseph D'Lacey has written a contemporary fairy-tale; here, in *Black Feathers*, you'll get everything you want to find in a work of dark, apocalyptic fiction: menace and magic aplenty, and characters otherworldly, scary and fantastic. A very special story, one to savour."

Paul Meloy, author of Islington Crocodiles

"A bold beginning to a new duology from the brilliant D'Lacey – where two children embark on a search for meaning that is riddled with ambiguity about the nature of the saviour they seek and which, ultimately, provides a siren call to live in harmony with the land."

Alison Littlewood, author of A Cold Season

"*Black Feathers* is poetic and compelling. It's a gripping story crafted around a deep core of eloquent anger. And it's scary – it's the scariest kind of fiction – the kind of fiction that rings true. D'Lacey has written a great book of and for our troubled times."

Tom Fletcher, author of The Leaping

JOSEPH D'LACEY

Black Feathers

THE BLACK DAWN
VOL I

**ANGRY
ROBOT**

ANGRY ROBOT
A member of the Osprey Group

Lace Market House,
54-56 High Pavement,
Nottingham,
NG1 1HW, UK

4301 21st St., Ste 220B,
Long Island City,
NY 11101
USA

www.angryrobotbooks.com
He who fears the Crowman

An Angry Robot paperback original 2013

Cover by Argh! Oxford
Set in Meridien by Argh! Nottingham

Distributed in the United States by Random House, Inc., New York.

ISBN 978 0 85766 345 0
Ebook ISBN 978 0 85766 346 7

Printed in the United States of America

9 8 7 6 5 4 3 2 1

*For Ishbel, without whose selflessness and support
the work could not have been done.*

PROLOGUE

When the final days came, it was said that Satan walked the Earth in the guise of a crow. Those who feared him called him Scarecrow or sometimes Black Jack. I know him as the Crowman.

I speak for him.

Across the face of the Earth, in every nation, great suffering arose and billions perished. An age of solar flares began, rendering much of our technology useless. The cataclysms that befell us, the famine and sicknesses, the wars – it was all the work of the Crowman, so they said. Yet it was ignorance that fuelled our terror of him and the rumours of his wickedness.

Ignorance and convenience; we needed someone to blame.

None who beheld the Crowman, whether in dreams or in reality, ever forgot him. Nor will he be forgotten now. We still recall his deeds of war and sacrifice. We tell his story to our children so that they may pass it on to theirs. Only in this way can we keep him close and dispel the lies. This you must understand: the Crowman is no more evil than you or I.

Hear his tale now. Take it to heart.

7

Though it pains me, I will tell it, clear and true.

I do not *want* to recount it. I do not want to recall the casting out of so much goodness, nor the reaping of so much pain. But, for the sake of all of us, I must and I will. Mark it well. Tell your kin and those you love his story. Tell them this: Satan walks nowhere on this Earth, nor has he ever, save where he treads within the human heart. Tell his story and let us keep the Crowman alive for as long as our kind walks the greening byways of this world.

Above all, make them understand one thing: the Crowman is real.

Where does his story begin? It begins in England, not really all that long ago. It begins with a nativity; the coming into the world of a special child. It was this infant who changed everything. This lonely boy, who became a man in the harshest of times; it was he who was destined to seek out the Crowman, only he who had the grace and strength to find him. It was this wondrous boy who revealed the Crowman to the world.

I am an old man now, broken and blind. But I still see the boy's journey. I see it with great clarity, as though I'm sitting on his shoulder or holding his hand. Sometimes I look out through his eyes, other times I watch from above. I see everything, even the things he couldn't. I find I want to shout to him, to push him this way or that, to warn him about what I know is coming. But I can't, of course. His story, and the story of the Crowman, is already over. It finished long, long ago and there's no changing any of it now.

All I can do is tell it. And in the telling, resurrect him for the good of all. For, without the teller, there is no tale. And without this tale, there can be no world.

PART I
AMONG CROWS

"Sometimes, when a bird cries out,
 Or the wind sweeps through a tree,
 Or a dog howls in a far-off field
 I hold still and listen a long time.

 My world turns and goes back to the place
 Where, a thousand forgotten years ago,
 The bird and the blowing wind
 Were like me, and were my brothers.

 My soul turns into a tree,
 And an animal and a cloud bank.
 Then changed and odd it comes home
 And asks me questions. What should I reply?"

HERMAN HESSE

"Scarecrow, scarecrow, fingers o' bone
 Here come the scarecrow
 Into your home
 Scarecrow, scarecrow, teeth o' glass
 Here come the scarecrow
 Let 'im pass

Scarecrow, scarecrow, eyes o' stone
Here come the scarecrow
When you're all alone"

"The high,
 the low
 all of creation
 God gives to humankind to use.
 If this privilege is misused,
 God's Justice permits creation to punish humanity."

1

I see the boy's birth.

There were signs; portents, if you will.

His two sisters were banished from the master bed-room where Sophie Black wished to give birth. It was upon the same bed where she had conceived the boy but for this, the moment of his introduction to the world, her husband was excluded. Sophie's closest friend, Amelia Porter, comforted her, squeezing her hand and massaging her sacrum with every accelerating contraction.

There was no sign of the midwife.

Downstairs, Louis Black paced the living room, checking his watch and sipping often from his whisky glass. He glanced at the inglenook and stooped to add a log to an already roaring fire. As he stood, he noticed the celebratory cigar poking from the breast pocket of his worn tweed jacket. He pushed the cigar out of sight.

On the mantelpiece stood a collection of photos. Louis's eyes were drawn to the tiny birth portraits of his daughters – wrinkled, red faces cocooned in white blankets and protected in the arms of their mother. A dozen times already Louis had thought of fetching the camera from his study. A dozen times he'd checked himself, deeming it hasty. Childbirth was dangerous, unpredictable.

He massaged his temples and took another drink.

Upstairs, in her older sister's bedroom, Judith couldn't sit still. She spun and danced while Angela sat cross-legged on the bed picking at the threads from a tear in the knee of her jeans.

"It's going to be a boy, Lella," said Judith.

"How would you know that? You're just hoping for a little brother you can fuss over."

"I dreamed about him. He'll have black hair and grey eyes."

"When did you dream that?"

"Can't remember," said Judith.

"You're making it up."

"Maybe I am. Want to see me skip backwards? I've been practising."

Lifting her arms with each step, Judith managed to skip backwards in a small circle. She stood, waiting for judgement and smoothing her fine hair back from her face. Angela didn't look up.

"What do you think, Lella? I can do a handstand too. But I have to be near the wall or I fall over."

"Mum has blond hair and green eyes. Dad has brown hair and blue eyes. We're both blond with blue eyes. It won't have black hair. And it won't be a boy."

Their mother's scream, from the other end of the corridor, left a hush in the room. Judith ran to the bed, climbed up and into the arms of her sister. A few moments later a longer cry pierced the entire house. Judith clung to Angela and whispered:

"It doesn't sound like her."

Judith felt Angela's warm cheek against her head. Her sister's hair smelled of shampoo and her cardigan was soft lambswool. Judith wished Angela would hold her more often until their mother howled again.

Judith cried out too, "You're hurting me."

There were deep red dents in the skin of Judith's arm. Angela released her grip a little but still hugged Judith hard.

"Sorry."

"It's OK, Lella. Was she like this with me?"

"I wasn't there. Maybe Dad knows. Come on, we'll ask him."

"But he'll shout at us. We're meant to stay up here."

Louis Black screwed the lid back onto a bottle of Dimple. When he turned he saw two pale faces.

"What are you doing downstairs?"

The moment lengthened, broken only by mellow crackles and hisses from the hearth. Louis smiled and they ran to him, Angela hugging his hips, Judith clutching one of his thighs. He placed his glass on the mantelpiece, knelt and put an arm around each of them.

"Is she going to be OK, Daddy?" asked Angela, trembling. "Her voice is so horrible. She sounds like... like an animal."

Angela began to cry. Seeing her big sister break down, Judith wept too. Louis Black guided them to his huge armchair and lifted them both up, one onto each side of his lap. He squeezed them to him and spoke in a deep, soothing rumble.

"Your mother is a very strong and healthy woman.

This is the third time she's done this, so she knows what she's doing. She'll be fine."

"But why is it hurting her?" asked Judith.

Louis sighed.

"Giving birth is painful. Anyone would cry out under the same circumstances."

"Does it always hurt?" asked Angela.

"Yes, always."

"I'm never going to have babies," said Judith.

"Or me," said Angela.

Louis nodded.

"A very wise decision. However, if no women ever gave birth again, all the people on Earth would die out."

"Why?" asked Judith.

Angela rolled her eyes.

"Duh! Because there would be no children born to replace them, stupid."

Louis's eyes silenced Angela but Judith had other questions.

"Does that mean that we'll have to have children even if we don't want to?"

"No. It doesn't mean that. The choice will be yours. Anyway, Jude, you're a little young to be thinking about it. But when the time comes, you'll know exactly what to do, just like your mother does. It's all perfectly natural and normal."

There was a vigorous rapping at the front door.

Louis stood, spilling the girls who followed him to the black-and-white tiled front passageway. Louis shivered and rubbed the chill from his arms. The girls sheltered behind him as he turned the Yale lock and drew open the door. Snowflakes and frosty air blew in.

Louis frowned at the weather. Filling the doorstep was a plump barrel of a woman in a navy-blue overcoat with the collar turned up. On her head was a starched white nurse's hat and in her right hand a battered leather medical bag.

"Mr Black?"

"Yes."

"I'm Frances Godfrey."

Louis blinked at her, blinked at the snow whirling around her.

"The midwife."

"Right, right. Come in."

He stood aside. Frances Godfrey was so broad he had to press against the wall to let her pass. She walked with a determined waddle and removed her overcoat in a series of impatient shrugs. Below it her nurse's watch lay upon a massive shelf of bosom. Her cardigan was ill-designed for such an enormous chest and it stayed back somewhere around her armpits. Louis noticed all this with a perplexed look and spent another few moments staring into the night. White flakes swirled in and out of view. A layer of powder an inch thick already coated the ground.

"Was this forecast?" he asked.

"I've no idea. Which room?"

"Sorry?"

"Which room is your wife in?"

"Oh, I see. First on the left at the top of the stairs."

"Nearest bathroom?"

"It's en suite."

"Fine. Will you be joining us, Mr Black?"

"Ah, no. No, I won't."

"In that case I shall see you later. I may call on you

to bring certain items from time to time. Will you be...
available?"

"Yes, of course."

"Some tea would be most welcome. I'm frozen to the
core."

She held out her overcoat, ice crystals becoming
beads of rain which dripped onto the hallway tiles.
Louis took the coat and she wobbled away from the
three of them, her feet pointing to ten and two. The
stairs creaked louder than usual as she climbed them,
her behind almost totally filling the gap between ban-
ister and wall. Her blue, drip-dry uniform crackled over
black nylon tights as she ascended. She drew the too-
small cardigan tightly around her against the chill. It
sprang open again straight away. Long before she
reached the bedroom, her pace had slowed and her
chest was heaving. As she raised her hand to knock, an
agonised stiletto of a scream cut them all.

"My god," whispered Louis. He took the stairs two at
a time. The midwife had already opened the door and
appraised the situation with a glance. She turned to
Louis and pushed him away.

"Stay out, please, Mr Black. This won't take long."

Louis had seen past her bulk, though, and he never
forgot the scene:

A freak gust had sucked open a window. Unexpected
winter breathed into the room. Snowflakes twirled in
and fell to the carpet. A fleeting impression of black
wings beating their way into the night was interrupted
by the curtains billowing inwards. In the reflective
black of the panes which remained closed, Louis saw
his own face, dazed by a glimpse of his wife.

On their bed, padded with layers of towels, Sophie

squatted with her hands thrust between her legs, intent on what was happening there. She wore the top half of an old pair of his pyjamas and was naked from the waist down. This was the position she most enjoyed when making love to him but beneath her now was a dark, wet stain of blood and mucus. Her ankles were streaked with fresh and drying spatters of her body fluids. Amelia Porter's hands were on Sophie's shoulders, either giving massage or merely support through her touch. Sophie's face, though shiny with tears, was not contorted by pain; she appeared to be concentrating. Louis was awed by the primal will he saw there. She screamed again, her face showing the strain, and his heart broke for her. His wife – so determined, so strong, so full of courage.

Then the midwife was closing the door on him.

"I'm sorry, Mr Black. You can be with her very soon. Why don't you go and put the kettle on?"

Louis shut his eyes, committing the scene to memory. It was sacred and extreme, both beautiful and base. A smell from the room lingered in his nostrils – the dry, almost Alpine chill of the air and the moist scent of Sophie's sweat and blood. My god, he thought again, there was a brininess to that smell; could it have been the smell of her tears? Perhaps the impact of the moment had brought some extra intensity to his perception. And those dark, beating wings at the window: surely just a misinterpretation of his own reflection in the glass.

Stunned, he walked downstairs.

His daughters stood unmoving in the hallway. They looked small and terrified. As he held his hands out to them and they began to walk towards him, there was one last scream from Sophie. It paralysed them all with its rawness. Louis could almost feel her throat bleed as it released that final, barbed howl. Some seconds later there was a smaller sound, also a cry, but that of an infant. The front door blew open and the panes of frosted glass in its upper half rattled in their frames when it smashed into the wall. The fierceness of the wind frightened the girls even more and they began to cry again. Louis walked to the front door, certain he'd closed it properly the first time. A living strength resisted him from the other side. He had to use his shoulder and much of his weight to make sure the lock caught and clicked.

He ushered the girls into the kitchen, filled the steel kettle and switched it on. From the cupboard he took down four tea mugs and arranged them on a tray. He made the girls get the tea bags and pot, sent them again for the milk and sugar. All this he did without being fully present, without conscious control, so that, when it was all arranged and the kettle had almost boiled, he barely knew how they'd done it.

There was a call from upstairs. It was Amelia.

"Louis? I think you'd better come up."

He walked up the stairs, aware that his movements were stiff and automatic. Amelia's face was tear-stained and full of care when he reached the top. She held the door open. The girls were right behind him but they waited on the threshold. The towels now lay in a tangled pile on the floor. Sophie was propped up with pillows, still in his pyjama top but now tucked under the bedcovers. In her arms she held what looked like a giant, mummified prune.

She smiled through crystal-tinted lashes.

"It's a boy, Lou. Our very own boy." She held the oblong parcel up high. "Say hello to Gordon Louis Black."

2

The girl erupts from the cover of the woods, scattering leaves, her face whipped by vines and tendrils. She feels no pain, only the imperative of flight and the animal will to survive.

Was it real? she wonders. Was *he* even there?

There are no answers.

To look back will waste vital moments. Focussing ahead she sprints for home through the cornfield, the stalks high and green around her, hearing nothing now but the rustle and snap of leaves as she passes, the tramp of her feet on the moist earth, the pounding circuits of her breath. She dare not even cry in case it saps her strength.

Her foot catches a fallen cornstalk. She takes long ungainly steps in an attempt to right herself and slides face first into the dirt. She's running again before she feels the pain of the soil-hidden flints which have pierced her palms and knees. Moments later the cuts make their presence known. The pain tightens her skin, slows her down.

She spits earth from her mouth and wills more speed to her legs.

The girl bursts from the cornfield, taking a few stalks with her into the meadow. The uprooted greenery falls away. Horses, cattle and sheep look up as she passes, before continuing to graze unconcerned. She's running uphill now, her thighs beginning to burn. At the top of the meadow there's a gate. She's already certain there won't be enough time to stop and open it. Not knowing exactly how, she vaults the gate, ecstatic to leave a barrier between her and it. *Him*.

She's in the village now, scattering chickens as she pounds down the main street. Faces look up and watch her pass. Someone shouts:

"Hey, Megan! You alright?"

But she's already left them behind.

And then she's at her parents' front door and through it and bolting it and leaning back against it. Panting, sagging to the floor. Crying.

Her mother wipes her floury hands on her apron and rushes to her daughter.

"Megan? Whatever's the matter?"

Sobs and gulps for breath have muted her. Megan's mother eases the girl to her feet and guides her to a chair. She ladles water from a stone ewer and hands it to the girl in an earthenware cup.

"Calm yourself down, Megan. I'm going to fetch your father."

Megan gasps and shakes her head.

"No, Amu... don't leave me."

"I'm not going anywhere, Meg. I'll ring the bell for him."

Megan's mother pushes open the kitchen window and uses a poker from the fireplace to whack a rusted metal tube hanging just outside. It releases a resonant,

melodious clang. Three short peals, the sign to come
home quick. And soon enough, Megan's father is
entering through the back, also panting, his face
creased with concern.

"What's happened?"

"I don't know yet. She's barely got her wind back.
Came in here like Black Jack himself was after her."

At that, the girl looks up and weeps anew.

Her father, a bear of a man with kind eyes and a gentle smile that even a chest-length beard can't hide,
comes to sit with his daughter at the table.

"It's all right now, petal. You're safe." He puts his
huge hand over hers and squeezes gently. "Tell me all
about it."

"I saw something… some*one*… in the woods."

"Who did you see?"

"I don't know."

"What did they look like?" he asks.

She looks at her mother again and puts her hand
over her mouth.

"Come on, Megan. If it's someone dangerous we
need to send people after them as soon as we can."

"Black."

That's all she says at first.

"What?"

"Black. All in black from head to toe."

Her mother and father exchange a brief glance.

"What else?"

"He…"

"It was a man?"

Megan nods and her blond hair shakes with the vig-
orousness of the movement. Her father's frown
deepens.

"He had a hat. A tall hat. It was flat on top – like a chimney. And his clothes were all black. A long black coat that poked out at the back. And black trousers and big, fluffy black boots."

"Fluffy?"

She nods again.

"Like… feathers or something. Black feathers. They came out of his sleeves and his collar too."

"And what about his face, Megan," asks her mother now. "Did you see his face?"

The girl nods. More slowly this time.

"It was like a bird's face. Pointy. And his eyes were grey. Like storm clouds."

Again, her mother and father look at each other. The father nods.

"You mustn't be frightened, petal. I'm going to fetch Mr Keeper."

"Mr Keeper? Why? I'm not sick, Apa."

"Mr Keeper has other responsibilities than tending the poorly. He knows things most folk don't."

"I thought he was a healer."

"He's that and more," says Apa.

"He can see into the weave of things," says her mother. "He'll know what's best."

Mr Keeper looks very odd.

Megan's never been this close to the man before but he's always been an object of fascination. He wears what Amu and Apa call a "boilasuit". For the winter there's a fur lining that buttons inside the boilasuit but in the October sunshine there's no need for it. The boilasuit is faded green and either it's too small for him or he's cut a few inches off the cuffs and legs. He wears no shoes and his hands and feet are always dirty. Mr Keeper wears a dun-coloured sack strapped over his shoulders which gives him a big humped back. The sack has many pockets sewn onto it and there are always interesting things poking out – strange plants that don't grow near Beckby village, small woven pouches with unknown contents, the bones of animals and the occasional brightly coloured feather. Megan always thought his bag was full of medicines but, now that he's been summoned to their cottage and knowing there's nothing wrong with her, she wonders what other purpose they might have.

Apa ushers him in, closes the door with a loud crash and then follows. A few folk have gathered outside the cottage, attracted by Megan's odd behaviour and the coming of Mr Keeper. Amu opens the door and makes eye contact with the bystanders. They all retreat.

Mr Keeper has had to duck to enter and now he shrugs his cumbersome pack to the floor. When he stands straight he's even taller than Apa and his hair is longer but much dirtier, matted and clumped together in what Megan thinks are called deadlots. As soon as he is inside their home she can smell him too. He doesn't wash, that much is clear, and yet he doesn't smell bad like the diseased, unwashed lunatics who wander from village to village begging scraps before moving on. He smells of work-sweat and of the very earth itself. He smells of dried wildflowers and wet sap. The whites of his eyes flash like lightning when he glances around and the wrinkles at their corners are deep and kind when he smiles – which he does as his gaze falls upon her.

"Megan," he says.

Is it a greeting, an accusation, a question? In her panic she doesn't know.

His tones are deep and soft, rumbling like the purr of a wildcat, soughing like wind through the trees. And she has a strong sense that Mr Keeper has not come alone. Even though there's nothing to see, she feels the lives of many things, or perhaps their spirits, moving around him as though he were their hub. She wants to trust him because she can see that trust is what Mr Keeper is all about. She wants to but–

"It's all right, little thing," he says. "I only want to talk with you. And after that… we'll see."

So saying, Mr Keeper approaches the heavy wooden table and sits on a small stool in front of Megan. His face is now about level with hers and she can smell his breath, all mint and wild fennel and smoke. The smell makes her pleasantly dizzy and a smile comes to visit the corners of Mr Keeper's mouth.

He turns to her parents.

"Do you wish to stay or would you rather be… elsewhere?"

Apa says, "I think she'll talk more easily if we're not here to distract her." He smiles at Amu and holds out his hand. "Come on, hen. Let's go for a walk."

When they reach the door, Amu turns back to Megan.

"Don't you be afraid now, Meg. Mr Keeper's here to help. You can tell him anything. Anything at all. Understand?"

Megan nods, but her stomach flutters.

3

On a Saturday morning near the end of October, when Gordon was two weeks old, the Black family were all outside in the rugged back garden. The scent of wild roses from the last blossoms lingered in the air. Aside from the snow flurries and gales of a fortnight earlier – events no one mentioned – it had felt like an endless summer. Mornings and afternoons were chill by now but it was still bright enough that none of them wanted to be indoors at the weekend.

Sophie sat in a deckchair reading a thriller. A wide-brimmed, floppy white hat kept the sun out of her eyes. Behind her on the terrace, well-insulated in his pram, Gordon slept. Angela was reading a magazine on a blanket on the grass and Judith was alternately running, skipping and dancing or stopping and losing herself for long moments in the tiny details of the life of the garden. For a full fifteen minutes she had been on her stomach watching wasps eat their way through a fallen pear. Each of them wore a skin-tight yellow and black uniform and walked with an agitated mechanical twitch. Their black antennae wavered unceasingly and their yellow mandibles cut through bite after bite of pear flesh.

Louis, walking past with a wheelbarrow full of hedge trimmings and fallen leaves, saw what she was doing.

"You be careful, Jude."

She looked up at him.

"They're like soldiers, Daddy. Look how pretty."

"They're not so pretty when they sting you. Don't get so close."

Mesmerised by the wasps and their work, she rested her chin on the backs of her hands.

"Judith."

"What, Daddy?"

"Back away from them a little, would you?"

Not looking up, she scooted backwards, somehow keeping her head on her hands. Her skirt rucked up, exposing the backs of her smooth thighs and white knickers. As young as she was he could already see her mother's shape in her. As he walked on towards the compost heap the wheelbarrow bumped up and down over the uneven grass, eliciting tinny rumbles. He wondered if Judith would still be so unselfconscious in ten years, and dreaded the complexities that time would no doubt bring.

When he'd dumped the load, he abandoned the wheelbarrow and walked over to Angela's blanket. She too was lying on her front, bending one leg up until the heel of her sandal touched her backside and then letting the leg straighten until the toe bounced off the grass. Louis squatted beside her and glanced at the article she was reading.

"Sports day diets?" He struggled to register the implications. "I'm sure we've got some *Bunty* annuals in the loft. Mighty Mo and Watson the Wonder Dog were great."

"I don't know what you're talking about, Dad."

"Wholesome children's books, Angela. Instead of pre-teen *Cosmopolitan*."

"It's not like that."

"How would you know?"

Angela tutted.

"It's just a magazine, Dad. I'm not turning anorexic."

When she said nothing else, Louis stood up.

"Fine."

He wandered over to Sophie's deckchair and sat down beside her on the grass. She didn't acknowledge his arrival.

"*You* still love me, don't you, Soph?"

He waited a long time for the reply.

"Hmm?"

"I asked you if, out of all the females in this family, you were the one who still loved me."

After a few moments, Sophie managed to turn her head from the seductive pages of her book.

"Female family what?"

"Forget it."

Rising, he walked the last few paces to the terrace where Gordon was warmly swaddled. He wanted to look into the lodestones of his eyes but the boy was deeply asleep, one tiny fist held beside his head in a baby power-salute. Louis smiled.

"I'm glad you're here, mate. Balances things up a bit. One day, we'll be able to discuss rugger and you can come home from school knowing there's a safe haven in your old man's study."

Louis thought about the suggestion. Half joking, he added:

"Don't take that too literally, by the way. I may be

working and not able to stop straight away. And you must always knock – everyone has to. But once you're in, well, *then* you'll be in the safe haven."

Suddenly content, Louis backed quietly towards the rear wall of the house and took in the scene; everyone who mattered in his life was arranged in this perfect landscape. He wished he could have had a painting, not a photograph but a unique painting, some rendering of his perspective that would seal in the satisfaction he felt in this moment of pre-autumnal perfection. Here was his family, his land and his life in silent rapture under a cerulean October sky.

Scanning the blue, he saw the tops of the trees and noticed one in particular, the horse chestnut that rose up to his left. It was the nearest tree to the house and had taken its share of damage over the years. Each winter it looked like it was dead and each spring the leaves came back leaving more and more branches bare. As he looked now, he caught sight of a large black bird sitting on the topmost barren branch. His satisfaction turned to ire and disgust. A haughty black crow was looking down on his son. A filthy carrion-eater.

An English vulture.

The crow hopped down to a lower branch, fixing Louis with a single obsidian eye. Louis frowned. Bold and unheeding of the presence of humans, the bird dropped from its perch and flapped to the lowest branch of the horse chestnut. The branch reached directly over Gordon's pram.

"Sophie."

When she didn't answer Louis didn't let the pause draw out.

"SOPHIE!" he shouted.

All of them turned around when they heard the command in his tone. Gordon woke up. Sophie struggled out from the sagging canvas of her deckchair.

Louis pointed.

"Have you seen this?"

"What? What is it?"

"It's a bloody enormous crow. They're evil. Have you seen them around here before? It's acting like it owns the place."

"I... I don't know. I suppose so. I think they're always around."

The crow floated down onto the edge of the pram like a kite of black silk rags, its talons curling over the navy-blue, waterproof fabric. For a moment, no one moved. Unconcerned, it regarded each of them without expression. Only when it lowered its head to test Gordon's blankets with its sharp beak did Louis rush at it, flailing his arms and screaming.

"Get away. Get out of it, you fucking *vermin*!"

The crow bated at the air but didn't take off until Louis was less than a couple of paces away. Finally it let go of the pram's rim and flew up. Gaining height fast, it rose once more to the topmost branch. There it perched, cool and untouchable, its tiny black eyes fixed not on Louis but on Gordon.

"Don't tell me you've left him out here alone, Sophie. Don't tell me you've just popped into the kitchen to put the kettle on and left him out here on his own for even a moment."

"I don't remember doing that. I might have, but only–"

"Don't say any more." Louis tried to hold on to his anger. His face was sick and grey. Gordon was crying now: a wail of fear and shock. It moved Sophie to run to him but Louis didn't even hear it. "You don't have any idea, do you?"

"Any idea of what, Louis? It's only a bird."

In the garden, both the girls had returned from the reveries that had so recently allowed them to ignore their father. They lay still in the places where they had been, but now they were jack-knifed on their sides and silent for other reasons than simple absorption. They shrank into themselves, hoping that their father wouldn't notice them and make them the target for his anger. Louis Black's rage was a rare thing but that didn't make it easy to forget. They watched as his eyes drove spikes into their mother, a figure who could usually ward off any of Louis's moods. He approached her and pointed again into the top of the horse chestnut tree as she knelt beside Gordon, trying to placate him. He spoke quietly and clearly, containing his fury.

"That 'bird' is a killer. At the very least, it is a maimer of the defenceless. Crows, ravens, rooks, jackdaws, magpies – all of them – are carnivorous opportunists. They peck the eyes from the heads of newborn lambs given half a chance. And ravens are hunters; they'll attack and kill small animals. And yet you let our child, our only son, lie out here unprotected, with one of them just waiting for us to turn our backs."

"Oh, come on, Louis. I'm sure it wouldn't–"

"Sure?" he screamed. "You're sure? What the hell would you know? You may enjoy the countryside, but you don't understand the first thing about it. I grew up on a farm and I've seen newborn lambs wandering blind with blood pouring from their empty eye sockets. Lambs with crows still sitting on their backs, waiting for another peck of flesh. Don't tell me what you're bloody sure of, right?"

Sophie was crying now, dismayed by his ire and terrified by the images. Angela and Judith cried their tears as silently as they could, fearing what might come next and not moving in case they caught his attention. The shouting didn't stop.

"Take the baby in the house right now and don't you ever leave him unattended in the garden. Never. Understand?"

"But Louis, I never knew—"

"I don't want to hear it, Sophie. You've risked my boy's life."

"He's my boy too," she half sobbed, half screamed at him.

Louis advanced.

"Get him in the bloody house now." He turned and caught sight of the girls. "You two. Inside. Go to your rooms until I say you can come out."

Sophie carried Gordon to the living room. He was screaming as loud as his tiny lungs would allow, barely drawing breath between each cry. She held him against her chest and bounced her knees, gently patting and stroking his back all the while.

"It's OK, honey, it's OK. Daddy was afraid for you and sometimes when he's afraid he gets angry. But it's OK, it's OK. Come on now, Mummy's going to keep you safe. You'll always be safe and we'll always take care of you. Oh yes, we'll always take care. Always, always, always. Settle down, my baby boy, settle down. Mummy loves you, we all love you and soon all the anger will go away, I promise."

On and on her soothing words went and it was the

tone, perhaps, more than the content that slowly calmed Gordon down. The girls, each silent and pale in their own rooms, heard their father stomp along the corridor to his study. They heard the clicking of the key in the glass-fronted cabinet and the sound of him breaking, loading and snapping shut his shotgun. Determined footsteps sounded back along the upper hallway and down the stairs at a trot. They ran to their windows and saw him emerge into the garden.

Sophie, too, saw him as he stalked from the terrace onto the grass not far from where she'd been sitting. She watched him raise the shotgun and take aim and she glanced up at the tree where the crow still perched, looking unconcerned. The girls at their windows also saw the crow. It wasn't looking down at their father or his gun. It didn't appear to sense any danger at all. Instead it seemed to be watching them. At the final moment, it looked earthward, but not at Louis. Sophie was certain it peered down through the living room window at her and Gordon. It opened its wings but not to fly; it looked as if it was settling itself into a more comfortable position.

When the shot came it was as though they'd all for-gotten what happened after a loaded weapon is pointed at a target, had never heard the sound of Louis firing his shotgun at the rabbits and wood pigeons they some-times ate. Sophie jumped back from the window, and Gordon, who had been near to sleep, snapped his eyes open to his second shock of the day. Upstairs, Angela and Judith started back too. All of them saw the puff of black feathers and splintered dead wood spray upwards from the crow. All of them saw it fall slowly from its perch, gathering speed until it thumped to the grass, bouncing once before coming to rest.

Louis approached the dead bird and saw how the tiny seeds of scorching lead had shredded one of its wings, torn a hole through the upper portion of its chest and taken half of its beak off. Ruby beads dappled its silky, coal-black feathers. He let the shotgun droop downwards and everyone jumped a second time as he released the projectiles from the second barrel into the fallen crow. Its body was spread out and flattened by the blast. More feathers flew into the air, some settling, others levitating on a soft breeze that had sprung up.

For the rest of that day, Gordon cried. Not the screams of shock he'd first made, but mournful wails that frightened Sophie and made her worry he was sick. Louis retreated to his study to clean his gun and be away from the people he'd hurt with his anger. He left the crow's body where it had fallen as a warning to other winged opportunists and also to his family. As was the way on the occasions when Louis Black lost his temper, it was Sophie who fetched the girls from their rooms because he'd forgotten about them. Louis drank whisky from the Dimple bottle in his study cabinet and spent the night on the small leather couch in the bay window, having swept all his files and papers onto the floor.

I do know the land, he had told himself again and again, I know the behaviour of carrion eaters. But he was afraid they would all think he'd over-reacted. It was strange that the crow had been so bold, not flying away even when it had seen the gun. He tried not to think about it, but the memory of it sitting there as if he did not exist wouldn't leave him until he collapsed half-drunk onto the couch and slept.

4

The cottage door shuts and Megan hears the sound of her parents' footsteps receding over the dusty track through the village. Down in the direction of the Usky River most likely, where they've always loved to walk and where, they sometimes tell her, she was created in the third quarter of the moon during the snows of February.

Mr Keeper is smiling as if he knows all these thoughts of hers.

"You've been to Covey Wood today," he says. "I can smell its soil on you. And you still echo with the chatter of the oaks."

"The oaks talk?"

"Oh, yes. Constantly. You'll hear them one day, I'm sure."

Megan's eyes widen.

"I think I'd like that."

"Well, sometimes you get to wishing they'd shut up, but it's great at first."

Mr Keeper is smiling and the lines beside his eyes have deepened into kindly cracks and his teeth are showing, much whiter and straighter than any she has seen, and it doesn't seem to matter anymore that she can't tell the difference between the tan and the dirt on his forehead.

"It's OK to tell me what happened out there, Megan. I have a sense that whatever it was is very important. That's why I've come to see you. But I don't want you to tell me a single word of it, not a breath, unless you can promise me faithfully right now that you won't leave a single detail out of your story. Can you do that, Megan?"

Megan nods.

"I need you to swear it, little thing. I need you to swear it on the body of the Earth Amu."

She doesn't hesitate.

"I swear it on the body of the Earth Amu, Mr Keeper. I will tell you everything."

His smile lines concertina even more and she suddenly realises that Mr Keeper is ancient. In spite of his height and his strong back and the speed at which he marches, Mr Keeper is a very old man indeed.

And Megan, careful to begin at the beginning and end only at the end, tells this very old man her story, without missing out a single detail.

"It started a couple of moons back. In the night country I dreamed about a boy. He was beautiful. I've never seen anyone like him in the day world, so I knew he was special. He was standing next to my bed looking down, and even though there was only moonlight to see by, I saw his face more clearly than I see yours right now by the light of Apa sun. His skin was as pale and smooth as the stones in the river. His eyes were grey as moon dust – I don't know why I say that but I know it's true – and they shone just as bright as the moon itself. His hair, well, I've never seen anything like that either, Mr Keeper. Black as Tor Caves on a winter's midnight. So black it was blue. And it shone too. His skin, his eyes, his hair; lit up my dream like purest starshine. He made me feel a little strange. I suddenly thought maybe not all boys are only good for wrestling and playing ball and hunting. Maybe there's other things they're here for. He made my chest fill up with something, like I had something to give away to him – to everyone – but whatever it was, it was stuck there for the moment, with no way to come out. I looked down at myself and I'd grown lovely soft mams as big as my amu's and I had hair on myself just like my amu. I felt lovely, Mr Keeper. It was the boy who brought them to me, so they only existed in the night country at first, but now…" She glances down shyly at the obviousness of her chest, "Well, they're real. They're coming. I shall be a woman soon enough."

Megan is crying. She doesn't know why. She's smiling too. Nothing makes any sense. But Mr Keeper doesn't say a word. He merely nods, and the nod says he understands everything she's telling him. Understands it better than she can now or perhaps ever will. She wipes away the tears with a knuckle and continues:

"Then, just this evening past, the boy brought me another night country gift. It was a feather, quite long and thin and straight, but shimmering blue-green in the moonlight. It was the tail feather of a magpie. He touched it to my forehead and suddenly I wasn't in my bed any more. Just for a moment – and I thank the Great Spirit that's all it was – I saw a man bound to a twisted old black tree, a tree long dead, I reckoned. The man was suffering a great torment at the hands of his captors. It was so terrible, what they were doing to him, that the moment the boy took the feather away, I forgot it. All I know is that they intended to kill this man and they wanted him to suffer. They wanted his death to be so awful it would be a lesson to us all.

"When the boy took the feather from my forehead, I was weeping. He gathered up my tears with the tip of the feather and flung them out of the window. The next thing I knew, my tears were sparkling in the night sky with a thousand other stars."

Megan shakes her head as she remembers.

"He was a bearer of gifts, that boy."

She puts a hand to her chest.

"And then he left. I couldn't bear to see him go so I got up and followed him. He was too quick, though. He flew. Somehow, the night gave him wings. By the time I was out of the front door, he was gone. I was so sad. And then I looked down and there on the track outside the door was the magpie feather. It was pointing out of the village, in the direction of Covey Wood. I made a promise to myself in the night country, then. I promised I would follow the boy to Covey Wood. Then I went back to bed.

"Come the morning, I'd forgotten all about the beautiful boy and his gifts and even my promise. You know how the night country is."

Mr Keeper's eyes gaze deeply into hers. He seemed to lose himself for a moment.

"Oh, yes, little thing. I know how it can be. I know it very well."

"When we'd cleared up the breakfast and Apa had gone to the fields, I decided to go for a walk. I found myself wandering to the meadow and saying hello to some of the animals. And then I walked around the high cornfield to the borders of Covey Wood. I remember thinking how dark it looked inside and how the wind flapped the leaves of the cornstalks ever so gently. The day felt lazy outside of the wood. But the breeze didn't seem to penetrate the trees, so inside the wood all was silent and still. I was frightened to go in there."

"But you went in nonetheless, little thing."

"I did. I know I had a choice. I could have turned around right then and headed down to the river to skim stones and paddle my feet in the pools. But I had this feeling in my chest, Mr Keeper, like it was full up to burst. I didn't understand it at all. But I had a sense I'd find the answer in Covey Wood. Seems silly now, that does."

"There's nothing silly about it," says Mr Keeper. "It was the night country breaking through into the day. It wanted you to return to the darkness even in the light. It wanted you to enter shadow. And, more than that, it wanted you to keep your promise. When you speak, little thing, the world listens. The Great Spirit, the Earth Amu and every other living thing hears your voice. Never forget that."

He takes a pouch from one of the many pockets in his boilasuit and a pipe from the top of his sack. He fills the pipe with a moist-looking herb and lights it with a burning stick from the stove fire. Once he has resumed his position on the stool and blown a few puffs of strange-smelling smoke at Megan – deliberately, she thinks – he says:

"What was your decision?"

"I walked towards the wood and the nearer I got, the

more puzzled I was by the shadows in there. Or the
light. It's difficult to explain. Inside the wood, it was a
different day to the day it was outside. The wood was…
charmed somehow. But it was dangerous too."

Megan sighs.

"I'm trying not to miss anything out, but it's hard to
describe."

Mr Keeper blows a big smoke ring and pops three
smaller ones through it before they all unravel.

"You're doing fine, little thing. I can tell you're keeping your promise, so don't worry. Once it's all out and
we've talked about it, you'll feel better. You'll feel
clearer. Right now it's all still muddy, isn't it?"

"Muddy. Yes, it is."

Megan stands up and fetches water from the ewer.
Even now she stands on the threshold of the forest and
does not want to enter. Mr Keeper is patient. She offers
him water but he declines with only a tiny shake of his
matted head. Megan resumes her place on the chair
and continues.

"The air inside the wood wasn't cool like I'd imagined it would be. It was warm, as though the sun had
made an oven of it. It was a lovely feeling to be so…
embraced. Entering the wood was like being welcomed
into the arms of strangers in a distant land. It's funny,
Mr Keeper. I've been in Covey Wood a hundred times
but I've never felt like that before."

Megan takes a sip of water and replays the events,
making certain that this part, most of all, is as accurate
as she can possibly make it.

"Time felt strange. Falling leaves took forever to
touch the ground, then moments later, I'd notice the
sun had shifted. I found a fallen tree. The roots were

exposed and the way they met the trunk made a natural place to sit. All I wanted to do was watch the magic of the wood in comfort for as long as the spell lasted. I climbed up and it became my throne. I sat like a princess surveying the territory that might one day be hers.

"Everything the sun touched lit up from inside and suddenly it was brighter in the wood than it had been under a clear sky. It doesn't seem possible now. The leaves of the oak trees glowed and where the shafts of sun touched the ground, those places were like pools of molten gold. I was tempted to dip a toe, but everything felt so fragile I stayed as still as possible. I didn't want to break the spell.

"My body felt strange too. The fullness in my chest was only part of it. The crown of my head was fizzing like a pint of ale and warmth spread down from there all the way to... well, all the way down. Everything was tingling, and then a buzz started. I thought it was a swarm of bees coming through the wood but the buzz was inside me. All the way through me. And the buzz got harder and stronger and I got scared it might do something to me – hurt me somehow.

"The moment I got frightened, some of the light went out of the wood and the buzzing went away. The whole thing was a trick to get me alone and far away from the village. Far enough that I'd be easy prey for that... man. That... thing."

Mr Keeper taps out the used herbs from the bowl of his pipe into his hand and places them into one of the many pockets of his boilasuit. Megan frowns at him.

"Ash can be sacred too," he says, as if that is some kind of explanation. "Now do tell, little thing. Tell me about this man. This *thing* that you saw. Leave nothing out, mind, or you'll be breaking your very important and significant promise."

"I've told you. I won't break my promise. Otherwise I wouldn't have made it in the first place."

Mr Keeper nods. Almost a bow. She finds, to her surprise, that she is happy to have pleased this man who, until a short time ago, had been no more than an odd character in the village. Not a stranger exactly but an unknown force. And he is powerful, she realises now that he is sitting so close to her. She also realises that much of his power comes from his ability to hide it from people. Now, Megan feels quite sure, he is allowing her to see what he's really like. It makes her feel special.

"So. Tell me what you saw and then we'll know, won't we, little thing? We'll know how we must proceed."

That's the first time in all of this – since the dreams, since the walk, since seeing what she saw and even since being alone with Mr Keeper – that she's felt all this has some inevitability about it. Things have been set in motion and now she must deal with the outcomes. What they might be she can't imagine, isn't sure she even wants to. From inside her a tiny voice says, This is what it means to grow up.

She doesn't really know if it's her voice but she knows it's true. No wonder she's afraid. She had no inkling when she woke up this morning that she would be taking her first steps into womanhood before the day was out. Her tone is suitably affected by the possibility.

"A cloud must have passed over the sun because the wood turned dark. The heat went out of the day. But I didn't even have time to shiver before that cloud passed and the sun was back, pouring into the wood through every crack in the canopy. But it was different afterwards. Things weren't on fire from the inside any more. Nothing glinted. Everything magical had fled. All that remained with me was the swollen feeling behind my breastbone, and that was just uncomfortable.

"And then he… it… appeared.

"He arrived like a player stepping from the wings of a stage. And for a few moments I wasn't frightened. I just watched him. He could have been a fool or a character in a comedy.

"He was there for me. That much was clear. He faced me, took off his tall, flat-topped hat and bowed my way. Bowed very low he did, as though mocking my thoughts of being a princess. I thought I was in my own little world but I wasn't. Not at all. I suddenly felt like it was his world I'd stumbled into, made myself at home in, elevated myself in. I was embarrassed and I was angry.

"He stood in a patch of brightness, a shaft of sunlight just for him. And the more I looked and the more I realised what I was seeing, the more my anger and embarrassment turned to fear.

"It was a man. At least, I thought it was to begin with. He was tall and thin with a proud chest. He wore black from head to foot: the black hat, of course, and about his shoulders a coat of black plumes which dropped to below his knees. The coat was open, though, and I could see his tight black trousers over his slender legs. The bottoms of his trousers splayed out over his boots, making them seem huge. At his cuffs, too, sprouted sleek black feathers and the sun, gone cold somehow, caught them and twinkled there like quartz on velvet. The feathers obscured his hands. His black hair was long and silky, like it was wet. And his face…"

Megan puts a hand over her mouth as she remembers.

"I imagined all this, didn't I, Mr Keeper? I fell asleep on the fallen tree and dreamed it."

Mr Keeper is silent for a time. Perhaps Mr Keeper will stand up now, heave his pack onto his shoulders and leave, having satisfied himself that Megan had nothing important to tell him. That Megan – "little thing" – isn't ready to grow up yet. That was what this is about, isn't it? Her growing up? Her not acting like a little girl any more?

When he speaks, he is kindly.

"You'd every reason to be afraid. You can't see such a thing and not be. But fear is only a sign of something else, a marker on a path. You mustn't let it rule you. You mustn't let it push you off course. Finish your story. Take your time."

Megan meets Mr Keeper's gaze and holds it for the first time since he entered her family's cottage.

"It wasn't the face of a man. I don't know what it was. I saw so much in his expression that his features weren't clear. He was full of sadness and rage and knowledge. He was kind and compassionate and mysterious. But how could he be a man? One moment his face was human, the next it was animal – a bird face, with a beak and sleek feathers and all. And his coat extended behind him as though it was his tail feathers and he stooped forwards a little and took a few steps towards me and he looked for all the world like…"

She weeps the words into her hands. She knows what she's said but she hopes Mr Keeper hasn't heard her. He hasn't.

"Be clear, little thing. What face did he show you?"

Megan sits up straight and takes a deep breath. She doesn't hide her tears from Mr Keeper any more.

"He was a crow. A huge black crow, and somehow he'd made me think he was a man. He tricked me, didn't he, Mr Keeper? The devil's come to our village and he's tempted me into the woods. It's Black Jack out there, isn't it? Come to take my soul? Come to take me away from everything I've ever loved. Why? Why me? I swear I've never done anything wrong, Mr Keeper, I swear it to you. You know I keep my word and I tell you it's true."

Megan is babbling. She stands up from her chair in utter dismay and looks around, but she knows there's no place you can hide from the devil. When he comes calling, it's your time and that's the end of it.

Mr Keeper is smiling. If she didn't know better she'd say it was scorn he wore there, hanging between those hateful wrinkles.

"Black Jack comes for my soul and you think it's funny," she shouts, and then she's weeping again. "Great Spirit, what am I going to do?"

"What you saw today was the Crowman. Black Jack, the Scarecrow – they're his guises too, little thing, but he showed you his black feathers. He's come to give you a message. I think it's time we went and found your parents. But don't you fret. This has been a good day. Not just for you but for the whole village. It's not often we get a visit from the Crowman."

Mr Keeper stands up.

"Come on, little thing. We must find your apa and amu and tell them the news. There's much to do."

5

Sunday began, as cloudless and warm as the day before. When Jude and Angela had helped to clear away the remains of breakfast – a quiet affair in the aftermath of their father's rage – Sophie took Gordon outside again. She placed him as she usually did near the centre of the terrace and she sat down next to him in a straight-backed chair to do some sewing. She checked the treetop before she did any of this and even scanned the other trees in the garden for signs of birds. There were none. In the place where the crow had fallen, there was no sign it had ever been there. She assumed a fox had snatched the body in the night.

After a couple of minutes mending a tear in Louis's gardening trousers, she glanced up. There in the horse chestnut tree, perched on the same branch as the previous afternoon, was another huge crow. If she hadn't known the first crow was dead, she would have sworn it was the same one; and Louis would have reminded her, had she said as much to him, that she wouldn't be able to tell one crow from another even with binoculars. The appearance of the bird disquieted her. One hand had flown to her chest in alarm, the other was already gripping Gordon's basket. The crow was a threat to her child. Since Louis's response the previous day, it was also a threat to the harmony of her family. Louis had always been a protective father – over-protective at times – but his rage in response to the crow had terrified them all.

She remembered in the instant she saw it that she had dreamed of a crow in the night, its black claws gripping the side of Gordon's carry cot as it peered inside. From her angle in the dream, she couldn't see Gordon but she knew he was in there and her fear was that the crow would peck out her defenceless son's eyes. She reached for the cot, which had become a basket of woven willow sticks, and as she did, the crow began to flap, its wingspan suddenly vast. She felt the downdraught from its wings as it lifted off, still gripping the basket in its claws. The basket rose up beneath the bird as it gained height and she awoke to find herself alone in the bed. From down the hall she could hear Louis's faint snores from the study. Gordon slept softly in his basket beside the bed but Sophie had pulled his cotton blanket up around his chin. Weeping, she'd clutched a pillow to herself until she fell back to sleep.

Seeing the crow now and remembering the dream, she felt her pulse quicken. She dropped the torn trousers to the ground, the needle still embedded in the fabric, a stitch half finished, snatched the carry cot and ran back into the house.

"Louis?" There was no answer. "Louis!"

"What?"

The reply was muffled and she knew where he'd be. Still clutching Gordon, whose nap had turned into a fairground ride, she trotted to the downstairs toilet and flung open the door. Louis looked up from the Sunday papers, surprise turning to annoyance.

"What the bloody hell is it? Can't I even have a crap in peace?"

"There's a bird in the tree again. A crow or rook like yesterday. I want you to get rid of it, Louis. I don't want them around here."

"All right." Louis glanced back at the article he was reading. "I'll be there in a minute."

"No, Louis. I want it gone. Right now."

Louis sighed, knowing his precious moment of solitude had come to an end.

"Can you pull the door to, please? I just need a moment."

Sophie went to their bedroom, closed the door and held Gordon's head in her hands to deafen him. Angela was watching television and Judith was playing in her room when they heard their father fire his shotgun for the second day in a row. They ran to the windows, too late to see anything.

Louis was the only witness. Anyone watching would have told him he was a useless shot, but Louis knew his skill. He'd been brought up with shotguns. He didn't miss. And yet, he couldn't explain what happened.

He'd stepped out of the back door carefully, not wanting to startle the crow. As it had been the day before, the crow seemed unconcerned by his presence. Louis, on seeing the corvid, was struck by the similarity it bore to the crow of the previous day. He had to force the thought from his mind, telling himself all crows looked the same. He had to tell himself because part of him knew it wasn't true; someone used to seeing crows and living around them would be able to tell them apart. When he raised the gun and sighted it on the crow, it half opened its wings and shifted position on the branch. As he aimed the bird let out a long, scornful cry.

"*Krrraaaaa*..."

Louis pulled the first trigger. The bird flapped, letting go of the branch. It fell backwards before gaining the air, turning and flying away over the trees in their garden towards the open fields. Certain he'd wounded it, Louis waited for a moment, expecting the crow to fall out of the sky. It didn't. It beat its wings with great might, unharmed.

He took a bead on it, aimed a little ahead and squeezed the second trigger. The crow was well within range and flying at an angle that had always suited Louis. The shot flew and nothing happened. Nothing except the crow shrinking smaller against the horizon and calling back an occasional caw of derision. Louis looked along the barrels, honestly wondering if he'd somehow bent them. They were straight and true, still hot from discharging. The satisfying, adrenaline-stimulating smell of burnt powder held no reward that day.

As he walked back past the bedroom, Sophie opened the door. Her face still pinched and concerned.

"Thanks, Louis."

"It's OK. No problem. How is he?"

"I covered his ears but he must have heard the shot. He's just started to cry again."

Louis listened to the noise: such a soulful, drawn-out squall that it brought him down to hear to it.

"Do you think he's OK?" he asked.

"I don't know. I think he's just scared by the noise. It's understandable."

"Should we take him to the doctor, do you think? I've never heard him sound this way."

"He was like this yesterday. You know… afterwards. But he was fine this morning."

"All right. If you think he's sick, though–"

"Louis."

"What?"

"He's fine. Relax."

"Yeah, OK."

He gave her a kiss on the cheek and took the gun back to the study.

That morning, the wind picked up and clouds burgeoned from nowhere. In one instant the sun was bright, illuminating every room with pure glare. In the next it would hesitate and fade. There would be a flicker of brilliant return followed by a deep gloom making the rooms dusk-dark in less than a second. Within an hour or so, the sun lost the battle with the weather. The house swelled with midday shadows and darkness and the Black family shivered and ran for extra layers. Soon the wind flung rain and hail against the windows and the roof, turning the house into a prison, and Sunday, usually a day that passed far too quickly, became long and tedious.

Outside on the terrace, Louis's ripped trousers lay crumpled and squashed to sodden blackness. Every crack in the fabric of the house became a mouth for the wind and it spoke to them all saying but one word over and over with every whine and moan:

Winter.

6

Down at the river the October sun lets the water break its smile into a million pieces of gold, each so brilliant they leave a mote of light inside the eye, each one unique and momentary.

Megan allows the motion of the water and the fragmenting of the sun to lull her. They're all sitting on the grassy bank and Mr Keeper is smoking his pipe again. She's only half listening to the adults talking about her. Some part of her is waiting for them to understand before she gives them her attention.

"You're certain she's all right?" asks her mother.

"She's taken a fright is all," says Mr Keeper. "And you should understand also that what frightened her meant her no harm."

"We can forget it, then," says her father.

Mr Keeper shakes his head mid-suck on his pipe, inhales deeply and then blows smoke.

"There's no forgetting such a thing, Mr Maurice. This incident is the start of something, not its conclusion."

Mrs Maurice is confused.

"What does that mean?"

Megan can hear the tension in her mother's voice.

Poor Amu. She's more frightened than I was.

Mr Keeper smiles and puffs on his pipe but it has burnt out. He palms the ash and deposits it in his pocket.

"I need you both to listen very carefully to what I'm going to say, and you need to let me finish before you ask any more questions. Do I have your accord?"

Her parents are already silent. They only nod in reply.

"Very good then."

He refills the pipe's bowl with deliberation before lighting it with a match. Only when it is well lit does he begin to speak and now, instinctively, Megan turns away from the river, its sparkles still glowing inside her eyes, and listens.

"I'm an old man. Older than you think. But I wasn't even thought of on the eve of the Bright Day. The first of the Keepers was there, though, and he showed those who followed him the way of remembering those times forever. We call it the eve of the Bright Day, but really those times went on for many years. Everyone thought the world would end and that people would be wiped out. It was a bad thing to dwell on. Belief can make things happen, you know. Perhaps that's why we came so close to making it true."

Smoke obscures Mr Keeper's face for a moment. He waves it away.

"Ha! Listen to me, rambling already. Never let an old man tell a story unless you've got all day, remember that.

"The point is, even though I wasn't there, I saw it all. Every Keeper returns to those times. There's a way back through the Weave but it only opens for a few. I wasn't born until generations later but I was there in the time of the Crowman and the Black Dawn. By moving between the strands of the Weave and retrieving the events of those times, I proved myself a Keeper. The Crowman said he'd live on in all of us, that he'd keep the land strong if we kept his story alive. And we do still tell Crowman tales at festival time, don't we? And we tell his stories at the fireside when winter comes.

"Children are still frightened of the Crowman and I think the grown-ups are too. If he knocked on your door after dark, you'd take a fright, wouldn't you? Anyone would. But that's not because the Crowman is bad, it's because he's powerful. All good and all evil exist within him. He was powerful before the Black Dawn and the mightiest of people were frightened of him even then. Scarecrow, they called him. Or Black Jack. They made him out to be a monster."

Megan sees a wild fire in Mr Keeper's eyes. She glances at her parents but they don't notice it. The old man points his pipe at his audience, then at his chest.

"He was just like you and me. A person. With a good heart. Good as ripe corn and pale ale. But he carried a burden – the burden of power. And that darkened him over the years. The more power you have, the more dangerous you become. Takes a strong back and a strong will to carry it. He had both, though I think sometimes he doubted it.

"He charged the Keepers with keeping his story alive, even though he's long gone. Before my own time comes I must find a new Keeper, a child with a strong back and courage enough to carry the story. They don't come along very often, I can tell you, but when one does the Crowman will show himself to them, he'll mark them out. That child must rediscover the story of the Crowman and keep it alive until they find the next Keeper. And that Keeper in their turn, the next. And so on. That way, the Crowman will always be with us."

Mr Keeper glances up as a cloud dulls the sparkles in the river. When it passes, he continues.

"You don't want to go back to a world without the Crowman. That really would be the end of everything.

"There's a little bit of him in all of us, you know. But he's stronger in some than in others. It's my belief that the Crowman came to Megan in Covey Wood today. This is nothing short of a miracle, because I was beginning to think a new Keeper for these parts would never come along."

"Are you saying that our M–"

Mr Keeper's glance at Megan's father is enough to silence him.

"She's been chosen. All I can do is find out if she's worthy. That will take time and it will mean no more schooling for her other than what she learns from me. I won't be able to feed or house her – you'll continue to do all of that. But she must spend six out of every seven days with me from before dawn until after sunset. If she's worthy, one day she will return to you, not as Megan any more but as Keeper. And if she fails then you'll have Megan back – as she always was but full of knowledge."

Mr Keeper didn't give them time to speak.

"You must talk it through. It's not a decision to take lightly, believe me. Megan needs to understand how difficult the role of Keeper's Prentice will be. The Crowman's story makes adults of children and she may not be ready. However, if she does complete the training, her contribution, not only to Beckby village but to everyone hereabouts, will be immeasurable. She will be a bringer of real joy and the land in these parts will love us all the more deeply."

Megan is sitting up straight, eyes wide, and something in her very blood is telling her that this is what she wants more than anything else in the world. There's something magical about Mr Keeper but she's not sure her parents can even see it. Yes, she is still frightened by the Crowman – terrified, if the truth be known. But the boy from the night country isn't terrifying. He is gentle. Just remembering him awakens a dormant recess in her, locked tight until now. Deep within herself, stronger than any desire she's ever known, the urge to follow the boy arises with crystal surety. This is her chance to find out who Megan Maurice really is.

"I want to do it," she says.

Her mother, as though slapped, is speechless. Her father's face reddens.

"Now wait a moment, young Megan, it's not your place to be deciding such things. You shall do as you are tol–"

Mr Keeper holds up his hand.

"In the end, Mr Maurice, the decision is entirely Megan's, and not yours or your wife's to make. You certainly cannot refuse her the right to proceed, should she be certain that is what she wishes to do. However, as I said, I think you should all discuss it very carefully before a… consensus… is reached. I will call on you in seven days' time, at which point I shall want an answer. If Megan is to undertake the training, she will come to me the following morning before dawn and we will begin. If she is not, then I shall trouble you no more about it. Please understand that there will be no second opportunities in either case. A yes is a yes. A no is a no."

Mr Keeper scans each face. Megan knows he can see the smile inside her eyes even though, for the sake of her parents, she keeps her face blank. He stands, collects his ash again and shoulders his pack. By now the sun is casting shimmering shadows of willow trees onto the bank and afternoon is giving way to evening.

Before he sets off, Mr Keeper says:

"Do you all understand?"

No one speaks, but Megan and her parents nod. Amu and Apa have calmed down enough to each place a protective, forgiving arm around Megan, and together they walk slowly home from the river bank where so much love has been made, so much that it became the most beautiful thing in her parents' lives and the thing, Megan knows, they believe they are about to lose.

That night, her small but swelling breasts ache, her belly knots and tightens. She bleeds for the first time. Amu brings her a bundle of moon cloths, quietly explaining their use. As to the blood and its significance, Megan has been expecting it. Pain is not the only sensation in the depths of her belly, there is a flutter there – excitement and expectation.

May 2004

The door to Judith's bedroom opened a fraction and a face, lily-pale in a thin bar of moonlight, appeared there. Lying on her right side facing the doorway, she watched through a tiny crack in her eyelids as Gordon pushed silently into the room. She felt a warm flush of anticipation and pride knowing she was his secret protector.

The door hinge creaked and Gordon froze. Judith saw the look of terror there. If Mum and Dad discovered him here, his nocturnal visits would end. Then what would he do when the nightmares came?

She'd loved him with a fierce loyalty the moment she'd seen his wrinkled, newborn skin and gentle grey eyes. So different to the feelings she had for Angela. Judith tested the love in her mind, especially on nights like this when Gordon came to her for comfort. She tried to quantify it, define it. If Angela was ever hurt or killed, Judith knew she would be sad. She would weep over her injury or loss. Without Angela, she was unguarded against the ways of the world. She would weep also because when they weren't arguing and when Angela wasn't being cruel or dismissive, they had a lot of fun. These things were enough to qualify as love.

With Gordon, her love was different. She couldn't have the same kind of fun with Gordon. With six years between them, playing with him was always a step backwards; the games themselves quiet, dramatic fantasies. She played with him because she knew he wasn't always happy playing alone, and his happiness was essential for her own. If anything bad ever happened to Gordon, Judith wasn't sure what she would do. She knew if someone hurt him she would calmly inflict upon them the greatest pain she knew how to give. Merely imagining that someone might seek to injure him made her fists clench beneath the bedclothes. And if he died, if she lost him, she knew all she would want would be to die too, to follow him to wherever it was that death took you.

She watched him, petrified halfway through the door. When no one responded to the creaking of the hinge, Gordon regained his courage and crept into her room.

He left it ajar so he could slip away through the same gap before anyone else stirred. So stealthy had he become that Judith often woke to find him in her bed, clutching her but already asleep. He came whenever he had nightmares, at least once a week, often more. She would take hold of his hand and squeeze it tight to let him know he was safe before returning to sleep. When she woke in the mornings he was always gone.

He approached now making no sound at all. If she hadn't been awake already, observing him through slit lids, she wouldn't have known he was there until his small, wiry arms had encircled her and his tight fingers had clutched her nightdress in a grip that would not relent until he left. She watched his eyes, wide and frightened, his pupils so dilated their blackness almost eclipsed the grey of his irises, watched his forehead crease with concentration as he used every muscle to move silently.

She lifted up the covers to let him see she was awake. His frown cleared and she saw the relief on his face, his fear gone in an instant. With great care, he climbed in beside her. She drew him close and tight. With an arm wrapped over him, she engulfed him in a warm cocoon. He pushed against her as hard as he could, expelling all the space between them, pressing his cold feet between her ankles.

The first time it had happened was almost two years before, when he'd had his first bad dream. Judith heard him walking down the hallway to their parents' bedroom, sniffing and sobbing as he went. She knew he must have tried to get in with Mum and Dad but neither of them wanted him in their bed. Mum had taken Gordon back to his room and whispered soothing words to him for five minutes before going back to sleep with Dad. It didn't do any good. Long after Mum had left him, Judith could hear Gordon weeping, even though he'd tried to stifle it in his pillow. She'd hated her parents for that, especially her mum. Judith had been the one to slip from her warm duvet and collect him that night. His small hand in hers, they had walked back across the hall. She'd climbed into bed and he had followed, hugging her so tight she thought he'd never sleep.

"Any time you're scared or have a bad dream you can come. But don't ever, ever tell anyone, Gordon," she'd whispered. "OK?"

"OK."

Now, here he was again, holding tight but already asleep and Judith, happy to be a shield against the dark of his own little mind, slept too.

In the morning he was gone.

7

The knocking is soft, almost surreptitious. Heather Maurice glances at her husband, a flash of worry passing over her face before he stands to open the front door.

"Mr Keeper," says Fulton, frowning. "I'm afraid you've missed Megan. She's out berry-picking with Sally Balston and the Frewin boy."

"I know," says Mr Keeper. "That's why I'm here."

Heather dries her hands on her apron and comes to her husband's side.

"What is it?" she asks. "What's the matter?"

Mr Keeper glances over his shoulder. Already, a couple of neighbours have taken an interest in his presence. He gestures towards the table and whispers:

"It might be better if we talk on the warm side of the door."

The Maurices stand back and let Mr Keeper pass. He sits at their table and loads his pipe. Fulton Maurice, usually placid, fidgets. Heather places her hand on his sizable forearm. Mr Keeper doesn't seem to notice. He lights up, takes a deep breath and clouds the kitchen with smoke in a single exhalation.

"There's something I couldn't tell you with Megan listening. Something that would make all this much harder for her."

Heather's brow creases and she squeezes her husband's arm. Fulton Maurice places his massive hand over hers, engulfing it. Mr Keeper leans towards them, his face solemn but kind.

"It's nothing bad, you understand. But it is so very important and you must swear to me that you will never mention it to her – whether she walks the Black Feathered Path or not." He searches their eyes. "Can you do this?"

Fulton Maurice nods but Heather is thin-lipped. When she speaks her voice is unsteady.

"You're asking a great deal of us already, Mr Keeper. And a lot more of our Megan. She's our only child and still just a girl. I'm not sure any of this is right for her. Or for us."

Mr Keeper's face becomes grave. Fulton Maurice shifts in his chair and looks away.

"This isn't simply about you," says Mr Keeper. "It isn't even about Megan. It concerns all of us. It concerns the land. And Megan is not so young as you wish to think. She is, even now, becoming a young woman and I can tell you, with the Earth Amu as my witness, that without Megan our future will be uncertain at best. The Crowman wants her – he's made that plain enough – and now it's up to her to decide what's right." Mr Keeper takes a pull on his pipe and looks out through the wind-eye beside the front door, staring far beyond the cottages on the other side of the track. When he looks back, as though returning from some terrible distance, neither of the Maurices can hold his gaze. "I can't make Megan's choice for her and I wouldn't want to, but can I at least rely on your silence? You must believe me when I say that much rests on your answer."

Heather sighs and leans against Fulton's shoulder.

"We're her parents," she says. "We can't help but be afraid for her."

Mr Keeper nods.

"I know."

Heather turns to her husband. Their eyes meet and, in time, Fulton Maurice speaks.

"We need to trust in the way of things, Heather. Strikes me none of this is an accident." He looks at Mr Keeper. "You have my word I'll say nothing to Megan."

Heather sits straight again.

"And you have mine."

"I thank you both." Mr Keeper put a hand inside his boiler suit. "There's something you need to see." He draws out a large, flat leather pouch which he lays on the table. Its ruby-dark surface has been polished smooth by years of handling and its edges are beginning to fray and crumble. With fingers roughened and wrinkled by constant foraging, Mr Keeper gently flips the pouch open. Inside is a pocket. He reaches for it and hesitates. Instead, he taps out his pipe and refills it.

"I need to tell you a story first."

"There was one Keeper who lived in the time when the Crowman walked this land. Just one. He remains the only person to ever meet the Crowman face to face – to be touched by his wings – and survive. The encounter almost killed him, left him crippled and blind. But the reward was great. The Crowman gave him new eyes with which he could see deep into the Weave. It was the gift of prophecy and it made him the first in our line. The Rag Man was his name.

"Now, every Keeper can see a little way into the Weave but the Rag Man saw everything. He saw us. And I think he saw Megan.

"In all the generations since the Black Dawn, there has never been a female Keeper. The Crowman has shown himself to one boy after another and their task remains unchanged. To tell the story. To keep it alive by journeying through the Weave and setting down the tale. This process keeps us all in touch with the Crowman. It keeps him alive inside us and that, in turn, keeps the land alive. But every Keeper so far has been fallible, even I. The risk always remains that one of us will journey in error and return with the story only half told. The farther away in time we travel from the days of the Crowman, the more likely that is to happen. Already, it may be that the story is not correct in all its facets. Already we may be forgetting the Crowman's true nature and how he links us to the Earth.

"But the Rag Man, he saw a girl in the Weave, generations in his future, when the Black Dawn was only a distant memory. The first and only female Keeper. He saw, too, that this girl would be the last Keeper. Either she would journey and rediscover the tale in its entirety, thereby keeping us united with the land for all time, or she would journey and fail. The story of the Crowman would be lost and our connection to the Earth severed as it was before the Black Dawn. Only this time, if that bond is cut, it will be final. Within a generation or two, all of us will be done for. The Earth Amu will die and the light from Father Sky will be snuffed out. For our lives and the life of the world are as one. We share the same destiny."

Mr Keeper pauses to reload and relight his pipe. Heather and Fulton Maurice sit, silent and still. Keeper slips his finger inside the pocket of the leather pouch and slides out a piece of paper. It is yellowed and its edges are nibbled and torn with wear. A pattern of thin, perfectly parallel blue lines covers its surface and between these, in a style too twisted to be readable, is a mass of spiky scrawl, apparently written in great haste.

Megan's parents lean forwards and frown over the handwriting.

"I know," says Mr Keeper. "Impossible to decipher without several years of study under your belt." He grins. "Which, fortunately, I have. This, as far as we know, is the Rag Man's only surviving inscription. There may be others but they have never been found. These lines are a prophecy, somewhat fevered, but nonetheless a vision of the future – the one we now occupy, if my instincts are correct."

He places the page in front of him on the kitchen table and is silent for a few moments before beginning to speak:

> *be watchful for an innocent*
> *guided by a black feather*
> *chosen in the shadow of trees*
> *in a time of harvest*
> *in an era of plenty*
> *fair of face and hair*
> *yet her name is black*
> *this is the keeper of keepers*

in whose journey the land may live or die
the boy cannot exist without the girl
without the teller, there can be no tale

Heather Maurice claps her hands with relief.

"Well that settles it, Mr Keeper. It can't be our Megan. Her name isn't Black!" She looks to her husband for support but his face is vacant. Mr Keeper shrugs with a resigned smile. "Fulton," she says. "Make Mr Keeper understand. It's all been a mistake."

"I think Mr Keeper may be right."

"How can he be right? She's not named Black."

Fulton sighs, his enormous frame shrinking.

"Maurice is a very old name. It doesn't mean anything now, but a long time ago it meant dark-skinned or black. I'm sorry, Heather. When I heard those words, my skin turned to gooseflesh. I don't know if Megan has the strength to—"

Mr Keeper holds up a hand.

"Please. I know it's distressing." He slips the ancient sheet of jagged script back into its pocket and closes the pouch, before returning it to his boiler suit. "There's nothing can be done right now. These are only words – from a time none of us can remember. They could be wrong. They may not even have come from the hand of the Rag Man." He leans towards the Maurices. "None of this is set. Not yet. But I couldn't let the matter go any further without telling you everything." He pushes his chair back from the table and stands, suddenly cheerful. "Let us wait and see what Megan decides. Let us see what rises inside her. One thing, at least, is clear, though – the Rag Man was very specific. She must be a girl. Still a child. If Megan is the one, her walking of the path must be swift – not years, as was my initiation, but months. I pray she decides soon."

October 2005

Sophie cleared the paper plates and discarded party hats, the leavings of cake and fruit jelly from the water-proof tablecloth; all the colours seeming dull in the cloud-choked October light. The kitchen was silent now, vacuous and forlorn in the wake of ten small children and their mothers. Streamers hung, pinned to the beams and thrown over the lights in the ceiling, some vague current of air animating them, giving rise to papery whispers.

A blue candle in the shape of the number 5 lay extinguished and partially burned in the centre of the table. Sophie lifted it, turned it in her hands for long moments before wrapping it in a paper bag. She took it to the bureau in the living room and unlocked the hinged writing panel with a key from a small vase on the mantelpiece. She placed the candle beside its four predecessors and a collection of other tiny relics – a lock of his hair, cut the very night he was born; several silky crow feathers; an infantile drawing of a ragged bird, in black crayon; the rattle Louis had made for him; his first pair of woollen booties. There were other mementos – lucky pennies and corks saved from champagne bottles and cards of congratulation – all relating to Gordon.

There was no glow of nostalgia around these arte-facts, merely a dark aura. Sophie ached, not with loss, but for something none of the family had had in the five years since Gordon was born: light hearts. They'd birthed him into an afflicted world. It was almost as if Gordon had brought its troubles with him: the changes in the climate and increased solar activity, the creeping totalitarianism of government, the epidemics and poverty, the undercurrent of fear. This was the joyless era Gordon would live through – if he survived. If any of them did.

In one of the bureau's hidden compartments was a growing collection of letters, sketches and poetry. The penmanship and craft of strangers. Sometimes they arrived in the post. Sometimes they were delivered by hand, or left anonymously on the mat outside the front door. Louis once had a tiny wooden carving of a scare-crow, about the size of a chess pawn, pressed into his hand by a crazed-looking vagrant outside Waterloo Station in London. On one of her shopping trips to Bristol with Amelia Porter when Gordon was two years old, a woman in the street had started screaming and point-ing at Gordon's pushchair.

"He's coming, you stupid bitch. Open your eyes. Black Jack's coming to damn us all."

The woman had dropped her own shopping in the road and run towards them, eyes suddenly wild, hair flying, only to be tackled at the last possible moment by an elderly ex-serviceman who'd witnessed the whole incident.

Everything about that day had been wrong – even before the lunatic woman made her lunge for Gordon. It was the first time Sophie had really noticed how tainted everything looked, the first time she'd admitted to herself that her family was living through dark times. Shop fronts were boarded up even in the most prosper-ous parts of the city, the graffiti covering them not merely profane but hallucinatory and prophetic. Each time she opened the bureau, memories from that day resurfaced, especially the defacing of derelict buildings and chipboarded windows: scrawled murals of bloody combat overseen by a screaming black angel and the strange poetry that accompanied the images. All of this so similar to the tokens which now filled the writing bureau's secret compartment.

Police had been everywhere but none had come to help them. Instead, they loitered in groups on street corners or in alleys, looking more like gang members than protectors of the public. Among these menacing coteries, she had glimpsed for the first time figures in long grey coats and broad-brimmed hats – now the Ward were everywhere. Bristol had smelled faintly of excrement that morning, the occasional waft making Sophie and Amelia wrinkle their noses. A few days later, following record rainfall in the South West, the sewers had backed up and Bristol suffered an outbreak of typhoid.

Sophie touched the compartment in the bureau, almost needing to check that the collection of strange gifts was real. But of course it was. She knew what she would see if she opened that cleverly crafted recess in the wood – what she and Louis privately referred to as the Crowman's coffer. Years of stored-up evidence that there was something different about her pale, sensitive little boy. Something strange. Something *foreshadowed*. Sophie drew her fingertips away, squeezing back tears of apprehension and fear. She folded the writing bureau's panel shut, locked it and replaced the key in its vase. Turning back towards the hallway, she screamed, her hands flying to her mouth.

Gordon stood there, still wearing his party clothes – blue shorts, and brown leather shoes now scuffed and muddy, a white shirt and small tie under a sleeveless green pullover. He held his hands out to her. In them he offered up the slack body of a jackdaw, its head lolling, its eyes glazed, its feathers dappled with tiny rubies of blood – Gordon's or the bird's, she couldn't tell.

"They're all dead, Mum."

"What?"

"It wasn't me. I found them."

Sophie's hands came away from her mouth.

"Take it outside, Gordon," she whispered.

Her boy turned away from her and she followed him into the hallway.

"Louis?" She shouted up the stairs. "Louis, come down. Quickly."

By the time they reached the back terrace, Louis had caught up and the three of them stared at the bodies of four other jackdaws, neatly arranged on the grey flag-stones.

Gordon's face was ashen with guilt.

"I didn't do it. They were just here."

Louis reached out a gentle hand, intending to bestow comfort on Gordon's back, when they heard the door in the garden wall creak. The hand never made contact. A figure slipped out of their property and pushed the old door closed behind it. All they glimpsed were the drabs of a hunter or poacher, probably a man.

"Jesus Christ, who's that?" He took a couple of steps into the garden. "Hey! What the hell do you think you're doing? This is private property!" There was no response. "Right, fuck this." He turned and ran into the house. Gordon and Sophie heard his footsteps pounding up the stairs and running down again moments later.

He ran past them with his shotgun, heading for the end of the garden. "Stay right there," he shouted back.

Ten minutes later, he returned.

"Did you see anyone?" asked Sophie.

Louis shook his head.

"Whoever it was is long gone. I couldn't even see which way he went."

He knelt down in front of Gordon.

"I don't want you coming out in the garden for a while, OK?"

"Why, Dad?"

"It's just for a while."

"But I didn't do anything."

"I know you didn't. I just want you to be safe."

Gordon began to cry.

"None of that. Come on, let's get rid of these birds."

Louis stood, broke his shotgun and placed it on the garden table. As he bent to retrieve the jackdaws, Sophie said:

"Should we call the police?"

"What can they do? Anyway, I don't want the police up here. They're more like government spies than peace officers. Let's not..." Louis allowed time for Sophie to meet his eyes, "draw attention to ourselves."

Gordon handed the dead jackdaw to his father before Sophie urged him inside and down the hall.

"Go on, birthday boy, I think you'd better wash your hands."

When she heard the water running, she looked at Louis, tears welling.

"What can we do?"

"Nothing. Just keep on loving him and keeping him safe."

Sophie gestured towards the dead jackdaw in Louis's hand.

"You call this safe? We have to tell him."

Louis stepped close, leaned forwards until their noses were almost touching.

"Put that idea out of your mind," he whispered. "Forever. Gordon must never know."

8

August 2009

Gordon's bedroom light flicked on, banishing the dark and its skulking army of terrors. It also blinded him.

"You all right, son?"

It was his father's voice.

"I think so."

"You were… screaming. Really screaming."

"Sorry, Dad." Gordon could hear whispering in the hallway outside his door – Judith and mum. He spoke loud enough that they could all hear him. "I'm all right now. Just a nightmare."

In the doorway, Louis turned to the others.

"He's OK. You can go back to bed."

After a few moments, two pairs of footsteps padded back along the upstairs passageway. Gordon heard the creak of bedsprings. Louis slipped into the room and shut the door behind him. He switched on the less glaring bedside lamp and turned out the main light before sitting on Gordon's bed. He placed his palm on Gordon's chest through the duvet.

"Getting a bit old for these bad dreams, aren't you? You'll be in double figures in a couple of months."

"I can't help it. I would if I could."

"I know, son. I'm sorry. It's not your fault." Louis sighed. "But we worry about you, you know. Mum especially."

"Mum worries about everything."

Louis chuckled.

"True."

He was silent long enough for Gordon's eyes to adjust to the brightness. His father looked tired, eroded. Gordon ground his teeth.

"How's everything at school?"

"It's OK."

"Yeah?"

"Yeah."

"No one's… making your life difficult?"

"No, Dad. It's fine."

"You never bring any of your friends home. You don't get invited to any parties."

"I've got a couple of friends. They're not like best mates or anything but they're OK. I'm just not into the stuff the other boys are into. Football. Cars. Fighting. I'd rather be outside. At the Faraway Tree or in Covey Wood. Doing stuff in the garden with you and Mum."

Louis was quiet for such a time that Gordon started to drift back into sleep. He came to with a start when his father spoke again.

"What, Dad?"

Louis looked over at him.

"I said, your happiness is very important to us."

Gordon put his hand out from under the duvet and placed it over his father's.

"I am happy, Dad. Honest."

Louis's face changed then, the care lines deepening,

crushed closer together. He looked like he was about to say something; something adult. A secret, perhaps. Late at night and sometimes on very still days when he was in the woods or watching the crows wheel and dance in the sky above the fields, Gordon felt there was such a secret, locked away in his parents' hearts, locked away in his own.

The moment passed and Louis's face cleared and opened.

"You know, I had some troubles when I was your age."

"What kind of troubles?"

"Oh… it doesn't matter what they were. Just my concerns about life, I suppose. About growing up. I used to write all my worries down in a diary. I found it helped me. I always felt better afterwards. Would you try doing that? If you knew it would help you sleep easier?"

Gordon shrugged.

"I suppose."

"OK. Good. That's good."

Gordon thought the conversation was over but his dad didn't get up.

"What were you dreaming about?" Louis asked very quietly.

Gordon wished there was some way he could pretend to be asleep but the tone of his father's voice made it clear there was no avoiding the question.

"I don't really remember."

Louis's gaze was stern.

"Try."

Gordon took a deep breath and closed his eyes for a moment. The image was there immediately, colossal and terrifying.

"It's a bird. A crow. And it's so big that its wings stretch all the way across the sky. It blocks out all the light and I know, deep down in my guts, that it's going to be night-time forever. It's like this crow has flown down out of space with his claws all stretched out, ready to…"

"To what?"

"I don't know exactly. To tear a chunk out of the world. To drag the world into the darkest part of the universe. That's it. That's all I can remember."

"You know that's never going to happen, don't you? You understand that it's just a dream, right?"

"Course I do, Dad. I'm not thick."

Louis's big hand patted his chest and he smiled.

"No. Thick is one thing you're not."

Under his breath Louis muttered something. He usually did this if he was swearing in front of Gordon or his sisters. What he said sounded something like:

Bloody crows.

"What, Dad?"

Louis looked at him and grinned, his eyes seeming to focus elsewhere.

"Do you remember the scarecrow we made?"

Gordon shook his head.

"I don't think so."

"You were probably too young. About two years old, I guess. We've always had a problem with crows and the like around here, and that year your mum decided to make a scarecrow to keep them away. I don't know why we didn't think of it before. Anyway, we put a lot of effort into this guy. We stuffed a pair of your mum's tights with straw for his legs and stuck them in an old pair of black trousers. She found some black boots at the tip one day and we used those for his feet. He had a big chest – a potato sack filled with more straw and over that he had an old black T-shirt. His head was a hollowed-out pumpkin with a creepy face carved into it…"

Louis paused and glanced at Gordon.

"Sorry, son. I'm not trying to give you more nightmares. I just–"

Gordon grinned now.

"I'm not frightened of a scarecrow, Dad."

"No. No, of course not. Well anyway, his arms were made from another pair of tights and we cut holes in the ends and stuck black twigs in there to look like bony fingers. Over the top he wore a ripped black overcoat that didn't fit me anymore and a crumpled black top hat from the charity shop in Monmouth. We even put some black feathers in his hat, like trophies I suppose, to ward off the crows. And we pushed his arms up a bit so it looked like he was clawing at the sky. We used an old bird feeder to keep him upright and put him right in the middle of the garden."

Louis smiled as he reassembled the phantom of the scarecrow in his mind.

"Did it work?" asked Gordon.

"Did it hell. The next morning we went out and he had a crow perched on each arm and two fighting for a place on his hat. There were droppings all over his coat and the apple trees were crammed with cawing, flapping bloody corvids. It scared your sisters half to death but not the birds. Complete bloody failure."

Louis laughed and shook his head.

"What did you do?" asked Gordon.

"I moved him up to the back wall of the garden and forgot about him. He stayed there for a year or two getting mouldy and falling apart. I think we chucked him on the bonfire in the end."

"I feel sorry for him."

Louis nodded.

"Yeah. I do too now that I think about it." His father's eyes filled with tears which didn't quite spill. "We do our best, Gordon, your mum and I. We really do."

"I know that, Dad. It's oka–"

Louis held up his hand.

"No. Just listen to me for a second. Life is hard enough even at the best of times. But these aren't the best of times right now. For anyone. I want you to know – to remember, no matter what happens in your life – that your mother and I love you very, very dearly. We'd do anything for you, Gordon. Anything at all."

Gordon nodded. He had no idea what to say. His father stood up from the bed, weariness overtaking him once more. Gordon had never seen him look so old.

"Think you'll sleep better now?" Louis asked.

"Yes, Dad. I think I will."

Louis nodded.

"Great," he said, without enthusiasm. "Goodnight, son."

"Goodnight, Dad."

Louis flicked the light out and moved to the door in the darkness, sure of his way. It wasn't until the thin light of morning seeped through the curtains that Gordon finally slept.

9

June 21st '13
My eyes only

When I woke up I thought I'd pissed myself. But the
dampness was everywhere and I realised it was sweat. Then
I remembered the dream. Replaying it, it felt like the first
time I've had this dream but while I'm dreaming it, it's all
so familiar. As though I've seen it a thousand times. Like
I've lived it a thousand times.

There's a dead tree. Its branches are like blackened arm
bones and blackened finger bones reaching up into the sky.
The trunk of the tree twists up from the ground, its black
bark spiralling as though the wood is contracted and taut.
There's a bend in the trunk like an old man's back, the sky
crushing it. Among the topmost of its dead branches sit three
watchful crows. One faces north, another south. The third
looks up into the sky. The sun is behind the tree, just above
the horizon. Terrible pain or total ecstasy seems to hinge on
whether the sun is rising or setting.

I hear people's voices, some crying as if they've lost
everything in the world. Others weep more softly but the
wound that caused their tears seems deeper. I hear the

tramping of feet. Not marching but the sound of people on the move. The road they travel is treacherous – behind the black tree I can see the snipped ribbon of tarmac stretching away over the low hills. In many places, the road is broken by huge cracks in the earth. There's a smell too, like overcooked steak. Smoke blows across the landscape. The crows caw, flap and settle, ever vigilant.

At the foot of the tree there is a single feather. The feather is long and thin, black at first glance. Then I'm holding the feather in my hand and it has a shimmer of deep blue-green. In the tree there's a rattled cackle and I look up to see a magpie bobbing its head and flicking up its tail in a lower branch.

That's all I can remember. Why would that make me soak the sheets with sweat?

Megan walks in almost total darkness along the track through the village. She wears lambswool underwear her mother has made beneath her roughest outdoor clothes. Over that she has wrapped a thick woollen blanket which doubles as a winter coat. She has never been up at this hour before and, with October's days running short, it is chilly before the sun rises. Despite all her layers she is cold inside and shivers as she hurries along. Dawn is still some time away as she reaches the edge of the village and leaves the main track. She hopes she has allowed enough time to reach Mr Keeper's place before the sun clears the horizon.

Amu and Apa have always been early risers, up at first light. Apa to go and work in the fields and Amu to make sure he has a good breakfast before he leaves. Both of them stand outside the back door each morning. They drop flour and barley onto the soil and make their prayers of thanks and ask for strong crops, a good harvest and peace between all creatures. Megan has always spent those few extra minutes in bed because children are not expected to pray formally until the time of their coming of age. Of course, the children are encouraged to talk to the Great Spirit in their own way and also to be thankful to and respectful of the Earth Amu. Maybe that was her parents' reason for allowing her to go to Mr Keeper in the end, knowing it was for the good of all and not just for her or them. But consent did not come easily.

"It's not the Crowman that worries me, Fulton," her mother had said the day after their talk by the river. "It's that Mr Keeper. How can we trust him?"

"What do you mean, trust him? What are you suggesting?"

"You know right well. What if he… hurts her?"

This had made her father angry. Whenever his voice dropped to a whisper following a venomous silence both Megan and her mother knew it was time to give ground.

"I'm disappointed in you today, Heather Maurice. I won't allow such words to be spoken in this house. If we can't trust our Keeper, we can't trust anyone or anything. You know that. Everything would fall apart like it did before. The seeds of another Black Dawn will not take root here. Do you understand me, woman?"

Her mother had nodded, weeping silently.

"The issue is, can we all live with the changes this will bring? Megan, you're going to leave childhood behind in a flurry of dust. That'll crack my heart a little, even if it doesn't yours. It will set you apart. Even from your friends. And if Mr Keeper decides you're not the one he's been waiting for, he'll set you free again to be neither one thing nor another. That's no life for anyone."

Amu's tears flowed ever more freely as Apa spoke.

"I'm sorry, Fulton," said her mother. "It's my fear for her that makes me say such things. I know Mr Keeper is a good man. I do trust him. I just can't bear the thought… can't bear the idea that…"

Megan had never seen Amu so upset. Her own tears came in response.

"…we're losing our little girl. Our beautiful little Megan."

Both Megan and her mother broke down then and clung to each other.

Fulton Maurice, tested to the edge of his own emotions at the sight of it, went in search of baccy and papers. It was a very rare thing that he smoked unless the occasion was special. He rolled a fat, crooked fag and lit it with an ember from the stove before returning to his wife and daughter.

"Listen to me, both of you. It's right to be upset and it's right to be a little frit. But we're not losing Megan if she goes. She's moving into a new phase, that's all. That was always going to happen. Maybe, if this is really what she wants to do, maybe she couldn't be in better hands." The smoke made his eyes water and he coughed, grimacing at the neglected, over-dry baccy. "Let it settle for now. It'll seem different tomorrow and then we can talk again."

And they had talked about it every day, with much the same intensity, until the night before when Apa, who had deflected all Amu's concerns and objections as they came up and who had needed to buy another ounce of baccy, said:

"I think we've made our feelings plain. Megan, you know we love you and hold you precious, more precious than anything else in our lives. Because of that we only want to see you happy and walking the right road. That's all any parents want for their children. But I think Amu and I have realised that Mr Keeper is right. This is your decision to make and whatever you decide, we'll stand by you. We'll do our best to help you see it through."

He rolled a slim, neat fag and lit it, blowing smoke with no small amount of satisfaction.

"So, it's up to you. Tomorrow you can have a lie in like you always do or you can rise while it's still night and walk that night road out to Mr Keeper's place. What do you want to do?"

Megan smiles now as she remembers that moment and pulls her woollen wrap tighter around her shoulders to pass through New Wood without catching her clothes on the pines. A lot of tears have been shed over the course of seven days. She even saw Apa cry once. But each night she dreamed of a small boy with moon-silver skin, tar-black hair and eyes of polished granite. A boy who held out his hand to her. A boy who always smiled.

New Wood is dense with trees, and despite her attempts to shrink, the branches of the pines snag and catch at her along the narrow path. The chill here is different. It breathes all around her and the silence is muffled by a frosty mist and a hundred thousand green needles absorbing all sound. The ground is soft and peaty beneath her brown leather boots and her way is defined more by touch than by sight in the darkness.

And then, quite unexpectedly, the trees end and the path opens out. Above is a circle of lightening sky in which the stars still observe her. She can smell smoke on the air and up ahead, near the opposite edge of the clearing, she can see a large, squat shadow from which a flicker of light escapes. This is the source of the smoke and possibly the source of the stillness in New Wood.

She has reached Mr Keeper's roundhouse.

August 10th '13
My eyes only

I'm such a saddo.

Even though I know I'm welcome in the world and even though I know my family loves me, I feel like a stranger.

At school I've never done well in any subjects except art, which doesn't count. Never made any really good mates. Never had a proper girlfriend. Never been in the football team. Never really been in trouble either. I'm just like this big... nothing. A loser. Even at home I feel like it's me who doesn't belong.

Why?

If I knew the answer to that I wouldn't be sitting here writing this stupid diary. I'd be out there doing something. Doing anything other than thinking. Thinking is all I do. And nothing ever comes of it.

There is still time to change her mind, even as she stands here on the threshold of the clearing where Mr Keeper lives. She could turn and walk back the way she came, back to the safety of her family and their small comfortable cottage. She knows there will be nothing comfortable about the work which lies ahead with Mr Keeper. It would be better, surely, to allow knowledge and adulthood to arrive in their own natural time. Even in her ignorance of the future and of where Mr Keeper may lead her, she understands that she will look back on these times and wonder, no matter what she does, whether she made the right decision. She already regrets the loss of a carefree mind. How much more of herself will she lose by walking forwards into this moment when she could so easily step back into the past? She thinks about this for several chilly moments, each out-breath unravelling in the still air. Her thoughts seem no more permanent than those same spent breaths.

But there's no undoing her visions from the night country, is there? No sending away the gentle boy with the black hair and grey eyes. And there's no unseeing of the thing in Covey Wood. If she turns away now these new presences in her life will never be fully addressed and she feels their import so very strongly. They are like parts of her already. Parts she neither wants to, nor is even sure she is able to, live without.

Before she realises what is happening she is walking towards the roundhouse, confidently despite the darkness, and her thoughts and fears only catch up with her just at the moment she rings the tiny bell beside Mr Keeper's squat doorway. Cracks of flickering yellow and orange are visible through the sticks and mud which form the walls, and between the doorway and its ill-fitting wooden frame, but she cannot see Mr Keeper. She is about to ring a second time when she hears a rumble from inside. She almost steps away until she realises the rumble has a voice – Mr Keeper clearing his early-morning throat. The noise goes on for some time and Megan finds herself willing the phlegm upwards so that the poor man can finally speak to her. The noisy proceedings end with a throaty *hoik*, followed by a massive-sounding wad of mucus leaving Mr Keeper's mouth at high velocity and landing somewhere impressively distant.

After a few more coughs and grumbles a croaky voice says:

"You'd better come in, little thing."

10

The weather's been getting strange again. We've had thunder storms and heavy rain all over the country. Even though it's October, the rain is warm, like a monsoon or something. Before the storms hit the air gets hot and heavy. It feels wrong.

Jude and I watched one yesterday. It had been sunny all day but then that steamy feeling made it hard to breathe. We huddled in the bay window at the end of the upstairs hallway and watched the sky go black. It was like nightfall. Jude and I held hands really tightly. The wind got up, whipping leaves into spiral flurries. Downstairs I could hear Dad locking windows and pulling the shutters closed. Angela was in her room, no doubt with her iPod wired into her brain, and the only light upstairs came from under her door. Mum was in the kitchen singing the chorus of some old song over and over to take her mind off things. She looks scared all the time now but I worry the storms will send her mad.

Down in the garden the wind picked up more leaves and

spun them into a vortex that danced on the grass near the horse chestnut.

Dad shouted up the stairs.

"You two be careful by that window."

The upstairs hallway window is still unprotected. Last year, Dad fitted roll-down aluminium shutters to every other window in the house but he hasn't got around to doing the one where we sat, even though Mum nags him about it all the time.

"And tell Angela to drop her shutters if she hasn't already."

Angela wouldn't have known a storm was coming unless someone hacked into her iPod and gave her an emergency bulletin. I left Jude on the window seat, knocked on Angela's door and walked in. She was multitasking – reading a magazine, texting her boyfriend and listening to music all at the same time.

"Fuck right off, Gordon. What are you even doing in here?"

I shouted "storm" and pointed to her window. She rolled her eyes and continued to text. I thought about telling her to unplug her computer but didn't bother. Let it fry, I thought.

After the brightness of her bedroom, it seemed like midnight in the hallway. I could just see Jude's black silhouette in the darkened window. As I walked towards her the sky outside turned white. I thought I'd gone blind at first but then an afterimage of her open-mouthed shock floated in front of my eyes. I started counting as I used the wall to guide me to where she sat. When I reached ten there was the loudest noise I've ever heard, a single boom like an explosion in the nearby hills. Ten miles, I thought. What's it going to be like when it's right overhead? I reached the window and Jude hugged me. Rain was falling slow and steady outside.

No light came from Angela's room. Even from so many miles away the storm had knocked out the power. Next thing I knew she was in the hallway.

"Dad? Dad! Can you reset the trip switch? My lights have gone out."

You could hear the disbelief in his voice as he shouted back up to her.

"There's a bloody great storm out there. Paint your nails in the dark."

She went back into her room, slamming the door. After the thunder, the bang of the door sounded pathetic.

The wind hurled rain against the windows, smearing it across the panes. The lightning was so bright we couldn't see where it struck and the thunder got so loud you could feel it in your chest and skull. With every flash, I saw the ground turned to water as the storm dumped inches of rain in a matter of minutes. Between the thunderclaps, I heard Mum crying and Dad trying to calm her down.

We're lucky to live on a hill. The rain's washing away houses and taking people with it. Every night we see it on the TV. It sweeps crops off the fields and carries them to the sea. It overflows from the sewers. All over the country there are emergency shelters for those who've been made homeless by the weather. Here in Hamblaen House we're still safe. For now.

Mr Keeper's roundhouse is a single circular room. They sit on sheepskins laid over a floor of woven rushes. At the centre, an iron stove like a fat cauldron with a flat top glows orange, giving off enough heat to make Megan's forehead prickle. She unwraps the woollen blanket from around herself and lets it fall to the reed matting. Opposite the front door, a small area of the roundhouse is partitioned by blankets hung across twine. This, she guesses, is where he must sleep.

A kettle on the stove top exhales a constant, forceful jet of steam. Beside it stands a small tool of some kind, the tiny handle of which pokes straight up from the hot plate. The chimney rises in a series of crooked black joints, straight out through the domed roof.

A heady confusion of scents fills the hot, dark space.

A hovel, she thinks. That's what it is.

Megan can't define all the smells. There's pine-laced wood smoke, of course, which escapes from several imperfections in the stove's chimney pipe, not to mention the burning baccy. She detects dozens of dried herbs, particularly sage. But there are fresher, more bitter scents too, like those that might rise from poisonous berries pounded to pulp.

Mr Keeper has gestured for her to sit and handed her a clay bowl of hot water, sieved from a charred-looking teapot on the stovetop. He flicked the catchings of the sieve to his right without looking and that is where the single wind-eye of the roundhouse is located. She hears the tiny patter of something landing outside. Drinking the hot brew now she tastes mint and fennel – she's smelled this on him before and it comforts her just a little. She is too nervous to speak.

As if picking up on her thoughts, Mr Keeper breaks the silence.

"It doesn't do to make a lot of noise and fuss in the morning. It takes an old man like me quite a while to get started. I like to do it slowly."

He looks over at her for the first time and in the dim glow of wood fire and tallow candles his face is defined only by its cracks. The half light does strange things to her perception and she sees in his face two centuries of age in one moment, and the freshness of a six-year-old boy in the next. He places his empty tea bowl to his right on the matting and turns towards her. His eyes, not cruel but intense to the point of terror, skewer her.

"I don't have to tell you that there's no going back, do I, little thing?"

Her stomach jittering, she says:

"No."

"Good. That's very good. I knew from the moment I met you that you'd understand how these things work. I have great faith in you, little thing. Great faith..."

He trails off, his eyes looking towards the stove.

"And that's why I want you to know that I would never hurt you for any reason."

"Yes. Of course." She's confused now. And suddenly frightened. "But why–"

He holds up his palm.

"Any pain this path holds for you is not of my making, little thing. It is in the nature of the path itself. I tell you this because you must trust me as your guide. Trust me always. Can you do that? Can you do it no matter what befalls you?"

In her panic Megan can't think. What is he asking of her?

"You knew this would not be an easy thing. You knew it would not be a game. You've been visited by the Crowman, little thing. Nothing will ever be the same for you. Nothing can ever be as it was. But I swear to you that I will guide you in the best way I can and with as much care as I am able. The path is not without pain, but neither is the path of life itself. I only need to know if I can rely on you to trust me."

She watches his face and sees uncertainty there for the first time. Here he is, this very tall, very old man. A man with grooves so deep in his face it is as though life cut him to put them there. He has been Mr Keeper to their community since before she was born – possibly since before her parents were born. This was not something that was bestowed upon him lightly. The lives of hundreds of people have been in his hands over the years. He has delivered children, healed the sick, tended the elderly, the crippled and maimed. He has driven out madness and given nothing but his love – though sometimes it is an angry love – to everyone hereabouts.

And he is the only one who can show her the path.

"I trust you to guide me, Mr Keeper. No matter what happens on the path, I trust you."

In the dark, his smile is like sunshine before the dawn.

"Oh, well done, little thing. That is so very, very good to hear." He sighs. "Now, I must ask you to be brave for the first time. And it won't be the last. It is all very well saying words and meaning meanings for the future. But you must be sealed into this future and sealed into your word. The Crowman has visited you and now he must mark you. Take off your jacket, little thing, and loosen your clothes a little."

By the glow of the stove, Megan reddens.

"It isn't what you imagine. Come now, do it quickly."

Unable to think at all now about what is happening, not knowing whether her trust is already about to be broken – maybe Mr Keeper exacts a price from the community that no one ever talks about – she does as he has asked.

"Come here to the stove where I can see, and expose your chest."

She moves as commanded, pulling open her cardigan and shirt, stretching down her lambswool vest. She is embarrassed by the fullness of her tenderly ripening breasts and does her best to hide them. It is only then that she sees what Mr Keeper is doing. He snatches the tiny tool from beside the kettle. Before she can react, he places one palm behind her back and with his free hand forces a faintly glowing piece of iron into the centre of her chest.

As she screams, the smell of her own skin burning mingles with the many other scents in Mr Keeper's roundhouse.

October 10th '13
My eyes only

Since the shortages have gotten worse, the vegetable patch has doubled, taking over most of the lawn. I've spent most of the holidays digging, weeding and hoeing. Most of the apples and pears usually drop and rot on the ground. This year, we've harvested the lot. Some are wrapped in paper up in the attic and mum has canned the rest or cooked them into sauce or chutney.

We also have a new chicken enclosure with six hens in it. They arrived with a nanny goat in the back of Dad's pickup and Mum says this is the only milk we'll get soon enough.

Everything in the garden is a reaction to what's happening in England and everywhere else. Mum and Dad act as if we might starve to death sometimes. Can they really believe that?

The other day we went into Tesco with mum. They have

*security forces in the store now. We saw them wrestle a
young mum to the ground, spray mace in her eyes and
electrocute her with a taser. Her baby was still in the trolley
screaming. It made me feel sick. We got out in a hurry.*

*You're not meant to hoard petrol but everyone does. We
started before the price rises put vehicles off the road, taking
five litres at a time. It's hidden in jerry cans in the hedge by
the back gate. There's enough to get us to the coast if things
get bad. But where would we go? More and more countries
are closing their borders as they try to deal with the weather,
fuel shortages and economic chaos. The only things going in
and out are trade goods under military escort.*

*Everything is scarce now. Gangs are stealing anything.
Not just TVs and phones but heating oil and diesel. They're
even chopping down trees so they can sell the wood. It
wouldn't take much for someone to break into the garden
and take all our produce, as well as the chickens and the
goat. Dad keeps his shotgun handy now. He bought a second
one for me and there's a whole wall of ammo boxes in his
study. You've got to hand it to Mum and Dad. They saw all
this coming and they were ready.*

I've got to go. I can hear shouting from downstairs.

11

Proof now, because I've already got it written down. I've definitely had this dream before!

Against a white sky streaked with clouds the colour of grey milk stands a skeletal tree, its branches blackened and dead. The topmost limb divides into three finger-like branches that look withered and dislocated. On the tip of each charred fingertip perches a large black bird. Crows or ravens, I think. One faces left, one right and one looks up into the sky. Then the three of them look down at something I can't see. On the horizon, far behind the tree, the sun is setting. It's the same red you see when you look at the midday sun with your eyes closed. Flesh red, shot through with veins of gold. I do not want to see the sun go down. I can't face the possibility of it not returning.

Someone is screaming. Hoarse, uncontrollable screams. The crows caw at something out of sight. Their cawing sounds like laughter.

When Megan opens her eyes she remembers the scorching of her heart but she feels no pain there now.

She is lying on sheepskins in the roundhouse and the morning sun penetrates the cracks in many places. Mostly, it comes in through the open front door and the tiny hole where Mr Keeper ejects unwanted things. He appears from behind the curtained area and kneels beside her. Only then does she become aware of something wet and heavy on her chest. He places a hand over it and the weight increases. With his other hand he holds hers. The skin of his fingers and palm is warm and dry but rough. From his hand radiates a thick aura that seems to envelop her hand and spread into her chest.

"What are you doing?" she asks, her throat dry.

"Making the pain go away, little thing. I'm sorry you had to suffer it but it was… necessary. From this moment forwards you carry the Crowman's mark and he is always with you."

He takes his hand from her chest.

"Now, let's have a look at the progress."

He peels away a green, muddy poultice from her sternum and lays it beside him on the matting.

"Ah, yes! Perfect! Have a look, little thing."

He holds a mirror so that she can see the place where the tool touched her. Already healing into a pink scar is a perfect symbol, forever part of her skin. Three claws pointing upwards to her face, one pointing down to her stomach. The footprint of a crow. There is no pain. She smiles and then cries.

"Can you sit up?" asks Mr Keeper.

She tries and finds it easy. He passes her more tea and she drinks it quickly, her thirst desperate.

"Dress yourself then, little thing, and we'll go out. There is much to be done."

• • •

February 7th, '14
My eyes only

I've had dreams of terrible things happening for as long as I can remember. When the news is on and I see the most recent earthquake or flood, or when some new disease starts to spread, I get this cramp in my stomach like it's in a vice. And I get that feeling, when you know you've seen something before.

I feel guilty too.

I know it sounds really pathetic and that's why I'm writing it down instead of telling anyone – I couldn't even tell Jude about this – but I feel like there's this huge blackness coming across the whole of the world. I imagine it's like the blackness on the dark side of the moon but it's a living, intelligent thing.

Crops are failing around the world and people are dying of hunger. Dad says that only used to happen in Africa. Now it's everywhere. I've heard stories about crowds of starving people in America storming corn fields or breaking into supermarkets and clearing the shelves. American police are allowed to kill those people. Sometimes they call in the army to do it.

All the terrible things I've always dreamed about are happening now. For real. I feel responsible. The worst one was the tsunami. I'd been having this nightmare about a huge wave. It's like the wave is made up of pure anger, like it wants to smash humanity when it hits. As it nears the shores, it rises up higher and higher. I'm on the land, high up on a hillside somewhere and looking down. Where the beach is, the water has all gone and I know what it means. I've been waiting for this day for a long time and that's why, in the dream, I live at the top of this big hill. All kinds of ocean animals are flopping around on the exposed wet sand and then, far out on the horizon, I can see a movement, some kind of distortion and I feel this terrible clenching in my stomach because I know that, even up here on my hill, I'm not safe from what's coming. The wave is impossibly huge and I always wake up before it strikes the land. The fear is too much to sleep through.

Last week there was an eruption in the Mediterranean. It was an underwater volcano but that didn't stop it blowing dust and smoke miles into the atmosphere. Within a couple of hours a tsunami hit every shore from Tunisia to Syria. In some places the tsunami arrived as a swell of a few feet that swept inland on low ground for miles. In other places, the wave was a giant wall. Footage from mobiles and handheld camcorders showed waves of up to seventy metres high racing into the land. Hundreds of thousands of people died in a few moments.

Did I predict it or is it just a coincidence? Do I tell Jude? She knows I have nightmares and she knows people die in them. But I've never told her about them coming true. That's only started to happen recently.

April 29th '14
My eyes only

Sometimes I feel like someone's here, watching me. I can't see them. I can't even hear them. I'll be standing somewhere, in the garden or looking out of the window in my room and it's like someone's right behind me. I've lost count of the times I've spun around thinking I'll catch someone creeping up on me.

There's something else. I've had it all my life, at least as long as I can remember, but it's only now that

How do I even write it? No one can ever read this.

I hear voices. There. I said it.

I'll be dropping off to sleep at night and I'll hear my name clear as anything. "Gordon." That's it. One word. I always thought it was just my brain going into that doze where your dreams begin. Recently, though, the things I've heard are like little proverbs or something. Really embarrassing. I cringe just thinking about them.

We are all stronger than we believe we can be

Shit, I hated to even write that down. I've never thought anything like that. I never would. Where does it come from? It's such an up itself way of saying something. Here's another.

Everything you need will come to hand in the very moment of its requirement

In the very moment of its requirement? What the fuck is that supposed to mean? I hate it. But I'm on a roll now. Check this one.

The Crowman is in all of us

I know. That's a step too far, right? The others could just be my subconscious bubbling up when I'm half asleep. But the Crowman. That's just too messed up. Who is the Crowman? Where does this stuff come from? It takes me back to the fear. That I'm responsible for bad things happening. Worse, that I'm going schizo.

Maybe I feel guilty that we're still doing OK up here on the hill. We've still got food – most people are on rationing now. We've got our own well water. And we don't get the crime and violence like they do in the cities. But we work hard to keep well stocked and we've been preparing for a long time. Mum and Dad were smart and they taught us to be smart too. Do I feel guilty about that? I don't think so.

Who or what is the Crowman and why do I hear voices telling me his name? Telling me he's inside me? Is he the one who's watching me?

12

When Gordon heard the crunch of tyres on gravel, he ran out to see what his father had brought back from the latest "supply mission".

For the last few weeks Louis Black had taken weekly trips as far as Bristol and Gloucester to buy goods of all kinds. The cellar was already stacked with bottled water, candles, torches and batteries, dynamo-powered radios, medical kits, ropes and bungees, tarpaulins, tents, waterproofs and other spare outdoor clothes. There was even an inflatable dinghy. The shed was full of timber, all manner of tools, vast coils of hosepipe and several car batteries.

This trip had yielded a more precious bounty. More precious to Gordon, at least. He could barely stand still when he saw the entire pickup burdened with all kinds of food.

"Wow. We'll be stuffed!"

"That's hardly the point, Gordon," said his father. "The idea is to eat a little bit for a very long time. When this lot is unloaded and put away, we all need to sit down and have a talk. Come on, grab some stuff." Louis shouted into the house. "Girls, you come and help too. Quickly now."

Sophie Black moved slowly and quietly, her face pale
and blank. Gordon lifted what he was able to: a few
cans in both arms or some bags of flour or sugar.
Angela was last to arrive and did the least to help, as
usual. Their larder, well supplied even at the worst of
times, soon looked like a canteen storage room. Gordon
helped to line up the tinned goods in rows: beans of all
kinds – including baked beans with sausages, he was
pleased to note – sweetcorn, chopped tomatoes, chick-
peas, potatoes, mushrooms, spaghetti, and even tinned
sponges, rice pudding and custard. Gordon could just
about drag along the sacks of rice, oats and other dried
goods, each in ten-kilo bags, but it was Louis who
hoisted them to the top shelves away from rodents.
Various kinds of flour and sugar were stacked in bags
eight deep on the next shelf down. Long-life milk,
powdered milk, condensed milk and all kinds of seeds
and nuts were ranked beside them. As the larder filled
and everything in it was arranged into order, Gordon
realised he was the only one excited about the latest
"haul".

Sophie Black put the kettle on, and when a pot of tea
was sitting under a woolly bobble hat in the middle of
the kitchen table and rounds of hot buttered toast lay
piled on a plate beside it, Louis Black called everyone
to sit down with him while they snacked and slurped
hot milky tea. Sophie sat down last, reluctant, it
seemed. Gordon watched his parents carefully, noting
that his dad only started to speak when he'd received
some silent eye-signal from his mum.

Louis took a deep breath and cleared his throat. Gordon thought his dad looked… embarrassed and, for the

first time ever, unsure of himself. He'd never known anything other than strength in his father. Seeing him like this was like losing his protection against the world. Only for a moment, but it was a terrible moment. He scooted nearer to Jude on the refectory bench and reached for her hand under the table. On the other side of it, next to their father, Angela shook her head in minute disgust.

"It seems that things have changed in the world. Even in this country," Louis began. "It looks like the Ward are here to stay. You've all seen the news."

They had. The Ward were the only party that looked capable of steering the country back to stability. In the previous election, their MPs had swept to victory in constituencies across the entire country. People were frightened. They wanted order restored. The Ward looked like an answer to their prayers.

Recession had been biting for years. Businesses folded every day and several banks had collapsed. Unemployment was soaring to record highs. The health service was now so badly funded it could only provide emergency care. Following the floods of the previous two years, the UK had a refugee population of close to a million and no way to look after them other than charity. Many of the homeless now wandered the country trying to stay alive. Crime was commonplace, the police ill-equipped or ill-disposed to do anything about it. Countries the UK had previously relied on for supplies of food were no longer exporting; they needed the food for their own people. Forgotten diseases had reappeared and spread, tuberculosis, diphtheria and rickets among them. Successive flu epidemics had wiped out tens of thousands of people in Europe and

steady rises in temperature had seen malaria cases
being treated in Cornwall, Wales and the west coast of
Scotland. Glasgow, Newcastle, Birmingham and parts
of London had suffered riots when water, electricity or
gas had been cut off, sometimes for days at a time. Fuel
prices were rising daily. Hauliers were the worst hit by
this and most people couldn't afford to use their cars
any more. An increase in solar activity had affected
satellites, phone networks and even the internet. On
two occasions, the world wide web had been inaccessi-
ble for several hours. People were calling it a new dark
age: the Black Dawn.

Only the Ward, representatives of which had
appeared in many countries when things began to look
irretrievably bleak, promised solutions to all of these
problems. The multinational corporations, threatened
by economic collapse in every market, began to invest
in influence rather than simple profit. Somehow they
needed to secure their positions for the future. Lobby-
ing and then infiltrating government wasn't enough.
They bought their way into the police and the army
and their management structure and organisational
skills began to look like a practical solution to many of
society's problems. People saw real passion in the
Ward, the ability to answer questions with a simple yes
or no and the gumption to follow through on things
they promised. Their Expulsion Bill of the previous
year, returning millions of migrant workers and their
families to their countries of origin, was the most radi-
cal political act in living memory..After that, support for
the Ward grew exponentially.

To Gordon all this had been no more than pictures
on a screen. They were stories about other people and

nothing to do with him. Now, before his father said another word, he knew the stories had reached Hamblaen House, that the Blacks had become part of the news.

"Most people are in favour of the Ward and it's dangerous to say you don't agree with what they're doing. But your mother and I don't agree with it. We oppose the Ward and everything they stand for."

Angela rolled her eyes at what she took for melodrama.

"I'm not joking, Angela Black. This is the future we're talking about. Yours too. If someone doesn't stand up to these people, they're going to turn the UK into a wasteland. The Ward have only one desire: to enslave us while we're on our knees."

Louis looked at Sophie and extended his hand to her across the table. She offered hers and he squeezed it hard.

"I've seen what the Ward are capable of. They've opened a branch in Monmouth – a substation, they call it. People go in there and they don't come back. Amelia Porter... she–"

Sophie shook her head.

"Don't, Louis."

He dropped his head for a moment, stared into his now lukewarm tea.

"What is it, Dad?" asked Judith. "What happened to Amelia?"

Louis looked up, stared into Judith's eyes until she looked away.

"It doesn't matter. What I'm trying to tell you is to stay away from the Ward. Far away. Don't even let them see you if you can help it."

Angela made a face of disbelief.

"I'm absolutely serious, Angela. If you see them, you hide. Understand?"

Everyone nodded. Angela started to get up from the bench.

"Sit down, Lella. There's something else."

For a moment, Gordon thought Angela would ignore their father and go to her room. Finally, she gave in.

"The thing is, I've…"

Louis looked from face to face around the table, unable to speak. Then he laughed.

"Oh, Christ. Look, I've shut the business. I've been thinking about it for a while. It was either that or go bankrupt. I thought it was better just to stop trading. Ha, what a joke. There's no trade out there anymore."

He ran his hands through his hair, a manic gesture he rarely displayed. His voice dropped to just above a whisper.

"We've all had good lives up here. But things are going to change. We won't starve and we won't end up like the people you see on the news every day, but from now on pretty much everything we do will be geared towards surviving what I suspect will be some very unpleasant times. If we work together, we'll do fine. I want you all to promise now that you'll commit yourselves to keeping this family afloat. Not just with getting food and water but with keeping each other's spirits up. If we pull hard, make a team effort, we'll be OK. I know we will."

The silence around the table was dour. Much of what Louis said that afternoon didn't really sink in for any of them until the changes he was talking about hit home. But Gordon hated the silence because it meant people were thinking about their answers rather than doing what they should have done.

"I promise I will keep this family floating," he said.

Louis smiled in a kind way but Angela laughed and would have followed up with words if her father hadn't silenced her with a vicious sideways glance.

"Me too," said Jude.

"Me too," said Angela without any sincerity at all.

Louis looked at his wife. Everyone did.

"Sophie?"

She didn't speak. She merely went on looking into her tea mug as though she had other things on her mind.

"Sophie, you have to say it. We all do."

She looked up, unable to hide that she would rather be anywhere else but here, in any other time.

"I promise to keep this family afloat."

Louis nodded, but Gordon guessed he would have more to say to Mum when no one was around.

"I promise, too," said Louis. "And not only that, I promise to protect you all."

13

In her bed that night, Megan touches her scar, tracing
its edges with a fingertip. She is exhausted by her day
with Mr Keeper and has come to bed straight after her
meal, barely saying a word to her parents about what
has happened. She knows they are worried but she's
too tired and too full of new things to talk about it.
What she needs is the comfort and warmth of her bed
and the time alone it will give her.

Mr Keeper kept her busy all day. Together they wandered across the borders of the community searching in
the hedgerows for various plants and herbs. Some of
them she recognised and others she'd never seen
before. It had been like searching for secrets and she
loved it. He had talked only a little about what lay
ahead. Perhaps he felt her branding had been enough
for one day. And yet, she had the feeling that somehow
the routes they took and flora they collected had a purpose, even though it was one she could not define.
Often Mr Keeper would stop and look up. She would
follow his gaze to a tree or fence post or a patch of
meadow and there she would see magpies, flicking
their tails and chattering out their raucous calls. And

each time this happened, Mr Keeper would smile and then return to whatever his business had been.

Before she left the clearing that evening, he said: "The magpies know about you. Did you see them?"

She'd nodded.

"You'll walk in the night country tonight, Megan. Mark it well. I'll want to know all in the morning."

He'd called her Megan ever since she'd woken from the faint caused by her scarring. He'd handed her a small sheaf of blank onion-skin pages, bound with twine.

"When you wake, light a candle and capture it all in here before you forget. Bring it tomorrow." He'd touched her on the shoulder. "Safe home, Megan. Safe home."

Then he'd turned, letting her go.

She touches the mark of the Crowman now, his footprint on her heart, and sleep comes so very easily.

August 3rd '14
My eyes only

Should I tell you about the shoebox in my wardrobe?

When I was ten, I caught flu. My body ached so much I couldn't get out of bed to go to the toilet and Mum had to bring me a bottle to pee into. The fever went on for three days and I was delirious with it.

When my temperature got really high, Mum put wet flannels on my head and neck and armpits. It hurt like ice-cold fire but it worked. I remember opening my eyes and she gave me a kiss on the cheek. My head ached so much I was crying so she told me a couple of stories.

On the day she gave birth to me, she saw a crow sitting on her bedroom window ledge. It was huge, she said, and it pecked on the glass and fixed her with one intelligent, black eye. That was the moment her contractions started. She said that later, as I came into the world, a snowstorm blew her window open. She believed it was a sign that the world had reached out a hand to welcome me.

She also told me about a crow that had perched in the chestnut tree by the back terrace and how Dad had killed it with his shotgun. She said I cried all night and she couldn't work out whether it was because I'd been frightened by the sound of the shot or if I was mourning the death of the crow. After that, no matter what Dad did, the crows and jackdaws always nested in our chimney pots, perched in our trees and did aerobatic displays over the house. In the end, Dad gave up trying to shoot them.

The first morning I felt well enough to get out of bed after the fever, it was to the sound of dozens of crows cawing away in the garden. When I sat up, still weak but out of pain for the first time in over a week, I found a feather on my pillow. I never asked Mum about it. I just assumed she'd left it there so I'd remember her crow stories.

It was the first feather I kept. And, from then on, whenever I found one, I put it in a shoebox with the one from my mother.

I suppose I ought to mention that the feathers I find are black. All of them. And they only ever turn up at moments when something important is happening or if I'm worrying about something or when I feel like everything is going wrong. I tell myself it's a hobby or that I do it because I like to collect things. But that's not really true. I do it because I don't want anyone else to find them.

14

Until Gordon had fetched the post from the wire box inside the front door, breakfast had been relaxed. Judith had stayed with friends in the village the night before and Angela was at university in Bristol. This left him, Mum and Dad to have a peaceful start to the day. The envelope, which Gordon knew contained something bad, bore the Evan Davies School crest. His father slit it and drew out a letter headed with the same symbol. The piece of toast he was halfway through sank back to its plate and Louis Black stopped chewing.

"What is it, darling?" asked Sophie.

Louis was silent a few moments longer as he finished scanning the document. Then he laid it on the table top.

"They're shutting the school."

"What?"

"They're shutting Evan Davies indefinitely."

His mother snatched up the letter but still asked:

"Why would they do that?"

"The attendance figures have dropped too low. Lots of people can't afford to drive in since the buses stopped running. The headmistress says the Ward are concentrating all their resources on schools in urban areas."

Gordon watched his mum read the letter, her eyes returning to certain passages over and over again when she lost concentration. She looked over at him and tried to smile but to Louis she said:

"Gordon's barely done a year at the school. What are we going to do?"

Gordon was surprised to see his father break into a widening smile.

"We're not going to worry about it."

"Not worry? How can you sit there and–"

Louis reached across the table and took his wife's hands in his.

"I understand why you're worried, Soph. I really do. But there are no jobs out there even if Gordon did finish school. And what were they really teaching him there anyway other than how to be a drone for some corporation? Or worse, a career as a Wardsman? We can get him a couple mornings of tuition a week – I'm sure there are plenty of unemployed teachers out there who'd work for food and a few quid. The rest of the time Gordon can get stuck into making the place run like a proper smallholding."

Sophie Black sat back on the bench, laughing without a trace of humour.

"Do you really believe you can dodge and weave your way through everything that's happening, Louis? The world is falling *apart*."

Gordon saw insanity flash in the whites of his mother's eyes.

"I have to believe it, Sophie. And I *can* do it."

"What, just like that?"

"Just like that," said Louis. "Times have changed. Let's not fight it, eh?"

Gordon watched his father's optimism growing as the moments passed. Soon he'd chewed down the rest of his toast, guzzled a full cup of tea and pushed his end of the bench away from the table.

"Come on, Gordon. Get that food down you and get your boots on. We've got work to do."

High winds had stripped both dead and live wood from the various trees. They spent the morning gathering fallen wood from every part of the garden, none of it large enough to be considered a log but the pile they created constituted almost a month's supply of fire-wood. Judith and Sophie both helped and though they worked mostly in silence, the common goal they strived towards made for a harmonious hour or two. They exchanged quiet smiles and occasional words but that was all. When the pile was complete, Sophie and Judith went inside to make lunch, while Louis and Gordon sawed and chopped the timber into manage-able sizes for the fires. They removed all the tiny twigs and set them aside for kindling.

It was as they covered the wood pile with a thick blue tarpaulin that they caught sight of two figures. The two strangers, men in long grey coats and broad-brimmed grey hats, entered the front gate, bypassed the front door and came around the side of the house towards them without any hesitation. Their eyes roved over everything they saw, studying, gathering in the details of both house and garden.

Louis pretended to bend down and resecure a corner of the tarpaulin. As he did so he whispered to Gordon.

"Don't say a single word, no matter what they ask you. Let me do all the talking. Understand?"

"Who are they?"

"Just answer me, Gordon. Do you understand?"

The men were too close now for Gordon to say anything. He caught his father's eye and hoped that would be enough. Louis finished fiddling with the tarp and stood up to his full height, feet planted slightly apart and arms folded. Even so, one of the men was taller than him by a good six inches. The other was a stumpy tub of a man, his spectacled eyes making a frog of him. They stopped a few paces away and Gordon studied their faces.

The frog, his tiny eyes magnified to bulging by lenses so thick he must have been almost blind without them, looked intelligent, his mind sharp and quick. The tall man's face was wasted and mean, his sick-looking skin tight over his cheekbones, the area between them and his jaw angular and recessed. His jutting bone structure cast shadows into the pits elsewhere in his face; the vertical crack in his chin, the squarish hollows of his cheeks, the caves of his eyes. This man, who might have looked incisive at first glance, exuded only numbness from his eyes, as though the soul behind them was imprisoned deeply within. Gordon noticed his massive hands and long strong fingers. The knuckles were rough and scarred, the fingernails thick but chipped. He smiled now, an automated expression, a machine coming to life.

"Have you lost your way, gentlemen?" asked Louis.

Gordon's throat tightened. He looked down at the ground, embarrassed. But he could only look away for a few moments. He wanted to see the response.

"Hardly," said the frog, his voice husky but effeminate. He reached into the pocket of his coat. Gordon tensed but the frog drew out a black wallet which fell open to reveal a photo ID card marked with some stamp of officialdom. He held it up for them to see, flipping it away before either of them could read it.

"My name is Archibald Skelton and this is my associate, Mordaunt Pike. We're Sheriffs of the Ward."

Louis shrugged.

"Never heard of it, I'm afraid. We don't go in for religion. Now, the Robertsons, they love all that kind of thing. You'll find them back towards the village on the right hand side. Lions on the gateposts. Can't miss it."

Louis nodded a silent goodbye, put his arm around Gordon and began to lead him away.

"I don't think you quite understand, Mr Black. Mr Louis *Anderton Richard* Black. Sheriff Pike and I are here on official Ward business. Government business. You'd do well to furnish us with a moment of your time."

Louis turned back to them, smiling again.

"Government?" He looked Skelton and Pike up and down. "Well, I suppose sending a couple of brogued, macintoshed civil servants into the countryside is the kind of money-wasting, time-wasting activity the government engages in these days. They could have spent that money on keeping our local school open, don't you think?"

"That would be a matter for your local councillor, Mr Black. Sheriff Pike and I have other... more pressing concerns."

"As do I. So, I'll politely request that you leave my property now. This is private land and, frankly, you're not welcome here."

Louis held out his hand, gesturing towards the front of the house and the gate through which they'd come. Neither of them moved.

"Right now, please, Mr Warden or whatever you said your name was. We don't want you here."

Gordon's throat was so dry he couldn't swallow.

"I'm very sorry, Mr Black, but we won't be able to leave just yet," said Sheriff Skelton. "This is a very sturdy-looking house you have. And I can't help noticing these are rather productive-looking grounds. If it turned out you were hoarding items that other people could benefit from, it might not turn out well for you. Did you know that?"

"Our house and what we do here is none of your business."

"I'm afraid it is. The Ward are very concerned with such things. If you don't acquiesce to our requests, we may decide to scrutinise your property. We may find the community would be better served if we shared what you have here with everyone in, say, a three-mile radius."

"You can't do that."

Sheriff Skelton smiled, exposing yellowed teeth.

"I hope it won't be necessary for you and your family to find this out through personal experience, Mr Black, but the Ward can do anything we like. Anything. We have what you might call a special dispensation."

Gordon, who'd been both proud of and frightened by his father's defiance, now felt a cold snake of dread in his guts as he saw the spirit shrinking from his father's stance. As if in response, expression came to Sheriff Pike's gaunt face. Until that moment he'd stood like a dormant engine. It wasn't a smile, merely a tiny flicker of interest from behind his faraway eyes.

"What is it you want?" asked his father.

"We just want to talk to you, Mr Black. You and your wife. And, if it becomes necessary, your children."

"If it becomes necessary?"

"If we don't hear what we want to hear."

Sheriff Pike's interest seemed kindled to a flame at the thought of it. Sheriff Skelton reached into another pocket of his grey raincoat and brought out an envelope. He handed it to Gordon's father.

"Call us within twenty-eight days to arrange an interview and we'll transport you to our substation in Monmouth. If we don't hear from you within that time, you and all the members of your family will be collected. Goodbye, Mr Black."

The two men turned and walked away.

Louis and Gordon stood watching them and even after they'd been gone for some time, neither of them moved. To move would be to enter the future.

This time, the boy who comes to Megan in the night country is not the same boy.

He looks the same and is just as beautiful with his pale skin and gentle manner, but he is troubled. He stands beside her bed and weeps the tears of someone who has lost something very precious. Not a possession, perhaps not even a beloved one, but something even more valuable. She sees the hole in the boy's chest. It is a ragged-edged wound. Something has sawn through his sternum and ribs. The hole has been made hastily and without care. A silvery light illuminates the cavity.

The boy's heart has been taken away.

The boy beckons and Megan rises from her bed, the touch of the night country on her skin and behind her eyes like liquid silver, cool and enticing. She follows him. Out through the front door again but as soon as it closes behind them she sees that they are not in Beckby village any more. Though she has never seen this landscape, she has heard about it. She knows what it is.

Ruins surround them. Buildings so great that even their smashed remains are four or five times the height of her family's cottage. The valleys between these fallen edifices, where the streets once ran, are blocked by rubble and things she doesn't understand. Things from before the Black Dawn.

The boy takes her hand. His fingers are cold as a plough blade on a winter's dawn but his skin is milk smooth and his touch is something like the flow of water in the Usky River. He leads her between the buildings in this broken world. Soon the buildings are far behind them and they are walking on roads of black stone avoiding great fissures which have split them apart – these they fly over at his behest. Farther along, the cracks deepen and widen until they are walking beside canyons which extend deep into the earth. The bodies of people and animals lie everywhere, decaying and pecked upon by grey-beaked rooks. Megan is undisturbed by any of it. She trusts this boy from the night country. If she had a brother, he would be like this.

The boy brings her to a forest of dead trees. The remains of their trunks and branches are either white, and glow bonelike in the darkness, or are black as soot. They walk through the dead wood and the moon lights their way, a silver disk shining through clouds of smoke. They come to a single tree in a broad clearing, gnarled and warped and blackened, straining under the weight of the night sky. In the tree sit three crows, cawing into the night, cawing at Megan and the boy.

He turns to her, weeping and smiling, and for the first time since she has entered the night country with him, Megan is moved. She steps towards the boy to embrace him and ease his wound. But when she reaches him he is gone. She looks around the clearing and all that is left is the black tree and its three cawing crows. The rest of the forest is gone too: a barren land rolls away in every direction, a land where fires burn on every horizon.

She looks into her hand. She holds the boy's still-beating heart.

15

Judith and Gordon stepped off the main track through Covey Wood, avoiding thickets of bramble and tall patches of nettle. The wind, which had torn so many limbs from unprotected or sickening trees, still shouldered its way through the canopy. Living timber creaked and complained overhead and Gordon found himself looking up often.

"Maybe this wasn't the best choice," he said.

They could have taken the disused bridleway and made the abandoned railway tunnel their goal or walked along the open and well-signposted track through the fields to what they'd always called the Yonder Tree. But they'd both agreed on the Thousand-Year-Old Oak in Covey Wood. Since the Ward had served their warrant on their family, the rest of the world seemed too exposed.

"It's fine," said Judith. "It's perfect. I can hear the wind blowing all the badness from the world."

It was an attractive idea but Gordon didn't believe it. All the wind could do was bring more badness with it. But letting Jude be happy was more important than arguing. Especially now. They moved with skill through the difficult landscape, knowing the way around thickets and finding paths through low yew and rhododendron that would have turned a visiting walker back to the main path. When the growth thinned and opened up they were on the far side of Covey Wood. Seeing the clearing in the trees and the giant at its centre, Gordon knew Jude had been right all along. This was the best place to sit and talk, in the protection of the Thousand-Year-Old Oak.

The oak was a gnarly giant. Rough-barked and ivy-covered on one side of its gargantuan trunk, it spread its thick limbs up and outwards in perfect, symmetrical subdivisions. In the summertime it looked like a vast green mushroom on a mottled stalk. Now, with October gales roaring and snatching at everything, all its leaves were on the forest floor. They weren't the only thing it had lost.

"Oh no," said Gordon.

Judith had already seen the damage. One of the oak's massive lower limbs had succumbed to the harrying of the wind. The bough had once extended from the main trunk almost horizontally, supporting a mass of smaller branches. Now it lay along the ground directly below its point of dislocation. It had made a deep score in the body of the oak, tearing a thick section away as it fell and leaving exposed a deep, almost white wound.

"This must have just happened," said Judith. She put her hands into the rent in the oak's trunk. "It's damp. You can smell the sap."

The oak had always been a symbol of power and longevity for Gordon. One thing that fascinated him about trees was that they could live for hundreds of years. They didn't know how old the oak was but it had always seemed a thousand years old to all of them, and now here it was, wounded by the wind.

"We can sit on the snapped bough," said Judith. "The oak would want us to use it. And it'll be safer too. I don't think there's much chance of anything falling on top of what's already come down."

Gordon didn't like to point out that it was more likely to happen here than anywhere else – especially if the tree was dying. But he sat across the log anyway, riding it, and Judith faced him in the same position. For a long time they did nothing but listen to the angry wind. It was as though the world were tearing out its own hair.

"Do you think we should go?" asked Gordon.

"If we don't go, they'll come and get us. It'll be like getting arrested."

"Collected."

"What?"

"They said they'd 'collect' us."

Neither of them spoke for a few moments.

"What do you think they want to find out?" asked Judith.

"I don't know. And I don't know why we have to go in there to answer their questions. Why couldn't they have asked us there and then?"

"Probably because Dad would have got his shotgun," said Judith, grinning.

"He wasn't far off it. But then all the anger just went out of him. He looked frightened, Jude. I've never seen him like that before."

Judith looked away. Not too far from the tree was the edge of Covey Wood and beyond that an expanse of field where no crops had grown for two years. Even now the field's surface was exposed and stony. Barely a weed would take hold in it, so spent was the soil. The wind had dried the top layer of the earth and whenever it wasn't raining, the wind lifted the soil and blew it away as brown ghosts shrieking across the land, as brown dust devils rising up in madness. Beyond these dead patches of land, dark mountains rose against the vengeful October sky.

"Angela's coming home," she said eventually.

"How come? I thought she had a job down there while she studies."

"She's coming home for good."

"But why? She hasn't finished. She won't get her degree."

"No. Probably not."

Judith leaned forwards and took her brother's hands in hers.

"I asked Mum and Dad to let me tell you." Tears swelled in her eyes. "She's sick, Gordon. The campus doctors don't know what it is and she can't get any tests done to find out more. She's too unwell to attend lectures. All she can do is come home."

"Why can't they just find out what's wrong with her and give her the right kind of medicine?"

"No one can get those kinds of tests any more unless it's part of an epidemic. There's no money for the hospitals now. You'd be lucky to get treatment for a broken arm."

"Well Dad can pay, then. He can get her to see a private doctor."

Judith looked away.

"Dad doesn't have that kind of money any more,

Gordon. All we have is the house and the garden and the animals. And that's a lot more than most people."

Gordon now looked out across the barren fields. He spoke with the voice of a little boy.

"Everything's changed, hasn't it?"

Judith didn't answer. She scooted towards him and wrapped him into her breast. She held him that way while they listened to the wood around them, listened to the trees trying to resist the power of the wind. From time to time, in other parts of the wood, they heard a splintering snap as more branches lost the battle. Something flashed down past them, fast on the air. It settled into the dry leaves and acorns covering the ground. Judith sat back and pointed.

"Look there."

"Where?"

"Just there. A white feather."

"So what?"

"Finding a white feather is a sign you've been blessed by an angel."

Gordon sat back.

"Really? Is that true?"

"I believe it."

He almost smiled.

"Maybe that means Angela will be OK," he said. "Maybe it's a blessing for her."

Judith nodded, happy for a moment in spite of everything.

"Jude?"

Gordon couldn't keep the tension from his voice.

"What is it?"

"What do black feathers mean?"

She shrugged.

"Black feathers? I don't know. Why do you ask?"

His grey eyes focussed in the distance.

"Those are the only ones I ever see."

Judith hopped off the fallen bough and snatched up the white feather before the wind could whip it away again.

"Not anymore," she said, poking it into the breast pocket of his coat. She gave him a small kiss. Standing back she smiled and cocked her head, looking at him in a way he didn't understand. She turned, kicking through the oak leaves as she walked away.

"We should go back," she said. "You know how Mum worries when you stay out too long."

Gordon slid off the log, landing evenly on both feet.

"She's never like that with you," he said.

"You're the youngest. They both worry about you the most."

They walked home in silence, Judith leading the way and Gordon losing himself in the landscape and the motion of the elements. Judith hadn't been able to answer his question about feathers. Her reticence on the matter made him think the worst; if white was a blessing then black must be a curse. Once he'd formed the idea, it was hard to think of anything else.

By the time they reached the door in the back wall of the garden, Gordon had made up his mind to sit down and talk to his mother properly about the crows and their feathers, ask her what she really thought it all meant. When Judith stepped through the door, having shouldered it to get it open, she froze, preventing Gordon from following her.

"What is it, Jude?"

"Go back."

"Why?"

She didn't turn to him but whispered as loudly as she could.

"The Ward. They're here. They've seen me."

She stepped through into the garden, turning to Gordon as she pushed the old door closed.

"They don't know you're here, Gordon. You should hide."

Her eyes spoke more than her words. Whatever she had seen in the garden had terrified her. Enough to tell him to get away. The door was almost closed now, her eyes were preparing to lie to whoever was approaching. She smiled first, though, wiping tears away and making herself look normal, like a girl coming home from a walk on her own.

"Run, Gordon!" she whispered. And as the gate closed, a softer breath passed through:

"I love you."

Not knowing why, Gordon did as he was told. The nearest cover was the hedges of the abandoned bridle-way. In thirty paces he was there, making himself tiny beyond a wall of blackthorn and looking back through the tangle of barbed branches. The old green door with its rusted hinges was still closed but he could hear voices: angry shouts and demands indistinct on the wind. Then the door was wrenched open and two men came out, one with his hand clamped around Judith's wrist. Gordon shrank and tried to be still but his body betrayed him, his heart beating so loud and hard he could hear nothing else. His whole body shook.

The men were dressed in the same grey raincoats, double breasted and tied at the waist with smart, stiff belts. They both wore the same grey, brimmed hats. But these were not Skelton and Pike; to Gordon they seemed like lesser versions, not sheriffs but foot soldiers.

"Where is he?" shouted the one holding his sister.

Gordon's fear turned to rage. He wanted to rush back and tear the man's hands from her, beat him with fists and feet and then drag Judith to safety. It was his duty to Judith, the one who'd always had the greatest love and care for him, more than his own mother. Yet rage wasn't enough and he already knew it. He wasn't strong enough to free her and his actions would only make things worse. In the moment when he might have rushed the two Wardsmen, he faltered. His fear returned, turning his limbs to lead.

I'm only a boy. I don't stand a chance.

He was too frightened to make good on what he knew to be right. That made him a coward, didn't it?

One of the men was demanding answers from his sister, yanking and shaking her by the arm.

"I've already told you," said Judith. "I haven't seen him since I went out. He's probably hiding in the attic."

"The attic?" said the other man.

"That's where he usually goes when he's frightened. You lot turning up like this has probably scared him half to death."

The two men pushed Judith back through the door. Gordon saw her looking his way but she couldn't see him. The green door was forced shut. He allowed himself a small grin; the attic? That was a brilliant lie. He had hidden in the attic once after an argument with his father but that was years ago. The smile dropped away fast.

The Ward had turned up a week early.

16

Gordon hunkered in the hedgerow until his legs ached. He heard occasional shouts from beyond the garden wall but couldn't make out the words.

What were they doing to them?

Keeping his head down, he sprinted to the green door, skirted the wall and dived into the bushes bordering their garden. His dive was blind and reckless and he caught his right thigh on a hidden thorn of rusted barbed wire. It tore through his jeans and into his flesh. Stifling a cry of pain, he tried to free himself and the spike ripped deeper. Grimacing, he backed up, his hands punctured by blackberry thorns, and lifted his leg free. He dragged himself through tiny animal runs in the undergrowth, leaving smears of blood on the soil.

Estimating he was about halfway along the length of the garden, he turned right and pushed through towards its border. Soon he could see the trunk of a pear tree. To his left, a little nearer the house, there was a laurel bush, probably the best cover in the whole garden. He crawled into the laurel, now almost in the garden. A Wardsman would only need to part the leaves and they'd see him crouching there.

He parted his shield of foliage a fraction. From here he could see most of Hamblaen House and look along its nearest wall, past the wood pile to where Skelton and Pike had first come in. This time they'd brought three vehicles: two four-wheel drives and a small truck, all grey. The truck had three tiny square windows along its side. Windows with black-tinted glass.

No!

Leaning against its cab was another greycoat smoking a cigarette. Conflict erupted from inside the house; shouting and slamming and things being broken. Gordon put a fist to his mouth.

Then his family appeared, each with their hands cuffed behind their backs, each attended by a Wardsman. His mother came first, her face streaked with tears and marked by a red hand-print. Gordon's rage swelled and he bit his knuckles.

I'll kill whoever hit my mother.

Judith came next; her hair, neatly wrapped into a bun on the back of her head when they went walking, was now loose around her shoulders, tangled and messy. His father was last to leave the house. Like the others, he was handcuffed but his head hung forwards and his face was bloody. Viscous drips still spilled from his nose and he could do nothing to wipe them away. The three of them were forced into the truck with the tiny windows. A Wardsman slammed its door.

Only then did Skelton and Pike appear, accompanied by another handful of greycoats. Skelton clasped his hands behind his back and his barrel gut preceded him, wrapped though it was by what must have been a specially tailored raincoat. He was smiling. Pike followed, something disjointed about the way his long, powerful

limbs moved. He removed a pair of grey gloves, each
with a slick of gore on them. Turning them inside out,
he placed them in a clear plastic bag which he then
slipped into his pocket.

Skelton spoke with the driver of the truck, who
stepped up into his cab, started his engine and drove out
of the entryway. Four Wardsmen climbed into one of the
four-wheel drives and followed. Skelton and Pike turned
and regarded the house, words passing between them
that Gordon couldn't hear. Skelton seemed reluctant to
leave, his eyes roving around the house and garden. His
gaze fell right upon the laurel where Gordon cowered,
right upon the parted branches. Gordon stopped breathing. Skelton looked away, still searching, but eventually
he turned and, with some difficulty, pulled himself into
the back seat of the remaining vehicle. Pike, too, struggled to get in the car, eventually folding himself in like a
contortionist. The remaining two Wardsmen sat up
front. One started the engine but for long moments the
car didn't move. Gordon had a sense that Skelton was
hesitating again, perhaps realising there were places they
hadn't thoroughly investigated. After minutes that felt
like hours to Gordon's crouch-weary legs, the car crept
away, out of the entry and turned right onto the country
road that led to Monmouth.

Gordon waited until the sound of the engines had
diminished to nothing. All was emptiness now but for
the insane wind, surging around the house and stream-
ing through the trees of their orchard, flaying the world
down to its raw flesh. Gordon collapsed back into the
laurel and wept.

17

Gordon hid for hours in the cover of the laurel bush. He couldn't erase the image of Judith's face as she shut the garden door on him, that change from fear and fierce love to a mask of nonchalance, the blinking and brushing away of sudden tears just before she was grabbed. Compared to that, his actions were those of a coward. They'd taken his family and all he'd done was hide in a bush.

I could have done something, he thought. I should have tried to stop them.

Gordon wanted to go into the house more than anything in the world, but wasn't it possible that they'd left a man or two inside to wait for him? If they thought he was still out here somewhere, didn't it make perfect sense that he would return? Gradually, an idea formed and, tired of hiding, tired of hating himself, but mostly very hungry, Gordon moved from his hiding place.

Beneath the laurel there was good clearance between the soil and the lowest branches and he made use of this by crawling on his stomach. The laurel brought him to within a few feet of the tarpaulin-covered wood pile which, if he stayed low, would shield him from anyone looking out of a window, even upstairs.

His pulse rising, he peered out from under the foliage. The house had an air of stillness about it. He scanned every window visible from his leafy hide and saw no movement, no watchful eyes. He checked what he could see of the corners of the back terrace. If there was anyone out there they were hidden and still.

He slipped out from under the laurel and slithered to the wood pile. There he gathered himself into a crouch and waited. No sounds came from the house. No one came out. He peeped around the edge of the tarpaulin. He was a few steps from the back terrace now. He looked up and checked the windows again.

Nothing.

A sprint of a few seconds took Gordon to the back wall of the house. Pain and stiffness around the cut in his right thigh slowed him down. Even pressed flat against the bricks he was exposed. He couldn't stay there. He was suddenly convinced there'd been a Wardsman patrolling all day.

Before he could progress, he had to put his mind at rest on one issue. Wincing as he dropped to a crouch again, Gordon crawled on hands and knees over the stone walkway which hugged the walls of Hamblaen House. He passed under the first living room window. Fear pressing down on him, he continued his crawl under the second living room window. When he had passed beneath it without event, he proceeded to the front corner of the house and stood up, once again laying his back to the wall and palming the bricks as though on a ledge. He gave his heart and breathing a few seconds to settle and then, as slowly as he could, and ready to pull back at any moment, he peered around the corner. More and more of the tiny driveway in front of their house came into view and the more he saw, the more his hopes rose. Finally, he was looking along the front edge of the house to the porch and it was clear.

He rested his head back against the wall and relaxed for a moment. It was no guarantee there wasn't someone waiting for him inside, but the absence of vehicles gave him a tiny reserve of confidence.

The windows at the front of the house were longer and lower, and getting past them unseen would be very difficult. Not only that, the entire area outside the front door was gravelled, making silent progress impossible. Gordon retraced his route, returning under the living room windows and placing himself once more against the back wall of the house. He wanted to peep over the sills of the windows, but he couldn't bring himself to do it. He'd known all along that returning to the house was a risk but, now that he had to make the play, he was seizing up again, stiffening with fear.

That's not going to happen. Not this time.

Crawling again, he crossed the back terrace under the windows until he reached the recessed area which led to the back door. He glanced around the corner, terrified by the recklessness of the move. There was no one there. The door was closed.

He crept towards it. There was a single, small pane of glass in it – like water frozen the moment after a pebble has been dropped into it. He peeped through into the hallway but the view was distorted. He thought he could see something at the bottom of the stairs. Whatever it was, it didn't move. He looked for a long time, trying to work out what it might be. The shoe of a man sitting out of sight on the third step? A man smoking, waiting? Gordon took a deep breath and put his fingers to the iron curl of the door handle. He pushed it down. Inside the mechanism, tiny springs creaked.

Then he was pushing the door open a millimetre at a time. Pushing it open and stepping inside.

The house *did* smell of smoke and this was enough to stop Gordon on the threshold, with the door still open. With each lengthening of the moment, his resolve leaked away. He had to close the door and either stay or leave. The wind wasn't helping his cause; the noise of its whooshing passage through the trees had entered with him. If anyone was here, they'd have heard it already. But leaving would only put him back where he'd started.

He wanted an escape route but he couldn't leave the door open.

What if the wind slams it? he thought.

A cold draught felt somewhere else in the house might be enough to give him away. He pushed the door closed behind him, gently shouldered it tight to the jamb and cringed when it loudly clicked shut.

He edged along the hall, pulse thudding.

The thing at the bottom of the stairs was Judith's coat, lying where it had been dropped or thrown. They hadn't even let her take something warm. Surges of anger accompanied his pangs of fear.

Ahead and to his left was the living room door, open as always. It was level with the bottom of the stairs and Gordon was able to peep up through the banisters and see that there was no Wardsman lying in wait. Reaching the doorway he forced his breathing to slow and craned his neck around the corner. The living room was empty. One of the wooden chairs beside the baize card table had been knocked over and the glass panel of the drinks cabinet had been smashed.

Gordon remembered his father's promise to protect them all and his hand went to his mouth. A noble oath Louis Black had been unable to fulfil. Gordon shared his father's shame.

By the fireplace was a set of wrought-iron hearth tools and Gordon crossed quickly to retrieve the poker. It was the first weapon he'd thought of – until he could get to a shotgun. With the poker in his hand, another small objective was achieved. Emboldened, he searched the rest of the house.

It took Gordon almost half an hour to establish the house was empty of agents but the Ward had not trod lightly through it. Every room showed signs of disturbance: drawers open, their contents rifled; mattresses still partially off the beds; clothes torn from wardrobes and left on the floor. The more he discovered, the angrier he became. Part of him *wanted* to find a Wardsman, perhaps napping on the job, and take him by surprise. He wanted to beat one of them – any of them, all of them – to the floor and keep bludgeoning until they weren't able to stand.

How can they do this? he wondered. We're not criminals.

Gordon had never witnessed real violence. He'd seen occasional scuffles and flares of temper at school but never serious harm. Footage of civil unrest was on the news most nights. Police raids were an increasingly common part of the bulletins and, now that he thought about it, Gordon remembered seeing grey-coated "bystanders" in many of those news items. He'd seen them attendant at demonstrations too – some of them mounted on horses in full riot armour of the same nondescript grey – but rarely involving themselves directly. Now, all Gordon could see was his father's bowed and bloodied face. He could only imagine what the Wardsmen had done, what more they would do. They looked coldly civilised in their neat, belted raincoats and brimmed hats. All of them moved with calm assurance, not a wrinkle in their uniforms, not a hair out of place. And yet they were capable of all this.

Even when he was sure the house was safe, Gordon still tiptoed. In his room he grabbed his camping rucksack and in it he placed the diary he kept under the carpet in his closet. The Wardsmen hadn't looked there but they had discovered and taken his collection of black feathers. What bearing would a box of feathers have on their "investigation"? He gathered some spare clothes and placed them on top of the books. In the study, he took the lock knife from the pocket of his father's tweed jacket. The shotguns and all the ammo were gone.

In the bathroom he took off his jeans and cleaned the wound in his thigh. It began as a scratch near his hip and deepened into a gouge. Some of the skin and tissue around the edge of it looked ruined and lifeless already. He took scissors from the cabinet and with a trembling hand tried to clip away some of the torn flesh. He realised at the first touch of steel that it wasn't dead tissue. Using a flannel moistened with hot water, he wiped away the dried blood and swabbed into the cut to try to clear away the dirt. When he'd finished, his whole leg was trembling and the flannel was filthy. He placed a disinfectant-soaked pad over the cut and wrapped a bandage around his leg. Down in the kitchen he hid the flannel at the bottom of the rubbish bin under the sink.

He made himself a large Ziploc bag of cheese sandwiches and stashed it in the pack. He took a leftover pot of chicken casserole from the fridge and heated some of it in the microwave. He ate it quickly, washed the bowl and cutlery and put it away. Everywhere he went in the house, he left it as he'd found it. He even opened the kitchen window for a few minutes to let the wind carry away the smell of cooked food.

He collected more supplies from the pantry, enough for a few days, just in case. He attached his waterproof sleeping bag to the bottom of the rucksack and strapped his tent onto the back of it. His father had ensured the whole family could survive outdoors in an emergency. Gordon would camp nearby while he waited for Skelton and Pike to bring his family home.

Before leaving, Gordon took the white feather Judith had given him earlier that day and placed it under her pillow. He doubted the Ward would search the place a second time. He wanted her to know he was OK.

18

Gordon kept to the edge of the garden as he ran to the green door and forced his way through. Pushing it closed again, he set off at a fast walk. He was determined and steadfast at first. Sheriff Skelton and Sheriff Pike became the central victims in a dozen brutal fantasies.

With every step he took from the house his outrage diminished. The cut in his thigh throbbed harder and the muscle around it tightened, slowing him down. The rucksack became a burden and he knew himself and his plans for what they were: the daydreams of a fourteen year-old boy who had no power in this world. Long before he reached the end of the disused bridle-way, long before the abandoned railway tunnel mouth came into view, Gordon was crying so hard he could barely see.

When he reached the tunnel mouth he slung off his pack. It landed and tipped over and he left it that way. On either side of the maw of the tunnel was a grass bank and there, to the right of the black opening, was where Gordon collapsed, sitting first and then lying down and curling in on himself with his arms covering his head.

The day began to die. Gordon didn't care. He could lie there all night, balled up.

What did it matter?

But with the sun paling and falling the wind was colder, and soon he was uncomfortable enough to sit up. As he wiped his face of tears, two magpies flew up over the hedge on the far side of the bridleway, fast-patting the air with black wings and flashing their white breasts. They both landed on his toppled ruck-sack and proceeded to flick their tails up, bob their heads down and broadcast their ratcheted chatter.

He was so shocked he didn't move. Magpies never got this close; they were far too wary of humans. And yet, here they were, not ten feet away from him and acting as though he didn't even exist. But there was still plenty of light and every now and again he was sure they were cocking their heads and looking right at him.

One for sorrow, two for joy...

"Well you've got that wrong," he said.

The magpies stopped calling and bouncing. They regarded him for a moment more and then took off. They flew into the mouth of the tunnel. Gordon scrambled down the grass bank after them. If they came back out now they'd have to fly right past him.

He stood on the threshold looking into the darkness and smelled the tunnel's cold, earthy breath pushing out at him. The magpies were gone. He waited there a long time, not believing that they would stay in there and then, terribly far away, so far he almost could have imagined it, he heard a single clicking call. Then all was silence.

He gave up the vigil when he saw how the darkness was gathering. If he wanted a decent place to sleep he needed to set it up right now. He cleared a space on the flattest-looking piece of ground nearby, throwing rocks to either side. Then, laying out the tent's base, he began to pitch his tiny, solitary camp.

October 5th '14
My eyes only

I shouldn't waste the torch batteries like this but I've got to write something or I'll go insane. I can get more batteries tomorrow when I go back to the house. I'm going every day until they come home.

I keep replaying this story in my mind. In it, I go back to the house with a shotgun and I see Ward vehicles parked at the front of the house. I sneak in the back door and there's a Wardsman standing in the corridor watching the front door. I shoot him in the back of the neck. A second Wardsman comes out of the living room fumbling for his gun. He gets the second round in the chest and slides down the wall, leaving a smear of blood. I take his pistol and reload the shotgun. I go upstairs. A Wardsman is coming down to meet me, pistol drawn and ready. I fire first, obliterating his hat and the top of his head. At the top of the stairs, two Wardsmen are running for the nearest door. My second cartridge hits both of them, knocking them down. There's no time to reload so I take the pistol and each of them gets a bullet in the spine. I reload the shotgun and clear the house one room at a time until eight Wardsmen lie dead. I remove all their weapons and ammo, find a set of car keys and drive to the Ward substation in Monmouth where I storm the building and rescue Mum, Dad and Jude.

It makes me feel a bit better and it keeps my mind occupied. Please, God, let them be safe and please, God, let me sleep.

19

After some days of rising before dawn and making her way through increasingly chillier mornings to Mr Keeper's roundhouse, a little of the magic goes out of Megan's new life. Routine takes the shine off the mystery. Each morning when she arrives, Mr Keeper shows her how to pray and make offerings to the Earth Amu, to the Great Spirit, to the animals and plants and to other beings who inhabit the woods. He makes her tidy up the mess inside his roundhouse and clear away any debris from outside while he smokes and drinks tea.

Then they walk out into the meadows and grasslands or into the many wooded areas or along the rampant hedgerows where Megan never knows what creatures she might see. Sometimes Mr Keeper brings his long-bow, teaching Megan to hunt. He's able to drop a rabbit at fifty paces or more, a deer at a hundred. They never want for meat. Each day is different, though the lessons are often the same. They collect berries from the many bushes which are in fruit, some of which they eat, keeping others for his concoctions. They collect herbs and fungi which they dry above the stove in the round-house. Together they visit the sick in the village and

Megan gets to know more of the people and learn a little about their troubles. Occasionally, she sees Sally Balston and Tom Frewin, friends she used to play with every day. Now all she can do is wave as they run to the meadow or the river to make mischief. Once or twice Mr Keeper is called to accidents and she accompanies him as he set bones, bandages sprains or rouses a woman from a faint.

In general, however, what started out as the most amazing adventure has become somewhat dull. Nor has she dreamed of the boy since the night he took her through the ruins to the dead forest and the black tree to give her his heart.

Now, as Mr Keeper rambles along a wall of hawthorn looking for something in the ditch at its root, Megan recognises the feeling she's having. She's bored. She follows along behind him for a while longer, trying hard to search with him, but she doesn't even know what he's looking for.

Finally, she says:

"Has the Crowman forgotten about me?"

Mr Keeper keeps shuffling along, bent to half his usual stature as he peers under the thorny branches and through their covering of deep red berries.

"Hm?" he says after a while.

"The Crowman. Do you think he's forgotten about me?"

He creeps along a little farther, as though stalking unseen prey.

"The Crowman? Oh, no. He hasn't forgotten."

"But how do you know? He's not doing anything. Nothing's happening."

Mr Keeper stops now and straightens up. He leans

back to stretch and she hears his spine cracking in a dozen places. He looks at Megan.

"You're impatient."

There's no point denying it. She nods.

"Well, you're young," says Mr Keeper. "You can't help it."

He bends down and continues his search. Fearing she's lost her opportunity to make a point, Megan hurries after him.

"What I want to know is when will... it... happen?"

Mr Keeper stands up again and faces her.

"When will what happen, Megan?"

"Well... whatever it is. Whatever's meant to happen."

"What makes you think it isn't happening now?"

"Now?"

"Right now. Right here as we speak."

Megan considers.

"Because I don't feel anything. Nothing is happening."

Mr Keeper looks up at the sky to see where the sun is. He slips off his backpack and lets it gently down to the grass.

"Let's sit for a while," he says.

Once he's descended the great height of himself to stretch out among the fronds of the meadow, Megan watches Mr Keeper run his fingers over and through the long grass, seed heads fully formed now on many stalks. He luxuriates in the contact, it seems, his eyes focussing elsewhere for long moments. Megan sits down too and waits for his absence to clear.

As the days spent with Mr Keeper have gathered behind her, she has been able to parallel his rhythms quite accurately. She knows when to stay quiet and when to volunteer help. She also knows he has episodes of removal from the moment; it isn't just a matter of him thinking of something deeply, it's as though his spirit leaves his body. During these episodes it is better not to interrupt him. Twice she's done so, thinking he was merely not concentrating and twice he has "come back" prematurely and been irritable and uncommunicative for the rest of the day.

So now, as he stares through the hawthorn and caresses the grass, she merely waits, listening to the throaty call of rooks in the nearby wood and watching the breeze touching the whole meadow as gently as Mr Keeper touches a few of its living strands. Megan's attention floats away too and she is surprised when it returns to the sight of something being offered to her.

"Here," he says. "Have some oat loaf."

Mr Keeper has come back before her. She takes the piece he's holding out, a half moon of pale bread about the size of her palm. He chews slowly on the other half. After he swallows the first bite he says:

"Have you ever been to Dulas Pond?"

"I've been fishing there a few times with Apa."

"There are some days when you can sit by Dulas Pond and everything is still. Winter days, usually. No insects hover over the water and no wind touches it. No kingfishers dive for food. And the land all around is quiet too, as though everything is asleep. But even though the surface of Dulas Pond is completely tranquil and undisturbed, things are going on down in the depths. All kinds of fish are feeding down there and their muck adds to the muck at the very bottom of the pond, day by day. If you took some of the slime from the bottom of Dulas Pond and put it on your pumpkin patch, you'd grow the biggest pumpkins hereabouts. That pond muck is richer than you can imagine."

Megan chews on her piece of oat loaf, knowing that Mr Keeper will get to the point eventually.

"You're like Dulas Pond, Megan. Nothing is happening on the surface and so you think nothing is happening beneath. But the truth is that all kinds of things you aren't even aware of are happening way down inside you. Sooner or later, those things are going to help you bring forth great bounties – not just for you but for everyone hereabouts. Do you see what I'm telling you?"

"I suppose so."

"Well, whether you do or you don't, I know it's happening. And when the time comes, many great and unexpected things will rise from the deep, deep pond that is Megan Maurice." He pops a piece of oat loaf into his mouth, chewing it slowly. "You just have to be patient. And the best way to be patient is to do other things so that you forget what you're waiting for."

While she understands everything Mr Keeper is saying, Megan still doesn't find it any easier knowing that, for now, all she can do is wait. She's about to ask if there's anything she can do to make "things", whatever they might be, happen more quickly when she hears the feathery swoosh of wing-beats – so close she imagines she can feel the downdraught from them. A grey-beaked rook passes over and lands on the lifeless branch of a tree poking up from the hawthorns that have choked it to death.

Megan and Mr Keeper are silent and still as they watch the rook. It hops up and lands again, turning to the right. Then again, turning to the left. Looking almost uncomfortable, it opens and closes its wings a fraction, as if trying to fold them more neatly. Then it pushes its head forwards, extends its throat and gives three long, loud croaks, its breast enlarging and its tail feathers stiffening with effort. Then it flies, leaving the dead branch bouncing from the force of takeoff.

Mr Keeper springs up and watches its progress until it disappears from view in Covey Wood. He puts the last of his oat loaf in his mouth and pulls on his backpack. Seeing the intensity in his face, Megan jumps up too.

"We need to go for a walk, Megan," he says through a floury mouthful. "And we need to go quickly."

He sets off, his long legs devouring distance, and Megan is suddenly running to keep up. Finding a break in the hawthorn, Mr Keeper plunges down into the ditch, through the rambling hedge and up the other side. By the time Megan has made the same manoeuvre, Mr Keeper is thirty paces ahead and striding out for Covey Wood. She hasn't been there since seeing the Crowman. After waiting all this time for something to happen, she suddenly finds that her legs are heavy and her feet clumsy. Keeping up with Mr Keeper, something else she's learned how to do over the span of their days together, now seems impossible.

When she finally catches up to Mr Keeper, he is standing on the threshold of Covey Wood, staring up into the trees. It began as a warm, clear day with a lazy breeze nodding the haw-berries. Now everything has changed. The sky is clogged with low cloud and the air is still and heavy. A shiver passes over Megan's whole body and she moves close to Mr Keeper's side.

The clouds must have come from somewhere but without a wind, how did they get here? The land all around has lost its colour and the trees of Covey Wood look black. Many have lost at least half their leaves and suddenly she remembers walking through the dead forest in the night country, led by the boy. The clouds press lower and Megan feels suddenly exhausted, all the strength in her legs sucked away into the earth. Her own small pack now feels burdensome. She wants to ask Mr Keeper what's happening but doesn't dare break his concentration. Soon the clouds have become an invading mist that slips down around them and into the wood, wrapping around the trees and entwining itself into their branches like vaporous serpents.

Unable to bear the stillness and silence of the moment, Megan takes a few steps towards the wood. Mr Keeper's hand firmly holds her shoulder as she tries to pass him.

"We haven't been given leave."

His hand, comfortable and strong but very definite in its intent, is an anchor in these suddenly untrustworthy waters. She takes confidence from it. This is just a change of the weather. Nothing to fret about. Autumn is making its presence known, rationing the sunlight and dampening the spirit. But if that's true, why is Mr Keeper so… vigilant? He still hasn't taken his eyes from the higher branches of the trees, even though it's now almost impossible to see them through the mist. What is he waiting for?

Somewhere deep in Covey Wood, so distant she might have imagined it, Megan hears a single gravelly caw. It can't be her imagination, though, because that's when Mr Keeper finally breaks from his own stillness and begins to walk towards the outermost trees of the wood. Leave, it appears, has now been given.

Before he reaches the trees, he turns back to her.

"You won't need to worry about nothing happening any more, Megan." His smile is almost sad. As though he's recalling some kind of loss. "Whatever you do, stay close to me – the mist will get thicker." He reaches out and plucks Megan's magpie feather from her hair where she's been wearing it at his bidding. "Hold this in your left hand. If we do get separated put the feather to your brow, think of me and call my name. I'll come and find you."

Before she can ask what is happening, he has stepped between the threshold trees and is in the wood. Already he is indistinct through the mist. Megan has no choice but to follow.

She wants to hold his hand; that's what would make her feel safest, but she knows she can't. Mr Keeper is not her father and she is not meant to be a little girl any more. But she is afraid. The mist is alive somehow. It presses against her, worms under her clothes until it chills her skin with its moist caress. She puts her right hand out to waft the vapour away like smoke, but the mist will not be so easily dismissed. Strands catch her fingers before tearing and melting away. What replaces the evaporated fibres is thicker, like wet, airborne web. After walking for some distance she notices that the less she thinks about the mist, the thinner it becomes and the better she can see.

Though she's been through Covey Wood dozens of times, she doesn't recognise where she is. One moment she'll see a familiar landmark and then the path leads somewhere unrecognisable. Either that, or something appears that shouldn't be there – a small pool, an area of marsh grass, an impenetrable bramble thicket or a stream. As she follows Mr Keeper she has the sense that they are being led by the mist. Accepting this, the way becomes easier. In the moments when she tries to remember the way, obstacles appear and the path becomes more difficult.

Mr Keeper stops and Megan comes up close beside him. As they wait, surrounded by the fibrous white-out, she begins to feel the mist tugging her. Mr Keeper, too, sways on his feet as the currents in the fog become stronger. The tugging is rhythmic, drawing the mist forwards and past them, releasing it and then drawing some more. Mr Keeper lowers himself to his knees, which makes him about the same height as Megan. He takes her hands in his making them seem tiny, and looks at her in the hypnotic, gently commanding way that he has.

"The time has come for us to part for a while, Megan, but you mustn't worry. I'm never far away and you have your feather if you need to call on me. The Crowman is up ahead. He's weaving the night country and the day world together so that you can understand your dreams. And he's weaving the strands of time, past, present and future, so that you may travel between them."

Megan shakes her head.

"I don't want to go to another time."

His smile is patient, amused.

"You won't go anywhere you can't return from. The Crowman wants you to see along the threads of time, backwards and forwards. He wants to tell you his story.

This is what we've been waiting for. Your training begins in earnest today."

Megan knows she cannot refuse. This is what she has promised to do. Not only is it her promise, she understands that this was what she was born for. To deny it now would be to discard the preciousness of her life. But it doesn't make being left alone in the woods with the Crowman any less terrifying.

"Are you ready to live in his sign?" asks Mr Keeper.

And even though she doesn't really know the answer yet, she says:

"I am."

Mr Keeper places a kiss on her forehead and gently turns her away from him, turns her into the future, just a few paces away, where the Crowman now sits, knitting dreams and reality, twining time into time.

Megan takes a step forwards, deeper into the woods.

20

Gordon kept all his clothes on in his sleeping bag. Even his boots. He thought it was unlikely that the Ward would pursue him at night, but if they had an idea of where he was, he supposed they might. Sleep did not come easily. After an hour of fidgeting and shifting, he sat up and wrote an entry in his black journal by torch-light.

One thing he'd overlooked was a mat to lie his sleeping bag on. He counted the cost in broken sleep. But even if he'd been lying in a warm comfortable bed in an expensive campervan with a safely locked door, he knew he would not have been free of the constant pecking of anxiety.

Within the partial hours where he did find rest, dreams awaited him.

He is running. Behind him are all the powers of the Ward. They come in four-wheel drives, on foot, on horseback, even in tanks and armoured cars. Everything about them is grey, even their mounts; their uniforms are suited to their mode of chase. Those on horseback wear riot gear with visored helmets. Those in tanks wear battle dress; the drivers and runners wear their long, double-breasted raincoats, buttoned and belted as always. Archibald Skelton and Mordaunt Pike lead the charge on foot, displaying superhuman speed and holding their pistols aloft.

Gordon is slow because he still wears his rucksack, because he is running through muddy ruts in cropless, barren fields. The soil is so spent from intense farming that it too is grey. The Ward close in and the first bullets sing past him. Gordon's footsteps get slower, the ground sucks at him. Tears of frustration soak his face.

In a last-chance bid to widen the gap between him and his pursuers, he drops his rucksack. The effect is instant and miraculous. His body is now the very wind itself and he surges forwards, power rising up in him from the earth. His feet barely touch the mud.

He chances a look behind.

Diesel engines grumble to a scream, horses accelerate from trot to canter to gallop, the tanks and armoured cars howl and tear at the dead earth, finding purchase and charging forwards. Skelton and Pike's feet become a blur. Once again the Ward close in. Tank shells explode to left and right, knocking the breath from him and sealing his ears with concussion. Bullets bite the dirt at his feet.

Gordon leaps, forwards and upwards, reaching for the sky. An updraught takes him, wind smoothes the tears from his face and he spreads his arms wide. He takes flight and rises fast. Looking down he sees the Wardsmen lose the fire of the chase and come to a stop. None can follow him now. As he sees this, he also sees that his legs are now tucked under sleek black belly feathers. His feet are black claws. Looking from side to side he sees his arms are outstretched wings, his wingtips spread like black razorblades. Minor adjustments of his feathers cause him to turn and dive or rise and roll. He is free and soaring up to the heavens, lifting through the clouds which have blocked out the sun for so long.

Above them there is only golden light from a sun so bright he can't look at it. This light descends from a sky of pure deep blue. Below him now is a land of brilliant white cloud, smooth and pure. He soars, knowing his blackness is beautiful against the white, against the light. Below him he can see his shadow speeding across the surface of the new landscape, keeping pace with every swoop or ascent.

Diving back towards the clouds to touch his own shadow, he flies through the cotton-candy clouds, their mist condensing on his beak and breast feathers. Something hits him and he lurches downwards. He tries to regain his lift by spreading his wings but they are restricted. A mesh has snared him. The Ward have fired their nets up into the sky and caught him. Now, he falls rolling over and over without any control.

Far below, the ground widens and gives up the details of itself like a map and then like an aerial photograph and finally he is hurtling earthwards at terminal velocity. He sees an army of Wardsmen waiting for him and blacks out just before he hits the earth.

Gordon woke to the sound of his own voice still crying out into the darkness. His bed was hard and jagged beneath him and it took a while for him to remember where he was. Anything was better than falling out of the sky into the hands of the Ward. At least out here in his tent he was still at liberty. At least he still had a chance to stay that way.

He rubbed his face. The light was returning. If they were coming for him, they wouldn't be far away. Feeling bruised all over from sleeping on the rough ground he sat up, unzipped his sleeping bag and stowed it. Within a few minutes he'd taken down his tent and everything else was packed away. He hoisted his rucksack, switched on his torch and entered the tunnel.

Ten paces inside, all traces of ordinary flora were gone. Grass and weeds could not survive the darkness and so he walked now upon bare, well-packed earth. His footsteps were muffled but they echoed away from him into the tunnel's endless snake-belly. He shone his torch left and right, above and ahead. In the cracks between the bricks grew some kind of damp rot which flaked like white scabs. In other cracks between the ground and the first course of brickwork, fungi grew in incestuous clumps. The air grew thick and tainted. He tasted wet dust on his tongue. The idea that trains had once thundered through this darkness unnerved him a little, even though he knew he was in no danger now. The tunnel's silence seemed to hold no memory of such powerful vibrations. Although he and Judith had explored the tunnel and even hidden in it before, neither of them had ever walked this far in. Gordon found it hard to keep moving. What if the tunnel collapsed, crushing or trapping him? Two forces fluxed in the darkness: one, like hungry black gravity, sucked him deeper. The other, his fear, and the menacing darkness, repelled him. He willed himself on.

When he thought he'd walked far enough, he dropped his pack and took out everything he didn't

need for his return to the house, before putting it back
on, almost empty. His torch lit the way back to the tunnel's mouth and from there he climbed up the grassy
bank on his right so that he could get to the other side
of the hedge. That way he could take the same route
home without walking along the bridleway itself.

If the Ward were searching for him, he'd see them
before they saw him.

From the hedge at the beginning of the bridleway
where he'd hidden the day before, the house and garden looked clear. But he watched for a long time before
daring to cross the open ground between the hawthorn
and the back wall of the garden. It was impossible to
open the green door quietly but he did his best, edging
and forcing it a few millimetres at a time until there was
enough space to squeeze through. Leaving it open was
risky, but he weighed it up before moving on. If there
was someone in the house right now, he might need to
get away quickly. If there was no one there he could
close the door again when he left and all would appear
undisturbed. He left it open and moved towards the
house, far more boldly than he'd done the previous day.

Nothing moved inside – at least, nothing he could see
through the windows. Limping slightly, he used the
trees for cover instead of crawling. When he'd reached
the tree nearest the back terrace he had a better view
of the windows on the ground floor and he took his
time, now, checking each one for movement or anything out of place. When he was satisfied, he checked
the front of the house. There were still no vehicles.
Once again he entered the house through the unlocked
back door and went in search of supplies.

He was upstairs in the bathroom changing the dressing on his cut when he heard the approach of a diesel engine. It came quickly up the country road, pulled into the entry and ground to a halt on the gravel. Gordon heard the handbrake ratcheted and two doors slammed. He froze. Part of him refused to believe his bad luck; the rest of him slipped into shock. No matter how fast he moved, there would be no getting out of the house. The front door opened and closed as he tied off his bandage and replaced the first-aid kit in the bathroom cabinet.

21

The house was old and its floorboards creaked but Gordon knew its foibles well. He already recognised one voice: the castrato tones of Sheriff Archibald Skelton. Shifting his weight stealthily from foot to foot, Gordon listened.

As he navigated the upstairs hallway, he heard Skelton say: "He'll be back today. I guarantee it. All we have to do is wait."

Sheriff Mordaunt Pike made some low growl of agreement. Gordon swallowed and kept moving.

"They're not merely protecting him out of love, you know, Pike. They know about him – the parents for certain."

Footfalls moved along the downstairs hallway, deeper into the house.

"The younger sister is interesting, don't you think?" asked Skelton.

If Pike answered, Gordon couldn't hear what he said.

"Utterly loyal," continued Skelton. "And yet, I don't think she really knows anything about it. She may suspect, I suppose, but that's about it. She couldn't help us even if she wanted to."

Creaking on the stairs made Gordon's heart somer-sault in his chest. He'd expected them to search the downstairs first. There was only one place he had time to get to. He made it to the threshold of his bedroom and crossed on tiptoe to the closet.

"Now, the sick one... she might make this easy for us. It's obvious she envies the boy. We could use her to bring him in."

Pike rumbled a response that Gordon couldn't make out. So they had Angela too? When had that hap-pened? Skelton was in his parents' bedroom. Gordon could hear him flinging items aside as he searched for something. Gordon stepped into the closet and stood to one side, pulling his winter clothes towards himself to hide behind.

Skelton's voice carried:

"It must be here somewhere, Pike. Our boys just didn't look carefully enough yesterday. Enjoying them-selves too much, no doubt. Find the book and we find the boy. Find the boy and all this is over before it starts."

This time there was no answer from Pike. Gordon heard Skelton step back into the upstairs hallway.

"Pike? Do you hear me, man?"

Pike didn't answer. Gordon felt something in the silence. He heard a second set of footsteps on the stairs. Slow. Methodical. A tall, heavy man in no hurry, approaching relentlessly.

What is it? What's wrong?

Gordon's sweat chilled as the answer came to him. He'd left his rucksack in the kitchen. He imagined the giant holding it up to his partner.

"Ah," said Skelton, his tone oily with satisfaction.

"That does put a brighter perspective on things, doesn't it?"

The sound of boots on worn carpet and loose floorboards came closer.

"Master Black," said the voice outside his bedroom.

From Gordon's place in the dark closet, Skelton's voice was that of a woman with a hoarse throat.

"We're so pleased you've come back. Your family is very worried about you."

The voice approached no closer. It sounded as though Skelton had turned away – towards the bathroom.

"They miss you, you know. Judith... *Jude*... is especially concerned for your welfare."

The motherly voice returned, coming closer than before. Skelton had to be in his room now. All Gordon had left was a tiny element of surprise; if he burst from the closet now, there was a chance he could duck past them and away down the stairs. He readied himself but he couldn't make the move. The possibility of escape slipped farther away with each beat of his heart and each extra moment spent thinking instead of acting.

"We've promised them we'll bring you back. Bring you back safe and sound."

The voice came from outside the closet door. Gordon shook, his stomach clenched. As he reached into his coat pocket and found what nestled there, the closet door was flung wide and the hanging clothes were swept away.

The sudden brightness defined the shadow of Skelton's giant accomplice, Sheriff Mordaunt Pike. Huge hands came for him out of the light and took his shoulders. It was like being lifted by a crane. He found himself looking straight into the death mask of Pike's face, its hollows and angles grim, its eyes lit only by the excitement of Gordon's capture. Pike's breath was tobacco smoke, whisky and rot. Behind him, smiling like a wide-mouthed frog, stood Skelton. The fat little man shook his head with a grin.

"So, this is the herald of the dark messiah, the boy we must all fear. There must be some mistake, Pike. He's nothing but a weedy stripling. A frightened, crying child."

Pike's mouth spread into a robotic grin exposing broken, infected teeth. The smile switched off after a second, as though its power had been cut.

"Still," said Skelton, "I suppose we'd better take him in. Bring him to the car."

Skelton led the way out of the bedroom and back towards the stairs. As though Gordon weighed no more than a walking stick, Pike transferred him under his arm. Gordon remained passive for a few seconds while his right hand worked frantically in his coat pocket. Halfway along the upstairs passage, his hand came free of his coat and he drove his father's lock knife through Pike's grey raincoat, towards his groin.

The knife was sharp and it slipped easily through the waterproof material. It cut through something meaty, before it struck bone and stopped. Pike stopped too and looked down to see Gordon pull his weapon free. He dropped the boy, as though discovering his walking stick was a snake. From where Gordon landed on the hallway floor, he had a moment in which to look up and see pain register in Pike's expression, hate rising in his eyes along with–

Pike screamed, a powerful but hollow sound, like a blast from a broken organ pipe. Everything about him was motorised and emotionless.

He's not human, thought Gordon.

The huge man's hands went to his wound and blood welled through his raincoat. Gordon could now see it was not Pike's manhood he'd damaged but something to the right. There was no way to tell if this was enough to stop the man from coming after him.

Gordon scrambled to his feet and charged at Skelton. The frog man was only now seeing what he'd done to Pike. At the top of the stairs Skelton crouched a little, spreading his arms wide to catch the boy or drive him back towards Pike.

Gordon didn't stop. He didn't turn. He rushed straight at Skelton, who seemed delighted that it was going to be so easy until he saw the flash of Gordon's weapon coming at him like a right hook. Even then he didn't raise a hand to protect himself. Gordon's blade pecked hard at his face.

For a moment, a tiny moment within the arc of the blade's onslaught, Gordon could see that Skelton believed he'd missed. His facial muscles were beginning to pull into a grin when steel sunk into the left side of his nose, above its bridge. Gordon withdrew the knife, watching pain register and blood pour forth. Skelton fell to his knees, raising his hands to the left side of his face. When he took them away, his cupped hands full of blood, he looked only through his right eye. The other was squeezed shut.

Gordon could see why. He'd sliced through Skelton's left eye, driving the point of the blade across into Skelton's nose. Now the man was trying to keep the ruptured contents behind his tightly closed eyelid. It did no good. Vitreous fluid leaked freely from the socket, mingling with his blood.

I should have stabbed forwards. He'd be dying if I had.

He should have, but he hadn't. Neither Pike nor Skelton was dead. Their screams – one like the wail of a steam whistle, the other like a woman robbed in the street – were testament to that. And before he'd reached the bottom of the stairs Gordon heard the mechanical giant snorting and stomping down after him.

"Get him, Pike," shrieked Skelton. "Bring him back to me. Then we'll teach him how to use a knife *properly*."

Gordon sprinted up the passage to the back door, raced out and slammed it behind him. Suddenly weightless with triumph, he flew across the back garden, knowing Pike still wasn't out of the back door. He reached the green door thanking God he'd left it open and tore away up the bridleway, his knife still slick and dripping.

When he could no longer keep up his sprint, Gordon looked back. He couldn't see Pike but he didn't stop. Even with Pike limping, his head start would be nothing more than a very few minutes. And Skelton would be calling in for more men. The running was hard and soon he slowed to a trot, looking over his shoulder every few steps. For the moment there was no sign of Pike. Long before he reached the end of the bridleway, Gordon was interspersing running with a fast walk to save his strength but maintain his advantage.

Finally, he cleared the last bend in the bridleway and saw the opening of the tunnel. Spurred on by making it this far, he found new strength in his legs and ran the last stretch with a growing sense of elation. He had, at least in part, paid Skelton and Pike back for taking away his family and abusing their home. He reached into his coat pocket for his torch, switched it on and ran into the tunnel. Even when he saw the Wardsman waiting for him in the darkness, he didn't quite believe it. His momentum carried him right into the man's arms.

22

The mist closes behind her and Megan is swallowed by the palpable whiteout. She can feel the direction in which the strands are pulled and she allows herself to be tugged the same way. The air is alive with a harmonic buzz which she feels more than hears. Against her face the ethereal threads of mist are damp and clinging. She fears she will breathe them in and suffocate. No amount of swiping at her face makes any difference. The earth tilts forwards, at least it feels that way – perhaps she is merely walking down a slope. The incline steepens, leading anti-clockwise. She descends, spiralling downwards, into some kind of crater. Even if she wanted to walk straight ahead she could not; whoever is manipulating the mist is drawing both it and her into a vortex.

Like steam from a kettle, the mist evaporates. In seconds it has thinned, torn and twirled into non-existence. Megan looks around her and recognises nothing. Wherever the mist has brought her, she is no longer in the Covey Wood she knows so well.

Instead of mist, there is snow. Night is falling fast. Megan stands in the middle of a huge expanse of bare, brown earth already dusted with a fine covering of powder. She is not dressed for this kind of weather and, as the light drains from the sky at unnatural speed, the temperature drops even farther. She holds her arms around herself, not knowing what to do. Finding shelter seems more important than anything else. She can see a line of trees against the darkening sky and she hurries towards them. From time to time she glances in the direction she has come from so she'll remember her way back. Only after several checks to ascertain her relationship to the landscape does she notice that she has left no footprints in the snow.

She reaches the trees with the same unnatural speed as the coming of the dark. The highest boughs are barely visible against the deep blue of night. The branches are partially naked, dying to the autumn and leaving skeletons behind them. Perched among the spreading fingers of the trees are hundreds of crows. There is an agitation among them; they lean close to each other in hushed conference, and hop from branch to branch as through whispering rumours. When they notice Megan, all movement ceases. She feels hundreds of quick bright eyes watching her. She is rising up from the ground, rising against the fall of fluffy crystals until she is among the branches.

She looks down at her body and she is a crow.

She is able to perch on a branch and balance without any effort at all. She knows the sleekness of her own face, sees the gleaming black curve of her beak. Unable to prevent herself she unfurls her wings and feels the grace and intelligence of their design. Without intending to, she rises from the branch. Spreading her wings has been enough to give her lift on the night wind that rushes unchecked across the now snow-covered field. She settles back to the branch again, laughing to herself. And then she glances to either side, and above and below and all around are her brothers and sisters of the black feather. All of them laugh silently with her. She is welcome in their shadow clan.

The excitement she noticed on the ground is even greater up here in the branches. The crows are expectant. Something wonderful is going to happen tonight.

At some spontaneous but agreed moment, every crow in every tree around her pushes up from its branch and flaps for height and speed. Megan rises too. She wishes now that she had always been a crow, that she will always remain one. If she never saw Apa and Amu again and could not continue her path with Mr Keeper she would not mind at all. She would rejoice. To be among crows, to be a crow, is all that matters now.

The flock gains height en masse. On other days, Megan knows, there would be aerial cavorting and gamesmanship, there would be tag and suicide dives. But tonight there is something to see and it is their duty to attend.

From on high there is much to see. This is not the world she has left behind in Covey Wood, though the land itself is the same shape, it seems. Below her are lights the likes of which she has never witnessed. They run in streams and rivers and they congregate in great numbers in patterns far below. Even though it is dark, the world below is busy. It is noisy too, releasing an endless hiss and roar upwards. Only in seeing this world away from the sanctuary of the trees does Megan sense the great danger and imminent threat. She cannot explain it. All she knows is that along with the great event of the evening, something terrible is also coming, a dark spirit summoned by this land, for this land; a spirit who will cast a deadly shadow over all who inhabit it. For the first time since she has changed shape, Megan is unsettled. These crows she flies with, noble though they are, live in treacherous times.

They do not fly towards the lights; the crows descend away from the noisy part of their world and fly towards the great comforting darkness of the open land. Soon they dip towards a smaller group of lights, this one much smaller. No noise rises here. The few lights shine from a single building surrounded by trees, and it is into these trees that the crows silently descend in their hundreds. When the trees are full, they land on the roof.

They are focussed on one particular light, a light emanating from a room in the upper part of the building. It takes Megan a while to understand that this building is a house with two levels. She has never seen such a thing before. She flies down to a branch affording her a view of the room from which the light comes. The snow falls harder and with it comes a rising wind; it escalates like music and Megan feels the most pressing agitation. She flies down towards the light and only realises at the last possible moment that she isn't able to fly into the bright room. Panes of glass larger than any she has seen in her own world form a barrier keeping her out. She lands on the sill and puts her beak to the window.

A woman squats on a bed in the throes of labour. Another woman supports her. A third woman wearing a tiny white hat on her fat head is struggling to kneel beside the bed. The baby is coming out at the very moment Megan arrives and its mother screams in triumph and agony as she pulls its body from her own, rocks back onto her blood-streaked heels and holds it up. At that moment the gale forces open a window near Megan and the snowstorm gains entry to the house. No one inside gives it much attention. They are all focussed on the baby boy who has just entered their world. Megan sees the boy's eyes are already open and so she pecks the glass, trying to attract his attention. In all the fuss, he is able to see her for only a brief moment before he is handed to the fat woman in the hat.

An opening appears inside the room and three faces fill it: the child's two sisters and his apa. Their faces tell stories. Megan pecks again, trying to get anyone's attention now. This is a sacred moment and none of them, despite their joy, seems to realise its true import. The other crows send her mental signals, telling her not to make her presence known because the humans will harm her, but Megan persists. Someone must see her. Someone must understand what the crows have always known.

Finally heeding the frantic but silent signals of the other crows on the roof and in the trees, Megan turns and flies to the top of the tallest tree, a horse chestnut growing quite close to the house. There, with a view into the expanding night for miles in every direction, Megan is filled with insights and emotions so strong she fears her crow body will split: this night is both the beginning and the end of something. It is the end of an age. The land knows it. The animals know it. Only the people, people who once were the guardians of the same land and its animals, seem blind to what is happening; what the arrival of this boy heralds. He will point the way to something. His life will bring change to the world and the change, like birthing, will be painful. His life will be hard and the life of the world will become tumultuous. He will inspire both love and hate and no one will ever be certain of him.

If only I could tell them there is a future. If only I could make them trust in him.

Even as she has these thoughts, she understands her place in all this is not as a messenger but as an observer. This is the beginning of a story. A true story. One greater and more far-reaching than the story of a pale, gentle boy; it is the story of the Black Dawn and the Bright Day, the story of the world's rebirth. And she must learn it. Only then will she be able to tell people there is a future. And only then will she be able to make them continue to trust. The idea is so strong it wants to explode from every part of her beautiful, sleek crow body. She has no choice, it seems, no choice but to rise on the whispering night wind and blend with the darkness of the black autumn sky.

The crows of Covey Wood, for she knows now that this is where they have always lived, sense her departure and she feels both their sadness at the cutting of this brief thread and their hopeful, optimistic salute to her.

Carry him, they call out behind her. Hold him in your heart as we always have.

Alone and high upon the openness of the dark Megan discovers that crows too can weep. Her tears become snowflakes and vanish among a billion others, the frozen tears of the world. She flies back to the Covey Wood of the day world and of her time with the first page of a story locked fast in her breast.

23

Megan's journey is not over.

Whatever has given her the body of a crow now takes it away. She is allowed to come to earth first and then her wings and long, sleek face vanish. Her feathers melt into black smoke. The crows, even though they could see the beginning and end of everything, even though they held the pain of the world in their beaks and claws, they flew light and free, they flew exultant, knowing they were magic, knowing their place in the world. Megan, human again, girl again, feels no such wonder or certainty. She wishes only that she could have stayed a crow forever.

She has a task, though, and a path to walk. She has a duty, and even as her body fills with its former solidity – and all-too-familiar frailty – she readies herself to move forwards and keep her word.

It is early morning and she stands in a hollow in a clearing among the trees. She thinks this is Covey Wood but she has never seen this part before. This is the vortex, she thinks, into which the mist was being drawn. She walks up the gentle slope. Partway up is a single crow feather, lying on the leaf-strewn ground and agitated by some breeze she is unable to feel. She leans down and lifts it up. The sun catches the filaments of the feather and it changes colours, rippling from grey to black to blue.

"They're the only ones I ever found."

Startled, she looks up. A few paces away is a small, slight boy with black hair and irises of stone. Her free hand covers her mouth to prevent a tiny cry from escaping.

"I always thought of them as black. Simply black. But they're not really, are they?"

The boy is beside her now, studying the way the light affects the feather. Megan can't help but take a step away from him.

"Don't be afraid. I would never do anything to hurt you."

She is embarrassed but doesn't know what to say. She doesn't want him to think badly of her. He smiles and shakes his head and Megan knows he knows what she's been thinking.

"This one is for you, Megan. You'll need it because you don't have language for the things you're going to see. You'll find it hard to keep their story alive if you have no way to describe them."

She thinks she understands.

"The crows showed me… lights. So many of them. Some were still and others moved in lines across the land."

"Yes. Cars and electricity. You haven't seen that before?"

Megan shakes her head and frowns. Why would she have? She's never been into the past before, where there were so many things that no longer exist. Things people didn't really need.

Again, the boy is listening to her thoughts.

"You shouldn't be so quick to judge, Megan. Just because you haven't seen these things in your time, it doesn't mean they're not there. And who's to say those things aren't useful, even necessary, if used in the right way?"

Megan is suddenly doubtful of the boy's wisdom and power. Maybe Mr Keeper has been wrong about the boy from the night country. Maybe he doesn't have so much to teach her. She can't help thinking this, and even as she has the thoughts she regrets it because the boy knows everything in her mind.

He doesn't appear affected. Certainly he is not angry. He smiles at her, his grey eyes watching her without any inhibition. She looks away.

"From now on," he says, "you must be ready to listen and learn at any moment and you must record everything that comes to you. Everyone has the ability, Megan, but few will ever become what you will become. You must never turn away from it, no matter how frightened you might be, no matter how alone it makes you feel. This gift is not just for you, it's for everyone."

The boy's face is grave now, an expression far beyond his years to possess. What manner of child could hold such knowledge?

"There's one other thing you must remember, Megan. Nothing will ever be simple. Nothing will ever be exactly as it seems to be now that the threads of dreaming and waking are woven, now that time is touching time. What you see will contain the truth but you will have to sift it out. There will be times when you cannot decide which world is real, the world you live in or the world into which you look. And there will always be a great darkness waiting to break through into your life and into your world. You must guard against it in all things. You must search it out within yourself and know it. You must embrace it. When you embrace the darkness within, you will always live in the light."

Megan strains to take in what he's saying, knowing all this must be recorded once she's found her way back to Mr Keeper.

"I don't understand the things you're telling me. I won't be able to remember it all."

"You will and you will. Your memory of this will be clear and accurate. You can't understand it now but in time it will make sense. Everything you need will come to hand in the very moment of its requirement."

The boy steps close and strokes Megan's cheek. His fingertips are like the touch of feathers.

"You mustn't worry. I chose you for a reason. And you agreed for the same reason. This is what you were born to do, Megan."

His final gesture is to touch the tip of the crow feather she still holds. The moment he does this, the ground beneath her begins to spin. It's as though something has wound the land into a tight spiral, humming with tension. Now the spiral is released and she pirouettes as the land unwinds. The depression she has been standing in rises upwards and the speed of the spinning increases until she is flung up, still turning, her arms flung out to her sides by the force of it. The bounce sends her up a few feet and then she falls to the earth, stumbling in a circle and then falling onto her bottom on a thick carpet of fallen oak leaves. She feels a little sick and collapses onto her side in the soft leaf litter. When her stomach settles and her equilibrium returns enough, she pushes herself back into a sitting position and brushes the leaves from her hair and clothes.

She is among the trees of Covey Wood, back in her own time and, she hopes, in the day world. The mist which came down so swiftly is gone and sun streams through the canopy, stamping broken pot-shards of light all over the ground. Her limbs are weary. When she looks around she sees Mr Keeper sitting with his back against one of the larger oak trees, its trunk veined with ivy. He is smoking his pipe and he nods an acknowledgment when she looks his way. The smoke rising from his pipe makes Megan just a little nervous, reminiscent as it is of the vapours that took her so far away from here.

"He's the little boy from my dream," is all she can think of to say in the end.

"Of course. Who did you expect it to be?"

"I don't know. I don't know anything." Suddenly Megan is crying. Shaking and crying and unable to stand up, she's so tired. "I don't think I can do this."

Mr Keeper is beside her and lifting her to her feet.

"Come on, Megan. You need to eat."

She is too exhausted to resist as he leads her out of the wood and back towards his roundhouse, making sure to skirt Beckby village and its nosy denizens.

24

Too late, Gordon tried to use his father's knife; too late because the Wardsman had seen him coming long before Gordon knew he was there. The grey-coat side-stepped. Gordon, whose breathless flight had in its final moment become a charge, stabbed without aiming. His knife hand was left in the Wardsman's influence as the rest of his body left the ground. He landed on his back on the rammed soil of the tunnel floor, all the breath driven from his body. The Wardsman stood over him, cleaning the blade on a grey handkerchief. Gordon scrambled away from the man and came up with his back against the tunnel wall. The Wardsman followed, glancing out of the tunnel's mouth for a moment.

Gordon knew he hadn't the strength to run again without being caught. Not yet. He needed a few more moments to recover. As the Wardsman approached, the blade of his father's knife catching the light from outside, Gordon felt the end of his life come into reach.

All this, and for what? They've taken my family and I haven't even lived yet. There's meant to be more than this. So much more.

The Wardsman knelt down in front of Gordon. He

folded the blade into its handle and held it out. Even in the tunnel's half light Gordon could see that the man's hand was trembling.

"I'm not going to hurt you, Gordon. Don't be afraid."

Gordon looked into the man's face. He saw not the cold eyes of a Wardsman, but the eyes of a beaten man; a gentle man who had done things he would always regret, things he had done in order to survive.

"Take the knife," the man said. "You'll need it."

Gordon searched his eyes for treachery but the Wardsman could not hold his gaze. The knife remained proffered and so Gordon took it, all the time expecting cruel recrimination. None came. The man only looked up again when Gordon had put the knife in his coat pocket.

"There's very little time. You must listen to me and then you must run. You must keep running and you must never let them take you. Do you understand?"

With what little wind had returned to his lungs, Gordon asked: "Who are you?"

The man, less and less a Wardsman as the moments passed, seemed close to tears. "I wish we had the time to sit and talk, Gordon, I really do. But if I give you my name and the Ward catch you, then they will know my name soon enough. We have to keep it like this." He touched Gordon's hand. "Whatever happens, I will cherish this moment."

"I don't understand."

"No. I'm sorry. Of course you don't." The Wardsman reached into his raincoat pocket and drew out some folded sheets of paper. The paper was wrinkled and battered but the Wardsman treated it as if it was a sacred artefact. He handed it to Gordon. "Letters from your parents. They'll help you to understand."

"You've seen them? Are they all right?"

The man looked away again, flint and iron rising in his eyes.

"They're fine. They send you their love."

"What about Judith and Angela?"

"There's no time, Gordon. Get up."

"Tell me about my sisters."

The Wardsman backed away and looked outside.

"Please get up. There are only minutes left, at best."

Gordon struggled to stand, his legs sore and fatigued.

"Just tell me if they're OK."

The man's eyes met his again. They were Wardsman's eyes now, hard and sharp with cruelty behind them.

"I haven't seen them."

The Wardsman grabbed his shoulder and hauled him deeper into the tunnel.

"Pike's coming," he whispered. "It's time for you to go. I've left you some things by your camping gear. Be sure to use them and be sure to read the book. Go into the tunnel as far as you can – it's a few miles long. You'll reach a pile of rubble eventually. You'll be able to dig through. Seal it up behind you and you'll be safe on the other side. I'll stop them from searching in here for as long as I can."

Gordon turned to go.

"Wait," said the Wardsman. "There's one more thing. Remember you can trust the Green Men."

"What? Trust the who?"

"Just don't forget what I've told you." The Wardsman's eyes softened for a moment. He held out his hand. "It's been my honour to meet you, Gordon Black."

Gordon left the hand unmet. The Wardsman nodded, not showing any wound.

"Go," said the greycoat. "And do us all a favour. Stay alive."

Gordon heard the limping machinery of Mordaunt Pike approaching, loud and surprisingly fast, his breath like steam and pistons. It was that which made him turn and run into the tunnel. He ran softly, touching the wall for guidance. Behind him he heard Pike reach the tunnel's entrance.

His voice was a growl.

"Where's the boy?"

"I haven't seen him yet, sir."

"He came this way. I saw him."

The Wardsman played it well. Gordon found himself grinning.

"If you had him in sight all the way, I would have seen him, sir. He'd have come right to me."

There was a pause.

"He was in sight when I left the house. I saw him come onto the bridleway. There's nowhere else he could have gone."

Gordon could feel Pike's eyes roving deep into the darkness like searchlights. He was certain the sheriff could see him.

"With respect, sir, these hedges are full of breaches and animal runs on both sides. He's only a puny runt and he could have squeezed through any time he felt like it. I suggest we send men into the fields as soon as possible, or we may lose him."

Pike's ranting breaths echoed into the tunnel behind Gordon as he ran deeper into the dark.

"What about in there, Knowles? It's the perfect

hiding place."

"It's perfect for us, sir – the tunnel's a dead end. We checked the Ordnance Survey maps before we came out. If he tries to hide in there, we've got him."

Pike's fire was going out by the sound of it. And with its dampening, some reason was returning. His voice was suddenly distant – he must have turned to look back from where he'd come.

"Damn him. He's away across the blasted fields, isn't he? Parker's in the car at the house. Tell him to get into the fields on that side and you take this side. And call in for more men."

"Sir?"

"What is it, Knowles?"

"You're bleeding. Shall I call for medics?"

"I've already phoned it in. They'll be here by now. Sheriff Skelton's need is somewhat greater than mine."

That was the last Gordon heard of the conversation, but he didn't slow down. He didn't trust Knowles not to turn him in. Couldn't it be that Knowles was merely setting a trap? All Gordon could do was get as far away as possible, and the tunnel was his only route. When he was sure that the torch could not be seen from the tunnel mouth, he switched it on.

Much farther along than he remembered leaving it, he came to his pile of equipment. Beside it was a small backpack, nowhere near the size of the rucksack he'd had to leave behind, but it would do. He crouched and opened the pack carefully, all the while expecting something bad to happen. It contained food, another torch with a spare battery, a book similar to his own notebooks, a jumper and a scarf. Strangest of all, his collection of feathers had been returned. Minus their shoebox now, they were bundled with string and wrapped in a piece of cloth. He repacked everything as best he could and shouldered the pack. He carried his tent separately and used the new torch to save the batteries in his own. Even shining the beam right into the centre of the tunnel, there was no end to it. He set off as fast as he could, wanting only the comfort of knowing he could sit down and read the letter from his mum and dad in safety.

As the adrenal high of fear and flight receded, Gordon felt the weariness of a soldier after battle. He had fought an enemy greater than himself in both strength and number, he had inflicted damage in the skirmish and he had escaped with his life. For now he was at liberty, though it wasn't the most princely of freedoms to walk through a tunnel as long and dark as a mine shaft. Nor did this freedom afford him any real choice about where he went; stop, turn back or go forwards wasn't a sparkling variety of options.

The torch was a luxury. He used his fingers and the wall of the tunnel for guidance to preserve the batteries. His legs were heavy and his right arm hurt from gripping the lock knife so tightly during his escape. His back was bruised by Knowles's throw and from lying on hard, uneven ground the night before. The worst pain was around the cut in his thigh. It pulsed, radiating heat and soreness with every step. The wound had reopened underneath the new bandage; he could tell from the dampness seeping into his trouser leg. He'd clean and re-dress it as soon as he found somewhere safe to stop.

Images of what the Ward might do to his family

sprung in his mind, each scenario worse than the one before. And now that he'd tangled with Skelton and Pike – blinded Skelton in one eye, for sure, and cut Pike to the bone – there was no telling what they might do, purely to satisfy their ire. Gordon knew he could save them. If he gave himself to the Ward, they'd probably let his family go home. When they realised he wasn't the person they were looking for, they'd let him go too – after some kind of punishment, no doubt. Maybe he'd even have to go to prison for a while, but when he'd completed his sentence, he could go home and he would always know that he'd done the right thing. It was his chance to make everything right.

Yes.

This was the way to do it.

Even though he'd made the decision in his head, his legs kept walking him farther into the darkness.

"Come on," he said out loud. "You've got to go back and give yourself up."

Still, he walked on.

"Stop!" he shouted. And then he was still.

The command echoed back and forth, disappearing away from him.

"I've got to go back," he whispered, but he couldn't move. Tears welled. How could he be so useless? Even now, knowing the right thing to do beyond any doubt, he still couldn't act on his conviction. His body aching, his brain no longer able to think clearly, he dropped to the tunnel floor and sat there, blind and exhausted in the darkness. The air smelled of mould and damp and broken open soil. It was thick and cold and hard to breathe. He shrugged the pack off and let it drop beside him.

Why is this happening to me? What have I done wrong?

There was no answer.

Suddenly, all Gordon wanted was his mum and dad. He didn't care about the future, didn't care about escaping or saving batteries or anything else. He just wanted them. And he had them, at least a small part of their thoughts, on those pieces of paper from Knowles. He pulled the sheaves from his backpack and switched on his torch.

The pages were crumpled and the writing had been hasty by the look of the scrawl. Still, he could recognise his mother's and his father's hand in the script and that alone was enough to bring a small smile to his teary face. Two letters: one from Mum and one from Dad. There was nothing from Judith and that brought fresh tears. How he'd have loved to read just a few words from her right now.

Needing his mother's comfort most, he read her message first.

25

My dearest Gordon,

I don't have much time, but someone sympathetic to the
future of the land, to your future, has offered to pass you a
message from me. There are two things you must know.
First, your father and I love you so very dearly. If you ever
have your own children, you'll know such love or something
close to it. You are different, though, Gordon. You're precious
in a way other children aren't. It makes our love for you all
the stronger. We've always protected you and will always do
so in any way we can, no matter where we are. Remember
that, won't you? The second thing is that you must not try to
find us. That is what the Ward want and expect you to do.
They're using us as bait. Don't give in, Gordon. You run, my
beautiful boy. You run until you have become a man. Then,
maybe, you can look for us. But never, ever let the Ward
catch up with you. Never let them find you. If you do, not
only will your life end, but so will the life of the land.
Everything will perish and time itself will be cut. I know you
don't understand any of this yet, but you will. You have a
journey to make, Gordon. It will be long and it will be
difficult, but you must never stop.

I know you have begun to awaken to your destiny. I

*know about your collection of feathers. The Ward ask us
about them in every interview and we say you've always
collected useless things – bottle caps, labels, rubber bands,
football cards. They don't believe us, of course. Right now,
the Ward know more about you than you do. So you must
learn about yourself. Those feelings, the ones that made
you keep your first feather, those are the feelings to trust,
always. The tiny voices and prompts that seem like whimsy.
For now, they are the only marker on your path. In time
those voices will be stronger and so will you. One day,
Gordon, you will discover a force no one can oppose. The
Ward know this and that is why they are trying to stop
you. They will make your life troublesome and lonely,
Gordon, because you can trust no one who cannot prove
their loyalty to you. Spies will be everywhere. Trust only
the voices that make no sense, the ones inside you, and that
way you'll always be able to spot friends and avoid
enemies.*

*I said there were two things, didn't I? Silly me, Gordon.
There are three. One, we love you more than any parent has
ever loved a child. Two, never let the Ward take you or that
will be the end. Three, find the Crowman. Who is he? I can't
tell you that. None of us knows. But you must find him,
Gordon. When you do, the future of everything will be
secure. He will leave you signs and clues. Follow them.
Listen well to those tiny inner voices, Gordon, and I promise
you will find your way to the Crowman and to glory.
Creation itself will be in your debt. It's a burden, I know.
But you were born to carry it, whether you believe that yet
or not, and no one else can do it.*

*So run now, Gordon! Fly away! We will see you again,
I'm quite certain of that. But for now you must travel alone.
Seek the Crowman and never give up until you find him.*

*Here's a strong hug and a strong kiss for you, my beautiful
boy.*

  With all my deepest love always
    Mum

Gordon hated himself for sobbing.

It echoed far away into the tunnel, far in both directions. He didn't have the strength to hold the tears
back, though. Nor did he have the will to stand up. It
was so good to read his mother's words and feel the
love that came with them. He hadn't realised how
much he craved that love in only this short time of separation, and now he missed her like a piece of himself.
The rest of her letter worried him very much. Perhaps
her capture and treatment by the Ward had weakened
her mind so much that she had nothing left to cling to
but fantasy.

Please let her be OK, he thought. Please let them not
have hurt her.

And this was swiftly followed by:

I'll kill anyone who touches her.

She really believed what she'd written; that was
clear. It was a deep conviction, something she was willing to risk her life over by keeping it secret. Wasn't that
the price the Ward would exact if she refused to talk?
He prayed not. So confusing, though, all this talk of the
Crowman.

Dear Gordon,

  *I never told you this enough – it's a failing between all
men, I think, but too often of fathers to their sons – I love
you. When you came into the world, you brought me a new
purpose and a new drive. Suddenly, I was not just a parent,*

I was a guardian too. It took me a lot longer to accept the truth about you than it did your mother. She knew something was extraordinary about you right from the moment you were conceived. I hope you can forgive me for being so slow to recognise you, Gordon. I hope you can forgive me for not telling you I love you more often. One thing about parenthood, it's filled with guilt and regrets. You have to be very strong to be a good parent and I doubt many people manage it. But I promise you this, Gordon, we've done the best we can and it was never your fault we struggled as parents, it was our own.

What a dreadful start to a letter!

Listen to me carefully, son. What I'm going to tell you is incredibly important. Over the years, things have happened, odd little things that would have been easy to overlook if they hadn't occurred so often. Those things point to the fact that there was something a little different about you. Not only that, from time to time we had letters and visits, even phone calls sometimes from complete strangers, and these communications were always about a dark-haired boy who'd been born in an October snowstorm. These strangers knew things about you no one outside the family could have known. Many of them said they'd seen you in dreams. Others said they'd met you when they were out walking in quiet natural places – impossible, I know. I had to accept that there was something unique, something precious about our own little Gordon. And, about the time you were born, the world we'd known for thirty-odd years, a world with its share of problems and tragedies, became suddenly very bleak indeed. You know what it's been like with the shortages and unemployment. The people freezing to death in their own homes in the winter, being flooded out or drowned after rainstorms, the people dying of heatstroke in the summer.

And then the diseases and viruses came and everything we'd taken for granted began to fall apart. To you it will seem quite normal that people starve to death homeless on the street and that the hospitals can't cope with the sick or that the police can't control the violence of a country that has lost its wealth and its rudder, a country whose land and weather are slowly killing its inhabitants.

And it's not just here, Gordon, it's everywhere. The world is descending into chaos and there's a simple reason for it. We've abused it. We've drained it. We've mined it. We've cut down its forests. We've over-farmed its land and turned it into a desert. There's no part of the world untainted by the touch of humanity. And the sad thing is, it wasn't always like that. It's only in the past couple of hundred years that our behaviour towards the world really got out of hand. Before that, most people lived in harmony with it and gave back to it rather than just taking from it all the time. And there are too many of us now for the world to sustain. She can't keep up. So there's only one solution and that is to rid herself of a giant swathe of humanity, like a dog shaking off fleas. And that's what she's doing, Gordon, she's purifying herself. Only those people who respect and look after her, who give back something for everything they take, only those people will have the smallest chance of surviving these times.

We've tried, Gordon. We've tried hard to live that way these last few years, but I'm not sure it wasn't too little too late. The main thing is that you are still out there, out of the hands of the Ward. If there is one agency that wishes to continue the pursuit of power at the expense of the Earth, it is the Ward. It has branches now in every country. They believe in subjugation. They believe in profit no matter what the cost. And they believe that when they die, none of their actions will matter. They're wrong, Gordon. They could not be more wrong. You have an opportunity to keep the world alive and you must take it. It's your duty and your destiny to do so. But the Ward know about you and they're coming for you. Listen to me now, Gordon. You must never, NEVER let them catch you. I can barely allow myself to think about what it will mean if they do.

I've seen your mum's letter and I must reiterate what she says. You go out and you find the Crowman. Find him at all costs. Become the man you were born to be, Gordon, and it will mean there's some kind of future. If you don't or if you can't, it'll be the end for everyone. But you can do it. I know you can and I've always known it. I love you, Gordon! Did I say that already? Here it is again: I love you! Take that with you, take strength from it if you're able, and go out into the country. Stay away from the cities if it's possible. And keep your head down. What your mum says is true: there will be spies and treachery everywhere. Our thoughts are with you, Gordon.

Fly, my boy! Fly to the Crowman!

Your ever-loving and very proud father

This was too hard. He wanted to do the loyal thing, the brave thing. To turn himself in at the Monmouth substation. To run away was easy. Surely there was no power in that.

He folded up the letters and this time stowed them in the inside pocket of his jacket, safe and close. There would be time to read the letters again when he reached the daylight at the other end of the tunnel. It was as though the earth had swallowed him. Still weary but partially renewed by the wishes and blessing of his parents, Gordon gathered his few possessions, loaded up and stood. Putting weight on his right leg was more painful now than it had been when he'd first cut himself. The wound seemed to radiate heat into the cool of the tunnel. But there was no choice: if he wanted to move, he had to walk.

Every now and again, when he could stand the tension of walking in darkness no longer and feared there might be some obstacle – or even some foe – waiting for him, he flicked on the torch for a few seconds. The tunnel had begun to make gentle turns first to the right and then to the left and it had developed a slight downward gradient. Down into the guts of the Earth. Into hell. Each time he turned the torch off, the darkness rushed back in and closed like a black sea over his head. It felt as though the stagnated, tarry air was drowning him and, as he trudged, the thumping ache in his right leg became an agonised tattoo. Thoughts of hell and of its denizens became more frequent and lurid. The Ward were in league with the legions of the underworld and they waited around every long, slow bend in the tunnel. Red-skinned demons with teeth like broken needles wore long grey raincoats and grey brimmed hats. Their twisted horns poked through the felt of their fedoras and their bony, spike-tipped tails protruded from beneath the backs of their macs. Slung over their shoulders were sets of chains and manacles or weighted nets, the mesh fashioned from barbed wire. A flick of the torch would send them scurrying farther into the darkness just beyond sight in the curvature of the tunnel, black hooves and snatches of grey fabric disappearing each time he used his light.

Gordon became thirsty and his face hot. He stopped and took several swallows of water. The heat in the tunnel surprised him. He had the beginnings of a sweat at his hairline but the rest of his face was dry and flushed. He took a few more sips and put the water bottle away.

Every step now sent a jolt of pain into the right of his groin, no matter how carefully he trod. Sometimes the jolt extended into every joint, sending a shiver along the skin of his back. Swirling images began to form in the blackness in front of his face, and blinking did nothing to dispel them. His fatigue settled heavier and heavier upon him. His pack might as well have been full of wet sand and his shoes soled with lead. His pace slowed to a shuffle.

Gone were the demons of the Ward now. In their place came sepia-coloured scenes played out against the screen of the tunnel's darkness. He flew over lakes and mountains, slow when he was soaring high, fast as he passed close to the land and the water. From a great distance he saw a volcano erupt, the earth roaring through the cone of a mountain and burning red phlegm spewing forth. The black vapours of the world's diseased lungs belched upwards, miles into the sky.

Every part of him was hot now. Images formed again from cream-coloured smoke so real he could almost touch its fibrous currents. He flew over the ruins of cities and the places where cities had once stood, now swallowed by the land – nothing but a scar upon the Earth's surface to show where a metropolis had been. But down below that scar, Gordon knew, millions of people lay, buried alive.

He flew over flooded fields and drowned forests. He flew over broken roads beside which the bodies of refugees rotted where they'd dropped, too sick or starved to keep walking. He saw armies of people fighting in the streets: a rabble of ill-equipped citizens on the one side, armed men in uniform on the other. Even without colours he recognised the force he was seeing, beating and shooting down civilians without mercy. The Ward. Men who believed the world and its people were there to be exploited, that power existed to make slaves of everyone who did not possess it. Not a government but a corporate army.

The visions kept him from thinking about the pain in his leg and the ache in his joints. He became aware that his hand had fallen to his side and he no longer touched the wall of the tunnel. How long had he walked this way? He had no idea. He was adrift on the night. And even then he did not put out his hand for the comfort of the wall. He merely stumbled onwards.

He kicked something hard and almost fell over. He took another few steps and kicked another object, heavier than the first. This time he switched on the torch and played its beam over what was in front of him. A hill of rubble rose from the ground to the roof of the tunnel, filling it from wall to wall. Thin bars of rusted steel fixing rose like dead stems from the debris. Keeping the torch on, he negotiated his way up the slope, careful not to stand on anything loose or trip over the larger obstacles.

As he neared the roof, he was obliged to crouch and then to crawl on his hands and knees. It would have been painful enough under the best of circumstances, but with his right leg so sore and every joint complaining, his greatest desire was to just roll over right there on the broken stone and sleep.

When his pack began to scrape the roof, he removed it and placed it and the tent beside him. Shining his light ahead, he could see the gap between roof and rubble extended into blackness on the other side.

There was a way through.

26

After Megan eats a heavily spiced stew, she falls into a hard, dreamless sleep. When she wakes, it feels as though she has slept for a month. She sits up, alert and energised, all her fear and weakness gone. Mr Keeper sits cross-legged on the reed matting, smoking, watching over her.

"Hello, Megan."

"Hello, Mr Keeper."

"How are you feeling now?"

"I feel like I could run from here to the ocean and back again. How long have I been asleep?"

Mr Keeper shrugs.

"An hour, perhaps."

"An hour? It felt like weeks."

"That's how it's meant to feel."

"What was in the stew?"

"It's Ricky Pot."

"What's Ricky Pot?"

Mr Keeper taps his pipe on his knuckles and drops the ash into his hand, pocketing it.

"Rook. Ale. Quick-bine. Salt and pepper."

"I ate a rook?"

"Three rooks, actually."

Megan grimaces, aghast.

"But the rook is hallowed," she says.

"Yes, it is. But it is not forbidden to the likes of you and me, Megan. When we have need, they come to us. They make us strong. I caught three this morning. They knew you needed strength and so they gave themselves. It's for the good of all. For the land."

Megan takes this in with as much poise as she can. She tries hard to understand the nature of the sacrifice, what the rooks have given just so that she might be renewed. Before she knows why or what she will do, she is rising from her sleep mat.

"I need to go outside."

Mr Keeper nods.

She opens the door, crouching to exit, and walks to the pile of debris where Mr Keeper composts his waste and leavings. There on top are the feathers, heads, entrails and feet of the three rooks. She gathers them up from the slowly rotting pile and takes them, slippery threads of gut beside horny grey beaks, greasy eyes beside pristine feathers and leathery claws. She carries them some way into the pines and digs a small hole in the soft earth with her bare hands. In it she places everything but one broad, unblemished feather. With the knife Mr Keeper gave her when they began their "gathering" trips, she cuts into the pad of her thumb and lets the blood from the incision drip onto the rook feather. Much of it dribbles away onto the recently parted ground but some of it soaks into the fibres of the feather, darkening it further and giving it unnatural weight. Not satisfied, she uses her cut thumb pad to smear the blood all along its grey shaft. Only then does she place it on top of the remains of the three rooks and cover everything with earth and pine needles. She kneels in front of the burial site and places her hands over her heart.

"Thank you," she whispers.

In the roundhouse, Mr Keeper is waiting with boiled water and a cloth. He cleans her cut and wraps it in a strip of muslin before handing her a steaming bowl of tea. As is often the way in the roundhouse, all is quiet for a long time.

Unusually, it's Mr Keeper who breaks the silence and her recollections.

"I've something for you, Megan. After I give it to you, you can go home for the rest of the day."

Megan brightens. Some time at home with Amu and Apa before bed will be an unusual treat. It's easy to forget she has any life beyond the Black-Feathered Path. The celebrations of the harvest have come and gone with her and Mr Keeper almost uninvolved but for his appearance to bless this year's reaping – the most bounteous crop in memory. The harvest is a season of rejoicing. The villagers spend time together in the streets and around the hub at the centre of the village. Bands play music all day and night and everyone dances and drinks ale and elderberry wine and Usky Lick, the local spirit. All the food is cooked outdoors and shared and eaten together. This year Megan has seen none of it. She misses Sally and Tom, too, misses playing and being idle.

Mr Keeper reaches behind the blanket that divides the roundhouse and keeps his sleeping place private. Now he brings out something large and heavy-looking. It is wrapped in black cloth which shimmers a little when the light catches it at certain angles. He places it on the matting between them and sits back. This is the correct way of giving. After a pause to let the gift settle, Megan leans forwards and takes it, drawing it close in front of her.

She unwraps the black cloth one fold at a time. Inside it is a box. The box is made of gleaming black wood. Scorched into the lid is the sign of the Crowman, the same crow's footprint she now bears on her chest. She lifts the lid, and inside are several items. The largest of these is a book, also branded with the Crowman's sign. It is bound in thick hide and tanned to black. Beside it are two black stones and a small black bowl set into carved depressions in the base of the box. Next to those are three long black feathers. She lifts the book; this single item is responsible for most of the weight in the box. The hide is smooth and cool beneath her fingers. She opens the book and stares at the pale, silky pages within for a long time. She closes and opens the book in several places and what she sees is always the same.

She looks up at Mr Keeper.

"What is this?"

"It's the *Book of the Crowman*."

"But it's empty," she says.

"No. The *Book* is full. The story is already there. Its words, however, have not yet been rediscovered and rewritten."

For once, Megan knows exactly what Mr Keeper is going to say next:

"That's your job."

For a while she runs her fingers over the items in the box, even the sleek wood of the box itself. She smoothes her palm across the surface of the blackened cowhide, and it seems to leave a trace of dust on her hand which she tests between her fingers.

"The feathers are from Anglesey ravens. I'm going to show you how to cut them into quills. You have a block of pigment, a grinder and a bowl. Before you leave, I'll instruct you in the making of ink. Tonight you must write the opening pages exactly as you have seen them."

He stretches for the kettle.

"More tea, Megan?"

"No," she says, adding: "Thank you."

"Tell me, then. The boy from the night country. Did he give you anything?"

"In the vision he gave me a feather. A crow feather."

"It was no vision, Megan. You must understand that. You journeyed to him and he gave you a feather. What did he say about it?"

"He said it would give me words for things I have not seen and do not understand."

Mr Keeper seems satisfied with her answer.

"Very good. May I see it, please?"

Megan doesn't know what to say. Protesting further will only make him angry and she doesn't want that today. So far, it has been overwhelming, special and exciting. She doesn't want to spoil it.

"I… I don't…"

"Where did you put it?"

She tries to remember what happened. As the world had unwound, she'd thrust it into the pocket of her coat so as not to lose it. The coat is beside her on the matting.

"You remember, yes?"

She nods.

"Then fetch it out. Show it to me."

Feeling stupid and embarrassed, worse than she ever has before, Megan pulls the coat to her and reaches into the outside right pocket. Her hand emerges with a single crow feather and a single magpie feather, the one Mr Keeper had given her before she entered the mist. Frowning, she hands them both to Mr Keeper.

He turns them in his hand, smiling as though he remembers something joyful. He returns them to her now-trembling fingers.

"The Crowman is with you, Megan. He has given you this feather so that you may write his story in the pages of his book, so that you may bring him to life once more. From now on, nothing will ever be simply what it appears to be. It is a burden but it is an ecstasy too. Magic is alive in the world, Megan, and it always has been. You must ensure that it stays that way."

When Mr Keeper has shown her the way to make ink and cut quills, she wraps up her bundle in its black, shimmering cloth and walks alone through the pines and along the paths towards home.

His final words to her are:

"Do not return to me here until you have written everything you've seen."

Her parents are delighted to see her and sit down to hear about her training – what little she is allowed to tell of it. Her mother feeds her well and her father regards her with both pride and sadness. As much as she wants to enjoy the extra time with Amu and Apa, all she can really think about is how she will make that first mark, a mark whose blackness will be both beauty and destruction, when she writes the first letter of the first word of the *Book of the Crowman*.

27

Whoever or whatever had blocked the tunnel had made a good job of it.

The space Gordon had in which to crawl would not have afforded a man passage. Even with his slight build aiding him for once he still got stuck from time to time. His aim was to clear blockages into cracks and crevices to either side of himself. This would save him having to drag debris back out. He tried to work lying on his left side to save his cut thigh from further damage, but it was impossible. After a few seconds or minutes of successfully and painlessly clearing chunks of rubble to either side of his crawlspace, Gordon would catch his right leg on something jagged and cry out.

The roof of the tunnel was never more than a couple of inches above him, causing moments of wild panic which made him want to crawl as fast as he could, without any care for his wound and without going back for his pack and tent. What if the earth above the tunnel shifted somehow and the tunnel's roof subsided just an inch or so? The bricks might settle down onto his back, not killing him but trapping him belly-down on the sharp-edged rubble and holding him there until he starved, suffocated or went insane. Fear kept him working with a cold efficiency.

The beam of his torch, once bright and crisp against the darkness, had yellowed and dimmed. Its light was oily ochre now and illuminated only the space immediately ahead. There was no end to his labours. The crawlspace just went on and on. As he moved a large nugget of rubble to his left, the torch flickered and went out. He tapped it and then hammered it against his palm. It flickered and died again. Hands shaking, he unscrewed the casing and removed the two batteries. He rubbed them in his hands and blew on them, prayed over them to stay alive just a little longer. He replaced them and the torch beam recovered long enough for him to shift one more obstacle. Then it died for good.

He sighed and laid his head against the broken rocks beneath him. They pushed up hard and cold into his face. There was no way to turn around. He would have to inch backwards, all the way back to the top of the rubble pile where he'd left his gear. Dust from the disturbed rubble got into his mouth, nose and eyes, making him cough and sneeze and send up more particles. Knowing how far he'd come facing the right direction made the mere thought of going backwards exhausting. There was no other option.

He pushed back with both hands, trying to raise his feet over the lumps in their way. Several times he got one foot trapped and had to move forwards to free it before proceeding backwards again. His temples throbbed with heat and pain and he caught the wound in his thigh often. He was weeping uncontrollably by the time he felt the space behind him widen and the coolness of the tunnel air spread up his legs and back. Before he'd had time to change the batteries and tie everything onto his pack, he was shivering, his head aflame but the rest of him encased in aching, gripping ice.

This time he dragged his pack with him, kicking back as much shifted rubble into the space behind him as he could. Knowles had told him to seal the space, but he didn't have the will to turn around and do it properly. He wasn't even sure he could make it back to where his batteries had given out.

The new challenge became hauling his backpack and freeing it each time the straps got caught on a protruding piece of mortar or bar of steel. He worked forwards like a fugitive animal now, no longer able to think, merely knowing that his choices had become very simple: keep moving and survive or stop and die. Something was wrong with him, he knew, but he couldn't allow himself to acknowledge it as anything other than a reason to keep going. He couldn't let it kill his hope. He had to make it somewhere safe and then he would rest. Stupid and spent with effort, he came to the place where his batteries had run out. He shone his renewed light ahead.

Tears came again.

He had already shifted the final obstacle with the dying of the torch batteries. Beyond, the blackness widened again and the air was cool and dust-free. He crawled onwards and was borne from darkness into darkness once more. Hauling his pack out behind him, he first rose to a crouch and then stood to descend a rubble pile exactly like the one he'd climbed. He could have been going out the way he'd come in – everything felt exactly the same. The rubble ended on flat, bare earth and the tunnel extended away into infinity. None of it mattered. For now his work was done.

At the base of the rubble pile he pitched his tent, forcing the pegs down into the earth without too much difficulty. At least here the surface below him was close to dead flat. He dragged everything inside the tent and unrolled his sleeping bag. Once again, not bothering to take off any of his clothes, he opened the bag, slid in and zipped it up around him. He took a cheese sandwich from the pack, somewhat squashed and battered now but tasting better than any meal he'd ever eaten. He tore into it and drank all his water. There was no way to resist the fire in his dust-lined throat. When he'd chewed down cheese and bread and grit from the rubble, he took his spare clothes out and piled them around himself inside the sleeping bag. He was frozen but his leg and face were roasting.

He lay down and succumbed to blackness.

28

A day after surgery, Mordaunt Pike limped into Sickbay 7 of the Ward's private hospital in Piccadilly looking for Skelton.

The boy's knife attack had damaged a tendon in the crook of his right groin and, though the surgeon who'd sewn the tendon up and the entry wound closed said he'd make a full recovery, Pike wasn't so certain. The sinew, which had been so nearly severed, felt badly repaired. Instead of a smooth line of cabling, a lump rose beneath the stitched lips of his wound whenever he moved his right leg. Given time, the surgeon had assured him, he would heal.

Time was what they didn't have.

He tried to walk normally as he made his way down the lengthy sickbay with beds to left and right. All were filled by Wardsmen injured while quelling riots, searching houses or arresting members of the Green Men. More wounded arrived from around the country all the time. Those who couldn't make it to London, Birmingham or Manchester died in transit. The Ward's influence was strongest in the cities. Medical facilities outside of them were basic: clumsy first aid applied in

Ward substations like Monmouth.

His and Skelton's injuries had been swabbed and dressed without much care or ceremony by a junior Wardsman trained in the basics. Then, looking like a pair of hastily bandaged soldiers returning from front-line duty, they'd been driven back to London.

Skelton had muttered and sworn and seethed the whole way.

"The demonic little cretin took my eye, Pike. He *cut out* my eye. I still don't believe it. The chief says we're to bring him to HQ. Interview him and put him down with an injection. Quick jab, end of problem. Not a chance of that now, Pike. Not a bloody chance."

Skelton wept then. Pike hadn't known which way to look in the back of the Range Rover. He tried to ignore it but Skelton's hand had clamped around his thigh.

"Don't you turn away, damn you. Don't ever do that." Skelton's grip tightened. "Look at me, Pike."

Pike had looked. Tears streamed from Skelton's remaining eye. Blood and mucus seeped through the bandages covering the space where his left eye had been. The grip on his leg released a little.

"I'm still the same old Skelton, see? A little piece missing but the rest is still me."

Pike hadn't been able to speak.

"Pike? I'm no different, honestly."

Pike had glanced into the front of the car. The driver didn't seem aware of what was taking place in the back seat.

"OK," he said.

And Skelton had smiled for the first time since their encounter with Gordon Black earlier that day. The grip had released and Skelton's claw became a soft, fat hand again, pale and well-manicured. The hand patted Pike's thigh, stroked it appreciatively before withdrawing. When Pike looked over again, Skelton was asleep, a small smile tickling the corners of his mouth. By the time they'd reached London, Skelton's sleep had deepened into unconsciousness.

Now, having asked to be notified the moment he woke, Pike still found his pace slowing as he neared Skelton's bed. Even one-eyed, his partner spotted him before Pike could change course or leave.

"Ah, Pike. You're looking better. Still limping, though, I see."

There was no point trying to hide it.

"Surgeon was a butcher."

"Well, you'll live. They tell me I will too."

Skelton's bandaging was much reduced compared to the half-mummification of his head the Wardsman in Monmouth had wrought upon him. A large white patch of bandage was held in place with strips of translucent tape. Black stitches were visible to either side of the bandage.

"It's a funny thing, Pike. Even though I can't see anything from the left side of my face, I feel as though my eye has been widened or opened somehow. It's like I'm looking into space or something. Very curious sensation." Skelton looked over at Pike, who had stopped walking in the middle of the sickbay and now stood there like a lost giant. Skelton gestured to a chair at his bedside. "Why don't you come and sit down here, Pike?"

Pike creaked into action and walked, one leg stiff and straight, to the chair. When he sat, the wounded leg stuck straight out.

"Does that hurt?" enquired Skelton.

"No."

When Pike didn't add anything, Skelton asked:

"What's been happening? Any trace of Satan's little helper?"

"No sign. Agents searched the fields and woodland all around the house. He vanished."

"Not possible, Pike."

"I know that."

"So he must still be there somewhere. I don't think he'll go far, knowing his family is in our hands. We should try to draw him in."

"How?"

"I don't know yet."

Skelton pulled back the sheets and blankets and hefted his short, stocky legs over the side of the bed. Pike had never seen his feet before. They were very pale, the skin soft and puffy. Skelton's hand resting on his shoulder for support broke Pike's gaze. Skelton was standing up now, his fat hairless chest close to Pike's face. His hospital pyjama top was unbuttoned. He had chubby breasts instead of pectorals and his belly was round, white and smooth. Pike couldn't stand because Skelton was using him to stay upright – the man was clearly still weak with shock and blood loss. Nor could Pike back away, because his chair was against the sick-bay wall. All he could do was remain intimately positioned as Skelton tested his balance.

"What are you doing, sir?" he asked eventually.

"Leaving," said Skelton. "Get my uniform, will you, Pike?"

"It's only been a day. You should rest more."

"If I rest, those Monmouth idiots are going to let the

boy get away. We have to get back there and find him. Get him quick and finish him at leisure."

Pike noticed a slight bobbing and swinging in the crotch of Skelton's pyjama bottoms.

"Come on, Pike! Get my clothes and let's go."

Pike rose very slowly from his chair until he once again dwarfed the man beside him. Nevertheless, he felt himself very small in the man's shadow.

29

Gordon feels a searing in his thigh, as though the lips of his wound are being prised open with glowing irons. Lava erupts from within and spills over his leg and groin, spreading the fire. Burning rivulets of this ichor spread radiant orange veins up over his belly and chest, finally setting his head aflame. Through all of this, he sleeps, his body too spent to respond.

The rest of Gordon's awareness is imprisoned in dreams.

He is beyond the Earth's atmosphere, looking back at the world in its protective bubble. All is silent and peaceful. Re-entry is pure white heat and then he is diving towards the body of the world, seeing the shapes of the continents at first and then recognising countries. Weather systems become visible and grow and he descends through layers of cloud until he can see Europe. But his destination is his own country, Britain.

From this height, the land of his birth is still tranquil but as he nears its surface, when individual fields and roads and built-up areas come into view, he begins to see signs of turmoil. In many places smoke rises, obscuring the view of the fires creating it. The cars on the roads have stopped moving. Instead he can see lines of people, miles long, snaking between the stalled vehicles. The roads themselves are cracked and, in some places, buckled and broken. In towns and cities, piles of rubble mark the places where buildings have collapsed. There are rifts in the earth where the green of fields is divided by black chasms. Some of them extend across entire counties. People, animals, cars and even entire homes have fallen into these new cracks in the world. Those who are not fleeing the cataclysms are at war. Men and women dressed in brown, green and black clash with cohorts of troops in grey. The grey troops are organised and fight in tight units. Their opponents, some kind of rebel army, are outnumbered and fight using hit-and-run tactics. Many of them fall as the grey troops advance across the country. Everywhere the bodies of the dead rot where they fell, food for the land and its creatures, carrion for the crows which populate every scene of chaos and conflict.

He sees the smoking ruins of his own home and the destruction of what was once his family smallholding. Even the garden wall and the green door with its rusty hinges have been knocked down. The trees in the orchard and the huge horse chestnut which had stood near the back terrace, even these have been cut down, and they smoulder now beside the wreckage of Hamblaen House, the house where he was born.

The wind sweeps him on a meandering course around counties and towns he has never seen before. And yet, aspects of each place strike a note of resonance in his heart. These are places where important things have happened to him, and yet he can't remember what they are. Finally, the winds take him south. A great reluctance rises within him.

He tries to resist but the wind is too strong. He comes to a hill where there was once a small forest. Now, all that remains of the trees is ebony stumps. At the crest of the hill, one tree remains, its trunk is contorted and squat, its boughs bunched and twisted. Its outer branches, every one charred to black bone, rise in supplication towards the unanswering sky.

The wind sets Gordon down at the very front of the tree. Behind it, the sun is setting. Against its dying fire, in the highest of the blackened branches, are three watchful crows. At the bottom of the hill, a great crowd of people is gathering. The crows call out to Gordon and he knows he has been here a thousand times before.

The earth is shaking. His body is being moved. Something takes hold of him. Gordon is unable to struggle against it. The shaking gets worse.

Someone whispers:

"Can you hear me? Tell me your name."

He tries to answer but his mouth won't work. He is being pulled now and he tries to resist, but his body won't respond. He tries to reach for the knife in his pocket but his body is as good as dead. He feels himself hoisted up and over a large shoulder. The movement reawakens the pain in his cut and he cries out, hearing the weakness of his own shout as it echoes in darkness. Somewhere there is light. Long before he reaches it, he loses consciousness again.

Recalling his story is not difficult, it lives in Megan like verse learned by heart, and when she comes to sit and write, it waits, as though the words are queuing up in her wrist. What takes the time, and what is more troublesome than she expected, is the physical act of writing with a raven feather quill.

With the responsibility of marking the story onto paper, she is nervous of making mistakes and so she writes very slowly. She can't help but think of the ink as the Crowman's blood, something he has given so that his story may be told. The ink takes a long time to dry, so she has taken to using one of her moon cloths to absorb the excess before it can smudge the pristine pages.

Mr Keeper has told her very little about the history of their world and almost nothing about the Crowman.

"You must see it for yourself," he always says.

She knows a little from school, though. Perhaps eight or ten generations past, no one knows exactly when, dark times befell the land. There was sickness and war, and the Earth Amu withheld her bounties. Floods, earthquakes and diseases wiped out most of the people from that time. They called it the Black Dawn. It was in those days of scarcity and death that the Crowman returned to the land – as he had whenever the balance between folk and the Earth was lost. He walked the woodlands and fields, the hills and valleys, and no one knew if he was for the good or if he was the devil himself. That's why they gave him other names like Scarecrow and Black Jack. Even now, no one is quite sure whether to love or fear the Crowman, but one thing is certain: everyone respects him. This, says Mr Keeper quite often, is exactly as it should be.

The feather the dark boy gave her is with her whenever she writes. Sometimes when she remembers a part of the story in which the images or events are impossible to describe, she takes the feather and lays it across her forehead for a few moments. After that, words always come. She doesn't know the new words but she knows that they are right. Her language grows.

The writing causes her pain – in her hand predominantly, which cramps and stiffens after being held for so long in the same position. But after she has sat for some hours, the pain extends up her arm and into her shoulders and down her back. Each time this happens she knows it is time to rest. Her mother brings her glasses of cool water from the stone ewer and sometimes warm milk if it's late in the evening, but Megan won't touch the drinks while she is writing. She is terrified she may spill them on the book and spoil it. She always finds the cool water warm or the hot milk cold by the time she is ready to take a break.

After nightfall, she continues by candlelight, the small flames casting flickering shadows of her hand onto the wall, transforming it into a monstrous, deformed claw. She notices little of what goes on around her each time the flow of the story has resumed. Nothing stops the story except her decision to finish writing, and nothing begins it other than her sitting at her table once the ink is ground, mixed and blessed.

While she writes the first part of the story her sleep is black and dreamless and restful. She wakes early each day and begins again feeling solid and happy in her purpose. Before seeing the Crowman in Covey Wood she had begun to wonder what her life was to be about. She had begun to wonder what meaning it could possibly have, things she sometimes talked about with Sally Balston, though not always with Tom

Frewin. She no longer has such questions or concerns. This lends her mind a calmness she had not known before and she senses this as another sign of childhood passing away. She does not miss it but she knows Apa and Amu do. She sees them looking at her sometimes, just a glance usually, and they always turn away when they know she has noticed the observation. The glances are sad and sometimes a little puzzled, as though her parents are wondering where their daughter has gone. If she had the time or the energy to spare, she would sit and tell them that here is Megan, the same Megan they've always known, only a little older inside and a little harder on the outside. She would tell them that there is more Megan now than there has ever been before, not less. And she would tell them to rejoice in that knowledge because it is a sign of things being right in the world.

But Megan has never talked to Apa and Amu in quite that way and she's not sure she ever will.

Sometimes she thinks of her friends and her days at school. Tom and Sally have been at her side like a brother and sister for as long as she can remember. All of that seems so far away now as to have been a part of someone else's life. The time she spends walking to Mr Keeper's roundhouse begins long before school begins and she always returns long after school has finished. It is as though Megan's world now and the world of Megan just a few weeks before have separated and drifted away from each other like continents separating, an ocean widening between them.

It takes three days for her to write the first part of the Crowman's story, and as she does so she is able to distance herself from the boy at the centre of the tale. But

when she is not writing, in those moments before she
falls to sleep and those moments before she rises, sometimes when she takes a break to eat or drink, she feels
the boy's presence intimately, like the soul of a recently
departed sibling. His story has started in troubled times
and with no small amount of secret drama. Already she
is terrified for the innocent child with black satin hair
and polished grey eyes, the boy with the pale skin and
destiny written in his very blood.

On the morning of the fourth day, it is with no small
weight of fear in her guts that she walks back to Mr
Keeper's roundhouse. Soon there will be more to write
in the *Book of the Crowman*.

It is to be a book of pain with sorrow in every chap-
ter.

PART II
TO WALK A BLACK FEATHERED PATH

"I seen Black Jack comin
Spreadin fire and flood
His black cloak flappin
Over bootprints o blood

I seen him bring down cities
Seen him wash away the fields
I seen him grinnin madly
While the mighty learnd to kneel

I seen Black Jack flyin
Leavin sickness in his wake
All he brings is death for us
And all he does is take

If you see Black Jack comin
Best you hide yourself away
When you see Black Jack comin
You've seen your final day"

GRAFFITI ON THE EAST WALL OF THE WARD
SUBSTATION, MONMOUTH, ENGLAND, PRE-BLACK
DAWN ERA, AUTHOR UNKNOWN

"The Great Spirit is in all things, is in the air we breathe. The Great Spirit is our Father, but the Earth is our Mother. She nourishes us; that which we put into the ground, She returns to us…"

BIG THUNDER (BEDAGI), LATE 19TH
CENTURY WABANAKI ALGONQUIN

"For the Lord your God is bringing you into a good land, a land of flowing streams, with springs and underground waters welling up in valleys and hills, a land of wheat and barley, of vines and fig trees and pomegranates, a land of olive trees and honey, a land where you might eat bread without scarcity, where you will lack nothing, a land whose stones are iron, and from whose hills you may mine copper. You shall eat your fill and bless the Lord your God for the good land He has given you."

DEUTERONOMY 8:7–10

30

"He looks so thin."

"The fever's wasted him."

"To look at him now, peaceful like this, he could be dead."

"He's not dead."

"I know he's not. I'm not stupid. But he looks like he could be. I've never seen anything more beautiful."

"What nonsense are you talking, girl?"

"You know what I mean. You know exactly."

A pause.

"Yes. I suppose I do."

"Think of it, if he's who we think he is and if what people say is right, he can never die. That's why he looks so perfect like this. Because even death won't take him away."

"I don't like to hear you talk about it. And anyway, it might not be him. Probably none of the stories are true. Everyone needs hope these days. People will believe anything."

"You've read the stuff he's got. You believe in him."

"I can't say one way or the other."

"You can, Dad. You *do* believe. Otherwise you

wouldn't have helped him."

"I'd help anyone in trouble. You know that."

"But this is risky. He's not just anyone. If they catch us..."

"I know. I know."

Somewhere, there was light. Rusty light. The smell of leaf mulch and wood smoke. Something cooking. Then there was hunger. And then there was thirst, unbearable thirst.

"I'll tell you what concerns me, Brooke. What if he's not for the good? You've heard the other stories. Some say there's a dark messiah coming, a destroyer – the son of Satan or Satan himself. Maybe that's who he is. Maybe we're tending Black Jack."

"It's the Ward who put those stories out. Everyone knows that, Dad. I don't believe it."

"Still."

"Even if there was such thing as Black Jack, this isn't him. He wouldn't be beautiful like this. He wouldn't be just a boy."

"This boy won't be a boy for long."

"That doesn't make him the devil incarnate, Dad."

A cool draught caressed Gordon's face and he heard the source of it, outside somewhere: the wind easing through the leafless trees. This was no dream. His body was more comfortable than it had been for a dark aeon. But it still felt heavy, lead bones without muscles to raise them. The rusty light was daylight coming through his still-closed eyelids.

"No. I suppose it doesn't."

There was another pause then. Much longer this time. Gordon felt their eyes on him. Then the girl, Brooke, broke the silence.

"I think he's awake."

No point in pretending now.

Gordon allowed his eyes to open. It was brighter than he'd expected and he blinked and squinted, unable to see anything other than what he'd guessed so far. A man and his daughter, perhaps, neither of whose age was apparent in the blur, sat side by side a couple of feet away from him. The light came in from behind them through a triangular opening. This was not a tent but a canvas shelter slung over a cord between two trees. He was in his sleeping bag and he was naked.

He tried to say hello but his voice was a dry rasp and the noise he made was unintelligible. Only in trying to speak did he realise just how parched his mouth and throat were. His next word came out with some urgency and though it was only a harsh whisper, both the father and daughter understood.

"Water."

It was the girl who moved first.

"Wait," said her father.

"No. I'll do it."

She was beside him swiftly. With one hand she raised his head a little and with the other she let him take water from a cup. The water was warm, not long boiled, but it was nectar to his dried-out palate. He wanted to tell her that she didn't need to help him but when she let his head back down and he tried to lift it again, he couldn't.

Naked and helpless.

"More," he croaked.

"You have to take little sips. And slowly. Too much of anything right now will make you worse."

She raised his head again, letting him take a few more small swallows.

"That's enough for the moment."

The water made him nauseous. His stomach cramped around its tiny cargo of fluid. Nevertheless, it had given his brain a charge, and he felt more awake and aware. These people, whoever they were, had made a camp outdoors and seemed to be there on a long-term basis. Through the triangular opening at the end of the canvassed enclosure he could see a well-established fire and a heavy-looking black pot hanging over it from an improvised tripod. Steam escaped from its lid – the source of the smell of cooking. The cramps in his stomach were hunger pangs. He was so ravenous, the pain of it was making him feel sick.

At his end of the shelter a wall of woven branches had been laid against the opening. Without it, wind would have been racing through the shelter, chilling him. He was lying across the shelter and there was plenty of space for the other two, but he could see no sign of their bedding. Either there were other shelters like this in their camp or they had their own tents. He didn't recognise the woodland outside. It certainly wasn't Covey Wood. He tried to gauge how far he'd walked in the tunnel. Hadn't Knowles said it was miles long? He could easily be in a part of the countryside he'd never visited before.

The man's face was lined and creased. He carried troubles there, unable to hide them. His hair was fair and thinning. It needed to be cut. The same was true of the sparse beard that grew mainly at his chin and below his ears. They might have been living like this for a while. The man seemed kind enough, though there was a hard edge to his gaze.

Both of them were dressed for outdoor life. Their boots looked sturdy and waterproof. They wore cargo-style trousers in lightweight, breathable material and tough-looking, waterproof jackets with hoods. Each of them wore several layers beneath, judging by the bulky look of their bodies. Curiously, though, their clothes were all drab colours. Greens and browns and charcoals.

Camouflage?

Perhaps he had something in common with these people. Like him, they could be hiding. Maybe that was why they'd helped him. Their kindness made him think of his family. He had to bite the inside of his cheeks to stop himself crying.

He watched the girl slide away from him and exit the shelter. She went to the pot, lifted its lid with a metal hook and stirred whatever was cooking using a whittled branch. The branch had seen plenty of use judging by the stain on its stirring end. More aroma wafted Gordon's way and his stomach groaned so loud that all three of them heard it. The girl and her father smiled but the man's smile faded quickly. The girl continued to grin, catching Gordon's eye for a moment and then looking away. He felt some other movement in his stomach at that moment, something that wasn't hunger.

His new carers had only spoken to each other when they thought he was asleep or unconscious. Now that he was alert they kept their silence.

They don't trust me.

He understood their reticence but he didn't like how it felt. He mustered a little willpower and took a deep breath.

"My name is Gordon," he said. The words came but without much force. For a moment they looked at him, frozen. While he had their attention he added, "Thank you for helping me."

Once the words were out he felt a heaviness cover him like a blanket, and though he tried to keep his eyes open – he really wanted to talk to them and he really wanted to eat whatever it was the girl was cooking – he wasn't able to do so. His mouth closed and his eyes closed and sleep rose up for him, dragged him down. The last thing he remembered was the girl's voice.

"I'm glad we found him, Dad. I think it's a sign, you know. A sign things are going to get better for us now."

If her father replied, Gordon didn't hear it.

31

Gordon woke to wetness on his arms and chest.

The girl, Brooke, was washing him with a warm, damp cloth. The abrasive but comfortable pressure was followed by the chill of the outdoors, and his skin prickled after every pass of her gentle hand. Where his skin cooled, the ache of fever sprang up and he knew he was not yet recovered. He kept his eyes closed, embarrassed that he was naked before her. She might stop if she knew he was awake and, though it wasn't entirely pleasant – the cold and the ache and roughness of the cloth were quite harsh – the attention was soothing.

The direction of his thoughts and the continued stimulation of his skin wasn't without its effects.

"You're not quite as sick as I thought," said the girl. Even with his eyes still closed he could hear the smile in her voice. He felt his face flush and burn.

"It's all right, Gordon. It's only natural."

She continued her work. His upper body complete, she rinsed the cloth in her bowl of water, lathered more soap into it and moved onto his legs.

"Probably best not to let Dad see, though."

Gordon couldn't help but open his eyes to see the mischief he thought he'd caught in her tone. She was smiling to herself as she worked, and when she saw him watching her smile broadened and softened. She moved the cloth from his undamaged thigh down to his knee and then cleaned his shin, calf and foot, lifting his leg to suit her work.

"I thought you were going to pass over. I saw my grandma's dead body in the funeral parlour when I was ten, but I've never actually seen anyone die. I was... scared." She stopped washing him and took his hand for a moment. "I've got this feeling about you, Gordon. I think you're someone extra-special. Someone who can help us."

"I will if I can," he said, his voice stronger than before.

She shook her head, her hair falling around her face until she pushed it behind her ears. She let his hand go and went back to her washing, more businesslike now.

"No. That's not what I mean."

No one had ever touched him like this and he didn't want it to stop. The efficiency of her work increased as she moved on to his wounded thigh. He cried out the moment she touched it and her eyes went automatically to the shelter's opening.

"Dad's out checking his snares. He doesn't like me... nursing you. You won't tell him, will you?"

Gordon shook his head. She moved quickly now, drying him a little with another cloth and zipping him back into his sleeping bag. She discarded the soapy water, made the shelter appear undisturbed and left.

Moments later she put her head through the opening.

"I'm sorry I hurt you, Gordon. I'll do it better next time, I promise."

Before he could respond she was gone again. It wasn't long before he heard the sound of running footsteps through fallen leaves and the sound of her father's voice, breathless and strained.

"Brooke? Brooke! I'm here. Are you all right?"

From some distance away he heard her reply.

"I'm fine."

The footsteps came to a halt, still out of Gordon's line of sight but not far away from where he lay, the throbbing pain in his thigh receding along with the pressure in his crotch.

"What happened? I heard a shout."

"More nightmares, I suppose. I looked in but he was sleeping. He'll be all right, Dad."

"I'm not worried about him, Brooke. I'm worried about you. It's not safe here."

"It's safer than home."

"We should move on soon. Find somewhere quieter, more remote."

"We can't go anywhere yet. Gordon can't even sit up, let alone hike."

There was a silence, and Gordon could only guess at what passed between Brooke and her father then.

"We can't take the boy with us, Brooke. You know that."

"But you said yourself it's not safe. He's got to come."

"He *can't.*"

"Then why did you bother to bring him here at all? Why didn't you just let him die in the tunnel?"

Her father didn't reply.

"We're still good people, Dad. It was the only thing

we could have done." Brooke's voice was passionate.
"We're going to get him well and then we'll move on.
And when we do, he's coming with us."

Her father's voice dropped to a whisper.

"No, Brooke. He's a liability. He'll slow us down and
he'll attract attention."

"You don't understand, Dad. If he doesn't come with
us, I'm not leaving."

Father and daughter didn't speak for the rest of that
day. When next he saw Brooke, she brought him a
steaming bowl of broth and fed it to him, a spoonful at
a time. He tried to whisper to her but she shook her
head and held a finger to her lips. When the soup was
gone, Gordon felt strength flowing into his muscles for
the first time. Before she left the shelter Brooke leaned
over him and kissed his forehead. Her lips lingered
there, soft and silent, for a long time.

They drink tea in the roundhouse, sitting close to the
iron stove. The smell of the place has become a comfort
to Megan: the aroma of drying herbs, the tang of pipe
smoke, the ever-present perfume of fennel and mint –
that smell seems to be tattooed into Mr Keeper's very
skin – and the earthier undertones of body odour and
reed matting. Returning this morning is a little like
coming home.

Mr Keeper is silent. He has given her no more than
a nod in acknowledgment before spitting a chunk of
phlegm through the wind-eye into the chilly early-
morning gloom. Now he sits in characteristic absence,
sipping tea from time to time. His mind dallies elsewhere, at some great, unreachable distance.

Is he in the Weave right now? she wonders.

In the smoky glow of the roundhouse, she feels the fragility of the membrane between this reality and that of her visions. Her pulse quickens in the knowledge that magic, the unseen and truest of realities, bides close at her shoulder.

As though he hears her accelerating heartbeat, Mr Keeper finally speaks.

"Have you brought the book?"

She reaches into her pack and draws out the cloth-wrapped box. She places it on the matting beside him. This is a moment she has been quietly in fear of ever since the raven quill first marked the paper. She watches him unwrap the box and lift its lid. She watches him draw out the black leather volume, his fingers touching it with love. His face is serene as he opens the book and looks into it, not reading it – his eyes don't move – but somehow absorbing what he sees there. He closes the book and leaves his palm resting on the cover for long moments.

He replaces everything with care and rewraps the box.

"When you're not writing the book, it must be kept in the earth. Then the land will know you are keeping the story alive. And the story will keep the land alive."

He pulls up a section of matting between them, brushes away a thin layer of soil and lifts a small wooden hatch. Beneath it is a hole, the walls of which are lined with wood. But the base of the hole is bare earth and into it Mr Keeper places the wrapped box to lie on the exposed soil. He replaces the wooden hatch, brushes the dirt over it and drops the matting back into position. He presses his hands to his face and breathes in deeply, his eyes closing as he inhales the scent of the earth. Then he brushes the crumbs of soil from his fingers.

"When the book is in your home, it will be enough that you place it in a box of earth under your bed."

For a few moments Mr Keeper wanders again, and she expects him not to return. Quite suddenly, though, his head snaps in her direction. When he catches Megan's eye he is smiling.

This always makes her nervous.

"We must make a journey."

"To where?"

"To the valleys."

She knows better than to ask why.

"Your parents will be concerned for you, so I'm going to go and tell them myself where we're going. I'll return with some extra clothes for you."

He stands up, easing the stiffness from his joints, and crouches to get out of the tiny doorway. Seconds after he's gone, he pokes his head back in and looks around.

"This place is a mess. Give it a sweep out before I get back. And hang up those new bundles over the stove before they moulder."

His head disappears.

It reappears.

"And make us a good breakfast. It's going to be a long walk."

When his footsteps retreat and fade, she stands and begins to attend to his tasks. It makes her smile, this affected strictness of his. She knows the chores are meant to be a kind of discipline for her but they are the easiest part of treading the path. Long before he returns, she's done everything he's asked of her and is relaxing with tea and keeping the porridge warm near the stove.

• • •

She hears Mr Keeper tramping across the clearing. He makes no attempt to disguise his approach – even though he's demonstrated he's more than capable of doing so if he chooses – and when he reaches the door of the roundhouse she hears him setting items on the ground before entering. She fully expects him to say that her parents have forbidden her to travel with him. They've already seen the draining effect a mere bit of writing has had on her. But if they've made any protest, he doesn't mention it. Instead he brings in items of her clothes and even some food in which she recognises her mother's trademarks – her wheaten loaf baked into a slab, some salted rabbit and chicken, a couple of balls of goat's cheese and some hard-boiled eggs.

Once everything is inside, Mr Keeper brings out his large and many-pocketed backpack followed by a second pack, slightly smaller but equally well furnished with extra hidey holes and straps for hanging items from. He divides items of food and equipment into two piles. When he begins to place items from his pile into his backpack, Megan does the same with her own. So much of what she's already learned from him is based on watching and copying. Only occasionally does he give her verbal instruction or talk to her about what he's doing. He saves that sort of input for later, when they're resting or eating or drinking tea.

Before midday, the two packs are stuffed with everything Mr Keeper thinks they might need for their "long walk". Twice he fetches his longbow and a quiver of arrows and changes his mind, packing instead what appears to be more food. The last things he takes from behind the dividing curtain are two floppy-brimmed felt hats with straps beneath them.

"One thing I've learned, Megan," he says, placing one on his head and walking towards the path, "is that it pays to have good headgear when travelling. Never underestimate the usefulness of a decent hat."

She is still waiting for an explanation of this when she realises he isn't coming back. She hurries after him, her pack already heavy and awkward, while she tries to adjust the hat strap under her chin.

32

It takes only a couple of hours for Megan to find herself farther from Beckby than she's ever been before. Mr Keeper has already broken these boundaries many times by taking her to the other side of the Usky River, beyond Covey Wood, to the far borders of New Wood and well beyond the village into meadows and copses rarely visited by anyone. Places where the grass and wildflowers are waist high in the summer and the undergrowth is alive with tiny movements, rustlings and snufflings. She thought her childhood wanderings gave her a great knowledge of the village and its environs, but Mr Keeper's understanding of the local landscape is far greater.

In the skeining of the day world and the night country and the winding of time into time, Megan has travelled in ways no one but Mr Keeper will ever understand. Yet to leave the borders of the physical land where she has spent all of her life so far frightens her more. He leads at a stiff pace and she is swiftly tired by the relentlessness of his steps. Even though he moves calmly and without any apparent hurry, his ability to devour the land with his footsteps is supernatural.

In trying to keep up she tires fast.

They walk now up a long, shallow incline for what feels like ten miles but is probably less than one. Her legs burn and she stumbles regularly. Her face heats up with anger despite the chill of the wind. There is no end to this hill and there is no clear pathway. The ground is hard and uneven.

The gap between Megan and Mr Keeper widens. She is hungry. She is thirsty. She is tired. She hates Mr Keeper and she wants to go home, to bed, for a month. The hill, though not particularly steep, goes on forever. Megan stops. Her legs buckle and she sits down hard on the ground, her pack pulling her backwards and anchoring her to the earth. She flounders there, unable even to sit up.

From very far ahead, Mr Keeper turns back and sees her. But it can't be that far away because in seconds he is kneeling beside her and helping her out of the pack straps.

"I can't do this. I can't go on."

She expects a scolding but his hands are gentle. He places a rough mat over the cold ground and helps her to sit on it, placing her pack behind her as a bolster. Once she's comfortable, he does the same for himself and sits beside her. They face down the long, shallow hill. And only then does she see how far they've come. She's astonished.

"Is that the village?"

Mr Keeper says nothing.

Between them and the tiny-seeming collection of dwellings there are great expanses of meadow, ridges of rampant hawthorn and blackthorn, areas of wood-land and small hills and valleys. Home is a world away already.

Mr Keeper sets about cutting some chunks of wheaten loaf and removes two hard-boiled eggs from their shells. He places their brittle, smashed casings in the pocket where he often drops his ash and hands Megan's share of food to her. He uncorks one of the water bags and offers her a drink.

"Not too much, Megan. A little at a time. Chew the water and don't fill your stomach."

She is surprised when three or four "chewed" sips are enough to slake her thirst. The hillside is exposed and the breeze that cuts across it cools her off, stealing the fire from her face.

"Eat your food as slowly as you can. It should be reduced to liquid before you swallow. Not so important when we're in the village, but out here on the open land you must conserve your strength and take every possible nourishment you can from what you have. Travel is an unpredictable thing."

"How far must we go?"

He smiles.

"A lot farther than we've just come."

"I don't think I can carry on. My legs hurt. My feet are sore and my back aches."

Mr Keeper is chewing. He seems to have put a small piece of bread in his mouth about a year previously and is still reducing it with his teeth. She tries to do the same while she waits for him to speak.

"You have to see things as they really are, Megan. Your apprehension makes everything worse than it is. This creates a struggle when, in reality, there is no struggle."

Her anger flashes hot once more.

"I am not imagining I'm tired. I'm not making all this up."

"Once again, the way you see things is causing you pain. Did I say you were inventing your exhaustion?"

"Yes, you did."

"Actually, I did not. I think you ought to shut up and listen to the actual words I'm saying for a moment, Megan. Can you do that?"

Megan swallows her fury. Only when Mr Keeper is satisfied with her silence does he continue.

"You're scared because you don't know where we're going. You only know that you've never been there before and that it means we must leave behind everything you are familiar with. That's true, isn't it?"

"Yes."

"Your fear makes you tired. And your fear triggers your imagination. What is beyond the next rise? How much farther must we walk? Am I strong enough to make it? Can I prove myself worthy? Why can't I do what Mr Keeper does?"

In spite of everything, Megan giggles. It's either that or cry, but she still hates herself for allowing the emotion to escape.

"Any of this sound familiar?"

"I suppose so."

"Good."

Mr Keeper takes a bite of egg and a bite of bread and Megan is almost convinced that the conversation is over, so long does it take him to liquidise and swallow his mouthful. In the meantime, though, she's beginning to feel the cold come through her clothes, she starts to enjoy the feeling of height and distance from the village. It is still there. It isn't going to disappear.

Nor is the snaking body of the Usky River. Nor will the forests and meadows. And from up here, taken together, they are beautiful in a way she hasn't appreciated before. There's land beyond them in every direction, land she's never seen before, could never have imagined until now.

"What I want you to understand is this…"

His voice snaps her back from the pull of the landscape.

"This is not a trial that you must pass by enduring hardships. Of course, the Black Feathered Path has its challenges and some of them will test you to your very soul. But you must save your energy for those occasions. And you must recognise each stretch of the path for what it is. Right now we are taking a walk through the land. It is a physical challenge but not too troublesome a one. We have food. We have water. If need be, we have shelter. Both of us are fit and healthy. There is no hurry. Do you see what I'm saying?"

"But you walk so fast. And you never stumble. And you know where we're going. You know everything and I know nothing at all."

"I walk at the speed I walk because it is comfortable for me to do so. You should do the same. The fact that you don't know where we're going should be a source of excitement to you, not a source of fear. Do you think I would deliberately lead you into harm or danger?"

She doesn't answer straight away.

"I don't know what you'll do. I don't know anything about you."

"Aha! And so you imagine things about me instead. You mustn't. And you mustn't imagine where this walk will take us either. If you are tired, rest. If you are hungry, eat. If you are thirsty, drink. If you want to stop

to appreciate the land or some animal or plant, do so. I
assure you, I will do the same. Don't imagine danger
lurks around every corner and don't waste your power
on false imaginings. Enjoy this. Every moment. As
much as you can. Will you try?"

Megan heaves a sigh.

"Yes. I will."

"Good. And as for me leading you into danger, let me
make this as clear as I can. If I didn't think you could
walk the Crowman's road, this Black Feathered Path
that I too have walked in much the same way, I would
not have allowed you to make the first step of the journey. I have great faith in you and great trust in the way
of things. The way of things comes from the land and
the sky and the greatness of spirit all around us. I don't
need to believe these things, Megan. I don't need to
believe them because I know them. Not in my head but
in my body. In my bones. Yes, there will be difficult and
dangerous times ahead for both of us, but I will do
everything I can to arm you, to train you and to protect
you from harm. The rest will be up to you.

"In the meantime, you really ought to try to have a
nice time."

So saying, Mr Keeper draws out his pipe, stuffs the
bowl with baccy and lights it with one of the matches he
has made especially for their journey. The look of con-
tentment on his face is almost comical and once again
Megan finds herself close to laughter. She lets it out. Just
a giggle at first. Mr Keeper grins to hear it. Then he
chuckles, shaking his head. Megan laughs out loud. Soon
the wind is carrying their laughter across the broad, flat
hillside, flinging it over the grasslands and away.

33

Each day, under her father's protective gaze, Brooke cleaned the wound in Gordon's thigh and redressed it. Once he was eating, he was soon able to sit up, and the day after that, when the camp sounded quiet, he slipped into his clothes, put his boots on without lacing them up and put his head outside the shelter. The air smelled of winter but the day was bright, dry and almost warm.

He took a few moments to take in the camp before trying to stand. The fire under the pot was mostly ash, having not been tended for a while. The blackened cookware was stacked neatly at the base of the tree which formed one of the anchors for his shelter. To his left was one large all-conditions tent, pegged out tightly and camouflaged like all the rest of the gear. Nothing was left lying around, and the clearing they were in was small. To find the camp you'd have had to be looking for it. Gordon felt a slight weight lift from him at that.

He crawled into the daylight and tried to stand. It was only then that he found out how much his body hurt. His lower back ached and was stiff. His right thigh

had limited movement, as though the muscle fibres
were gummed up. His knees, elbows, hips and shoulder
joints complained, and he felt flashes of fever jolting
through his spine and neck. Still, he was alive and he
knew he was mending. When he reached his full
height, the world turned grey for a moment and he had
to bend towards his knees to avoid fainting. Once the
dizziness had passed he was able to stand upright. If
someone had pushed him he'd have collapsed, but for
the moment it felt like progress.

A few yards away was a smooth-barked beech tree,
the grey skin of its exposed roots lit up by the sun. Gordon stepped carefully towards it and sat down in the V
where two roots joined the trunk. There his back was
supported by the wood and the sun illuminated him.
The warmth seeped into him and he felt its comfort and
charge.

It was a still day and the trees were silent above him.
Nevertheless he felt their presence. They seemed to
stand guard. Far away he heard rooks calling to each
other across the fields, optimism and energy in their
cries. From time to time a leaf fluttered to the already
well-littered ground. He thought about his parents and
his sisters. He thought about Skelton and Pike, who
would surely be looking for him even now. He thought
about Brooke and the way she cared for him. He
thought about what she and her father might be running from.

For once, none of these thoughts bothered him too
deeply. Right now there was nothing he could do about
any of it. If a dozen Wardsmen burst into the clearing
now, he hadn't the strength to fight, or even to run.
Right here in this instant he had no power over

anything at all, and that was fine. What he had was a moment of peace, a moment which might prove to be very short; he had the sun and the trees and the sound of rooks, he had a place to rest.

For once, giving in was easy.

They ate rabbit, pigeon and pheasant. They ate wild mushrooms and sloe berries. They drank tea of mint or lemon balm. Gordon's strength returned quickly and soon he was helping around the camp: collecting wood, cleaning the pots and bowls after meals, fetching water from the stream.

He was so grateful to them that he didn't mind the wary way in which Brooke's father still watched him. He'd had to ask her to tell him the man's name in the end. He doubted John Palmer would ever have introduced himself otherwise. Each time he left the camp to check his snares, he lingered before leaving, watching his daughter and watching Gordon. It was uncomfortable not to be trusted and yet not know exactly why.

Since he'd recovered so quickly after they started feeding him, there'd been no more "bed" baths and the only time Gordon had been close to Brooke was when she changed his dressings. There had been opportunities to talk but Brooke had been evasive ever since the day her father had come running back into camp. The mood between her and her father remained tense, somehow on hold.

What little talk there was between the three of them was usually reserved for discussing the practicalities of the camp. When she was able to, Brooke shared long, open smiles or happy glances with Gordon, but that was all. He knew that John Palmer was suspicious of him. If that didn't change, he might have to leave these people before he was made to.

There was one last thing he could do, though. One morning, as John Palmer collected his hunting gear and began his routine of mistrusting, regretful glances at him and Brooke, Gordon approached him.

"Can I come with you?" he asked.

John Palmer couldn't hide his surprise.

"Hunting?"

"Yes. I know about snares and I'm good at being quiet. I won't get in your way."

It only took a moment or two for Brooke's father to register that if Gordon was with him he wouldn't be with his daughter.

"It could be a long walk. Can you manage it?"

"I feel fine. If I get tired, I'll just turn back."

John Palmer shouldered his gear and moved off without saying goodbye to Brooke. He turned back once.

"Are you coming or not?" he asked, and before Gordon had answered he was out of the clearing and moving out of sight.

Gordon looked at Brooke, their first private moment in many days.

"He's not a bad man," she said. "He's just frightened."

"I know."

Brooke put her hand to Gordon's cheek and smiled. He wished he could understand what she was thinking. The sound of John Palmer's footsteps was almost gone. Gordon leaned forwards and kissed Brooke, just a peck really and a quick one, but on her lips. He turned away before he could see the reaction.

"I'll see you later," he said.

John Palmer's route took them along the edge of the wood but just inside its boundary. It was an old wood with many huge beech trees, their muscular trunks sheathed in leathery grey bark. Smaller trees and shrubs gave the camp good cover, but out here the trees were large and well spaced. John Palmer moved through them not like a hunter but like prey, eyes watching the open spaces all the time. Gordon walked behind him, silent as a panther, and often John Palmer would turn – pretending to check far behind them but really, Gordon knew, to see if he was still there. The more Gordon watched John Palmer, the more he wondered what could have scared him so much that he would bring his daughter out to the forest to live wild.

Finally, John Palmer broke from the protection of the beech wood. There was an expanse of lumpy land in front of them, broken by patches of deep green, spiky marsh grass. To their left was the River Usk, which, like most of the rivers in the country, now constantly threatened to breach its own banks. Its waters swirled by, muddy and spiralling with currents. Fortunately, there had been no rain for a few days – at least, Gordon didn't remember any – and the grass of the hummocked flood plain wasn't too waterlogged.

John Palmer got as close to the river as he could, descending the bank a little to maintain cover as they crossed the exposed field. They had to jump across runnels of water draining from the land, the muddy bank sucking at their boots. Gordon, so confident and fleet of foot through woods, began to tire, his strength caught and washed away with the passing eddies.

When they reached the opposite side of the marshy land, Gordon's lungs heaved for air and his muscles burned. He struggled up the bank behind John Palmer, but where the bank ended another rise began. His legs began to shake and when he reached the top he fell to his knees. John Palmer turned and Gordon saw great concern in the man's eyes. This he had not expected. The man ran back to him and helped him into a sitting position.

"You all right, Gordon?"

"Fine. A bit weak, that's all."

The man looked annoyed with himself.

"I shouldn't have brought you. You're not well enough."

"I'm OK. I just need to rest for a minute."

"You're trembling all over. Here, I brought a snack."

John Palmer handed him a dozen or so sloe berries and Gordon chewed them hungrily. They were bitter but what little sweetness they possessed cooled the burn and soothed the ache in his legs.

"More?" asked John Palmer.

Gordon nodded.

When he'd eaten a second handful of berries, John Palmer handed him a strip of meat.

"What's this?"

"Smoked rabbit."

Gordon bit into the wrinkled meat and chewed fast. It tasted good and it must have been obvious.

"Not bad, is it?"

"Tastes amazing."

"It lasts for ages too."

John Palmer sat down beside Gordon and joined him

in chewing a string of rabbit meat. For a long time the only sound was the swollen rush of the passing river and the distant calling of rooks.

"It doesn't take much for people to become animals, Gordon. Just a bit of hunger and discomfort and fear. Then it all breaks down."

Gordon didn't say anything but he agreed. He'd seen it all over the news every night as the country ran short, first of luxuries and then of necessities.

"Seventy-two hours from anarchy, that's what they say."

Gordon stopped chewing.

"What does that mean?"

"It's a social theory, I guess. If you cut off the food, the water, the power and the fuel, it will take seventy-two hours for people to turn into savages. Civilisation breaks down. Remember the floods in Cumbria last year?"

Gordon didn't remember any floods in particular. Hardly any areas had escaped the consequences of storm rainfall.

"There were parts of the Lake District unreachable by any means. Areas where water and power were cut off for weeks. Lots of people didn't manage to get to the supply drops. It wasn't reported on the news but I heard every abandoned house was ransacked for food and water. They took the valuables too. When the tins and dry goods ran out, people ate their cats and dogs – raw if they didn't have means of starting a fire."

Gordon was pale at the thought of it.

"Is that true?"

"I can't say for certain, but that isn't the point really. Far worse things have already happened in this country." John Palmer stared out across the landscape beyond the small ridge where they sat. "Things no one will ever talk about."

Whatever had lifted John Palmer's barriers now brought them down, hard. He stood and looked down at Gordon.

"It's very hard not to like you," he said. "You certainly seem like a decent boy. But you're not a Palmer, Gordon. You're not… one of us. Don't forget that."

The man turned and walked down the ridge into the area of untidy brush and shrub that stretched to the base of the hills. Beyond, the land rose into heath and heather, more forest and higher peaks beyond. Gordon stood too. He was unsteady, but the food had returned much of his strength to him. When he felt able, he followed John Palmer.

34

When Gordon caught up with John Palmer, he was staring at a strange catch. Rabbits should have been in the carefully laid wire slipknots. Instead, they found three rooks.

Cautiously, John Palmer approached the snares and Gordon advanced with him. The wires glinted through the grass, one end anchored to a peg in the ground, the other tight around a black, bony foot. The rooks didn't move.

"Maybe they're in shock," said John Palmer, more to himself than to Gordon.

While he puzzled over their catch, Gordon enjoyed a physical proximity to the birds that he'd never known before. Rooks were generally shy and wary of humans. This close, Gordon could see their intelligent eyes and the powdery grey of their long, curved beaks. Feathers extended down from their broad breasts like fluffy plus fours, from the bottoms of which poked comically skinny legs and long feet. The rooks seemed to watch him carefully. Only when he bent down close did they try to hop away from him, tripping over their short tethers.

"I've never eaten vermin," said John Palmer.

Gordon was swift to reply.

"Rooks aren't vermin."

"Course they are. Farmers shoot them on sight."

Gordon let the matter pass. Some things weren't worth arguing about.

"We've got enough food for a few days," continued John Palmer. "Maybe we should just let them go."

"No. They're here for a reason. We should take them back."

John Palmer regarded him with some surprise.

"You going to kill them, are you?" he challenged.

Without speaking, Gordon stepped forwards, knelt and put his hands over the first rook. It barely struggled. In his left hand, he smoothed its wing feathers and feet into a tight grip. He took the rook's head between his thumb and index finger.

"Wait," said John Palmer.

Gordon looked up. The man's face was full of confusion.

"We could still release them. They've done nothing to us." The words sounded feeble.

"That's not the point, really, is it?" said Gordon.

He stretched the rook's neck and twisted its head in his hand. There was a quiet grinding and a faint snap as the bird's lightweight bones separated beneath his fingers. The feathers were warm in his hand as the rook's nerves twitched and its wings spasmed in his grasp. Soon it was still. Its head hung limp. Gordon placed it in the ground and moved to the next snare.

John Palmer didn't speak to him for the rest of the day.

• • •

After their rest and food, Megan keeps pace more easily. At the top of the slope – not endless, as it soon turns out – she sees a huge expanse of countryside spreading into the distance like a broad canvas, more colours and textures of green than she can count laid over it. She stops to take it all in. This is another world.

This new land stretches to the horizon under a vast sky. She knows from school that the world is a sphere but she imagined it smaller than all this. She experiences a moment of dizziness, utterly overwhelmed by the possibility of the size of the Earth and suddenly realising her own tininess in relation to it. The dizziness turns to fear. She flings out her hands to either side but there is nothing to hold on to, and so she sits down, anchoring herself to the land.

In the distance a huge flock of rooks takes off from a stand of poplars. There must be hundreds of them, wings seeming to flap in slow motion as they rise. Moments later the sound of their calls reaches her. She is comforted.

Mr Keeper has noticed the halt in their walk, and he looks back towards Megan with a smile.

"Beautiful, isn't it?"

She can only nod, tears spilling from her eyelashes.

They walk along the crest of the gentle ridge for quite a while, and Megan absorbs the landscape at leisure, feeling less fear and more awe the farther they progress. They are moving uphill but it's a barely noticeable gradient. Then they run out of ridge and a path appears: exposed dirt, worn down between two banks of grass. The track winds upwards more steeply and the going requires effort again.

This time Megan is steady, not forcing herself to

tramp harder but only putting one foot in front of the other. After a while, this rhythm causes her to disappear from the world and she becomes a detached awareness. Megan is the tide of her lungs and the beat of her soles on the exposed dirt. Megan is the sensation of heaviness and the pull of pack straps. Megan is a winding pathway, only a few steps of which are visible up ahead. Megan is gone.

For a long time, a time she neither cares nor is able to measure, they rise upwards. She does not stumble. Nor does she look up to see how far ahead is her guide. The gradient levels out and the path lengthens in front of her. She can see without having to look up that Mr Keeper is not too far ahead. She glances to either side and in doing so, she returns to herself. They have crested a new ridge. This one is much higher. To either side the land falls away gradually, but if she were to try to walk straight down, the walk would become a scramble and then a fall.

To her left is the same vast bowl of land stretching out to a horizon now even more distant. Mr Keeper has stopped walking. He is looking to the other side of the new ridge. As she draws level with him, Megan lets her eyes be drawn into yet another new landscape.

Her hand flies to her mouth, too late to stifle the small cry that has escaped.

She looks at Mr Keeper and sees in an instant that this is no surprise to him.

Written in his features she recognises an expression she has never seen there before. Nor could she ever have predicted such a man as he would have cause to display it. Something akin to shame. He says nothing and turns his face out across this new landscape, scrutinising it.

A procession of skeletal towers, cages rising high up into the air, make an angled line across the land. From each tall framework, three pairs of arms stretch out to either side. These arms grip black ropes which connect every tower. Where the ropes are broken they hang earthwards like whips. A few of the towers are damaged too or buckled, leaning to the left or right. Megan thinks of giants: blind, drunken giants using ropes to guide themselves across the land.

Following the motionless march of the giants is a huge slate-grey path with lines painted onto it. Dozens of people could walk abreast along it. In many places the path is broken or cracked, black chasms like hungry mouths wait for travellers to fall in. Along the path are things she has only seen in her visions – enclosed carts without their horses or oxen to pull them. Cars. That was what the boy had called them.

The path and the giants have one destination: a village. But a village so large it would hold more people than Megan knows how to count. The outlying areas of the village are made up of dwellings around mazes of smaller tracks. Hundreds and hundreds of dwellings in each area. Hundreds of tracks leading back to the main path like streams feeding a river. The tracks lead to buildings many times the height of those nearest to Megan. Hundreds of dwellings rising high into the air, thousands of square wind-eyes, like black lifeless sockets.

There is more, much more, but all of it is silent and dead. She's never seen an absence of life like this in the day world. It makes her cold inside.

"I've seen this," she says. "I've seen it in the night country. But it was alive then."

"Yes. It was alive. A long time ago."

"Is this where the boy comes from?"

"Not here, no. But somewhere like this. Somewhere not too far away. That's why his presence is so strong hereabouts."

Hereabouts.

To Mr Keeper, even this distance from home must still seem nearby. Megan wonders how far he has travelled. Even standing beside him, she doesn't feel safe so close to this dead place.

"Is anyone still there?" she asks.

Mr Keeper shakes his head.

"No. There's no life there. None at all."

"Does anyone ever… go there?"

"No. Never."

"What happened to it?"

There's no answer. She looks across at Mr Keeper and sees that expression of regret again. She's never seen his face so troubled, so much age hinted at in the many lines and cracks of his face. He looks at her now, knowing his emotions are visible for once but not seeming to mind. He smiles and puts a hand on her shoulder.

"I could tell you, but you'll find out for yourself soon enough. You'll see it. I will tell you this, though," he says and turns to the path again, walking away. "It was something we did."

"Us?"

"People."

Megan's imagination overloads. People did all this? Built it and destroyed it?

She hurries after him.

"But why?"

Mr Keeper stops and turns back to her. He looks so sad and so tired that Megan is suddenly very afraid for him. His eyes take on that other-world stare and she thinks she'll lose him to one of his absences, but then his eyes sharpen and his pupils contract. His look cuts right through her.

"Because we forgot where we came from."

A moment passes, and when she recovers from the feeling of everything being her fault – it can't be me, can it? – Mr Keeper is far ahead on the path along the ridgeway. She can only wonder where she's been this time. She rushes to catch up before remembering what he has told her. She lets her steps fall back into a comfortable rhythm, allows her eyes to wander left and right – mostly they are drawn to the dead place on the land where people once lived in immeasurable numbers – allows herself to breathe deeply and without strain. Gradually the distance between her and Mr Keeper begins to close.

Brooke plucked and gutted the rooks with less distaste than Gordon expected. She discarded the feet and the heads but used as much of the birds as she could to make a kind of stew with herbs gathered nearby.

When the food was ready, John Palmer ate with reluctance and complained the meat was tainted and bitter. He didn't finish his meal. Brooke ate slowly and thoughtfully and finished her portion without serving herself any more. To Gordon, the stew tasted better than anything his mother had ever made. He took a second helping and ate with gusto while the other two looked on. Each mouthful seemed to charge him. All the weakness he'd felt that morning evaporated, to be replaced with a sense of vitality and clarity. It was how he imagined people felt after too much coffee. When John and Brooke Palmer continued to decline more food from the pot, Gordon finished it and said a silent prayer:

Thank you for your strength and sacrifice.

35

They walk for the rest of the day, stopping sometimes to look across the land. The ridge path seems endless. At some point in the afternoon Mr Keeper finds another path, barely noticeable, which leads off the ridge in a zigzag.

Going downhill is hard work on her knees and Megan takes it slowly, resting often. She has never walked this far before and certainly the load on her back is heavy. When the gradient levels out she almost cries with relief. The path disappears but Mr Keeper seems to know where he's going. The land becomes dense with broad areas of bramble, rambling wild roses, now autumnal and flowerless, and hedgerows that have become impenetrable walls of thorn. They pass through it all, Mr Keeper finding gaps where she sees only barriers, and enter a woodland of birch, the bark of every tree curling and peeling like dead white skin. The breeze causes the bark to rustle and Megan is reminded of the book and the sound its pages make as she turns them.

The broadly-spaced birch trees give way to oak and pine and then sycamore and beech. They reach an open tract of marsh grass. She sees willow trees and knows they must be close to water.

"I need to stop," she calls to Mr Keeper.

He turns back.

"It's not much farther, Megan. Just into this wood." He points to a grey mass of beech trees only an acre or more away across the tussocked grassland. "Can you make it that far?"

She nods and follows. They pass willows to their right and she can smell the river beyond. It's the Usky – she would know the scent of its waters anywhere. Its familiarity is a comfort that makes the last part of the hike more bearable. They enter the beech wood and the trees there are majestic, silent grey beasts which rise high and noble into the air. Mr Keeper stops, shrugs off his pack and lowers it to the ground. He stretches forwards and backwards a few times and then squats to ease out his legs. Megan drops her pack as though she has been carrying a boulder, and collapses to the ground.

The beech trees have left a space among themselves, roughly circular and clear of obstructions, save for the odd fallen branch. These Mr Keeper gathers together in preparation for a fire.

"Don't sprawl for too long," he says after a while, "or you'll have no energy left at all. Come on, I've got a job for you."

She groans and rises to her feet.

Mr Keeper is searching among the beech trees and soon he finds what he's looking for: a clump of hazel. Its long, thin branches reach straight up from a central stump of trunk. The nuts have fallen and many remain untouched, though it's obvious the squirrels have had their share. She pockets several handfuls of the nuts while Mr Keeper uses a long, heavy blade to separate the hazel branches from their trunk.

Together they carry bundles of hazel back to their clearing and Mr Keeper begins to build a dwelling for them. First he marks out a circle by forcing the thicker ends of the sturdier hazel branches deep into the soft earth, twenty-eight uprights which he then bends towards the centre in opposing pairs, lashing them together with twine. He weaves the thinnest branches between the uprights, creating five lateral rings which hold the dome together. From time to time he takes a feather or some dried herbs or the claw of an animal and builds them into the weave of the roundhouse.

When this is complete Megan helps him wrap the structure. They use a fine, sheer cloth the colour of dried lichen. This Mr Keeper has carried underneath his pack in a cylindrical bolt, which Megan had mistaken for a bedroll. They place this roll of material, thinner than paper but as strong as her coat, around the hazel branches as tightly as they can, turning the whole structure into a bubble of pale, dusty green. They secure the wrap with twine at three levels, pulling it tight and tying it off.

Mr Keeper crawls inside the roundhouse to burn sage and pine. She hears him praying in whispers. All at once she feels very safe in the presence of this ageless man. A man who seems so much like a naughty boy in the skin of an elder.

Dusk is coming.

Mr Keeper keeps the fire small but well-fed, and they boil water in a blackened pan to make tea. The temperature

drops and they sit inside the roundhouse to drink it. Mr
Keeper smokes in silence, baccy fumes mingling with the
scent of sage and pine. Soon the only light she can see is
the glow of Mr Keeper's pipe and the flames of the small
fire flickering outside the roundhouse. When Mr Keeper
finishes his smoke, he rations out some food. They eat
quietly and the darkness deepens.

As Megan sits, she drifts and dozes, her back resting
comfortably against her pack.

She slips away.

"Do you feel him?"

Megan snaps to wakefulness. It is dark but for an
indistinct and shapeless orange glow coming in from
outside.

How long have I slept for?

"He's here, Megan. Do you feel him?"

Mr Keeper's voice is a whisper. She keeps her voice
low too.

"I... I don't know. I must have been–"

"Shh." His voice drops so low she can barely hear it.
"Listen, Megan. The Crowman is with us."

Megan strains to hear and her heartbeat quickens.
Her senses focus. Her mouth is bark-dry in an instant.
But she listens, though. It isn't footsteps she hears outside the roundhouse – its "walls" now seeming more
flimsy than a layer of web – it's the swoosh of huge,
distant wings.

The wings quicken their beat, slowing some massive
airborne form for landing. The wind buffets their shelter. The dome shifts and settles and the noise outside is
gone. The sound of stealthy footsteps progresses near
and then begins to circle the roundhouse. What flew

now walks. Is this the same Crowman she saw in
Covey Wood?

The footsteps stop.

She can see nothing but she senses Mr Keeper reach for
some talisman at his neck and clasp it in his gnarly hand.
She hears him intoning whispers so faint they might only
be her imagination. Suddenly, she wants to pray.

Pray, she thinks. Before it's too late.

Great Spirit, if this is a test, if this is part of my path
then make my footsteps upon it sure and strong. Help
me to endure this. Let me have the will to be everything I can be for myself and for this world.

Her terror vanishes. Gone like a pebble to the bottom
of a lake. In its place she feels a radiated peace. It comes
from outside the makeshift roundhouse, where the
stealthy footsteps stopped. She knows – knows – that
whatever is out there is for the good. A dark light of
benevolence streams into the shelter as she hears
words, spoken distinctly but in utter silence, both outside and within herself.

*Have no fear, Megan Maurice, for everything you need will
come to hand in the very moment of its requirement and you
will fulfil your purpose here.*

There is movement by the entry flap and something
enters with a breath of cold air. She stiffens at the intru-
sion in spite of herself. A hand takes her wrist. The grip
is soft and soothing, its touch blood-warm in the darkness. And all about the fingers of this hand she feels a
cuff of silky feathers. Feathers, she knows without
needing to see, as black as the void.

Come, Megan Maurice, I have much to share with you.

The hand draws her out into the night. She finds
herself stammering.

"B-but the book. How will I remember it all?"

You can never forget. Not even the smallest detail or sensation. It is your gift. It is your curse. That is what it means to walk the Black Feathered Path. All you need is the strength to hold it, Megan, no matter what you see, no matter what you feel. Can you do that much?

There is no hesitation.

"I can. And I will. I swear it."

They are in the night. The fire's life is a waning glow, cooling beneath a crust of ashes, barely visible and yet the one thing that Megan can see. When this faint radiation begins to shrink she realises that she has been lifted away from the grip of the Earth by the hand of the Crowman. She rises up, feeling the branches of beech trees passing on all sides. She looks to where the arm and body of the entity which holds her must be, but she can see nothing of him. All she can feel is the rise and fall of vast wings above her and the sensation of being held near to the warm, soft breast of a bird. The Crowman rises and rises and Megan is drawn with him. Higher than she has ever risen before. Into the very beyond.

They are flying over time itself and over the woven threads of the day world and the night country. Megan is dizzy with fear of falling, not to earth – that would be to die, that would be *something* – but into oblivion where she would fall forever, away from the Great Spirit, away from time and the beautiful Earth, abandoned, irretrievable and forgotten.

They ascend through the Weave towards the stars. The Crowman takes her back once more.

Back to the boy.

36

Each morning when John Palmer went hunting and checked his snares, Gordon joined him. He didn't ask to go along and John Palmer didn't tell him he wasn't welcome. The man regarded him with something like fear now and always looked away first if ever their eyes met.

Gordon shot wood pigeons, pheasants and rabbits with John Palmer's air rifle, and he showed him better ways of placing and concealing his snares. Meat became plentiful. Since eating the rooks, Gordon's healing had accelerated. He felt stronger than he'd been before the fever. He was a little taller now, a little broader. Living wild appeared to suit him.

With his returned health came the urge to move on. Not simply a need but a sense of duty. Fear of the journey and a reluctance to say goodbye to Brooke stopped him acting on what he knew to be right.

In moments when he wasn't hunting or helping out around the camp, Gordon took his pack down to the stream where he could be alone. He would sit and look through the book Knowles had given him.

It was a sinister thing. Like a diary to which many

people had made contributions, none of them knowing exactly why, or what it was they were recording. Everything related to the Crowman, but sometimes he was referred to as Black Jack, other times the Scarecrow. There were drawings in pencil, drawings in biro or even crayon – anything that had been to hand at the moment inspiration struck.

The themes of the drawings were always similar, like the nightmares he'd had ever since he was tiny. Barren forests with blackened trees and exposed earth; fallen buildings and collapsed city-scapes; bodies being washed away in flood water; lightning striking the land like warheads; dark clouds rolling over bald hillsides; diseased people crying out to heaven; starving, naked refugees with hollow bellies and pits for eyes sitting beside broken highways; cars and people and buildings falling into great cracks in the earth; lava flowing through parks and streets.

In every depiction of cataclysm, sometimes in the foreground, sometimes a tiny representation watching from afar, stood the same figure. Long dark hair hanging over his features, arms stretched wide and upwards as if in summoning, a long coat covering most of his body, and at his cuffs and ankles something like black straw or black lightning instead of fingers. Some sketches were portraits in close-up. A beak for a face, grey eyes fixed on the artist or viewer, hair like skeins of black silk and everywhere black feathers falling like snow. A few of the pictures weren't of a man at all but were merely studies of crows, some in flight, some sitting in high branches, some lying dead in the deserted streets.

The writing was just as eerie, just as focussed.

"*The Crowman Feeds upon the Blackened Stump of England*" was the title of one of the landscape drawings. There was poetry too. Pages and pages of it in dozens of different hands, all stuck into this scrapbook by some strangely obsessed chronicler:

> 'Tis a black dawn brings the Crowman
> 'pon a black dawn only will he come
> To the Bright Day will he lead us
> On that Bright Day will his work be done

The prose entries were lurid and apocalyptic:

> A dark man is coming and his coming signals the
> end of everything we know. He is tall and his skin
> is pale. His hair is as black as the wings of a
> raven. His basalt eyes are mined from the centre
> of the Earth. They sparkle even as he watches the
> world destroy itself. I see him high on hillsides
> watching death sweep the valleys. I see him in
> trees, perched and cackling. I see him among the
> ruins of the towns and cities, striding between the
> heaped-up dead, his ragged coat flapping behind
> him like feathers. Walking, always walking,
> pausing only to see the annihilation, through the
> long darkness towards some weak light far in the
> distance where he will exit, leaving only smoking
> remains. Surely, Satan himself is come among us.

But some were not so bleak:

> When the Crowman returns to our land you will
> know that the dark times are at an end. For he

will spread his wings across this nation and draw
away the black veil that has covered it for so long.
It will be a cleansing. It will be death and rebirth.
Pray for his swift arrival that we may be deliv-
ered. Pray for the coming of the Crowman that we
may be, at last, transformed.

Reading the book made him remember his own nightmares anew. With the recollection of a lifetime of bad dreams, all the strength he was gaining would evaporate. Who was it that his parents were suggesting he should go and seek out? Were they telling him to find and confront the very devil himself? Or was it simply a man they wanted him to find?

One thing Gordon knew for sure was that he was just a boy. A boy alone and without any influence. All he could do was try to find this man, as he had been asked to do. What he suspected was – and the more he thought about it the more sense it made – that many people were out there searching for this Crowman. Sending many might ensure at least one of them succeeded. Probably, they were boys and girls his age because they'd be less likely to be suspected and caught. Perhaps children all over the country had received letters or instructions just like this from their own parents and were searching for the Crowman right now, just as confused and frightened as he was. Thinking about it this way made it easier to live with what he had been asked to do.

After every reading of the scrapbook, he sealed it, the letters and his own diary inside the Ziploc bag that he'd brought from home. He stowed it all at the bottom of his pack. He knew Brooke and her father had been through his stuff but he doubted they'd studied it, and it was best they didn't see any more, best they trusted him right now, until he was strong enough to move on alone.

Until?

Who am I trying to fool?

Gordon was fully healed and fit right now. The wound in his leg no longer gave him any pain and the muscle had ceased to be stiff and unresponsive. He had a feeling he was heavier than he'd been before his escape through the tunnel, and he was certainly stronger. Each trip out with John Palmer proved his increased fitness and stamina. Nothing slowed him now, no hill or marsh or thicket. He seemed able to negotiate the landscape without it sapping his energy. Quite the opposite, in fact; the more time he spent outdoors, the more the landscape fed him. Sometimes his body hummed with power and enthusiasm, and he was tempted to run fast and long just because he was certain that he could. All this in just a few days.

No, there was no excuse for staying other than his infatuation with Brooke and his fear of walking the land alone in search of the Crowman. What sane person would want to do that?

But the more he considered his situation, the more he had to accept that it was time to take responsibility for himself. If finding the Crowman was the one way he could save his family, he had to begin now.

He came to this decision as he sat alone by the stream one afternoon. Resolved, he stowed his diary and scrapbook in the pack, slung it over his shoulder and walked the short distance back into the camp. Brooke was busy at the cook pot, adding wild parsnips and

herbs to a stew of rabbit and pheasant. Gordon scanned
the camp.

"He's gone off somewhere on his own," said Brooke.

"Oh. Everything all right?"

Gordon felt himself to be at the root of every problem or disagreement, no matter how small.

"He can't show his emotions around me," said
Brooke. "He's too... closed off. I'm sure he thinks that
if he ever let go of his feelings to me, he'd cry for a
week. So he goes off and cries alone somewhere from
time to time." She stood up and brushed her hands on
the seat of her trousers. "It's nothing you've done.
Well, not directly anyway. Having you here reminds
him there's a world out there. The one we left behind.
Trouble is, he can't let go of how it used to be and who
he was."

"What about you?" asked Gordon, placing his pack
on the ground between them.

"I've done my best to put the past behind me."

She sighed, and the strength went out of her usually
upright, noble posture. Gordon saw for the first time
that she had been playing the role of a woman and
now she was reverting into girlhood. Stuck between
being a boy and being the man he needed to be was
such similar territory that he felt an unhealable sadness
for Brooke. The woman would always carry the little
girl within, a little girl who had been hurt and could
never grow up because of it.

She was speaking to him, telling him her story with
great openness before he'd fully registered what she
was saying.

"We were attacked in our home. I didn't realise it
until then, never even thought about it really, but

we're wealthy. At least we used to be. I didn't realise because there was nothing to hurt me and nothing to worry about. I've thought about that a lot ever since.

"Every day you could see more and more people living on the street, but I never understood what that meant. We had food. We had petrol. We had heat and running water. All because we had money. Mum and Dad used to walk through town as though they were shrinking. As if they didn't want anyone to notice them. I know why now.

"When you spend money, people notice. If your clothes are clean and smart, people see it. And so many people are going without things now that they hate you if you have what they need. Dad was an investment banker and that probably made people hate him even more. He stopped going into the local pub and Mum started ordering everything we needed online or over the phone. Then they took me out of school and hired a private tutor for me. Jenny Latham. She was lovely. She was there the day they came into the house."

Brooke stopped, her eyes focussing on a place of memory. She seemed to lose her way, but Gordon didn't want to let the moment go. He wanted to know what had happened, of course, but he also knew it would be good for Brooke to tell the story. Otherwise it would be locked inside her the way it was locked inside her father.

"Who were they?" he asked.

His voice was a whisper, but it was enough to bring Brooke back to the present, drawing the thread of the story with her.

37

Brooke cleared her throat.

"We don't know for sure. Dad has his suspicions. They must have known us, or known him at least, because they all wore balaclavas. They arrived in a big white van and Mum opened the door when they pulled into the driveway. She thought it was a delivery vehicle. Six men jumped out. Well, four men. Two of them were... smaller. Just kids really. They didn't bother with the door. They smashed the downstairs bay window and climbed in. Mum was running for the kitchen when they caught her. I always think it was the knife block she was going for. That's what I'd have used if there'd been time.

"The two who'd knocked Mum down dragged her upstairs. I was up in my Dad's office doing maths problems and talking about boys with Jenny. It all happened so quickly. I saw them dragging Mum to her bedroom before we slammed the office door and put a chair under the handle. It didn't hold for long. I went to the window to see if we could jump down, but I didn't have the guts. By the time I'd decided that, they'd broken through the door.

"Two of them had taken Mum, which left two men and two boys in the office with us. Jenny grabbed Dad's letter opener – it was only ivory but it was still enough of a weapon to make them back off. I snatched a pair of scissors from the pencil holder. Better than nothing. The men spread out so that they could come at us from all angles. Every time they made a move, Jenny slashed the air with the letter opener, making them jump back.

"I noticed a few things about them. Long belts with extra holes held up their jeans, and their wrists were bony. They weren't proper thieves either. They way they hesitated, you could see they hadn't done this before. They lacked confidence. Thinking back now, I suppose if Jenny and I had rushed them then, waving our silly weapons in their faces, they might have backed out of the way and we could have run out of the house. But I couldn't have left Mum, not even using the excuse of calling for help. Anyway, we were terrified so we didn't try to charge through them. We just held them off. And then the men who'd taken Mum arrived in the office too. After that we had no chance.

"They came towards us and the next time Jenny slashed at them, one of them caught her hand and twisted the letter opener out of her grip. Then they trapped her hands behind her back. The same thing happened to me except I started kicking and screaming and banging my head to make them let go. They lost their grip on me a few times. I broke one man's nose with the back of my head, kicked another one who got too close right in the balls. He dropped to his knees and didn't come near me again after that. But they did get me and it only took a minute or two. The feeling of those scrawny arms and bony fingers around me. It was horrible.

"They took us into Mum and Dad's bedroom. Mum was tied up with dressing gown cords and her cheek was bleeding. They'd tied a scarf around her mouth to keep her quiet. When I looked in her eyes I could see she was already close to breaking. Her breathing was all wrong and she didn't seem to recognise me. They tied us up with bits of clothes too. I don't think they wanted us out of commission for long, but they hadn't brought any rope with them. I saw what they were doing from out of the bedroom window. They were taking the food. Everything we had. Tins of soup and fruit. Pasta and rice. Even what was in the fridge. They took all of Dad's wine and spirits too, filling plastic boxes they'd brought with them in the van. I looked for a licence number but the van had no plates.

"The boy who'd been left to keep an eye on us saw me looking out of the window, and realised everything I saw made it more likely they'd be caught. He came across the room and pushed me down onto the floor with Mum and Jenny. But not before I'd seen them shut the van's doors. They hadn't taken anything that I would have considered valuable – the TV or the stereo or games console. It only struck me later that they probably lived somewhere without electricity.

"They all trooped back up the stairs and began taking our clothes then. I just couldn't believe it. They took coats and jumpers mainly, things to keep them warm. They took my stuff and Mum's too – they must have been collecting for their women. They even took the blankets and duvets and some of the thicker curtains.

"On their next trip upstairs they came into my parents' bedroom and stood there silently, their eyes peeping through their balaclavas without any expression. But I knew what they were thinking. They looked at each other as if waiting for someone to make a decision. The boy who'd been making sure we didn't escape had been keeping an extra-close eye on Mum. From time to time he'd gone over to her and checked her gag to make sure she could breathe OK. He'd also checked the bindings at her wrists and ankles, and I'd seen his skinny hands touch Mum's feet and linger on her calves through her tights. But he'd always backed away after a few moments. He was the one who edged forwards again and knelt beside my Mum. He stroked the hair from her eyes and face and touched the cut over her cheek. Mum's breathing suddenly quietened and her eyes widened. She looked right into his eyes and the boy looked down and away.

"But even though he couldn't meet her gaze, he couldn't stop his hands from exploring her. It was like watching a devotee touch a goddess. His fingers were… reverential, somehow – first holding the material of her dress and then feeling the soft flesh beneath. When he touched her breasts, she flinched and I had to turn away.

"They moved Jenny and me into my bedroom and tied us together back to back. They left us there and closed the door. But I could still hear my Mum trying to scream through her gag, trying to make them stop."

Gordon heard all this as a story, something that wasn't real and could never have happened. And yet, he knew it could. He knew it had. It shamed him. Like the boy who'd broken the trust between human beings by touching Brooke's mum, Gordon looked down and away. He didn't have the right to hear any of this.

"They were careless in the end. Spent too long with my mum when they should have taken their spoils and run for it. As it was, Dad came home. We all heard his car turn into the driveway, and Jenny and I heard the raiders thumping down the stairs to get out to their van and away. Dad says he knew what was happening the moment he saw the van. These kinds of robberies had been taking place a lot. Instead of coming into the house, he ran to the garage and got his shotgun. By the time the raiders came out of the house, he was armed. He shot one of them in the leg. It was the boy who'd first touched Mum. They grabbed the boy and threw him bleeding into the van. As they backed out of the drive, Dad blew out one of the wheels. They drove away on three tyres and one rim. The Ward caught all of them a couple of miles down the road, but the boy died of blood loss.

"Nothing happened to Dad. These days, defending the home is one right we do still have, but the families of the thieves have all sworn revenge – especially the boy's father. They were all living in a derelict building in town, pooling their goods after each raid. Now the families are on the run. And we're on the run from them. Dad reckons they're not country types, don't know how to survive on the land. He thought we'd be safest far away from town."

"You left everything?"

"All of it. Dad said, 'What price could you put on our lives?' He's got stuff, money and things, hidden away, but the house is there now for whoever decides to squat in it until we get back."

"What about your mum, Brooke?"

"She couldn't come with us. She's with my grandma in Cornwall. Dad says it's the safest place for her."

"And you and your Dad are just going to live out here in the countryside forever?"

"I don't know what we're going to do. Move on, probably. And then keep moving until he can think of something. Maybe we'll find a new home somewhere else and Mum can come and live with us again."

Gordon wanted to do something, to say something at least, but what words or actions could answer what she'd told him? The kiss he'd given her before going off with her father to check the snares: it was a kiss for him more than her. Now she needed to be held in the strongest and most sincere way, something just for her, and Gordon couldn't make his body work to give her that comfort. He wasn't worthy of her pain. Encouraging her to talk had seemed like a good idea to begin with. Now he knew it was folly – his desire to do the right thing by others neutralised by his inability to deal with the realities of their need.

But he couldn't just stay silent and stand still in the vacuum her words were creating with every passing second. All he could do was tell the truth. It was pathetic-sounding to his ears but it was better than nothing.

"I can't believe what you've been through, Brooke. I don't think I'd have the strength to deal with that."

"It's not about strength. It's about not having a choice. I miss Mum but I've got to look after Dad. He thinks he's the strong one, my protector, but he's the one who has to hide every few days when he breaks down. I don't know what he'd do if he was on his own.

I think he'd just give up. Everything he's ever worked for and everything he's loved is either gone or damaged. There's no fixing any of it. I've got to keep him going until he can start something new, find something worth living for."

"What about you? You need a future too."

Brooke's face was blank, almost as though she didn't understand.

"I'm still young. I've still got time."

"Time for what?"

"I don't know exactly. When Dad's feeling better and we know we've found somewhere safe to live, then I'll… start again."

Everything she said made giving her a hug impossible. Instead, Gordon looked away through the leafless beech trees, knowing his time with these people would soon be over. He knew he mustn't get stuck in the past. He had to keep moving and fulfil his parents' wishes. What they'd asked of him was their only shot at freedom. He might be young and lacking in strength, but he knew he would search until he died if it meant there was a possibility of saving them.

Brooke's voice and the directness of her question took him by surprise.

"You must have a family somewhere. What happened to them?"

He wished he'd never started all this. But there was no way to back out of it after Brooke had been so open with him.

Where to begin?

"The Ward took… collected them. Wrecked the house. Hit my father. Cuffed them all and took them away."

Brooke's expression was pure fascination, though Gordon could see she tried hard to hide it.

"The Ward? What did your family do?"

"I'm not exactly sure. It's like the Ward think they're part of some conspiracy."

"When was this, Gordon?"

"I don't know exactly. Before I went into the tunnel plus however long I was in there plus however long I've been here."

"Don't you want to go and see them? At least find out what's been happening? I mean, the Ward aren't... you know, known for their hospitality."

This was the question he hadn't wanted to answer.

"I can't go back. That's what the Ward want me to do. They're using my family as bait. If I go back they'll have all of us and that'll be the end of it. The end of everything."

"How do you mean?"

"A Wardsman smuggled some letters out. One from my mum and one from my dad. They both said I should get as far away as possible and never go near the Ward. Never trust them. They said if I did come back to find them, they'd be as good as dead."

"But you can't trust what's in those letters. They could have been written under threat."

"I've thought about that a lot. I know in my heart that the letters were genuine, Brooke. And anyway, if the Ward had forced them to write something, it would have been to tell me to come in and save them, wouldn't it? Then the Ward would have all of us and they'd have won."

Brooke didn't say anything for a while. Gordon hoped the conversation was over.

"So what about your future, Gordon Black? What are you going to do without your family?"

It was a harsh question. A challenge. He thought for a long time before answering. Could he trust her? After all she'd done for him, after her honesty, didn't he at least owe her the truth?

"It's simple, Brooke. I'm going to find the Crowman."

Horror and delight lit up her face.

"The Crowman's real? I knew it! I knew you were connected to him."

Gordon gestured to his pack.

"Only because you went through my stuff," he said, locking eyes with Brooke. "How much did you read?"

Brooke looked away.

"Hardly any, honestly. I'm sorry, Gordon. We had to find out who you were – to see if we could trust you."

"Your dad doesn't trust me."

"He doesn't trust anyone." Brooke's eyes were suddenly bright with anger. "Why should he, after what's happened?"

He couldn't answer. There were no words. He picked up his pack and turned away. Her hand took his arm and he looked back, seeing her rage had become tears.

"Don't walk away," said Brooke, finding her smile again. "Tell me more about… him."

"I don't really know anything. But my parents said I had to find him. They said he was their only hope."

Brooke shook her head in wonder, whispering:

"The Crowman."

She stared off into the trees.

"Do you know anything about him?" asked Gordon.

After a while she came back to herself.

"Not really. You hear good things and you hear bad things. I mean terrible things. I thought it was all just a silly story to start with, but you can't help wanting it to be true."

"Why?"

"Because wouldn't it be wonderful if there really was someone out there with that kind of power?"

Gordon was exasperated.

"What kind of power?"

"I don't know exactly. The kind that changes the world. The kind that changes the way people think and behave. He's like this great leader or something. It's just that no one knows for sure whether he's good or bad."

She knows something about him, Gordon thought.

"What does he look like?" he asked.

"No one really knows. But I think he's very tall. And he wears a long black coat. His fingers are all straggly and he has long black hair too. Some people say he's like a scarecrow and even the ones who think he's for the good say he's terrifying to look at. I think maybe he's deformed. A man who looks like a raven."

"He shouldn't be hard to spot, then."

Brooke took his sarcasm as a joke and giggled.

"Seriously, Brooke. Someone who looks like that is going to be hiding, not walking around in plain view. Especially if he knows the Ward are after him."

"What makes you think they are?"

"I think they're scared of him. They believe he has power and that if he uses it, their own power will be destroyed. I think they want to kill him before he has too much influence."

Brooke was about to say more on this when they both heard the shuffle of footsteps over the leafy ground. Brooke busied herself around the cook pot before John Palmer came into view. Gordon placed his pack inside the shelter, pretending to rearrange things inside until John Palmer had time to notice he was nowhere near Brooke. Then he crawled back out. The man's eyes were bloodshot and the skin around them was rubbed and red.

He pretended joviality.

"What's for dinner then? Coq au vin? Paella? Steak and chips?"

"Anything you want, Dad," said Brooke. "With chocolate ice cream for dessert."

Rather than making him smile, her words brought new cracks to the man's face. Gordon took out his lock knife and began to sharpen it so that he didn't have to watch.

38

Megan collapses to her knees but her weight carries her forwards.

She puts out her hands but still lands on her face in the long grass. Once there, she can't push herself back up. She only has the strength to roll onto her side, stranded. Soon Mr Keeper is kneeling beside her. She feels him loosening her pack straps and freeing her arms. He helps her to sit up, and as she looks into his benevolent, slightly amused face, she is hit by a wave of dizziness and nausea.

Mr Keeper grips her shoulders.

"Breathe, Megan. Long, deep, slow. It will pass."

She does what he tells her. A few moments later her head has cleared and she feels a little better. But her weakness persists.

"I can barely hold myself up," she says.

"It was a long absence. You're not used to it. You haven't eaten since he came for you."

"When was that?"

"Last night. You could probably do with some breakfast."

He hands her a water skin, cuts her bread and

cheese. Megan is suddenly ravenous, and even though the bread tastes a bit dry, she relishes the effort and reward of chewing it. She washes each mouthful down with water.

"Steady, you'll make yourself sick."

With some effort she slows her rate of attack. She glances in the direction they've come from, not recognising the landscape.

"Did I disappear?"

"No."

"But didn't you see me leave the shelter? He took my hand and we…"

She smiles to remember it.

"You didn't go anywhere. At least, your body didn't. You sat there staring for a while. When it was time to sleep, I made you lie down. In the morning, I woke you up and got you out of the shelter. You stood there while I made some tea and ate some food. Then I packed everything up, helped you put your pack on and we left. We've been walking ever since."

"I can't remember any of that."

"That's because you weren't there, Megan. You were with the Crowman. Do you remember where he took you?"

"Oh, yes! I remember everything. Everything he showed me. How it looked. How it felt. Every detail. He said I'd always remember it. For the book. He said that was my gift."

"And what did he show you, Megan?"

"He showed me more about the life of the boy, Gordon Black. Much more. I feel like I've been away for days. Weeks even."

"Time spent in his story seems much longer than

time in our own world." Mr Keeper squats and brings out his smoking gear. With practised fingers and in no hurry at all, he loads the pipe bowl with tobacco and lights it with a match. After a few puffs, he settles into a cross-legged position. "Tell me, Megan, if you can, what is it like to be shown these things?"

Megan doesn't hesitate in giving her description.

"They come to me like living visions, and are full of things I've never seen before and do not understand. And yet, now that I have the feather, I have words for everything I see. But there's a feeling that comes with all of this, a feeling I don't understand. It's as though someone else has seen the story before me. Many, many times. Is that possible?"

"It's more than possible. It's true. Many have seen before you and many more will see after you. The Crowman will make certain of that."

"There's something else. The boy – Gordon – he's so… alone. And such terrible things have happened to him. Is it because of me somehow, Mr Keeper? Am I doing these things to him? I don't want to hurt him. I don't think I can bear to see him hurt again. And the visions, well, sometimes it's like I *am* Gordon Black. Like I'm right there with him, *inside* him. I feel his pain and his loneliness. I feel his powerlessness. I don't know if I have the strength to keep doing that. He's afraid and I'm afraid for him. I have this feeling something terrible is going to happen to him. I don't want it to be because of me. And I don't want to be there when it happens."

Mr Keeper reaches across and takes her hand.

"It's not you creating this, Megan. It comes through you. Your function is to allow it to pass, commit it to memory and record it. Do not involve yourself in it or you may distort it. That alone would be grounds for me to end your training. You must do nothing other than be as open to what comes as the river banks are to the river."

Mr Keeper smokes, journeying far away himself for the briefest moment.

"All you need to realise is that Gordon Black's story has already happened. You must merely rediscover it. That is what it means to walk the Black Feathered Path. You have the strength to be with him as he makes his journey. If you didn't, you couldn't have come this far. The Crowman knows you, Megan. He knows what you're capable of." Mr Keeper squeezes her hand while he puffs on his pipe. "I know too. You're going to be a Keeper one day, Megan. One of the best we've ever seen. In the meantime, I will help you and protect you in every way I can. If we each do what we were born to do, if we keep to our truths, all will be well. You have the strength to do this. I know it in my heart."

Megan sits quietly. She doesn't feel strong or power-ful, but the boy's presence lingers now, like a familiar scent in an empty room. She cannot help but love him a little, having felt his pain and known the depth of his sorrow and loss. He seems far too young to have lived so much tribulation. Megan's life has been slow and comfortable. It has been safe and happy. At least until she met the Crowman. Gordon's life has been over-shadowed by the dark form of his destiny. His agonies can only increase, the responsibilities he carries become greater and heavier.

As if reading her thoughts, Mr Keeper says, "Your part in all this is just as important as his, Megan. Without you to tell his story, the boy suffers for nothing. He labours in vain. What you do keeps Gordon Black alive."

She nods without conviction.

Exhausted as she is by the return to her body, it's hard to give too much thought to any of this. She watches Mr Keeper smoking his pipe and that becomes a simple, pleasurable focus. As the old man's eyes begin to stare somewhere in the far distance, something occurs to her.

"Is that where you go?"

It takes a moment for him to return, even though his own absence has only just begun. This is the first time she's ever interrupted him intentionally, and she is frightened now that she has angered him. But when he is once more within the boundaries of his own body, Mr Keeper is smiling.

"Sometimes."

He inspects his pipe bowl and sees that it is spent. He knocks the ash into his hand and it disappears into a pocket. He puts the pipe away.

"At first, Megan, your journey was the one I made. The only one. But once that journey was complete, I began to make journeys to other places and times. For other reasons. Occasionally, I travel just because I can. We mustn't be working all the time, you know…"

"And when you go, you're not here anymore?"

"Part of me is rooted. The rest of me flies."

"Will I ever get used to it? I feel so heavy now. So tired."

"You'll recover more quickly each time you return. This was a long absence, Megan. It's no wonder you're worn out. Here, eat some more bread and cheese. Take a little more water too, if you can."

Mr Keeper holds out these things to her, but Megan has gone away for a moment:

She sees a broken road. She sees a barren hill. At its crest is a blackened, twisted tree. Three crows sit in the tree. The sun is setting, angry and bloody over the scarred, sickened land. This is...

There is bread and cheese in her hands. A water skin, beside her.

"What do you see, Megan?"

She shakes her head.

"Tell me."

She draws breath deeply.

"I know this from somewhere. Or maybe he's seen it... or will." She puts down the food and drinks a few sips from the skin, gasping because her throat is so dry and the water opens it like a torrent through a rut. "Wait. I've seen this. It's from his night country." She looks at Mr Keeper and her eyes fill with tears. "He has nightmares. The most terrible nightmares."

Mr Keeper nods but not without compassion.

"Your world and his world are woven now. You may walk in his night country and he, perhaps, may walk in yours. Do not let it deter you from your discovery, Megan. See his story. Bring it back. Write it down. That is all you are for now, a conduit for the boy's life. Transmitting it is all you must do – all you can do until the story is told."

Megan, suddenly grim-faced, feels a tiny surge of pride. She has her place in the world. She has her purpose. How many can say that? She will do as she has promised to do. She will bring back the boy's story for the good of the world.

39

It was a long and fruitless morning. All the snares were empty, and Gordon and John Palmer saw no game for a couple of hours. When they finally came upon a group of rabbits playing near a warren in a steep bank, John Palmer insisted on taking the shot with his air rifle. He missed a simple kill and the rest of the rabbits scattered into the many entrances of their home. The man laid his forehead against the rifle stock, and Gordon thought he would cry again, this time in plain view. It wasn't that they needed the food – the stocks of cured meat were plentiful – it was the weight of John Palmer's powerlessness settling heavier on his shoulders. At least, that was what Gordon supposed. The man was on the run with more fear of what was behind him than hope for what the future might hold. Gordon tried to feel some sympathy for him, and couldn't. John Palmer's coldness in the face of what had happened to his home and family worried him. The man's pain was greater than his own, the crimes committed against him more brutal. Their shared misfortunes ought to have brought them closer, but John Palmer was still suspicious of him and that kept them apart.

But when he got right down to it, there was something about Brooke's father that Gordon just didn't
like. He couldn't specify what it was, he only knew it
was true. His instinct told him to be wary.

For the first time in many days, they returned to
camp empty-handed. John Palmer led the way. Suddenly careless of being spotted he took the direct route,
foregoing the river bank and walking straight towards
the area of forest where their camp was hidden behind
a screen of trees. Gordon sensed John Palmer's failure
to provide seething within him and turning to anger,
anger that would soon come his way.

"You've done a lot for me, Mr Palmer. I could have died
in that tunnel if you hadn't found me when you did."

John Palmer muttered something gruff that Gordon
couldn't decipher. A verbal waving-away of his own
kindness? An oath of regret that he'd ever set eyes on
Gordon Black? It didn't much matter now.

"I'm going to move on tomorrow," continued Gordon. "I didn't want you to think I wasn't grateful for
your help. I really am. I hope you and Brooke find a" –
he was going to say "safe" and was glad he didn't –
"good place to live soon."

John Palmer took a few more steps and then
stopped. He turned and looked down at Gordon.

"You're going off on your own?"

"Yes."

"But where are going to go? How will you survive?
This is a dangerous country now. Everything's scarce.
Even food and water."

Gordon looked around at the land. A grey blanket of
sky stretched to every horizon. To the west the
landscape rose into high, purplish hills. Everywhere

else there was woodland and fen, smaller hills and the valleys between. Plenty of places to travel quietly. Plenty of cover for him and for the animals he would stalk. Plenty of water in the swollen streams and rivers. The land called to him, and suddenly this man John Palmer and his sad story were a weight that Gordon wished to cast off and leave far behind. The land called to him to enter it deeply and lose himself there. We will make you strong, the trees seemed to say. I will feed you, said the voice of the Earth. All over the sky, crows and jackdaws and rooks and magpies were suddenly on the wing. Not a call from any of them, not a swoop or a dive, a mere hanging upon the air in anticipation. We are your dreams, they seemed to say.

Follow us.

"Did you hear what I said?"

John Palmer seemed insulted by Gordon's confidence.

"I'm going to find the Crowman," said Gordon. "Do you know anything about him?"

At the mention of the name, John Palmer resumed his walk, opening a gap between them. Gordon caught up easily, his legs stronger now than they'd ever been before.

"Anything at all would be helpful. What you've heard about him. Where he's been seen. Anything."

John Palmer wouldn't look at him.

"This is nonsense."

"If you don't know anything, it's OK. I only wondered. I have so little to go on, you see. Just rumours, really."

John Palmer tried to walk faster, but Gordon paced him without effort, his gait casual against the grown man's hasty trot. Brooke's father seemed not to notice the host of corvids dotting the sky in every direction. He saw nothing but the ground right in front of him. Gordon knew he'd get no answer. The man was too closed off. Even if he knew something, he wasn't going to share. He was too afraid of everything.

Gordon stopped walking and watched John Palmer stalking away across the uneven ground, walking so fast he almost tripped every few paces. This was the condition of John Palmer's mind. Trying to escape everything: the past, the truth, himself. Gordon let him pursue his folly and slowed to enjoy the last part of the walk back to camp. The beech forest was slate grey and silent away across the fields.

When John Palmer broke into a run fifty yards ahead of him, Gordon knew it wasn't an attempt to avoid the truth. He'd seen something among those quiet, leafless giants.

Gordon ran too, his booted feet finding easy purchase in the lumpy field and striking the earth surely every time. Without really trying he was running faster than he ever had in his life. And though he began far behind John Palmer, he could already see what the older man had seen.

There were figures moving amid the trees that hid their camp. Gordon drew level with John Palmer and overtook him. He heard the shouts of men. Something zipped past the right side of his head. A figure in the beech wood stopped and reached towards its neck as if stung. The figure took its hand away and Gordon saw a red palm and a red throat. The man – Gordon could see his beard now – fell to his knees, one hand picking frantically at the wound under his chin. Blood came fast and pressurised beneath trembling, slippery fingers. It must have been John Palmer's finest shot. For once, John Palmer's instincts were correct. Gordon could sense the malevolence emanating from the men in the trees, men who now retreated farther into the wood.

The wounded man's neck pumped arterial blood in comical arcs, as though from a water pistol loaded with cheap wine. The portion of his face not covered by hair drained pale as he plucked at the entry wound for the tiny lead pellet that had already ended his life.

Another shot passed beside Gordon, and he heard a man groan in immediate response. As he cleared the tree line and plunged into the woods, he saw more and more of what lay before them. There were several men in the camp, six more at least, and they had already begun to destroy it. At first he couldn't see Brooke, but that was because he was looking for a blond girl dressed in sturdy outdoor gear. There was no evidence of that there.

Gordon dodged to his left on a sudden impulse as something in the camp exploded in his direction. He side-stepped again, instinct guiding him as he reached for his father's lock knife and unclasped it. A second explosion erased a low branch beside him. One of the men had fired a shotgun at him and was now slipping two more cartridges into the still-smoking weapon with calm, sure fingers. Gordon came at him as the man locked the gun shut and raised it.

He dived low as both barrels discharged right over his head. His momentum folded the man in half, causing him to sit down. Gordon punched the knife blade upwards into the man's stomach. He had no idea what he was aiming for; he merely wanted the blade to enter as deeply as possible. He was aware of the man drawing a sudden in-breath and stiffening. He withdrew the knife and rolled away. The man sighed with the exiting of the steel and sat staring straight ahead.

There wasn't time for Gordon to wipe the blood from his clenched fist or from his red-greased blade. Another of the men ran at him, a dirty machete raised high over his head. He too was bearded, his hair thin and grimy, his furious eyes wide and glaring. The pellet which obliterated one of them did not stop the man immediately, but it gave Gordon the opportunity to rise to his feet and skitter from his path. By the time the pellet had entered the man's frontal lobe, he'd stopped and stood, blinking, arms still held high, the machete poised to fall. Ruined ocular mucus, the mess of one angry eye, leaked from his left orbit with each confused blink.

"You're lovely," the man said, and sounded surprised by the utterance. "You're so beautiful." He sat down with the machete still wavering on high. "Yes, that's it. I hadn't realised before. I want to love you. It hurts so much and I want to be with you and I forgive you because you are so lovely. So lovely."

Blood followed the dregs of the deflated eyeball, the flow of it increasing until one side of the man's face was streaked with it. Gordon stood, expecting him to attack at any moment. The deranged man muttered about beauty and peace and love, all the while his weapon pointing upwards like an antenna receiving divine transmissions.

Four other men, equally shabby and wild, all of them so thin their clothes flapped around their limbs, had grouped by a tree. They had knives. One carried a small hatchet, another a bloodstained hammer. A pellet slapped the tree by which they stood, and their group became a huddle on the far side of its trunk. Their anger and confidence were gone. They seemed ready to scatter. One of them called out.

"We know you, John Palmer. We know what you did. You can't run from the past, man."

John Palmer entered the clearing, his gun barrel preceding him. His voice quavered.

"I was protecting my own. That's any man's right, and you know it."

"You're a murderer, John Palmer. A child-killer. I hope you die of shame and burn in hell."

Gordon looked across at Brooke's father. Eventually John Palmer said, "I probably will."

It was so quiet, Gordon doubted any of the men could hear.

"We're even now, John Palmer," said the speaker from behind the tree. "All debts cancelled. All bets off."

"What do you mean?" shouted John Palmer.

"You'll see."

As soon as John Palmer turned away, the men raced into the woods. In seconds they were out of sight. Gordon considered pursuing them, but there was blood cooling and coagulating on his hand and already the fire of conflict was going out of him. Whatever had happened between these men and John Palmer was not his business, except in as much as he owed John Palmer his life.

The man with the shotgun was on his back, his weapon tight in the grip of his dead fingers. He still stared but straight up now, through the leafless canopy and into the featureless grey sky. Gordon sensed rather than saw the circling crows up there, and for the first time in his life he recognised the feeling this gave him. It was as though he had not only been watched over, but studied by something both distant and close by, something unseen high above and also invisibly at his side.

The machete man had stopped speaking of love. He sat with his mouth open. His hands had finally sunk to rest between his legs, the edge of the blackened machete blade biting through the leaf mulch into the earth. From his sightless eye he had seen something wonderful before he died, but Gordon knew it was no more than brain-damaged hallucination.

The noise John Palmer made was a howl of ultimate disappointment.

Gordon turned now, walked a few paces and saw why.

Brooke was hanging outstretched, with her face to the bark of a large beech. At first he thought they'd tied her to the tree because her feet weren't touching the ground. But the blood that ran in such plenty, down from her upstretched arms, over her bare shoulders and down her naked back and flanks, told a different story.

40

They had stripped her and, judging by the welts and
raised areas of redness on her skin, they had beaten
her. Her head hung back, no strength in her neck. Her
eyes stared up. Her hair hung, streaked red and brown.
It was clear that they had done the things that, under
very different circumstances, men were created to do
to women, but they had done this, and worse, to a girl.
The order of these acts was unclear, but the worst of
them was the nailing of her hands and wrists to the
grey body of the beech tree. The nails had been hammered in carelessly, and there were several. In their
haste to complete the act they'd mis-hit some of the
nails, bending them over before they were fully home.
This had not stopped the hammering. Most of Brooke's
fingers were pulped and broken, her left ring finger
hanging by torn skin against the back of her hand. Four
nails had flattened each of her palms to the bark, and
the natural shape of her hands, the hands that had
washed and tended him with such delicate surety, were
destroyed. Two nails penetrated the backs of each wrist,
and it was from these wounds that most of her wasted
blood originated. From these twelve nails, Brooke was

suspended, her unclothed body pale and elongated like an animal hanging in the slaughterhouse.

Gordon was almost too frightened to approach. Then he saw that her whole body was vibrating. Brooke was shivering.

She was alive.

John Palmer was on his knees, staring up at his daughter's ruin as though the pain was all his. Gordon was disgusted.

"We have to get her down," he said.

John Palmer didn't move. Gordon walked over, placed his boot on the man's shoulder and sent him sprawling.

"Now!"

John Palmer looked up, crying as though Gordon's shove was the most painful incident of the day.

"Find something," said Gordon. "Quickly. Help me get her down."

John Palmer stood up, dazed. Gordon took his shoulders, pleaded to his face.

"Tools. A crowbar. Anything."

John Palmer ran into the tiny clearing and upended a small leather bag. He returned with a pair of yellow-handled pliers between his quivering fingers. Their eyes met. Gordon took the implement, his own hand showing no trace of a tremor.

41

They buried Brooke beside the tree.

The removal of the nails reopened her ruptured arteries. The blood leaked in meandering pulses as Gordon lay her on the earth.

She spoke for several minutes to both of them before falling silent.

"The pain isn't so bad now."

She was shaking so hard, every word came out juddered. Gordon wept because he knew how much pain he'd caused in trying to release her. The renewed bleeding was his fault too, but there'd been no choice – they couldn't have left her hanging.

"It's just the cold," she said. "I can't bear the cold."

They'd placed a foam camping mat under her and two sleeping bags on top, tucking them tightly around her, leaving her arms untouched. Her blood leaked straight onto the leaves and into the earth. John Palmer ran to fetch the last sleeping bag. Gordon wanted to hold her hand. Instead he placed the palm of his hand over her heart and tried to send warmth and comfort into her body. Her shaking seemed to settle.

She looked at him, and he could tell Brooke knew

she was dying. Something held the terror of that approaching darkness off, some strength she had that her father did not possess.

"I wish we'd had a little more time together, Gordon."

"I wish we'd had a lot."

She smiled.

"You're a good person. Don't ever think you're not." She was nodding, more to herself than him it seemed. "I know you'll find him." Her eyes closed for a moment. "Yes, you'll find the Crowman. And he's for the good, Gordon. I'm sure of it now."

John Palmer returned with the blanket and rested it over her. She smiled at him, but he couldn't look at her face.

"So cold," she whispered.

John Palmer's face creased further into grief.

"Hold her," said Gordon.

John Palmer didn't move.

Very gently, Gordon took the man's hand and placed it on Brooke's forehead.

"Just touch her," he breathed.

John Palmer shuffled closer and placed his face beside Brooke's. He cradled her head. Gordon watched the smile this elicited slipping from her face. And then it was peaceful. Gordon stood and left the man with his murdered child.

It was more than an hour later that John Palmer walked the few yards back into camp, his face pale and his hands still dirty with Brooke's dried blood. It took Gordon a long time to convince him that they needed to bury her and even longer to persuade him that the tree she died beside should be her final resting place.

Eventually, John Palmer gave in.

But Gordon was sincere in what he told the man:

Brooke needed to return to the land that had birthed her. Now that her spirit was flying and had no use for her body, it should be left to nourish the tree.

The burial took until dusk. By the failing light the blood on the beech tree's bark became charcoal on grey. They didn't try to remove it. John Palmer muttered some half-remembered Christian solemnities and fell once again to his knees beside the freshly-turned earth.

Gordon whispered:

"The crows will carry you home, Brooke."

He felt stupid saying it, but on a level he couldn't consciously access, he believed it.

Whatever had held John Palmer together since he'd lost his home and sent his wife away was now unravelling. What he'd run away from had caught up with him. It looked as though, at any moment, he might claw away the earth from his daughter's body and try to pull her back from death.

"We've got to move the other bodies," said Gordon.

He stepped away from her graveside towards the clearing, hoping he could draw John Palmer away. The man looked up at him, pale and sickened.

"I'm not burying those *murderers*. Those… raping, *child*-killers." His words came out clogged with tears and fury. "They've taken… everything."

Gordon stood silent for a few moments.

"I know," he said. "And I'm sorry. We don't have to bury them. But we have to move them. How far is the tunnel from here?"

Gordon hadn't been back since they found him. John Palmer shrugged.

"Not far."

"Can we carry them there before it gets dark?"

"We can drag them."

Gordon didn't wait for John Palmer or ask again. He walked to the nearest raider, the one with the machete, and grabbed hold of the man's ankles. The trainers he wore were muddied and the laces had been replaced with garden twine. The soles were almost worn through. The man's bones weren't encased in much flesh. The attackers were starving. They may once have been respectable men with jobs and families and hobbies, but they'd become homeless marauders, thieving to stay alive. Gordon wondered how long it had taken for their moral codes to break down. Denied what they wanted or merely angry at their lot, violence would have come next. Perhaps with that violence came a certain reinstating of the illusion of power over otherwise unrelenting circumstances. And then taking not only goods and money but taking more precious things like dignity and chastity. Their own lives annihilated, they had become destroyers of other people's existences; rapists and murderers, as John Palmer rightly stated. This was one of the ways evil spread, a disease of the will that anyone could contract. Gordon couldn't condone what the men had done. There was no excuse.

And what of his own guilt? Violence against his family and against Brooke and John Palmer had given birth to violence in him. He had stabbed three men now and one of them lay dead a few paces away. Was there any way back from that? Would he become nothing more than a starving survivalist? He could only console himself with the knowledge that each aggressive act he'd committed had been in defence. Had he not fought with enough conviction, he could easily be dead. Surely he had the right to protect his own life.

All these things he thought as he dragged the machete man over the leafy forest floor. In a few minutes the sun would be beyond the horizon and this job would be impossible. He looked towards the place where John Palmer still knelt beside the grave of his daughter. The man didn't move.

"Look," he said. "Just show me where the tunnel is and I'll move them. I want to get it done before it's too dark."

The John Palmer who stood up to help him was an old man, his hair suddenly greyer and thinner, his face slacker, his body weaker. For once, Gordon was glad of the silence that existed between them as they hauled the dead men from their clearing, through the quietly observant beech trees to the darkness in which Gordon himself had almost died.

Gordon moved the third body on his own, leaving John Palmer to sit once again beside Brooke's grave. Once he'd reached the tunnel mouth he pulled each of the bodies as far inside as he could and laid them beside each other in the darkness. He knelt there with them for several minutes, praying in silence. He prayed that their spirits would travel to somewhere less terrible than the world they'd left behind. He prayed for their families. And he prayed for their forgiveness.

42

In the morning, John Palmer was gone.

Gordon checked Brooke's resting place first. It was undisturbed. He made a circuit of the tiny camp and spread his search in a widening spiral. He checked inside John Palmer's tent. All his gear was there but there was no sign of the man. The camp fire was cold. No food was missing.

The day lengthened, and John Palmer didn't return. Gordon set off thinking that perhaps he might have gone to check his snares. He knew this was unlikely. John Palmer had a knife on him at all times, and Gordon didn't think it was unreasonable to suspect that the man was walking back to the town he'd come from, back to the place where the men who'd escaped still lived. Like those men, John Palmer had nothing left but hate and a desire to put things right with violence.

Gordon stayed in the cover of the trees all the way down to the river, following the path they'd taken the first day he'd accompanied John Palmer to check the snares. For the first time in some days there were heavy-looking clouds in the sky. Through the denuded branches above him, Gordon could see the mass of iron grey thickening and darkening as it proceeded across the sky. The same wind that forced those clouds onwards pushed through the exposed arms and fingers of the beech trees, waking whispers from their bones.

He reached the edge of the wood where it opened onto the wet grassland and the river bank. The water had receded from the flood plain and the level of the river had dropped. Willows grew beside the water, some of them straight and tall, others leaning out over the water. It was in one these far-reaching willows, its trunk close to horizontal, that Gordon found the body. Many of the willow's leafless branches draped into the water, their sinewy tips depending from thicker boughs like hair. The tree made Gordon think of a woman washing herself by the riverside. It would have been beautiful but for the ugliness of John Palmer.

He hung from a thick bough, his face swollen, his eyes red. His head rested on two fists thrust under his chin, giving him a slight pout and the aspect of a man who'd died of boredom. In his struggles he'd managed to hook the fingers of both hands between the tightening cord and the skin of his neck. The fingers had been trapped there and then broken by the weight of his body and the pulling of the river water at his legs. The rope he'd used was lightweight nylon and thin: useful for outdoor pursuits. It had cut quite deeply into his neck, far enough to disappear but without breaking the skin. The fatness of his face had given him a pumpkin-headed appearance. His body turned first a little to the right and then a little to the left as the current of the river tugged at his calves and waterlogged walking boots. The branch he hung from bounced very slowly, dipping him, extracting him.

Two magpies landed in the willow tree, breaking Gordon's almost-dreamy exploration of John Palmer's suicide. They clattered and chattered at each other in great excitement, their tails flicking high, before hopping towards the place where John Palmer's rope was secured. One of them fluttered down onto the dead man's head. It looked at Gordon, rattled out one more cry and then pecked into John Palmer's eye. Soon its partner joined it and their cries ceased as they feasted on the fresh carrion.

Gordon turned away.

He remembered the last time he had seen two magpies. Their message then had seemed to be to enter the tunnel. Circumstance had caused him to do exactly that. He had come close to death in that darkness. Until the man who now gave his flesh to the magpies had found him and his daughter had nursed him back to health. Surely, if it was a message those two magpies had given him, it had been a sound one. They had led him in the right direction. What was their message now?

He looked at John Palmer one last time and watched the magpies tearing at his face so hungrily and with such relish. He approached the river bank some distance away from the tree.

At the water's edge he took out his father's lock knife and unclasped it. It was flaky with the dried blood of a dead man. He submerged it in the river and used his fingernails to chip at the encrusted gore. The water soon rehydrated and loosened the blood. Streaks and flakes swirled in the water and were gone. The knife came out clean, the blade gleaming even under the deepening shadows cast by the clouds overhead. He shook it out, blew into its cracks to clear the water, and dried it as best he could on his trousers before folding it away and putting it back in his pocket.

He walked quickly back to the camp. By the time he was there he had an idea of what the magpies might be telling him. The more he thought about it, the more sense it made: in happening upon death, the birds had secured a little more life for themselves through the bounty of John Palmer's flesh. Gordon knew he could respond positively to the situation too – there was an opportunity here.

In the camp he dragged all the equipment into the open and dumped everything onto a groundsheet. He took his time discarding what was not useful and what was too heavy to carry, calmly measuring the value of every item before keeping or abandoning it. By noon he had dismantled the camp. What he could not use he carried to the tunnel and placed it far enough inside that the rain would not spoil it. With luck, someone who needed the equipment would find it one day. When everything but his new pack was stowed, he brushed the camp with a branch, redistributing leaves where they'd slept or cooked so that the mark of their habitation was minimal.

He hefted John Palmer's rucksack onto his back. For a long time he stood at Brooke's graveside, not wanting to leave her. Not wanting to be alone again. When he knew there was no more reason to stay, he whispered some words to her and set out to the edge of the forest. He stepped into the open just as the rain began. In the distance, obscured by cloud, were the hills.

That was where he would begin.

43

Sheriff Skelton and Sheriff Pike arrived at the Monmouth Ward substation mid-morning, with a handful of their own men. They commandeered the profile room and pinned maps, photos and charts to the walls. When Skelton was ready, Pike summoned the local Wardsmen to join them.

Skelton made a presentation using his laptop, relying for much of his talk on enlargements of the physical "evidence" the Ward had gathered over the previous three or four years. He showed photos of their objective at many stages of his life from birth to present – all collected from Hamblaen House. He predicted, based on artists' sketches, how the boy might look with longer, shorter or different-coloured hair – they fully expected him to hide now.

Skelton also displayed the better-known images of the Crowman from several scrapbooks of collected eschatological predictions and displayed transcripts taken from hundreds of identified prophets from the past ten years. Skelton exhibited excerpts of poetry and prose on screen, reading it out in his disdainful feminine tones, now flat with restrained rage. He showed artistic impressions, drawings and paintings by people of all ages from toddler to centenarian. Again and again, Skelton reiterated one point: the boy must not find the Crowman. They must never be united. The prophecies varied in many ways, enough to make a single cohesive story almost impossible to pick out, but one thing was agreed upon by every author. When the boy came into contact with the Crowman, the end of civilisation – already in motion – would begin in earnest. Eighty per cent of the world's population would be erased in a matter of months. Infrastructure would be destroyed, power would cease to flow, water would run dry in every tap, gas lines would be severed, roads would be impassable, crops would fail, rivers would find new courses, the earth would split, the rain would fall and fall, disease would rise in every city, the air would be poisoned and humanity would cry out as one for mercy.

The boy had to be found. The Crowman had to be stopped.

This, Skelton reminded his London crew (and the rural Wardsmen he trusted as far as he could see from his blind left socket) was the purpose of the Ward first and foremost. Yes, they served the global economy. Yes, they served the New World Order. Yes, they believed in harnessing the Earth for the gain of men, and the conquering of men for the gain of the Ward. But if they couldn't find Gordon Black and bring him in, if they couldn't root out the Crowman and end him before he ended the world, then there would be no point in serving and nothing left to serve. The Crowman was here, in England, and that made England the final arena. There would be some assistance from the Ward in other nations who could spare it, but this was now an English fight. It was up to every Wardsman in the country to put this mission before anything else, to lay down their lives if that was what it took. Otherwise, all possibility of power would be rested from their grasp forever because the world and all its bounties would be no more.

They were opposing the suicide of the planet. They needed to master the world, chain it, mine it, own it and its peoples. Only then would their task be fulfilled. Only then, Archibald Skelton told the assemblage of men in the profile room, would he take a day off.

After showing Ordnance Survey maps and aerial photographs of the area around the Blacks' smallholding and telling his men not only where but how he wanted them to search the terrain, he dismissed them all but for Pike.

"We need to take a trip downstairs," he said to the skull-faced automaton that was Mordaunt Pike, the most reliable and relentless Wardsman he'd ever worked with.

Hard on the outside, thought Skelton. Soft on the inside. And mine. All mine.

The cell system below the Monmouth substation was extensive but by no means the largest Skelton had seen. Many in London were four or even five times the size. There were mass holding cells for those just passing through and single cells for longer-term collectees. There were enough well-equipped interview rooms that twenty individuals could be processed simultaneously. An incinerator ran day and night to accommodate waste.

Skelton still hoped keeping the Blacks under lock

and key might be enough of a lure to bring the lost little boy in. Gordon was no street kid and he was used to the love and attention of his kin. A boy alone in the countryside or in the town with the nights drawing in: how long would his nerve hold? How long before he ran back to Mummy? Long before he reached the four cells where the Blacks were held, Skelton had formed a plan. He would keep them all alive for a little while longer.

Pike walked a little behind him, almost like a dog at heel, disciplined, dangerous and loyal. Skelton grinned to himself but the movement in his facial muscles caused him to wince in pain. He couldn't think of his robbed left eye without hate squirting into his veins from some deep poison gland he hadn't known he possessed. God, but he would make the boy suffer when he got hold of him.

Skelton and Pike stood on the gravel outside the Black residence and waited for the final search to be completed. This time the ten Wardsmen inside the house were leaving nothing untouched. They arrived with hammers and crowbars. Doors were torn off their hinges. Walls were stripped of their paper in search of hidden stores. The attic was scoured and so was the basement. Floorboards were lifted. Carpets ripped up. Everything of value was removed.

Skelton listened with satisfaction at the sound of breaking wood and glass. All the while he worried the edges of his bandage, trying to get at the itch beneath it. As the day passed, his finger had wormed under the tape, and his nail could now agitate the crusty black stitches at the outer edge of his left eye. The itch never quite went away, and his fingernail explored deeper all the time.

Pike watched without expression, but twice during the day when food was offered, he turned it down and Skelton gleefully devoured the taller man's portion, not noticing the grey pallor of Pike's sunken cheeks. Nor did Skelton notice the watery gruel of pus on his cheek until a drop pattered to his lapel, causing him to fumble for his hanky and mop his face and coat. Even this didn't prevent his finger from seeking to explore the maddening pruritis where his eye had been.

"Shame about Angela Black," Skelton mused. "We could have used her."

Pike shrugged.

"She wouldn't have lasted long on the road anyway," he said.

"I suppose not. Frustrating, though, Pike, because she'd have made a difference. Didn't take much to turn her. She must have hated her brother, eh?"

Pike said nothing.

"And then she dies. Without her, luring him in will be that much harder."

"We can use the other one," said Pike in monotone.

"I don't know. Judith Black will take some persuading, I think."

"So let's persuade her."

Pike's eyes caught Skelton's and momentarily flickered with dead light. Skelton's heart raced to see it. He was about to ask Pike about his proposed methods when Knowles, one of the Monmouth Wardsmen, trotted up to them.

"There's no sign of the boy. Doesn't look like he's been back. We found some more hoarded items behind a panel in the attic – food, water and ammunition for the shotgun. There was cash under the floorboards in the study. Other than that, nothing."

"Remove everything of value," said Skelton. "Then take all their animals into the house."

The Wardsmen worked with less enthusiasm to bring the hens, geese, goats and pig indoors, even though the animals were tame and didn't particularly resist. None of the men were able to avoid muddying or fouling their otherwise pristine grey raincoats. Skelton grinned at their muttered oaths. Even Pike's teeth peeped, a brief flash of tainted ivory, from behind his flat lips for a moment. When Skelton moved off towards the rear of the property, Pike followed, his limp unimproved. As they made their way between the apple trees towards the green door in the garden wall, Knowles caught up to them.

"What now, Sheriff Skelton?"

"Burn it. But don't hang around watching the fire like a bunch of kids. I want you to recommence the search immediately. Exactly as I've outlined. Understood?"

Knowles frowned.

"Shouldn't the animals be redistributed?" he asked.

Skelton leaned close, causing Knowles to recoil.

"The sooner the people starve, the sooner they'll do as they're told."

"Yes, Sheriff."

"Pike and I will retrace the boy's last footsteps before he disappeared. I want to see if he's left anything behind."

"The bridleway?" asked Knowles.

"Correct."

"But we've already checked that very thoroughly, Sheriff."

"I want to see it for myself."

Knowles appeared to be about to add something before deciding against it. What he actually said was:

"If you need any assistance out there, Sheriff, I'll send whoever's nearest."

"We'll be just fine, thank you, Knowles." Skelton watched Knowles nod, about-face and hurry back to Hamblaen House. "I don't like that man."

Pike shrugged and forced open the green door. This time the hinges of the garden entrance gave up and the door fell out of its rotting frame. Pike let it drop to the ground and Skelton stepped through. Rags of black smoke began to rise from the house and, for a moment, he watched as the flames lanced up below twisting smoke-devils. Skelton turned away and waddled towards the bridleway as the first squeals and bleats of panic escaped the house. After a few paces, he glanced back to check on Pike. The grim cast of his partner's face was like a sculpture.

The tunnel mouth came into view around a bend, marking the end of the bridleway.

Skelton reached it first and began to check the area. He stopped and stood straight when he heard Pike's uneven gait over the rough, weed-infested ground. The man approached with his good leg taking a decent-sized, straight step, but he had to lift his wounded leg by raising his hip and swinging it forwards. Regardless of this encumbrance, Pike moved like a thing pro-grammed. He was focussed and inexorable and it was beautiful to watch him, advancing as though he was wrought of pistons and gears and unyielding, lifeless materials. The man was terrifying. Never had a human been so much like an engine. Pike was his tool, his machine, fuelled by duty, loyalty and the desire to inflict pain. Pike would always do exactly as he was told. Skelton's heart beat a little faster.

When Pike arrived, there was a tiny slick of sweat at his hairline. He looked a little nauseous but said nothing.

"So, this is where he ran to?" asked Skelton.

He watched Pike's brain replaying the events.

"He came up this path but he was ahead of me, making ground. I lost sight of him."

"Do you know how far he came? Did he make it to the tunnel?"

"I can't say."

Skelton nodded to himself, lips clamped tight. They'd come close and they'd missed a very good opportunity. If anyone else had allowed the same thing to happen, Skelton would have made sure they were disciplined. But the ferocity of the boy's attack had taken them both by surprise. The fourteen year-old, and a puny one at that, had shown real fight. Still, they were forewarned now; Gordon Black would never surprise them again, nor would they ever be under-prepared for an encounter with him.

Skelton glanced around and noticed how a space near the tunnel's mouth had been cleared of rocks. Looking closer, he found entry marks in the ground.

"He must have slept here," he said, pointing. "Far enough away that he'd be out of sight but near enough to easily return."

Pike saw the marks too.

"What did he do with his tent?" he asked.

Skelton looked around.

"What would you have done?"

Pike gestured with his chin into the darkness of the tunnel.

"Quite right. There's nowhere else except the ditch under the hedges. But why risk getting wet gear when you've a perfectly dry place right beside you?"

"Then why didn't he pitch tent in the tunnel? Safer. Drier. Out of the elements."

"Fear, Pike. Fear of the dark. He camped here and returned to the house, leaving his gear stashed inside the tunnel. He had to come this way in order to pick up his stuff."

Pike shook his head.

"Why lead us straight to it? Wouldn't he have hidden somewhere else until we'd gone and then come back?"

Skelton could see the logic, but what difference did it make?

"He still had to come back here at some point, whether we were here or not. Right?"

"Right."

"So when he came back what did he do?"

"He went into the tunnel to fetch his gear," said Pike.

"Let's take a look."

The tunnel's opening gaped like a monstrous throat, and Skelton hesitated, experiencing a moment of unease as he crossed its threshold. Chained in the flooded dungeon of his subconscious, a paralysing fear of the dark writhed like a vast eel. He'd done much to overcome his weaknesses over the years, to forget them – Ward training had eradicated almost all of them – but something about the silent, observant *life* in darkness still disturbed him. Mastering himself, lest Pike notice his nervousness, he strode into the blackness.

Only a few paces in, he stopped. The light of day plainly showed recent disturbance to the ground.

"What do you make of that, Pike?"

The giant moved in closer, his limp eliciting pride and protectiveness in Skelton – and something else he wasn't ready to name. From his lofty vantage Pike surveyed the earth beneath their feet.

"There was a disturbance here. Not a fight. More of a struggle." Pike's eyes roved the shadowy tunnel mouth; he switched on his torch. "This is the print of a size ten, standard-issue Ward brogue. Over here, the prints of smaller hiking boots." After a few more seconds he made eye contact with Skelton then looked away. He retreated towards the light. "The boy was here. He went up against one of ours. Neither was seriously hurt."

Skelton moved after him, glad to leave the sucking darkness behind.

"Wait, Pike. What else?"

"That's it."

"But if neither was injured, what happened?"

Pike's words were a flat hiss of escaping pressure.

"Someone let him go."

"Not one of our men," said Skelton.

"Couldn't be," said Pike.

"One of the Monmouth crew, then."

Pike's silence said it all. Skelton knew his partner believed in the Ward. It was his life. The very purpose of his existence. Even to utter an accusation toward another within its ranks was to commit some small betrayal of the whole. The Ward existed in every nation of the world, and their remit was to protect the world from the coming age of darkness at any and all costs. Now that the prophecies showed England to be the land from which the darkness would spread, the mission had fallen to Skelton and Pike. The responsibility rested squarely on their shoulders. Pike, Skelton knew, carried that burden in a very special way – it was like a power source. The idea that one among them might have made a mistake was shame enough. To think that they had a traitor in their number was far worse. Pike took it personally. Everything was personal with Pike.

"And I think I've an idea who it might be," said Skelton.

Pike ignored this.

"We need to search the tunnel."

Skelton cleared his throat.

"You and I can't do it," he said. "We don't have the equipment."

Skelton reached into his pocket and withdrew his grey mobile. One bar of reception winked in and out of existence. He dialled Knowles but the call failed three times. Instinctively, he looked into the sky. There was nothing to see, of course. He threw the phone into the hedge.

"What are you doing?" asked Pike.

"Accepting the facts," said Skelton. "Haven't had a signal anywhere we've been for a week. Christ knows what we'll use from now on. Bloody carrier pigeons or something."

He walked away. Pike followed, the sound of his footsteps determined but broken.

"Where are we going?" he asked.

"To fetch some high-power torches and a few more men," said Skelton.

Pike grunted behind him and stopped. Skelton turned back.

"What is it?" He asked.

"Make sure Knowles is one of them," said Pike.

44

The rain fell steady and hard, and soon the comfort and dryness of the previous few days was a distant memory.

Gordon tried not to think about the events which brought those dry, safe days to an end. But from time to time a flash of the strangest or most painful of those moments would enter his mind and blot everything out: the mutilation of Brooke's hands, the sound her father made when he found her, the blood caked to her buttocks and the backs of her thighs, the smell of the earth as they dug her grave.

When he was angry, and he was angry for much of the time, he remembered how the attackers had died. Death had been almost comical: a man trying to pick a tiny pellet from the artery in his neck, a raging man speaking of love. And the one Gordon had killed. What he remembered of that was only the sensation of punching his knife blade hard and high and the disbelief at its effectiveness. He was fairly sure the tip of the knife had stopped against the man's spine. So deep. So very, very deep. He could recall the intimate warmth of the man's blood coating his right hand, but he didn't even know his victim's name.

He expected the rain to chill him, but it did not. Wherever his new power came from, it made him warm as well as strong. His pace never faltered, though he climbed both gentle and steep slopes. And though the rain slickened the rocks and turned the earth to mud, his footsteps were sure and solid. His waterproof jacket had a peaked hood, which he tightened to his head with hidden straps, and it kept most of the rain out of his face.

He chewed smoked game as he walked. Around him the world was cloaked in swirling cloud, low and grey and heavy with moisture. Sometimes the landscape emerged, to reveal moments of deep-green vegetation or glistening black rock, perhaps a distant grove of trees or glimpse into a valley, but mostly the world was shrouded and wet, and Gordon was glad not to see too far into it. He put as much distance between himself and his past as possible. Somewhere, the Ward were searching for him; on the path behind him right now, perhaps. He would walk and he would search until he found the Crowman. Only that could save his family. It was the one thing worth doing in the world.

Either that or lie down and give up.

45

After three days of walking with barely a break, Gordon's newfound strength had waned and his hike became a trudge. He watched for signs of followers and other travellers but saw none. Exhaustion settled on him and when he found a decent spot, he decided to stop a while and build himself up again. He pitched his tent in the shelter of an outcropping of smooth stone. The rock formed a barrier against the wind, which was strong everywhere else on the hillside, and the overhang kept the rain off.

The view east from his camp was expansive.

Standing on the far side of his fire, approaching a ledge which gave onto a steep drop, the space between him and the horizon was abundant with England's varied splendour, and yet the land was somehow drab and spent-looking. Immediately below the ledge were the leafless tops of trees on a steep hillside. Their canopy angled swiftly away from him – to fall from the ledge would be to break every bone long before he hit the ground. Beyond the deciduous forest there was a thicker band of pine, richly green despite the approach of winter. Beyond that, only visible in a few places, was a dark snake of river, this side wild, the other flatter and more habitable. There was a small town beyond the flood plains of the river. Gordon could see the steeple of a church and plenty of houses.

On the roads around the village no cars were moving. All seemed still. Beyond the town and its environs, the land rolled out in a patchwork of sick-looking fields. There was a dullness over the Earth and he couldn't put it down to the cloud-filtered light. In the distance to the left and right were other villages and hamlets, and far away, almost straight ahead, there was a larger city skyline, little of which could he make out. The closer to the horizon his gaze travelled, the more low vapour was in the air and the less distinct were the features of the land. At the edge of his visible semi-circle of world, the land and sky merged in a haze.

Far to his left, which was north, and on this side of the river, a thin genie of smoke rose above the pine forest. From here it was impossible to tell if there was a house hidden by the trees or a bonfire or someone's camp. He had the feeling it was the latter, however – the middle of a wood was a better place to hide than it was to build a home. Going to the town was too risky and unpredictable. It could be crawling with the Ward. Taking a peek at the wooded encampment seemed a far safer option.

When he'd regained his strength, he planned to investigate.

Smoke rose from the pine trees all day.

Gordon spent time climbing the smooth-skinned rocks overhanging his camp and wandering from place to place on the hillside. He found thickets laden with sloe berries and filled his pockets with the ones he didn't eat straight away. Every now and again he would stop and scan the land around him for movement. All he ever noticed was the same thin wraith of smoke above the pines, sometimes pushed over by the wind, others rising vertically before thinning into nothingness against the ash-grey sky.

That evening he ate well on berries and dried meat, treating himself to a few strips of rook breast. He heated water over his fire and made a tea of sorrel leaves. It warmed him and cleared his head. For the first time in three nights, he slept deeply and dreamlessly, but he slept with his knife open and ready within easy reach, thinking always of the Ward.

Dawn came, and with it apprehension. In the daytime he could be seen. He crawled from the warmth and relative comfort of his sleeping bag out into a cold, clear morning. Mist covered the land on either side of the river like a thin layer of dry ice. In the evergreen forest the fire was still alive, though the ghost it threw up was pencil-fine and pure white.

He packed everything up and shouldered it easily, having scattered the remains of his fire as best he could. He knew his strength had returned as he walked away, feeling light despite the rucksack, his legs springy and renewed. He breakfasted on strips of dried meat and looked for a safe way down into the leafless hillside forest.

From there he planned to make his way into the pines.

He smelled the camp long before he saw it.

The mingled scent of grilling meat, burning fat and wood smoke led the way. Gordon's belly responded to the smells with loud squirts and gurgles as the walls of his stomach moved against each other in anticipation. The savoury aroma reminded him of barbecues but smelling it on the cold morning air gave an edge to his hunger, making him realise he would fight for food if it ever came to that. He hoped it would not.

As he approached the smell, he slowed and then stopped. There'd been plenty of time to think of a way of announcing himself to strangers, but he hadn't come up with something he was confident about. Now that he was nearing the camp, he felt a genuine sense of his own trespass and the danger that brought with it. His instinct was to leave other people to themselves, to respect their boundaries. Yet here he was, crossing the outer boundaries of someone else's territory.

There was a moment in which he calmly and coolly decided it was time to turn back. He stopped and listened. He thought he could hear the crackle and spit of grease on hot ash. He imagined what it would be like to put a piece of charred meat to his lips, to bite through its heat-dried crust and into the tender, dripping flesh beneath. To chew hard and swallow a thick lump of hot nourishment. But he mastered himself and turned back, feeling a flood of relief and a release of tension in every muscle. Self-preservation was more important.

The way he'd come was blocked by two men.

46

Gordon tried to gauge the threat the men posed to him.

The most obvious danger came from the shotguns. Each of them carried a double-barrelled twelve-bore. However, the guns were broken and carried over the crooks of their arms. Their faces were heavily bearded, making them appear ancient, yet their eyes were bright and young, and Gordon guessed the men to be in their twenties or thirties. Unlike the raiders who'd attacked the Palmer camp, they were well dressed and equipped for the outdoor life. They both wore the same brand of sturdy calf-length lace-up black boots. They looked like army issue. Their bodies were covered by fur-lined waterproof boiler suits of olive drab, suggesting a military origin. At their necks he could see thick woollen roll-neck pullovers and their jackets were skiwear – padded, hooded, many-pocketed and colourful – out of place in the pine forest. Their hats were similarly garish, with ear flaps and bright Scandinavian designs. Both men wore fingerless gloves, keeping their hands warm but allowing them to manipulate either their guns or their traps; Gordon was fairly sure they were hunting game, not him.

Fairly.

He assessed their eyes. Mostly what he saw there was surprise and even a little curiosity. One of them, a man with a beard almost black, seemed to display a slight mistrust but not enough to mean trouble. Gordon thought it better to take the initiative.

"I saw smoke," he said. "Thought I'd come and see who was down here." He gestured in the direction he'd been going. "Is that your camp through there?"

The man with the black beard said:

"Why did you turn back?"

What could he do but be honest?

"I changed my mind," he said. "Felt like I was trespassing."

"Trespassing?" The way black beard repeated it made Gordon think of the Lord's Prayer. That hadn't been what he meant. But black beard didn't mean it that way either. "You can't trespass. The land is for sharing. For everyone."

"I just… it felt wrong."

The second man, whose beard was straw in the centre, ginger at the sides, said:

"That's respectful."

Black beard nodded.

"So what do you want?" he asked.

And Gordon was suddenly stumped. What *did* he want? Some company? The next part of his life? Directions to the Crowman? Or just a bellyful of flame-seared meat.

"Nothing," he said in the end. "I'm only passing through."

"What's your name?" asked black beard. Any mistrust the man had felt towards Gordon had been replaced by amusement. Perhaps the thought of a four-teen year-old boy just "passing through" struck him as funny.

And his name. What was his name? Could he tell them?

He put out his hand.

"I'm Louis Palmer," he said. The name sounded good. Even Gordon felt convinced by it. Something about the sound of it must have impressed black beard too, who now responded with his own hand.

"David Croft," he said, unable to hide his surprise at the strength in Gordon's grip. "And this is Beckett Adler. Dave and Beck."

Gordon found himself grinning at the sudden break-through of camaraderie. They seemed like good men, men who loved and respected the land, and they were friendly – far more friendly than John Palmer had ever been. They weren't his family but they seemed decent and honourable.

"You hungry?" asked Dave. "We've got some deer cooking in camp. There's plenty."

Gordon couldn't hold back his tears. The strength left his legs and he reached out to a tree to hold himself up.

"Come on, Louis. Let's get some food into you."

He saw the look that passed between them, a look that said "he's just a kid". They tried to take an arm each and help him along, but Gordon shrugged them off. He stumbled into their camp red-eyed, all too aware how weak he must have looked. Two other men watched him arrive: a thin one with grey streaking his beard – though he was probably no older than Dave or Beck – a man who rarely spoke to begin with, other than with his eyes. His mandible was arrow-shaped, his sparse facial hair barely concealing its barbed angles. Even his cheek bones looked sharp enough to puncture his face from within. His name was Grimwold. To Gordon it sounded like a nickname, not a surname.

The fourth member of their group was an old man, old enough to be any of these men's grandfather, it looked like. He had trouble getting around but his eyes were full of smiles, with deep, cheery wrinkles at their corners. They called him Cooky.

When he arrived, snivelling and trudging into their camp that day, Grimwold's head snapped up from the branch he was whittling to a point. His eyes caught Gordon's, but Gordon was too drained to try to decipher what he saw in them. Grimwold's eyes flicked around Gordon's body, as though measuring him somehow. Cooky turned from the fire where he was turning deer steaks and racks of ribs. The smoke was making his eyes water, but when he saw Gordon, it seemed those tears were of recognition and welcome.

Gordon forgot all of this when Cooky handed him an enamelled plate laden with a steaming lump of meat and a chunk of aromatic bread, freshly baked under a pile of coals. They made space for him to set up his tent, and Dave, who seemed to be the alpha in the group, told him he could stay as long as he wanted.

47

As she walks, trying to tread in Mr Keeper's footsteps, Megan's strength returns. It is as though the land feeds her energy through the soles of her feet. Soon the aches in her body, brought on by walking with so much weight on her back, become a kind of comfort to her, a reminder that this is the world she is in right now: the real world.

Up ahead Mr Keeper stops and turns back to face her. He is smiling but it is one of his knowing smiles, which means something is coming. When she reaches him, he lays his hands on her shoulders.

"You can't be a Keeper if your only experience of the world is the village where you grew up. Your connection with the other worlds, powerful though it is, isn't enough to broaden you. For that you must travel, see other people and how they live their lives. You must know this world and its people for what they really are."

Behind Mr Keeper there is a downward slope. Megan is aware that the landscape beyond it is not some vast, silent plain or expanse of woodland. There are dwellings there – she glimpses them around the side of his body. Smoke rises in a number of places, but he has deliberately placed himself in her line of sight and her view is blocked.

"Remember one thing, Megan. Stay with me and you'll be safe. No one will ever interfere with a Keeper. Whatever happens, do not allow yourself to be separated from me. Where we're going, not everyone is as friendly as they were back home."

For a moment, Mr Keeper's face pinches with an emotion Megan isn't used to seeing there. Worry?

Fear.

He takes her shoulders in his strong but gentle hands.

"You'll be tested here, Megan."

She frowns.

"On the Black Feathered Path?"

Mr Keeper can't hold her gaze. After some time staring at the ground his eyes return to hers, hardened.

"To see if you are able to continue. You will have to prove yourself."

Megan stands straight, opposing the weight of her pack and squaring her shoulders.

"What must I do?"

Mr Keeper shakes his head.

"It is not for me to decide. But know this, Megan Maurice: everything depends on your success. *Everything*. All I can say is, no matter what happens, no matter how alone you may feel, I will be with you." He smiles, though it seems to cost him some effort. "Do you trust me, Megan?"

"Of course."

"Well, then. Let us be on our way."

He steps clear and Megan looks upon Shep Afon for the first time. Mr Keeper sets off at his usual pace, but

Megan hesitates for a long time before following.

Like the dead village they passed, Shep Afon is huge, but very much alive. Most of the dwellings are benders, leaners, roundhouses or thatched crofts. There's little sense in the layout but the roads between them are like the cables of a spider's web. Spirals lead in circuits, linking one group of dwellings to the next and the next.

From each area of dwellings, roads lead to the centre of the village. Around the centre, the buildings are larger; not as large as the ones in the dead village – the city, as Mr Keeper calls it – but far bigger than anything in Beckby. Many of the houses have windmills – something she's heard of but never seen. The smaller ones are three blades on an upright post, two or three times the height of the dwellings they stand beside. But nearer the centre, and in certain areas outside the village, they are much larger – as tall as the framework giants marching past the abandoned city.

A river passes right through Shep Afon, a meander forming one-half of the open hub at the heart of the village. Along the river banks are more wheels than she can count, all turned by the passing of the water. People, carts and animals, tiny from this distance, throng the streets. The flow of traffic has two directions: into the village centre and away from it. The central circle of the village looks like it is full of tents, but Megan has already guessed that the hub is also the village's market. From roads all around the village, carts and trains of people and animals are arriving all the time. Despite what Mr Keeper has said to her, Megan is suddenly keen to be among them.

• • •

Mr Keeper ties a cord from his waist to hers and she walks close to keep the connection loose, but he has told her to yank hard if she encounters any "trouble". He tells her to be watchful, to remember as much as she can about what she sees and not to make direct eye contact with anyone.

At the edge of the village they encounter the first shelters. Many of these are places where traders have stopped and set up temporary bases. Some are merely blankets slung over an A-frame of sticks – small enough to be carried by a single person. Others are sturdy benders with well-crafted poles and covers of fine cloth and felt. Outside every home, mobile or permanent, large or small, burns a fire. On most of the fires black pots boil with water or broth. Others boast metal grates on which sizzle strips of meat, and above the rest are spits or skewers where larger cuts and sometimes whole animals are roasting above the flames. Greasy smoke and heady steam mingle in the cool air. Megan's eyes sting and drip tears, and all the while her stomach gurgles and gripes.

Curiosity keeps her eyes on everything except the road ahead, and often she finds herself yanked along because she has paused while Mr Keeper has continued to walk. These jerks occasionally draw a stare or titter from the sidelines. Sometimes her observation of the campers is met with hostile glares, sometimes with blankness. Occasionally, she realises she has met some stranger's gaze and looks away before they begin to move towards her.

Many of the travellers and settlers along their path make way for them. Then she realises it is Mr Keeper they clear the road for. She can't decide if it is out of respect or fear. Perhaps a little of both. It makes her feel safer, but not safe enough to engage any of the strangers with even a nod or a smile.

She has never seen so many people before. As they progress along the dusty byway more travellers join them, some they pass and others, hurrying, pass them by. Traders and buyers also march away from the village centre, creating turbulence in the flow of traffic. Most of the faces she sees are grim, dirty and determined. Hardly anyone smiles. Mr Keeper was right: this place is not as friendly as Beckby, it is not friendly at all.

At first, the sounds in the village were distant and far-flung: a pot clanging, the hiss of meat dripping fat into embers, dogs barking somewhere in the distance, people calling to one another, pack animals grunting or baying, the curses and cajoles of their masters. Longer range and muffled, the sound of stones being broken, metal being worked and timber sawn or hammered. Now they have become part of the throng, and the noise is chaotic and loud, closing in on them from every direction. Other pedestrians and their animals jostle and push. An unseen hand grabs at her and she scuttles close to Mr Keeper, reaching for him and then hesitating. He seems to know and turns to her.

He mouths:

"Stay close."

But if he shouts or whispers, she cannot tell over the hubbub.

Megan lets her hand fall away but she stays as close as she is able. She chances a look behind to see if the owner of the hand is nearby. In the blur of faces she cannot tell who it might have been. With the density of human and animal traffic becoming a crush, the noise

is everywhere and almost indistinguishable from itself.
The smells which were once appetising are now nause-
ating when mingled with what rises from the crowd.
The people are unwashed and the smell of their bodies
packed into the throng is rank and sour. The animal
smells are strong too and she knows she has stepped in
half a dozen kinds of manure already. There's no helping any of it. All she can do is hope that Mr Keeper can
lead them through.

They shoulder their way along the street, leaving the
temporary dwellings far behind them. Now they pass
between cottages like the one Megan's amu and apa
live in. Beyond those they walk past houses with second and third storeys, and the light reaching street level
diminishes. Faces stare from wind-eyes with scorn or
boredom, the people they belong to dressed in bright,
clean clothes whereas the pedestrians wear mostly
greens, browns and drabs.

As they near the village centre the streets darken further, the buildings pressing in on both sides. Then,
night gives way to daybreak; they spill into the great
circular hub of the village, and the press of bodies on
all sides eases. Before them are spread hundreds of
stalls, each one with a roof of cloth or canvas and a sign
or banner bearing the trader's name and the wares or
services offered. From where they've entered the great
marketplace, Megan can see fishmongers, butchers,
fruiterers and grocers. There are kinds of meat and veg-
etables she's never seen before. Nearby, a butcher
specialising in squirrels, rats and rabbits brings a cleaver
down onto a bloodstained block, halving an already
skinned, gutted squirrel and sending up a squall of flies.
On the nearest fruit stall a colourfully-robed woman

buys a bunch of curved, elongated yellow items, paying
the stallholder in dried beans. To Megan's right a man
sits and has his feet measured beside a stall selling boots
and shoes. Along every curving aisle, stalls sell snacks,
boiled, grilled or deep-fried in oil and handed out on
skewers.

Megan assumes she's been standing with her mouth
agape because Mr Keeper tugs on their cord and gives
her a stern look before moving away along one of the
outer aisles. Here, between the stalls and the buildings
forming the edge of the hub, there is more space for
people to pass. Judging from where he's chosen to
walk, Mr Keeper doesn't look as though he plans to
buy anything in the market.

As they dodge between buyers and sellers and those
bringing more stock to the market, Megan notices a
woman approaching them. The woman wears a head-
scarf of faded blue and her eyes are a similar colour.
The woman's face broadens into a smile and Megan
thinks she recognises her in that instant. The woman
holds out her hands and Megan finds her own arms
reaching out to meet them.

"You've a good clear face, girl. A fine face. Tell your
fortune? I can see who you'll marry and the tally of
your children."

Mr Keeper turns to Megan then, his face fierce and
his eyes smouldering.

"What did I tell you, Megan?"

"Oh, now, there's no harm in it, sir. It's merely–" The
woman stops when she sees his face, her hands still
outstretched but not yet touching Megan's. Megan sees
the scarf-headed woman glance up and down, taking
him in. "Great heavens. A Keeper. I am sorry, sir. I

didn't know the girl was with you."

In that moment, the woman's momentum carries her an extra step and the contact she'd always intended is made with Megan. At the touch of Megan's fingers the woman's grey-blue eyes widen and her mouth opens in shock. She snatches her hands away and makes a gesture of warding-off that Megan has never seen before.

"Save me," she whispers. "Save us all. The girl's got the Scarecrow in her."

"You'd do well to keep that kind of talk to yourself, woman," says Mr Keeper. "Now, leave the girl alone."

"Oh, you can be quite sure of that, Keeper. I'll not set foot near this girl nor look upon her face again."

The woman scurries away into the crowds and is lost.

Megan stares down at her feet.

"I'm sorry. I didn't mean to look at her."

She feels his hand, gentle on her shoulder, and finally meets his eyes. They're kind again, the anger gone.

"It's all right, Megan. All this…" He gestures around at the market and the village. "It takes a little time to get used to."

48

It was difficult enough being a stranger, but to be a boy among unknown men, on their turf and therefore bound by their rules, put a strain on Gordon which he hoped did not show on his face.

There was, of course, no way to check this, and so he settled for an expression somewhere between friendliness, which he hoped would not make him seem weak, and a scowl, which he hoped would not mark him out as looking for trouble. If his father had been here, he would have told a joke or two. He would have known just how to lend a hand and to whom without getting in the way. Louis Black had always been a man among men, though Gordon had only seen it on rare occasions. And if his father had been here now, Gordon would have watched him for cues at the same time as hiding behind the rock of his confidence and strength.

But there was no hiding now, other than behind a feigned maturity which Gordon knew was fooling none of the men in the camp. The first thing Dave had said on entering the camp was:

"Everyone, this is Louis Palmer. He's just passing through."

Dave's gloved hand had clapped him on the shoulder. Unexpected as it was, the blow sent him off balance. This had elicited a show of teeth from Grimwold. A frown from Cooky's watery eyes. Gordon sensed enemies and allies shifting on the chessboard of his life.

As they sat eating, Grimwold had glanced at him from time to time, a viscosity to his gaze that made Gordon's fist tighten around the fork they'd given him. He hoped for silence because he didn't want to answer their questions. He hoped for talk because the silence knotted his gut. He felt responsible for every sly look, every notch on the measuring post of hush. In the cold air, his cheeks glowed, revealing him. He hated himself, all the while knowing such feelings made him even weaker. One thing he'd learned early at school was how the jagged flints of bullies gravitated towards the weak. At school he'd always got away with it because he was cheerful and friendly. Even if he could regain that demeanour now, he wasn't sure how effective it would be against someone determined. Against a determined man.

And then came the questions.

"So, where you from, Louis?" asked Dave. It was a friendly enough question. A fair one, given the circumstances.

"Near Monmouth. In the hills."

His voice sounded weak and scratchy in his throat. His embarrassment spun out of control, making him dizzy, wrecking the experience of eating the freshly grilled deer meat and warm bread.

"Monmouth?" said Beck. "That's a fair stretch. Must be, what, seventy, eighty miles?"

Gordon shrugged. "Dunno." He really didn't.

"You walk all that way?" asked Dave.

Gordon, who'd filled his mouth with meat and bread so that he wouldn't have to speak, nodded.

"How long?" asked Beck.

Gordon swallowed a bolus of half-chewed food. It took its time going down. When the blockage finally cleared, his eyes were watering.

"Three days," he said in the end.

Across their circle of five sitting figures, Gordon noticed Dave and Beck exchanging a glance he couldn't read. A little respect at last? He could dream, couldn't he? More than likely it was suspicion. Anyone covering that distance in that time was in a hurry. Why? That's what they were wondering – and not just Dave and Beck; all of them.

"So, uh…" began Grimwold. Gordon hated his voice long before he finished his question. It sounded like someone had put gravel in a blender and switched it on somewhere far away. In a basement somewhere. "Where you, uh, passing through… to?"

Cooky caught Gordon's eye, and must have read so clearly his discomfort that he broke in.

"Gents, the boy's been here less than five minutes. Let him get some grub down his neck before you give him the third degree, eh?"

Gordon noticed how Cooky didn't level the criticism directly at Grimwold.

"Hey, Cooky, he's resting his arse in our camp, eating our rations. The least he can do is give account of himself." The gravel spun in the drain of Grimwold's throat. "He could slit our throats in the night and take all we've got."

"He's just a lad, Grimwold," said Cooky, his hands held up, placatory. "You know as well as I do how tough it can be on the road. Give him a moment to settle, will you?"

Grimwold hadn't finished.

"He could have mates out there, just waiting until dark. Waiting to come in here and... and–"

Dave held up his hand. In command, this time.

"That'll do, Grim. Cooky's dead right. Give the boy a chance."

Gordon looked from face to face. Wouldn't it be easier just to stand up, his meal half-finished, and say thank you? Stand up and walk away before they all came to hate and mistrust him? He thought about it and he almost did it. What stopped him was the depth of his loneliness. Without someone else to look at, without someone there to talk to, even just a few words of purposeless exchange, he would surely implode into the vacuum growing within himself. And a circle was a circle, was it not? If he didn't hold with these men, if he couldn't be a part of this group, it meant there would be nothing for him but the crows and rooks and magpies. The earth and the trees and the streams. The rocks that poked like broken black bones from the flesh of the mountains. He wasn't ready to be that displaced yet, didn't have the strength to be that alone, that insane.

His voice surprised him. It was clear and strong, if quiet.

"I'm on my own. I'm not here to hurt anyone or take what belongs to you. I'm grateful for the food you've given me. But I'll go if you don't want me here."

He put his plate down, the meat and bread still

steaming in the chill pine air. Looking from face to face, he saw mild shock on all but Grimwold's. Grimwold was leaking disdain.

"Finish your food," said Dave. "And help yourself to more until you're full. We're not short of supplies. All I ask is that you make a contribution to the camp while you're here. Is that fair?"

It was more than fair, and it embarrassed Gordon further to have to answer such a question.

"Course," he said. "I won't stay long."

"Stay as long as you want."

He filled himself until he could eat no more of their food, and still there was meat left over. Erecting his own tent gave Gordon a skin of protection from the scrutiny. Once he'd crawled inside and zipped the outer flap shut, his stuffed belly sapped his energy. Though he felt nourished, he was tired too. He wanted to sleep and shut out the stares and questions just for a while.

He lay on his back with his laced fingers cradling his head. Heaviness spread from his turgid gut into every limb. His eyes closed and he drifted. As though his mind were snared on a fishhook, something reeled him back to consciousness again and again. Sleep, tantalising and a mere threshold away, would not come. After a time the fullness in his middle began to ease and the sluggishness went from his thinking.

He sat up, slipped the black diary from its Ziploc bag and began to write.

October (I think) '14
My eyes only

Realised just now that I'm probably fourteen. Totally lost track of time, though. I'll have to ask what day it is. That'll be awkward.

I'm a long way from home. Men I neither know nor trust have fed me and let me stay in their camp. They're eating meat – I never knew deer would taste so good – and bread made in tins right in their fire. They seem well organised. Their gear looks like army surplus – maybe they were all soldiers. Perhaps they still are. I haven't found out anything about them yet. They know a lot more about me but it's obvious they're suspicious. Especially Grimwold. But Grimwold would be suspicious of an egg in a bird's nest. I don't like him.

Cooky's older and less intense. Maybe I can ask him where they came from and why they're here. Or maybe I'll be moving on before I have that chance. Beck and Dave seem hard somehow, hard on the inside. Can I trust any of them? I don't think it even matters. If all I do here is eat, rest and move on, I'll be happy.

Happy.

That's such a lie. I have to find a way of staying strong.

I was about to write that I feel like the whole world is against me, but that would be wrong. The world, the actual physical land and all the animals in it and the feelings I get from them all, that world is like a friend to me. A friend that never asks for anything but always gives something.

No. It's time that's against me. And people.

The Ward are hunting me. Brooke's father didn't trust me, didn't like me, probably only saved me because Brooke insisted. The men who raided their camp would have killed me, and they didn't even know me. Every time I think of the one I killed, I remember the feeling of the blade in his stomach. I had no choice. It was him or me. He deserved what he got. They all did. But that feeling of metal through flesh, the warmth of his blood all over my hand, how it went tacky, all of that, it makes me sick to think of it. Sick with guilt. Sick at the violence of it. Sick that there has to be so much loss. Three raiders dead. Brooke and her father dead. And now these four men. Dave, Beck, Cooky and Grimwold. They don't trust me either.

I'll give it another day. See what I can discover. See if they'll chill out.

But I've got my knife beside me just in case.

And Mum, Dad, Jude and Angela, I'm praying for you all. Praying to the land and the life in everything that you're OK. I'll find the Crowman, just like you asked me. I'll find him and I'll bring him back.

49

When the tunnel search yielded nothing but a dead end in the form of an impenetrable pile of rubble, a strange sound escaped Skelton's lips: a mewl of frustration, a manic whimper. Knowles caught a glimpse of Skelton's puffy, pale face in the yellow torchlight. The look he saw there terrified him. Skelton was looking right at him.

Knowles knew he had to get away, far away. Now. He'd rather take his chances on the run than in an interview room with Skelton and his bolt-together sidekick, Pike. More than any sheriffs he'd ever met – and there'd been plenty, and all of them were freaky – Skelton and Pike scared him the most.

If he could make it back out of the tunnel, he could run for it – be the first back to the cars and take one. He had to make his break soon.

Skelton's effete voice intruded again:

"Is there any chance the boy might have got through?"

Knowles decided not to have an opinion. Jones, the freshest Wardsman among them and with plenty to prove, scaled the hill of rubble until he was lying on his stomach at the top of the pile, inspecting the hardcore with a torch.

Jones had opinion enough for everyone.

"It's completely blocked, sir. No one could get through here without some decent equipment. A brick hammer and a crowbar, for starters. I can't see through to the other side. A couple of JCBs would need a week to go through this lot." Jones looked back down at Skelton and the rest of them – to see if he was making an impression. "Young boy like that – what is he? Fourteen? – he'd have no chance."

Knowles grinned in spite of his own panic. Jones himself was only seventeen, a recruit straight from school.

"Thank you, Jones," said Skelton. "You can come down now." He turned to Pike in the gloom. "I want you to look. I need to be certain."

Pike lumbered through the darkness and mounted the incline of debris. Knowles watched his strange, clunky way of moving. With his huge hands, Pike could have been some kind of earth-moving machine. A nervous smile visited Knowles's lips in the darkness. Jones's agony at having his opinion ignored was plain even in the torchlight. Pike's injury hampered his progress. He looked like a broken robot, his muttering and grumbling the sound of its noisy, misfiring motors.

When a pair of arms took hold of each of Knowles's elbows, he jumped. Pike, on his mission, did not look back. Jones watched in puzzlement, out of the loop of secrecy. Knowles glanced at the faces of the men who held him. These were his peers from school. The men he drank with in the pub before he joined the Ward. Now he drank with them in the substation rec room.

They were his colleagues. His friends. Their eyes, once the affable, trustworthy eyes of comrades, were closed to him now. He was the enemy they'd all worked so hard to root out and destroy. Suddenly he was just another day at the office for them.

Skelton moved in front of him, appraising him with his good eye the way a butcher sizes up a fresh carcass. How long had Skelton known? What exactly did Skelton know? These were questions to which he might never find an answer. Skelton, on the other hand, would soon have Knowles regurgitating knowledge and facts as though he were reciting well-loved poetry.

"We haven't really had the opportunity to talk much, Wardsman Knowles," said Skelton. "And I regret that. I regret it deeply. I like to get to know the men… under me. It makes working with them more fulfilling somehow."

Every word slipping from the Sheriff's delicate lips was both a death sentence and an intimate caress. Knowles shuddered at the thought of such a man touching him. Skelton took a step closer and Knowles flinched. The grip on his arms tightened and he felt a gun muzzle caress the skin of his neck. Gooseflesh rose in a wave from his scalp to his toes. Skelton was shorter than him, and the soft-faced slug of a man now looked up at him as though he might go on tiptoe for a kiss. The Sheriff's cold, fat fingers took hold of Knowles's hand, making him recoil again. The fingers tested his skin the way a librarian might explore the covers of an old and valuable book. Knowles's stomach tightened at this exploratory, almost reverent touch.

"I'm going to get to know you… Knowles," said Skelton, almost giggling over the similarity of the word and the name. "I'm going to get to know you very well."

In the silence that followed, Knowles heard Pike scrambling back down the rubble pile. Skelton turned to watch his partner. At the bottom of the slope, Pike stood and limped back.

"There's no way through," he said, towering over all of them in the yellow torchlight. "He must have gone another way."

Knowles noticed how deathly Pike looked. The man always looked sick, but the shadows and bad light in the tunnel made it worse. He was a risen ghoul, animated bone-machinery. Behind him, Jones looked relieved that his assessment had been validated. All eyes now turned to Knowles, most particularly the one Skelton still possessed. The eye bulged, toadlike and manic, already seeing too far inside, already unearthing his betrayal for all to witness.

"That leaves us with just one lead to investigate," Skelton said. "We must concentrate on it with diligence."

He nodded, and Knowles was about-faced in a heartbeat. They let go of his arms and marched him ahead of them. Knowles could sense the pistols aimed at his back and he did not have the courage to run before them. They wouldn't kill him anyway. They'd merely shoot his legs out from under him and carry him back, keeping him alive for Skelton.

He wanted to put off that moment for as long as he was able.

50

Mr Keeper leads Megan around the outer edge of the village hub until they reach the river. Here the banks have been built up with rocks so large it must have taken teams of oxen to shift them. Mr Keeper allows his hand to trail along the backs of the huge stones and then stops.

"This will do."

He drops his pack over the highest rock onto the one below and motions for Megan to remove her pack too. She hands it to him and he places it beside his. The unburdening is a great relief, and both he and Megan spend a few minutes stretching out tight calves and compacted bones. Then Mr Keeper mounts the rock he's chosen and sits cross-legged upon it. Megan glances over at the packs, balanced on the rocks. Beyond and quite steeply below is a small stretch of beach and then the river.

"They might fall and roll in," she says.

"They're safer there than they are in the market."

She climbs up beside him and together they survey the river. From this high point the creak, splash and thump of waterwheels is loud. The water along both

banks of the river is churned up by their movement.
On the other side of the river there are very few buildings, and they and any other dwellings are sparse and
well spread. Three wooden bridges arch over the water
connecting the severed, less-populous section of the
village to the hub.

"Why is that side so quiet?"

"It's where they send folk who don't fit in."

"What does 'fit in' mean?"

"Could be lots of things. They might have hurt someone or taken something that didn't belong to them."

"Why would anyone do that?"

Mr Keeper considers his answer for several
moments.

"Because they've forgotten the abundance of the
world."

"Do they have to stay there forever?"

Mr Keeper shakes his head.

"If they can prove they have something to give,
they're allowed back."

Megan watches the waterwheels and loses herself in
their motion for a long time. Now she understands why
Mr Keeper placed their packs away from the market,
but she still can't believe that anyone would actually
try to take something that belonged to someone else.

Eddies swirl past in the disturbed water. Behind her
the noises of the market come and go as she enters and
leaves places in her imagination, many of them conjured by the things she has seen in the last few hours.

A tiny boat bobs towards the section of river above
which they sit. The boat is almost circular, propelled by
a white-haired man so ancient he could be Mr Keeper's
grandfather. He moves a single paddle, swishing it like

a tail and making the boat move to his will. He brings
the boat to the edge of the river and bumps it against
the sandy bank. Nimble as a cat, he leaps out of his
diminutive vessel and pulls it far onto the shore where
the water can't reach to pull it back in. He lifts a pack
from the boat, much like the ones she and Mr Keeper
carry. With this obviously heavy weight slung over one
shoulder, he climbs the rocks which reinforce the hub
side of the river, making right towards them.

Mr Keeper, shaken from his reverie by this, stands up
and waves his pipe. The ancient man waves back. Mr
Keeper grabs his pack and signals for Megan to pick
hers up, but the old man shouts out.

"No need. I'm coming to you."

"Go and help him, Megan," says Mr Keeper. "Can't
you see the man's older than time itself?"

Megan leaps to her feet and begins to stumble down
over the huge rocks to the old man. Once again he
waves her off.

"Nearly there now," he shouts. "And I'm quite sure I
don't require any assistance climbing this piddling little
slope. I'm fitter than the pair of you."

Megan hesitates and looks back at Mr Keeper. He's
grinning.

"Might as well leave him to it then," he says.

Moments later the old man is standing before them
and placing his pack beside theirs. Megan notices he is
not even panting. And though his face is so wrinkled
and leathery she couldn't count all the lines on it in a
whole day, his eyes are like those of a child: bright,
playful and mischievous. He jumps onto Mr Keeper's
rock and they embrace tightly for a long time.

"It's good to see you again, old friend," says Mr

Keeper. "You haven't changed at all."

"You have," says the old man. "You're getting old." The old man turns to Megan and inspects her with his boyish eyes. "And who have we here?" he asks.

"This is Megan Maurice."

The old man takes both of Megan's hands in his and closes his eyes for a moment. His palms and fingers are weathered and dry but the skin is warm and intense. She feels a welling of emotion at his touch. When he opens his eyes he is smiling.

"What a great pleasure it is to meet you, Megan Maurice. You are a light for the world. I can tell you have much to give."

She can't hold his gaze.

"Megan," says Mr Keeper, "this is Carrick Rowntree."

Overwhelmed, she doesn't know what to say. In the end she says nothing.

"Come," says the old man, jumping down from the rock and shouldering his pack once more. "You must be hungry. Allow me to furnish you with a repast."

He trots away as though his pack weighs nothing and Megan and Mr Keeper struggle to keep up. They follow him between the concentric aisles of the marketplace, and he leads them to the very centre of the hub. Here he finds a larger stall than many of the others with chairs and tables made of logs ranged nearby.

"Make yourselves comfortable," he says.

They watch from their seat as Carrick enters a fierce negotiation with the stallholder. When he returns, the stallholder is red-faced but the old man is smiling.

Mr Keeper nods in the direction of the irate man, who is now moving around at high speed behind his stall, his hands a blur as he reaches for ingredients from all directions and adds them to pans Megan cannot see. Smoke and steam rise. The man wipes his face with a rag slung over his shoulder, his anger evaporating as he cooks.

"What was his trouble?"

"Oh, he'd forgotten why Keepers don't pay for anything."

This is new to Megan.

"You don't pay? Why not?"

The old man grins.

"Well, it's simple, really. We don't pay because we don't get paid. Keepers don't have any money."

"Oh," says Megan. It was simple but it didn't make much sense. "But why is that?"

"Ah. Now that's a little more... esoteric. Not something the gentleman making our lunch would have understood – though he was curious. No, I had to threaten him with the law." Carrick grins again, delighted by the reaction he's provoked in the stallholder. "It goes back to the times of the first Keepers. Do you know when that was?"

Megan shakes her head.

"You'll find out soon enough, I'm certain." The nod he and Mr Keeper give each other is barely perceptible, merely a half-closing of the eyelids. "At the time, money had been a very important thing to everyone and suddenly it became worthless. People soon realised what the Keepers had to share with them was much more valuable, and so they made sure the Keepers were well looked after. Keepers became living symbols of the giving and receiving nature of the universe and of the land. And so that they could travel safely and confidently, everyone agreed that they would be welcome wherever they went. Nothing they ask for can be denied."

It is Megan who grins now.

"So if I felt the need to twist that man's nose," she pointed to the stallholder, "he'd have to let me?"

The old man nods with feigned seriousness and then holds up a finger of warning.

"But it would be a terrible abuse of your power."

All of them laugh, Megan especially hard.

"You know," says the old man, "there's a saying that everything you need–"

Megan can't help but interject.

"–will come to hand in the very moment of its requirement." She puts her hand over her mouth. "Sorry."

Mr Keeper looks surprised – not an expression she sees on his face very often. She thinks perhaps he's angry until he puts an arm around her shoulder, leans over and squeezes her as though he were her own apa.

He looks at Carrick and smiles.

"That's not something she's ever heard from my lips."

"Nor should it be, Mr Keeper. And good for you, Megan Maurice."

At that moment the stallholder arrives with a tray and thumps a steaming bowl of food in the centre of the table. In front of each of them, he places a wooden bowl and spoon. Smaller bowls of the same hollowed wood serve as cups, and he places an earthenware pot next to the old man's bowl.

"Enjoy," he says. "And please forgive my ignorance, Keepers. It's a long time since I've seen your kind here in Shep Afon. I hope you'll eat with me again if you ever return."

"So do I," says the old man – the aroma from the steaming bowl is delicious – and the stallholder departs, his good humour renewed. Carrick points to the food and tea on the table. "Now doesn't that just prove that old saying to be true?"

Megan peers at the heap of food.

"What is it?" asks Megan.

"Barley bowl," says Mr Keeper. "In the centre and underneath everything else is a mound of steamed barley. Over that is poured a broth and on top of that the cooked meats. It varies from place to place but this one does look particularly good. I'm suddenly ravenous."

Carrick ladles food for each of them and makes a short prayer of thanks to the Earth Amu and the Great Spirit. He pours them each a cup of scalding tea and they begin. The food is so good that no one speaks for quite some time, other than to utter mewls of satisfaction or ask for more. Between them, they demolish the entire barley bowl. Megan is sitting back with her hands feeling her stretched tummy when the stallholder returns with three bowls of stewed fruit and custard. The three diners shrug and set to again.

When their pudding bowls are empty, the conversation is flagging and the remaining tea is long cold, the old man rises and they follow him back to the river bank. The three of them descend the rocks to the sandy shore, and the old man erects a hemispherical canopy with the opening towards the water.

"When you get to my age, a nap after lunch is essential."

Mr Keeper, still groaning with the weight of food in his belly, clears his throat.

"I wouldn't normally, of course, but I think I'll join you."

Megan, so full she can barely keep her eyes open doesn't say anything. She unfurls her bedroll from her pack and lays it half inside the canopy. She is the first to collapse, hands clutched around her stomach.

Soon all three of them are snoring.

Megan wakes to a hand pressed over her mouth, and something cold and sharp against her neck.

Mr Keeper grumbles in his sleep and turns over. The old man, Carrick Rowntree, still snores. Much of the light of the day has gone and there is a chill rolling off the river. These things are incidental to the knife and the hand, both of which belong to a figure wearing a ragged black hood. Two holes have been cut in the material from which stare intense eyes.

Three other black-hooded figures stand to one side. One of them beckons for her to stand up. It holds a finger to where its lips must be before drawing the same finger across its throat. Megan stands, still groggy from sleep, her head thumping and her legs jittery.

For a moment the figures stand and watch her. The four hooded heads turn to each other. The one she has obeyed so far nods and another steps forwards, pulling a hessian sack over Megan's head. Her world goes dark. The knife and the figure holding it to her throat impel her away from the sleeping men and down the gentle incline of the beach towards the water.

51

Gordon woke often, reaching for the reassurance of his knife in the darkness on every occasion. When morning came, he stayed in his tent. Its isolation and safety were flimsy, though, and soon produced a new weakness, a new fear. They couldn't see him, true. But he couldn't see them either. If they were plotting to evict him, or worse, it would be impossible to get a sense of it from inside the tent. Though he hated the exposure, his youth denuding him in front of these men, he made himself unzip the flap and step out. Dave, Beck and Grimwold were pulling on backpacks and checking their guns – rifles this time. They looked like the real thing too, not air-powered toys for hunting pigeons or rabbits. When Grimwold caught him looking at his firearm, his lips peeled again from his dull-surfaced, dirty teeth. Gordon looked away immediately, unable to hold the man's greasy, penetrating gaze.

Cooky sat in the mouth of his own tent, a well-used but sturdy canvas construction which looked like it had survived from the early days of the Boy Scout movement. He was reading a book, or so it seemed at first glance, but he had a pen in his hand too. Dave led Beck and Grimwold to the perimeter of the camp, where he looked back and called to Cooky.

"See you in a few hours."

Cooky didn't look up from his book. He merely raised a finger in acknowledgment.

"I'll have some grub and coffee ready," he said.

Only Grimwold looked back as he left the camp, fixing Gordon in his reptilian stare, blank features betraying contempt and want. Gordon's fingers touched the open knife in his pocket, drew strength from it.

When the sound of their footsteps receded, swallowed by the pine forest, Gordon still stared after them, thinking that now would be a good time to leave. Now, while he was well fed and Grimwold was out of sight.

Cooky was absorbed by his book, occasionally underlining sections with his pen. Gordon watched him for a while, but if the old man knew he was observed, he never once looked up.

"Where are they going?" asked Gordon in the end.

At first he thought Cooky hadn't heard him. He was about to ask again when Cooky looked up and clicked his pen shut.

"Hunting," the old man said.

"Deer?"

"Maybe."

Gordon wondered what that meant. He was silent for a while, this time under the scrutiny of the older, less dangerous-seeming man.

"You're young to be travelling," Cooky said. "Especially on your own."

Gordon didn't respond.

"These are dark times," continued Cooky. "No telling

what people will do to each other now."

Gordon almost nodded.

"Seen that for yourself, have you? I thought as much. Why else would you be on the road?" Cooky closed his book, distracted enough now for a conversation, it appeared. "Where's your family?"

Gordon didn't answer. Cooky pressed his lips together and closed his eyes in understanding.

"Got some relatives where you're going, have you?"

Don't. Don't ask me these questions.

"Friends then?"

Gordon felt the weight settle back into his limbs again, but it was different this time. This was the weight of realisation. He had no one to help him. He did not know where he was going. He was a boy abroad in a world of men. Men like Skelton and Pike, like the raiders at the Palmers' camp. Men like Grimwold. He could trust no one.

He had no awareness of running back to his tent or diving inside. All he knew was some moments later his head was half buried under his pack and he was weeping into his hands while his body writhed. It occurred to him, quite a cold observation, that his fit of tears was so severe it resembled hysterical laughter. Indeed, from time to time a laugh escaped between the sobs and the thought that he, too, might be insane made his tears flow more freely than ever.

Some time later, Cooky's voice came, soft and calm outside his tent.

"You all right in there, Louis?"

Gordon barked out another short giggle-sob at the idea that he had taken his father's name without having the strength or worth to carry it. But he was able to reply.

BLACK FEATHERS

"Yeah. I'm OK."

"Come out and have a hot drink. You don't have to say a word if you don't want to. I'm nosey. I ask too many questions. Always been my problem. I won't do it again, I promise."

Gordon cleared the remaining tears from his face and the snot from his nose, wiping his hand on his trousers. He backed out of the tent to find Cooky crouching there with a steaming mug in his hand. He held it out and Gordon took it.

"It's got some whisky in it," said Cooky. "Don't mention it to the lads, eh?"

Gordon took the tea and sniffed it. The fragrance of the whisky wasn't as unpleasant as he'd expected it to be. After a few sips it didn't taste too bad either.

His sadness became something more subtle, melancholy brought on by the aliveness of the trees all around them and silence of the forest. In the simplicity of the setting there was great moment and presence. Every branch and every hidden creature had something to say to him. The message, though silent and wordless, was clear: everything that had happened was behind him and he was still alive. One day this pain would be a memory too. What mattered now was the search, the keeping of his promise to his parents. And with this message came something else for the very first time. He knew if he listened, he would always hear this silent voice speaking to him. And if he heeded it always, he would fulfil his mission. Everything that seemed so wrong and so cruel in his life now seemed like a piece of something bigger and more significant. This journey wasn't about him. It was about the world. This message shouted itself from every tree trunk and every pine needle and every patch of winter sky. Far above him he heard the mellow cry of a single rook, aloft on chilled winds, confirming out loud what every other living thing was saying to him silently: this, all this, was meant to be. All this was right. When Gordon moved, the world would move with him. He knew it now. In his marrow. In his blood.

The knowledge made him get to his feet. If Cooky hadn't placed a gentle but restraining hand on his arm, he might have walked out of the camp and continued his journey right then. The bony but insistent grip of the old man brought him back. Gordon looked at Cooky, knowing his eyes must have been wild. Then he smiled and sat down. There was time. There would be time for all of it.

He drained the rest of his tea, relishing the heat and elation that now ran in his blood. He looked Cooky in the eye and said: "Have you ever heard of the Crowman?"

After a moment in which Cooky didn't respond, a moment in which the whole experience almost collapsed, Cooky began to speak. He spoke for a long time and Gordon took it all in.

52

Megan's hearing reaches out for clues. The sounds of shouting and bustle from the market have diminished almost to nothing. By now the stallholders and hawkers and all their customers will have gone home or back to their camps. The clunk and splash of waterwheels seems louder now and comes from all around her.

She feels the sandy bank soften beneath her feet. They are at the water's edge. From all sides, hands lift her and for a moment her feet touch something that feels like a solid wooden floor. Then she is forced to her knees and from there onto her belly. The knife remains pressed against her neck. She hears the sound of oars gently cutting water and feels the rocking of the river beneath her.

Only a few moments later she feels the bottom of the boat hiss to a stop on the sand. This bank of the river is very different. It's quieter than the market side and smells of sewage and rot. The air is cold and still, somehow stagnant. It feels like a different world.

She is lifted from the boat and marched up the bank. Near the top she is manhandled from the sand onto an outcropping of grass. She is propelled by hands from all

sides. Megan considers screaming now that the blade
has been withdrawn, but what good will it do? Even if
Mr Keeper hears her, they could slit her throat long
before he can cross the river and intervene.

They come to a halt. Megan hears the sound of a
canvas flap being pulled open. Hands force her to bend
and she is pushed through a low opening. Close, dirty
heat replaces the cool air of nightfall. Her captors with-
draw and the flap falls shut behind her. She tries to
stand upright and her head comes into contact with a
low roof made of what feels and sounds like woven
reed or rush. Unsure what to do, she stays bent at the
waist and half crouched, waiting.

Although the others have certainly gone, Megan
senses she's not alone. The air in the space around her
is too charged. Somebody observes her in silence, of
that she is certain.

"I'd like to sit down, please," she says, her words
weak and unconvincing.

Silence swallows them. Perhaps she is alone, after all.
Alone but for her imagination, which has always been
a little too active to be useful. And if she is alone, then
there's no reason why she can't–

"Now that you're here, you can be at your ease.
Remove the covering from your head."

It's a female voice. A commanding tone with an edge
of impatience and weariness. That it is a woman she
shares this new space with brings Megan a wash of
relief. She removes her hood to find herself in the
warm glow of tallow candles, the greasy scent taking
her all the way to Amu's kitchen in an instant. As she
lowers herself to the filthy reed matting, she sees
whose dwelling it is.

The woman sits cross-legged, everything below her waist wrapped in torn, grimy blankets. Above her waist, she is naked. The folds of her belly suggest she has born many children, and her breasts, hanging drained and limp, are testament to this. Now, though, her nipples have been pierced and short wooden dowels the colour of peat poke horizontally from each teat. They look to Megan like dams, either symbolic or actual, to prevent any more of the woman's milk from flowing.

Her skin is the kind of brown that only comes from spending every day outside for the whole arc of the sun to touch. It has the look of hide about it, and the wrinkles and cracks it bears are deep. Dirt fills each fold of skin, especially at her armpits, where dense hair bushes. Her neck is a mess of fold and wattles, each crease gritty with filth. When she speaks these loose rolls of skin shake and wobble, making Megan think of turkeys. Her face, too, is a sagging succession of dewlaps, the weight of her skin pulling her lower lids away from her eyes, exposing jaundiced sclera and capillaries that look like rusty fractures in polished ivory. Her septum is pierced with the same dark dowelling as her nipples, and her ears, twice the length they ought to be, hold polished wooden discs the size of Megan's palm. Much of her torso is tattooed with curling symbols and ancient glyphs, now faded to a filthy blue. Like Mr Keeper, her hair is long and matted.

What has she done, Megan wonders, to put her on this side of the river?

"It's some lofty company you keep, girlie." The voice is wheezy and laboured. Somewhere deep in the woman's chest, something vibrates. "Not that most hereabouts would notice. What brings you to Shep Afon?"

Megan's jaw clenches.

Girlie?

"My name is Megan Maurice. I walk the Black Feathered Path and that is our business here."

The woman makes a long reedy noise, catching something thick and wet in her lungs and bringing it north. She grumbles a gobbet of phlegm into her mouth, reaches for a wooden bowl and spits a deep green lump into it as if that's what she thinks of Megan's introduction.

"So you say. So you say."

The woman reaches around beside the blankets that cover her legs until she retrieves a baccy pouch and some papers. She rolls a fat, loose cone, crumbling dark aromatic herbs into it as she works. When she lights up from a nearby tallow candle the smell is unfamiliar to Megan.

"It's my medicine, Megan. Keeps me right."

She inhales deeply from the cone, holding the smoke inside. When she finally lets the breath go, she appears to relax and shrink. The wheeze sounds just as bad.

"When Mr Keeper wakes up, he's going to come looking for me."

The woman regards her through baggy-skinned eyes.

"Perhaps he will. But not on this side of the river. He has no business here. Neither of them does, and well they know it."

"I don't believe you."

"You will when they don't turn up, Megan. Believe me, they're not coming for you. Not here."

Is she telling the truth, wonders Megan, or just trying

to frighten me?

The fear she has held down, ever since the hand slid over her mouth and the knife dug into her neck, now surfaces out of control. She begins to back towards the door flap.

"Don't bother. They're waiting for you right outside. All they're going to do is bring you back – tied up. Is that what you want?"

Megan shakes her head.

"Sit back down and be still, then."

Megan returns to her place on the reed matting. So that the woman won't see her crying, she bows her head and lets her hair fall in front of her face. Smoke fills the small space entirely and she feels light-headed.

After a few moments she peeks out between locks of hair but nothing much has changed; the woman still sits there smoking her cone down to a nub, holding each breath before letting the smoke go. Megan relaxes a little. The lightness in her head is quite pleasant and some of the knots of tension go from her shoulders.

"Who are you?" she asks after a while.

"My name is Bodbran. Folk call me Bran."

Bran places the last piece of her smoking cone, too short to suck on without burning her lips, into the bowl where she spits her phlegm. It sizzles out. For the first time she smiles, and Megan sees a deep kindness written in all the winkles and bags of her face, as though it is smiling and laughter that has put them there.

"Has the moon touched you yet, Megan?"

At first Megan doesn't understand. A moment later her face flares and reddens. As though in response to the old woman's question, she senses a familiar dragging deep in her belly. She will bleed soon.

Bodbran nods and says: "Time is short."

"I don't understand," says Megan.

"There's something you must do, Megan. Something very important. I can't let you return to the other side of the river until it is done."

53

"Heard of the Crowman?" Cooky said with a guarded look. "Oh, I've heard of him all right. Most people have, though you don't hear many admit to it. Why do you want to know?"

For once Gordon managed to deflect a question with a lie.

"I'm just curious," he said. "I keep hearing about him. My family used to talk about him before they..."

"Before they what?"

Gordon looked down at his feet, hiding his lying face from Cooky and knowing that the gesture would be interpreted as shame and reluctance to speak. He left long spaces between his words, hoping this would draw Cooky further into his untruths.

"Things weren't... good... at home. I had to leave. When they weren't... hurting me... Mum and Dad were always talking about this Crowman. It seemed like he was something to do with why everything's changing now. It was like he made everything worse. I keep thinking if I could find out the truth about him I might be able to understand why they changed so much. I might be able to..." Gordon put his face in his hands and sobbed, "… go home."

Cooky patted Gordon's back without confidence. He didn't let his hand linger. Gordon knew what he was thinking. He didn't want to be anything like Gordon's "parents". He didn't want to be dyed their same sick colour. He wanted to make things right somehow, and so his words spilled out. Like he was answering the boy's need with a story, as though his words were soothing medicine.

"I'll tell you as much as I can," he said. "As much as I know. The trouble is…"

Gordon looked up, knowing his eyes were red and wet, allowing himself to look as lost and frightened as he really was.

"The trouble is what?" he said with a broken croak.

"The trouble is no one really knows the truth about him. No one knows if he's real or just an urban myth."

"What's an urban myth?"

"It's like a folk tale but for modern people. People who live in cities."

"My parents believed in him but they didn't live in a city."

"Fair enough, Louis. But cities are the place where these stories usually start. They're like rumours that might be true. Do you see what I'm saying? Telling you everything I know may not help you at all if none of it is true."

"It will help me. It'll help me understand my mum and dad better. That's all I want."

Cooky went to the fire where the tea stayed warm at its edge in a white enamel pot with blue edging. He poured them both a cup and added a little whisky to one of them. The one he handed to Gordon was just tea.

"You've had enough drink for one day," said Cooky, winking. Then he sat down beside Gordon and took a drink from his mug. The fire, down to a pile of nicely glowing coals, exhaled a muted, continuous hiss. Gordon listened in the pause before Cooky began to speak, and there was nothing but the long dying breath of the fire. No birds singing. No branches snapping in the distance. No rustling of small animals in the undergrowth. The forest seemed expectant.

"The first I ever heard of the Crowman was in my local on a Friday night lock-in. There were about ten of us in the Half Moon that evening, mostly farmers and one or two younger lads with nothing better to do of a weekend than drink until they couldn't stand up straight.

"Conversation was lively and raucous, as you'd expect for that time of night with that amount of beer swilling in every gut. But the atmosphere in any pub can change in a flicker of a moment and one by one everyone gets drawn into the new mood. Could be laughter. Could be sadness. Could be grief. Could be triumph."

Cooky clicked his fingers.

"It can happen like that."

He took a thoughtful sip of whisky-laced tea, his eyes focussing into memory as he relived the lock-in.

"But it wasn't like that this particular night. The ambience in the place changed gradually. I can't remember what started it – maybe I didn't even hear what it was – but soon we were discussing what we'd do if it was our last day on Earth, how we'd want to spend it. That got a few laughs going for a while, but in general the mood of the place went downhill.

"Now I'd had a lot to drink that night. You don't stay for a lock-in and sip tonic water, after all. Nights like that are always a blur the next morning – especially the conversations. All I tend to remember is the feelings of a night out; it's like someone mutes the soundtrack and I can only remember how it looked and felt. But the next morning I woke up and I remembered just one thing: the words Bill Tatchforth spoke.

"'The end times are coming,' he said.

"He had hands like shovels, Bill Tatchforth, so callused and hardened from working outdoors the skin was more like horn, tougher even than leather. When he picked up his pint it would disappear behind his fingers like a child's cup. Everyone shut up when Bill spoke, because apart from 'how do' or 'pint of the usual' or 'nice again today' – which he'd say in even the foulest weather – Bill never said a word to anyone. He would just sit and drink quietly and steadily from the moment he arrived to the moment he left. Fifteen pints. No more or less every Friday night. In that time he'd get up for a piss only two or three times and he'd walk out of there steady as a rock and walk home to Manor Farm through rain or hail or snow or fog. It was like nothing touched him.

"But *something* touched him all right, and that was the night he talked about it while everyone else in the pub, even Jim Chivers the landlord, listened in utter silence, not daring to laugh or interrupt in case it shut Bill up for another twenty years.

"'The Black Dawn,' he said. 'That's what's coming. No one alive will ever have seen a time like it and most of us won't live to tell about it.' He took a long, deep pull of his beer and nodded to Jim Chivers for another.

'I've seen it in my dreams almost every night for the last ten years or so. And when I'm out attending to things come the morning, I can feel it in the land all around me. Something's coming. Something bad.'

"Jim Chivers put Bill's next pint on the counter top. I remember watching the foam overflowing and sliding down the sides of that pint glass like something dying. There wasn't a sound in the Half Moon. Everyone was listening for what might come out of Bill's mouth next. I think most of us were hoping it would be some kind of a joke. Except Bill Tatchforth had never told a joke in all the years I'd known him. Everyone approached the bar, where we were standing like believers at the feet of a prophet.

"'There's a dark man coming. I've seen him in my dreams too. Fingers like black straw poking out of torn sleeves. Sometimes I see him standing at the crest of some bald hill, those arms and fingers stretching up and out like he's reaching for the edges of the world and crying out to heaven. His coat blows out behind him like dark wings. Like a scarecrow, he is. A ragged, walking scarecrow. But he's a message for us. He's the one bringing the Black Dawn, the end times. Where he walks there's death. Sickness, starvation, war, the land broken and changed forever. I've seen it all.'

"Bill Tatchforth drained his next pint in one and then he pointed one of his huge fingers at us. I'd never seen him do that before either.

"'You'll mark my words if you've any sense between the lot of you. The Crowman's coming. And you'd better be ready.'

"And then he stood up, like he was coming out of a trance or something, and the old shy half smile he usually wore returned to his face. He said goodnight with a small wave, just like he always did, and let himself out of the Half Moon's back door. It was so quiet we could all hear his footsteps as he walked away up to Manor Farm.

"The next Friday he came in, just the same as always. Ordered his usual and stood at the bar like nothing had happened. No one asked him about it and nothing was ever said. I never heard it mentioned again."

Through all of this Gordon sat unmoving, his second mug of tea untouched. It had cooled between his cupped hands, and now he drained the mug and set it down beside him on the ground.

"Do you think Bill Tatchforth was... mad or something?"

Cooky's sips of tea were more leisurely, more savoured.

"No. I don't. We – the regulars in the Half Moon, that is – didn't see quite as much of him over the coming months. Sometimes he'd miss his Friday-night drink and that would mean a fortnight could pass without him tipping his flat cap at you. But when he was in the pub he was just the same as he'd always been before that one strange night. Even I began to find excuses for his outburst – maybe he'd had no dinner that night and the beer had gone to his head for once. Maybe he was taking medication for something and it had made him a bit peculiar.

"For almost a year that's what I let myself think. We saw Bill less and less over that time. When we did see him, though, he was the same old Bill we'd always known. Then there was a stretch of several weeks when no one saw him. Not in the Half Moon, not out on his tractor hauling hay or moving his beasts from one pasture to another. Weeks became a couple of months, then three. Jim Chivers started to mention it every Friday night.

"'Haven't seen Bill for a while,' he'd say, and there would follow a silence in which some of us remembered that one odd night and all of us would wonder if any of the others had bothered to go up to the farmhouse door and knock to see if Bill was OK. None of us had. Shameful, when you think about it. Just because Bill was quiet and a little aloof, just because no one really knew anything about him, looking back that really isn't enough of a reason not go and see if a person needs some help. I'm still ashamed of it now, Louis. If there's one message I could pass on to a young man like you, something I knew he'd always remember, it would be 'look after those around you, no matter who they are'. Treat them the way you'd want to be treated if you were the one in trouble. If everyone did that one simple thing, the world would be a different place. It wouldn't have come to... this."

"Do you mean all the rioting and stuff?"

Cooky looked angry for a moment and then his face softened. Gordon could guess what his thoughts had been: "How can he be so stupid?" followed by "Well, he's only a boy". Heat prickled his cheeks.

"I mean everything. The way this country's gone. The way the world's gone. The weather, the economy, the self-serving government, the crooked legal system, the diseases and food shortages, the rise of the Ward. All of it. It shouldn't have come to this, Louis. If only we'd cared a little more for each other and a little less for ourselves it could have been..."

Gordon thought he saw a glistening around the corners of Cooky's eyes and he tried to look away, not wanting to see a grown man show weakness – embarrassed by it.

"…it could have been paradise. And we fucked it all up. Bill Tatchforth wasn't mad. He knew all this. And what he said about the Crowman, well, I can't say I've seen the Crowman but I can agree with Bill about the bad times and the Black Dawn. It gets closer every day. I think what he saw wasn't a man at all but a spirit or an energy that will stay here until we learn how to look after it and each other. Only when we get back to a state of counting the simple blessings of each day and the importance of our friends and families. Only when we give something back for every time we take something. Only then will this dark energy or spirit leave us alone. I think the Crowman is some kind of teacher or caretaker. And I think he's going to be here for a long, long time.

"Bill was getting ready. He'd told us to get ready, but none of us did. He'd dug a shelter under his farm and lined it with concrete. I can just imagine him down there of a night time, stripped to the waist and mixing concrete in a barrow, shuttering it all up himself and getting old Margie to hand him his tools. He'd stashed enough food to last three or four years for the pair of them and Patch and Gilly his sheepdogs. He had extra shotguns and tons of cartridges and secret ways in and out of the shelter. I heard he even had ways of listening to what was going on upstairs in the farmhouse so he knew if it was safe to go out or not."

Gordon had to interrupt:

"But what was he afraid of? What exactly?"

"No one will ever know now. Nuclear war. An invasion. Some kind of natural disaster. Maybe just lawless times. But he was ready. Just like he told us to be."

"Why will no one ever know? What happened to him?"

"The Ward happened to him. He was collected and charged with hoarding. They took all his livestock away, all his provisions. They demolished the farm and the shelter with explosives. There's nothing left of it now. And no one's ever seen Bill Tatchforth since the day they took him away. They never will, either. No one comes back from collection. Ever."

Gordon was on his feet before he knew what he was doing. On his feet and walking away from Cooky. Walking anywhere that he wouldn't have to hear another word from the man's mouth. Cooky came after him.

"What is it, Louis? You all right, lad?"

Gordon ran into the trees but Cooky stopped at the edge of the camp. In the old man's silence Gordon could hear him adding it all up. Cooky would know the Ward had something to do with why Gordon was "passing through". As soon as Cooky told the others, it would be time to move on. Weeping angry, heartbroken tears and shaking his head against what Cooky had said, Gordon stopped and rested his head against the trunk of a pine tree. Please, please, please. Make it all stop. Give me back my family and my life and I'll–

What? What could he offer in return for the impossible?

There was nothing.

The Crowman was his only hope. Cooky had to be wrong about it being just an energy or some kind of spirit. And he had to be wrong about the Ward too. Mum and Dad had both told him the Crowman was the key. He had to believe them if no one else. Find the Crowman and they had a chance. That's what they'd written. It was all he had now: the road to the Crowman.

And now that Cooky had guessed what put Gordon on the road in the first place, it was time to gather his gear and move on.

54

Knowles heard footsteps in the corridor and his heart stuttered. His stomach tightened and sweat lathered his palms.

The first thing they would do was extract his teeth. All of them.

It was standard interview practice. Knowles knew the thinking behind it and how effective it was. Other torturers in other eras might have taken one tooth at a time, hoping to maximise the effect of the pain and debilitation, but the Ward had discovered that a full clearance at the outset sent clear messages:

We're serious.

This is only the beginning.

It also disfigured interviewees in a very personal and obvious way. Teeth were somehow like guardsmen, and taking them all away created instant vulnerability and demoralisation. There was no posturing. There were no threats. No questions were asked to which an answer was expected. Interviewees were restrained and a Wardsman would empty their heads of teeth as quickly and efficiently as possible. Only then would an interviewer enter the room and begin to probe for information. Knowles was perfectly aware that most interviews were successfully completed in that very first meeting.

His problems were twofold:

First, his only contacts within the Green Men were already incarcerated in the Monmouth substation. He'd been part of the team that visited them for collection. There was little or nothing more he could tell his interviewer about them that the Ward didn't already know. However, the Ward didn't know that yet.

Second, he was a traitor. No. That was an exaggeration. He had loosely aligned himself with the Green Men. He wasn't a fanatic. He wasn't a diehard. He just didn't go along with his employer's view of the world. What he should have done was go on the run and join up with the Green Men. That would have been a commitment to a cause. It would have been dangerous but it would have been simple. Why he'd thought he could play both sides, be the double agent, he couldn't fathom.

One thing he'd learned during the interviews and collections he'd been involved in was that people didn't always know why they did the things they did. They didn't always have reasons they could put into words. Not until the end, anyway. By that stage they would have thought everything over a thousand times, with great care and in great detail. They would have asked themselves over and over if what they believed in was worth dying for in agony and humiliation on someone else's terms. Usually, just before the end they would rally a sense of self far greater than they had displayed at any other time. In that moment they would necessarily be defiant but they would be certain beyond any doubt what had motivated them to risk everything for the sake of a principle. And they would usually state it calmly and plainly in the minutes before they died.

Knowles knew in his gut that he'd made a good decision to pass information to the Green Men and aid them whenever he was able. His contribution to their cause had been great because of his position within the camp they opposed. But he still couldn't say why he'd done it.

His twofold problems afforded him twofold certainties.

First, the Ward would interview him until they were absolutely certain that he had not a scrap of useful information left inside his mind.

Second, they would kill him as slowly and as painfully as they possibly could.

After that, the Ward would release stories about the way he had died, knowing the information would ripple and circulate. They would use it to spread fear and tighten their control over the fallen nation this once-Great Britain had become.

Knowles considered his part in these machinations and realised he was little more than a speck of grease on the engine of history. With or without him the engine would continue to run. And whether he'd done anything to alter the course of this engine's progress would always be a mystery.

In fact, he admitted to himself as a set of keys rattled in the lock of the interview room where he now sat on the wrong side of the desk, he doubted his destruction at the hands of the Ward would contribute anything at all to any of it. He would hold what he knew about the boy inside for as long as he was able. There was nothing more he could do.

Three Wardsmen entered. Two approached and belted him tightly into his chair. The third remained with his face to the door. A mandibular depressor was inserted into his mouth to ensure it remained agape. The two who'd restrained him left. The third did not yet turn to face him.

What was that? An attempt at menace? That wasn't the way they were supposed to work. The figure in the grey uniform was somewhat diminutive in stature. He didn't recognise the shape of the man. Was this an escape plan being put into action by another mole he wasn't aware of? How his heart leapt at such a hope until the man turned around to face him.

It was Jones. The boy. It wasn't an air of threat he'd been trying to create. It was his merely lack of confidence causing him to hesitate and, Knowles now saw, his embarrassment that his first ever dental clearance would be performed on a fellow Wardsman. These thoughts had given him a slumped appearance but now he stood straight, if not equal to his task then resigned to it.

Jones approached Knowles's chair.

At some point during the procedure, probably after Jones's inexperienced, sweat-slicked fingers had snapped or crushed rather than cleanly removed the fourth tooth, Knowles had a small realisation. Something that gave him a little satisfaction and elevated him from that speck of grease to, perhaps, a small moving part. He could, if nothing else, buy the boy some time. And if the boy got away from the Ward, it might mean things turned out differently.

It might mean they turned out better.

• • •

"You don't have to go, you know."

Gordon packed as fast as he could. He didn't answer. Cooky seemed misty-eyed. Maybe he'd had more of the whisky. He still stood with his enamel mug and drank from it in small sips. No steam rose from it but each sip made him gasp a little.

Gordon's tent was down and tightly stowed. He made sure the rest of his gear was just as neatly packed and that there was nothing missing.

"We've all had trouble with the Ward, Louis. That's why we're out here."

"Not the kind of trouble I've had."

Cooky's tone dropped to a growl.

"You'd be surprised."

Gordon stopped what he was doing and looked over at the old man. He was swaying slightly. His face had sagged and he radiated exhaustion. The skin around his eyes looked looser, and gone was the jovial, approachable demeanour. Here was the damage now, thought Gordon, rising to the surface the way it did with everyone he met. Pus ready to leak from wounds that would never heal.

"No," said Gordon. "I wouldn't be surprised by anything the Ward do. When Dave and the others find out they're looking for me, they'll kick me out anyway. I'm not waiting for that. If you've all had trouble with the Ward, you won't want them sniffing around here." He gathered up the last of his things and stashed them in his backpack.

"You don't understand, Louis. We… oppose the Ward. Actively. There are people like us all over the country."

Gordon was still for a moment. Here was something.

"Like a resistance movement?"

"Yes. Exactly like that. We call ourselves the Green Men."

The Green Men.

"Could you…"

Cooky sharpened up, stood straighter.

"Could we what?"

"How many of you are there?"

"Not many yet. But the numbers are growing all the time. You should join us. We need bright ones like you. Young men with some determination and strength."

Such words had never applied to him. Gordon was aware of the power of flattery all of a sudden. It was very hard to disregard what Cooky had suggested about him because "bright, strong and determined" was exactly what Gordon wanted to be. What he wanted more than that, though, was the power to change the past.

"Could you break my family out of the Monmouth substation?"

The question was enough to deflate Cooky.

"We don't have that kind of influence – or numbers – yet. But one day we might."

"You've got spies, though, right? There was a Wardsman who helped me after they took my family."

"Yes, we've managed to get a few moles inside the Ward," agreed Cooky, "and turn a few others to our way of thinking. It won't be enough influence to get your family out, though. I'm sorry, Louis."

Gordon stood with a leg either side of his backpack. Shouldering it would mean he was leaving. He wanted to know more first.

"Can I have another cup of tea before I go?"

"Course, lad. Course you can."

Cooky brewed a new pot and poured a mug for Gordon.

"Whisky?"

"No thanks."

They sat down side by side again not far from the fire.

"Why do you call yourselves the Green Men?"

"After the Green Man. Heard of him?"

Gordon shook his head.

"He's an old myth. A symbol of every living thing in the plant kingdom and a sign of rebirth. To us he represents the importance of the land. He's like a bridge between men and the Earth."

"Is he a spirit like the Crowman?"

"I'd say that was pretty close to the truth. The Ward are grey like concrete and steel. They believe in profit and exploitation. They want one corporation to govern the whole world. They believe in technology and they want nothing but power for the sake of it. They take but they never give anything back. If that was the spirit of the twentieth century, the Ward are its body here on Earth. They're real and they're dangerous. They'll destroy the future just to be in control for today.

"The Green Men stand against that in every sense. We see that without the land, there'll be nothing for anyone. Care for the land, live with it closely and give back to it in every way. If you can do that, the land will keep on caring for you, keep yielding its fruit and bounties. The Ward are going to destroy the natural bounty of the land, they're going to kill the very Earth itself with their greed. Someone's got to stop them, and it's going to be us."

Quite obviously drunk now and not bothering to hide the fact he was drinking whisky any more, Cooky had become an evangelist.

Cooky put an arm around his shoulder.

"So, Louis, now that you know all about us, can we count on your support? Are you one of us?"

"I'd like to be. I really would, Cooky. But I have to keep moving. I have to find help for my family."

"Just because you're on the road, it doesn't mean you can't be a Green Man."

"All right. What do I have to do?"

"You've to swear a simple oath and spill a little of your blood. That's it. But it's a promise you can never go back on. The Earth will always know you cheated her, and when they bury you at the end of your days, she'll never let your bones rest."

Gordon shrugged. He didn't require threats to make him loyal to the land.

The cut hurt more than he'd expected, and it worried Gordon that Cooky had used the knife he butchered the deer meat with to do it. He winced each time he thought of the blade being drawn across the skin of his palm. The blood had spilled lavishly onto the pine needles and then soaked down into the earth. Cooky had made him speak a few words of fealty and Gordon spoke them solemnly. The bandage Cooky applied was grey and a little greasy, and the palm of his left hand throbbed hotly. When Cooky noticed him holding the wound, he said: "If it didn't hurt, it wouldn't mean much, would it? Don't forget who you are now, will you?"

"I won't forget."

"And don't talk about it unless you're in the right kind of company, understand?"

"I won't, Cooky."

"And there's a sign so you'll recognise other Green Men. You stroke the skin at the outer corner of your eye three times." Cooky showed him. "Like you're brushing away some grit, see?"

Gordon nodded.

"But what it signifies is the tears we cry for the land and the tears she cries for us. Remember that."

Gordon was smiling now. Cooky was like a fussy parent.

"I'll remember."

He left the camp before the others returned from hunting, his pack laden with smoked deer meat. Drunker than ever, Cooky hugged him as though Gordon was going to the gallows.

55

At first light, after an uncomfortable night on the damp, insect-infested matting, the same hands that took her from sleep beside Mr Keeper and the old man do so again. This time they drag her from Bran's filthy hovel into the chill of early morning. Megan shivers; her coat is still on the other side of the river. She can hear the waterwheels tantalisingly close. If she broke away now, she could run to the river and dive in. She's a good swimmer and could easily make it to the other side. But she's not such a great runner, and she is still stiff with sleep and aching from the hard ground.

As Bran has instructed, they hand her a small pack with some provisions and a leather sleeve which contains a map. Once these items have been given to her, the five hooded figures stand back with their arms folded across their chests. It is only then that Megan thinks she can see the swellings under those folded arms. Her kidnappers are all women.

One of them points the way out of the ramshackle gathering of tents and shelters, and Megan can do nothing more than turn and walk in that direction.

She hears footsteps run up behind her, and one of

the hooded figures is there. It holds out something in
its hands, and Megan hesitates before taking it. After a
brief pause, in which Megan is certain words will come
out of the hood, the hooded figure runs away again.
Megan turns and keeps walking, all the while tearing
into the cut of cold meat that has been saved for her
from someone's meal the night before. Having not had
any food since lunch the previous day, she is ravenous.

Before the last dwelling is behind her she is gnawing
the bone clean. When there's nothing left she tosses the
bone to her right, towards the water where she knows
some animal will extract what little nourishment the
bone has left to offer. The river tempts her. It would be
a swift and simple matter to run for the bank now,
throw away the map and knapsack, dive in and swim
to safety.

She keeps walking.

Something in the way Bodbran threatened her keeps
her away from the river. A curse, the woman had said;
a curse so profound even death would be no escape
from it. The only way to cross back to Mr Keeper and
the old man is to make this journey first and bring back
what Bodbran seeks. Then she'll be free to go.

One advantage of a light pack is that she makes good
time. Soon the sun is up and Shep Afon and Bodbran's
hut are miles behind her. To her right, on the other side
of the river, the land rises up into a ridge and she recognises that she and Mr Keeper arrived along that same
ridge to find the bustling market village. She looks at
the map and sees the ridge represented there, a path
running along its spine. As Bodbran has said she
would, Megan begins to understand the map and its
purpose.

By the time the sun is as high as it will get given the time of year, Megan has crossed many meadows and picked her way through or around thickets of hawthorn and blackthorn. Sloe berries are abundant and she collects them as she goes, enjoying their bitterness. The map shows a huge forest and soon Megan finds herself within it. It's far too large to go around and its trees border the river right to its bank. All she can do is go through.

What little warmth the sun has afforded her over open ground is quickly dissipated once the trees block it out. Most of the leaves are gone now but the growth above and all around her is dense. The expansive feeling of walking over meadowland is gone and now any sound she makes is reflected right back to her from every tree trunk. Each rustle and snap sounds as though it comes from behind her or from cover, and she whips her head around often to check. There's no one there, not even a fox or a badger, and when she stops walking the forest is utterly silent. Not a single bird chirps anywhere.

Megan is thirsty and she's fairly sure she can hear something sloshing in her knapsack. On the map, about halfway through the forest, there is a clearing and in that clearing some kind of tree, larger than all the others.

If I can make it to that tree before nightfall, that's where I'll rest and drink.

The forest slows and saps her. Thorns catch at her and fallen logs trip her. Megan stumbles and stops walking, feeling the strength drain out of her legs. Nearby is a moss-covered log and she sits down on it, resting her elbows on her knees and her head in her hands. After a while, she opens the knapsack and removes the water skin. It is much smaller than the one she usually carries and so she takes the tiniest sips to make it last. If she can find a spring she'll be able to refill it, but she doesn't know the river water here and suspects that, even this far away, it will be rich in waste from the village.

The knapsack also contains a gauzy tarpaulin which she assumes is for shelter, though how it will keep out the elements is a mystery. There is no sleeping mat or bedroll, only a light poncho. Maybe Bodbran expects her to make the journey in a single day. The afternoon light shows the forest in darker and darker tones. She'll be lucky to make it to the clearing before nightfall at this rate.

Once the water skin, tarp and poncho are out of the knapsack, there's very little left. Bodbran has provided tinder and flint to make fire but there is nothing to boil water in. A small knife in a soft leather sheath lies at the bottom of the pack. The sheath is branded with the motif of a feather and beside the sheath there is another leather wallet. Inside this is a single, large black feather.

She studies the map and reconsiders what it is Bodbran has asked her to find:

"It is a thing of power, ageless and unchanged since it was created. All about it will be destruction and decay and this alone will shine. You will know it by its purity. Bring it back to me and you will go free."

"And if I can't find it?" Megan had asked through the aromatic smoke haze.

"If you fail, you are cursed, Megan. You must find it."

"But where exactly is it? How long will I have to

search for it?"

"Beyond the forest is a place where no one goes. I have seen it in the Weave but I can tell you nothing about it. It is the kind of place not shown on any map. Do you understand what I'm telling you?"

"No. I don't understand any of this."

"You will soon enough. All you need to do is find the very centre of this place beyond the forest. Go to its heart. That's where you'll find it."

Looking at the map now, the task seems hopeless. Beyond the forest, what the map shows is indistinct. Megan tries to make sense of what it represents. It seems to show gradual ruin and decay. The trees at the other side of the forest are small and withered or burned. The path becomes broken and peters out. From there the map shows nothing but shading or blank space. Beyond it the grasslands continue. The river runs beside the missing area on the map and on through to the other side where the land becomes distinct again. Something else runs across the blank patch in a diagonal line. Neither a road nor a river, it is depicted merely as a connected series of curving lines, like teeth marks. Somewhere within the blank area on the map is what Bodbran has sent her to find.

At its heart.

The light of day is waning and there's still a good way to go before she reaches the clearing and the tree where she plans to camp. Megan takes another couple of small sips from the water skin and rolls the fluid around her mouth many times before swallowing. When everything is back in the knapsack, she shoulders it and walks on, trying to find a little brightness within herself and give her steps a little bounce.

The best she can manage is a fast trudge, each foot-
step overshadowed by a growing sense of dread.

Alone again. Walking. But at least he was alive. At least
he could still search.

Cooky had pointed him away from the hills towards
the midlands. There would be more people and that
might mean more danger, but there would also be
more clues, more knowledge he could glean. Along the
way, he might find allies too. Green Men, people who
might help him search.

Gordon walked fast away from the camp. He moved
through the pines along a tiny path between the trees,
hoping it was a different direction to the one the hunting party had taken. The feeling of vitality in his
muscles, his ability to carry a pack and still make good
time, had grown. He felt taller, and perhaps he was. He
willed strength to the limit of every limb, imagined
himself filling out and rising up. To be a man, he
needed a man's stature. It was coming to him. He knew
it.

But to be a man he had also to be strong on the
inside, and this was where he felt a terrible vacuum.
Within himself there was only fear and loss and despair,
nipping at every thought, weakening every hope.

About a mile beyond the edge of the pine forest the
path angled down a small slope, and he found himself
beside the river he'd seen from his rocky, hilltop camp.

"Cross the river. Head east." That's what Cooky had
said. "You'll find more of us out that way. And any
Green Man you meet will tell you all he knows about
the Crowman. It's him we fight for. But don't trust
anyone just because they say they're a Green Man. Use

your instincts."

Gordon followed the path down until he was walking beside the river, against its flow. He scanned the banks for boats, bridges or anything else that would afford him passage across.

56

When the light began to leave the sky Gordon knew he wouldn't make it across the river before dark unless he swam. That wasn't an option: his equipment would sink and probably take him with it. There had been places where the river had broadened and the water had become shallower, but not shallow enough for him to wade across. There was still too much rainwater coming down from the hills.

He'd have to try again in the morning. He ground his teeth. It was only twenty or thirty yards across the water, but it was twenty or thirty yards of impossibility. He set his mind to finding somewhere secluded to pitch his tent.

To his left, one field after another sloped upwards towards hedges and lines of small trees. When he saw a thicker stand of hawthorn and a few small birches, he turned up the hill following a hedgerow until he was among them. He wouldn't be able to see out from where he planned to put the tent, but it seemed safe enough.

He decided not to light a fire. He had water and dried meat. There was no real need for any of it to be hot. He sat watching the river as he chewed deer strips and drank a few sips of water. The moment he finished, he pulled everything inside the tent and zipped himself in.

Darkness came sluggishly, and every few minutes he inspected his hand in front of his face to check if he could still see. Not wanting to make himself visible writing by torchlight, he got into his sleeping bag, made a pillow of some of his clothes and lay back. When sleep did come it was light and restless, ushered in by dream wraiths. As the night progressed the wraiths became more substantial, taking the faces of his enemies and his fears.

Angela came up from the river bottom, her clothes torn and dripping, weeds wrapped around her ankles. They trailed back into the water as she walked up the slope to his tent, a slew of green entrails in her wake. He heard the squelching of her waterlogged shoes and the splash and squirt of fluid leaking from her pores as she walked.

She stopped outside his tent, seeming embarrassed about her condition – most unlike her.

Perhaps it isn't Angela at all, he thought.

Despite the tent being zipped up and the darkness of the night being complete, he could see very clearly how she looked: bedraggled, hesitant, distracted.

She tried to speak but no sound came at first. Eels as black and oily as tar slithered up from her throat and out of her stretched-open jaws. They passed from her lips in skin-wrenching spasms, dropping to the grass to slither away, silver reflections gleaming off their backs from a moon Gordon couldn't see.

Finally, the eels were gone from Angela's stomach

and she was able to whisper to him. He didn't recognise her voice.

"I come with a message of hope for the future. A Bright Day is nigh."

Even in his sleep, Gordon giggled at her solemnity and the triteness of her speech.

"I wish I could believe you," he said. "And that's the truth."

The old Angela, sarcastic and dismissive, returned.

"OK, you got me. What I came here to say is the end of the world is just around the next bend and there's nothing you can do about it."

The end of the world.

No one had ever said it to him like that before. Not even he and Jude had ever spoken of it in quite that way. But wasn't that what they'd been thinking all along? Wasn't that what his parents had been preparing for? And wasn't this the same fear that motivated the Ward?

The end of the world. That was the end of everything, wasn't it? The end of history, the destruction of every human memory ever made. Not only the end of the Earth but the end of its story, its erasing from the memory of time itself. He imagined this end then as an explosion on a galactic scale, an event that blew the world apart and left nothing but dust to drift in the space the planet had once occupied. But he knew it wasn't really like that. Really, it was a sickness. If the world were a person, the sickness would resemble leprosy. Superficial initially, now the rot was deepening. Areas on the surface were dying but as the sickness burrowed deeper into the flesh, huge areas of the world's body would become necrotic.

The end of his life. The end of his family's lives. The end of everything. He couldn't make sense of it, couldn't fit the idea in.

He saw the amused leer on Angela's water-ruined face.

"You're lying," he said.

"I might be. But you'll never know if I am or not. What would you rather do: spend your last days on the run, or see Mum, Dad and Judith one last time before the end comes? You're going to die, Gordon. Just because you're only a boy isn't going to stop it from happening. Do you want to die alone, or surrounded by the people you love?"

Lies or not, her words were powerful. The one thing he didn't allow himself to consider in the daytime was never seeing his family again. Separation forever. But here in the privacy of sleep there was no way to escape his feelings. He didn't want to cry in front of his merciless sister but he couldn't stop himself.

"Well," she said. "I guess there's your answer."

Gordon snivelled, on the edge of wakefulness now. As Angela retreated back to the river she had one more thing to say:

"Turn yourself in, Gordon. The Ward are everywhere anyway, so you won't have far to travel when you give yourself up. Or you could just stay here. They'll catch up with you soon enough."

Her footsteps on the grass were stealthy and soft. Not the sloshing gait she'd arrived with. They got louder as she backed away. The noise of her re-entering the river was wrong too. It sounded like the opening of a zip. By the time Gordon realised why, he was pinned to the floor of the tent by the weight of a tense body. A hard, sharp point dug into his throat. Hot breath, scented with whisky and cigarette smoke, blew across his face. Tense, excited, aggressive breaths. Laughter, terribly loud in the silence of the night even though the intruder tried to keep it hushed.

Gordon thought of his own knife, only a few inches from his fingers and left locked open for exactly this reason. There was no way he could reach it, though. Not before his own throat was cut. For the moment all he could do was lie still. The body on top of him shifted, tense and edgy. Gordon felt an intimacy to the weight. It made him nauseous but the knife at his neck kept him still.

"Unzip the sleeping bag."

The whisper was a wheezy rasp. Gordon didn't recognise the voice. Nor did he move.

"Do it."

This was a chance.

Given leave to move his hands, he could try for the knife. He might even be able to grab it in one swift move, but would he then be able to turn and use it? He didn't think so. All the intruder had to do was push his blade upwards and Gordon was finished. The longer he thought about it, the harder his heart beat. Soon it was all he could hear.

Slow enough not to create alarm, Gordon began to unzip the sleeping bag as he'd been asked. The breath of the knife wielder quickened. The knife trembled at his neck.

"All the way down."

The accent. That was familiar.

Gordon did as he was asked.

The man rolled further onto him and used his free

hand to peel away the sleeping bag from his body. Gordon found his voice, not much above a whisper.

"What do you want?"

"Shut up."

"I've got food. Money too. You can have it."

The harsh breathing became a spasm of giggles. The whisper became speech.

"What I want, I'm going to take."

A rattle in the throat like pebbles shaken in a glass. The intruder forced his free arm under Gordon's throat, locking his neck into the crook of the elbow. The force was enough to squeeze his windpipe. Gordon's voice became a strained wheeze.

"You're strangling me," he said, his voice a pressurised gurgle in the darkness.

"No," said the voice, more confident now and rattling like stones. "No, no, no. If I was strangling you, you'd be dying. It'll be a while before we get to that."

57

The transition from woodland to open grassland is abrupt. The trees stretch out to Megan's left and right in a long slow curve, meeting on the other side of the clearing, perhaps a mile away. The sudden sense of space is welcome but dizzying. She sets off with renewed speed and a lighter step towards the centre of the clearing where a single tree, impressive even from this distance, rises and spreads in solitude and splendour.

Looking back at where she's come from, Megan thinks she sees movement among the darkened trees. She stops and turns to look properly. The wood is silent and still. She hurries on her way. The sooner she can reach the tree and make her camp, the better. Every few steps, Megan glances over her shoulder.

Soon, though, the majesty of the tree is enough to take all her attention. How a tree ever grew to this size is a beautiful mystery. She stops, still some distance from the tree, and sees how mightily it fills its space here at the heart of the clearing. Though leafless and ready to sleep for the winter, it is like the ruler of all trees: ancient, strong and wise. A true sense of majesty exudes from the tree. Megan quiets herself and asks permission to approach. She feels an almost jolly acquiescence from the tree and hopes she isn't misinterpreting it.

Respectfully, she moves closer.

Between the ground and the lower branches there is an almost uniform space making the outline of the tree look like a giant, dark mushroom. These lower branches are twenty feet or more above her head, and once she is under them she feels like she has walked inside some kind of spiritual interior, a place to worship the land and all creation. The air under the branches is charged. This is not her imagination. She feels a kind of vibration on the skin of her face and along every hair on her head. When she holds her hands out, the buzz is in her fingertips.

Astonished by this palpable power, she covers the last few paces to the tree's trunk. There's nothing she can compare this to. It is the largest living thing she has ever seen. Still uncertain about touching the tree, she walks the circumference of its trunk, counting her paces. As near as she can get without touching the bark, the tree is twenty-five paces around. She makes the circuit three times: one extra time to be certain and another just to appreciate again its vastness. The smile returns to her face, a smile of awe.

Finally, she allows her fingertips to penetrate the buzzing aura of the tree, which seems somehow thicker the nearer her hand gets. Her fingertips make contact with the hard, gnarled bark and the buzzing stops. She lets her palm sink flat against the surface and what she feels now is no longer a vibration but a flow, a tide beneath her hand. The sap of the tree in motion, like

blood, only far more slow-moving and beating a
rhythm in time with the heart of the seasons. This flow
pulls her into the time of the tree, which is a time exist-
ing long before Megan began, long before the coming
of the Crowman, a time which will continue in this
slow beat long after Megan has gone.

When she finally pulls away from the tree, she finds
her initial touch has become an embrace, her whole
body pressed against the body of the quiet giant.

Darkness isn't far away.

Megan is fortunate there is no wind. With no other way
to secure her muslin-fine tarpaulin, she makes a simple
framework of heavy fallen branches, propping them
against the trunk of the tree and wrapping the light
sheet over them. What she ends up with is a tiny lean-
to. Fallen branches also make the fuel for her fire. While
it gives her a sense of security and gives off essential
heat, a fire at the centre of a huge clearing like this can
be seen from every direction. It is also conspicuous
because of its noise. Splits, pops and hisses echo back to
her from the distant wall of trees all around. If she had
a drum she doubts she could make more noise. She is
relieved when the high, bright flames reduce to a glow.

Neither star nor moonlight penetrates the cloud-
choked sky. Once the fire burns low, it is a marbled
orange eye staring into total darkness, fading, dying.
Sitting inside the lean-to, wrapped in the poncho,
Megan follows its closing: into sleep, into the night
country.

Grimwold. Even in the dark, Gordon was almost certain
of it.

The thin man's knife hand was empty. Gordon knew because Grimwold had used it to find his crotch. The man now squeezed what he found there, hard between his palm and fingers, twisting Gordon's developing genitals into his fist and making him scream.

Laughter was loud in Gordon's ear now, the gravel spinning and clattering in Grimwold's food-processor throat. Now he knew what Grimwold's gaze had meant, the oily stares and sneering, greasy appraisals: the man despised himself but not enough to change. A man like Grimwold would never change.

The mashing of his penis and testicles worsened. Grimwold put all his hate into it and Gordon, rising out of himself and seeing the whole attack unfolding, knew that it could only get worse. When Grimwold was finished with him, he would kill him.

With calm objectivity, Gordon realised this rising up from his own body was probably due to oxygen starvation. He felt his pain but he saw himself feel it too. He did not have the strength to fight Grimwold off.

His mind screamed: *I'm just a boy.*

Still a boy after all that he'd witnessed. Still not man enough to save himself, let alone his family. Gordon didn't believe in God – at least, not the way other people seemed to. He hadn't prayed much in his life but he prayed now. There were forces greater than himself. That little he was certain of. There were creative powers at work in the world, the intelligence and influence of which he could only guess at. He called upon them then and there:

In the name of all that's good and right in this world, help me. I'm not meant to die here. There are people depending on me. I must survive. I ask the land. I ask

the trees. I ask the sky. Give me strength. Send me your
power.

Gordon felt a wind on his face as he dropped back
into his body and back into his pain. Grimwold still
laughed like a maniac, his saliva dripping onto Gordon's face. He was shaking his clenched fist now,
wrenching Gordon's genitals, crushing them as
though wringing water from a sponge. Agony
expanded in every direction from his groin and a sick
ache filled his guts. The wind increased and, over
Grimwold's sadistic braying, Gordon heard the whine
and swoosh of huge wings.

The darkness turned bright. Gordon's fear and pain
became a white rage. The criminality of his family's
arrest, the shame of his running away, his failure at
every turn to fully respond to what was happening, to
deal with it, to alter it; all this rose up within him,
blinding him with fury.

Enough!

He didn't know if he screamed the word or merely
pronounced it in his head, but Grimwold's grip loosened for a moment and in that fractured instant,
Gordon became an animal. He twisted, bucked and
writhed so hard that his neck came free of Grimwold's
headlock. Gordon beat the hand that had tormented
him with his own hammer of a fist. The clench withered under his pummelling and Grimwold snatched his
hand away. Free now, Gordon sprang to his knees in
the dark of the tent and reached for Grimwold's neck.
He screamed in fury, his voice becoming the screech of
a thousand crows. It filled the tent and Grimwold
stopped fighting.

Suddenly, Gordon could see as though it were noon

daylight in the middle of a field. Grimwold lay on his back, his knees drawn up, his hands outstretched blindly against the noise and frenzy. It was obvious he could not see as his eyes flickered, trying to focus on anything at all.

Gordon saw Grimwold's abandoned blade on the floor beside his sleeping bag and his own knife, its handle peeking from beneath the jumper he'd used as a pillow. He ignored them both and leapt onto Grimwold. It felt as though he flew. He battered the man on both sides of his head. His blows came so quickly they looked like the fluttering of wings. His arms moved like fronds of black silk, whipping Grimwold wherever he was exposed – his upper arms, his ribs, his ears. Very soon the strength went out of Grimwold's upheld legs and his knees dropped. Gordon now kicked at Grimwold's legs and groin. Each time Grimwold tried to roll to one side or another, attempting a foetal ball, Gordon flipped him easily onto his back. Soon Grimwold's arms were held up without any strength and his head lolled to each blow. His heels scrabbled on the floor of the tent but he had no strength left to raise his knees.

Only when Grimwold no longer moved did Gordon cease.

58

He dragged the limp man out into the night, and the darkness filled his spirit like oil in a lamp. It expanded inside him until his body ached with power. He held his hands up into the night, certain that feathers sprouted where his fingers should have been, and he thanked the land and the trees and the sky. As if in answer, a wind came up and bent every tree with its force. Live wood groaned and branches whined for the harsh, dark breeze.

Gordon carried Grimwold to the trees behind his tent.

Gordon sat beside Grimwold until first light. The man still breathed.

When he could see well enough to walk, Gordon stripped beside the river and entered its beige currents. The chill tightened his chest and hoisted his shoulders. Just beside the banks the pull of the river was gentle but insistent, and he planted his feet wide on the reedy bottom. As he washed, rusty stains swirled away downstream and in them he saw shapes, perhaps the shapes of the future. For the thing he had been was dying and the thing he wanted to be was being born. Their forms mingled in the gently churning waters. He saw for a moment a small boy drowning, his hand outstretched for help. He saw for a moment the form of a vast black bird taking flight, its wings unfurling in the eddies. He saw armies of ragged men defeated by sleek grey troops. He saw cities crumbling to earth. He saw blinding light and endless darkness. He saw the bodies of a hundred thousand people strewn across the land and left along the highways. He saw a tall, dark man walking the land, and everywhere the man strode was devastation.

With the last of the stains whirling and melting into the brown of the river water, the visions ceased. Behind the hills was the risen sun and for once the day was cloudless. All around him the birds sang as if this were the first day of creation. The first, or perhaps the last. Gordon submerged himself in the river for a moment to wash his face and hair. When he surfaced he pulled his hands back across his head to squeeze away as much water as he could. His fists closed around the thick uncut strands, driving out the water. By the time he'd climbed back onto the bank, all traces of his deeds had been taken away by the movement of the river.

He stood naked in the cool morning light, shivering and waiting for the air to dry him. He dressed slowly and carefully and returned up the gentle slope to break camp. A bloody human form lay under the thorn trees a few paces away, its solar plexus rising and falling only slightly. Gordon felt nothing for it. When his tent and gear were stowed, he hefted his pack, shouldered it and walked away.

He stayed close to the river, enjoying the comfort of its ever-changing nature, knowing that it knew him and carried his message in its waters. But all the while he searched for a bridge that would take him to the Crowman.

59

Within seconds of being conscious, Grimwold wished he were dead.

It was still night, darker than it had been before he entered the boy's tent. Every part of his body hurt but his agonies were worst around his temples, eyes and groin. He already had a creeping sense of what the boy had done to him but his mind could only scream denials.

For a while he didn't move. Dawn's arrival would make an inspection easier. At least he wouldn't have to move his hands around and hurt himself in the darkness. But dawn, if it was coming at all, was taking all the time in the world. Suffering took him into other rhythms of existence in which his body's natural painkillers flowed. Not enough to take the pain away, but enough to let him travel away from it. In this half awareness it was easy to ignore the truth: that he was so badly hurt he could barely move.

The boy had battered so hard on his ears Grimwold didn't think he could hear any more. The only sound was a continuous metallic whine. Listening to it was another distraction from a pain that engulfed his nerves like flames. He became aware of other noises, timeless beats behind the constant echoing in his head. It took a while to register that these noises were coming from outside of him. He recognised the call of blackbirds, sparrows and tits. They must have been in the hedgerows all around him. It was soothing and diverting to hear them until he realised their deeper significance.

Daybreak had come and still his world was black.

Now he *had* to move, had to explore himself, regardless of the pain it caused him. He reached up to his face, new agony awakening along his arms. It felt as though he'd been smashed by a claw hammer, not the fists of a boy. Something was wrong with his hands; his fingers wouldn't move properly. Still he brought his palms to his face. Before they touched the place where his eyes should have been they met a thin, splintery resistance and the touch sent lances into his head.

Oh no. No, no, no. What has he done?

He tried to touch the things in his eyes with just his fingers but his fingers had grown spines. He brought one hand to his mouth to find it barbed. He began to whimper. Suddenly he needed to do this very quickly and it hurt so very much. Several long straight thorns had been pushed right through every finger. Grimwold had to find the broader end of each one, bite on it and pull his hand away to extract it. None of them came out easily. His palms had also been impaled many times, from front to back and back to front. The effort of turning his smashed arms and wrists first one way and then the other in order to allow extraction of each thorn was almost as bad as each removal. All the while the hedgerow birds trilled their chorus in the black dawn.

When his right hand was free of piercings, he brought it trembling to his face. Again, the sharp, prickly resistance and the skewering pain deep into his eye only confirmed what he'd suspected for a while. The boy had put out his eyes with spikes of hawthorn. Nearby, a murder of crows cawed and cackled before taking off and flying away. The sound drew a rattled gasp of terror from his throat. He heard their laughter fade as they left him. He had a sense they'd been watching.

Grimwold removed both thorns, damaging his eyeballs further. They leaked onto cheeks already wet with tears. He made no attempt to stifle his crying. He doubted he could have stopped himself even if he'd tried. Whimpering and sobbing, he removed the thorns from his left hand and then the ones from his genitals and the soles of his feet.

Ruined, bleeding and exhausted, he slept until the cold woke him. The boy had stripped him to perform his operations and he shivered as he regained consciousness. Grimwold wished for death again, but death did not come and he sensed it would not. He stood up, so much pain in his body it was hard to isolate where it began and ended. He began to stumble, mud pressing into the many wounds in his feet and everything he touched with his outstretched hands sending lightning bolts of agony all the way to his spine. After an hour of faltering reconnaissance, he had a vague idea of where he was in the field where the boy had camped. The tent and the boy were gone but Grimwold's night persisted.

Through its darkness he tried to find a way home.

60

Megan is aware of movement in the darkness. Stealthy, cautious creeping. Deliberate, purposeful sliding. The blackness of the night is complete and all-encompassing. Someone or something is close by and they've approached this near without waking her. She feels the heat of anger and embarrassment rush to her cheeks. This is the second time in as many days that she has been caught napping. She lies still.

Can they see me?

There's certainly more than one of them. The sounds come from all around her.

She thinks; tries to control her breathing and quiet her heart.

What can be out here, in a clearing, under a tree in the middle of the night?

Badgers. Foraging badgers.

The thought calms her respiration and eases her fluttering heart. With it come other answers: rabbits grazing. Foxes on the prowl. Mice nosing through stems of grass. Deer moving across the wide open space, safe under cover of the night. Hedgehogs hunting slugs. Moles pushing up the earth. These are the sounds of the animal night country, the natural world she never sees or hears during the hours of light. She has never been this close to them before, never experienced them alone like this.

In her sleep she has slid to her right a little, and now she sits up straight so that she can listen more comfortably to the night symphony of the animal.

Except there's a problem. In trying to sit straighter, she finds it difficult to move. She knows this feeling, a kind of numbness that comes over her when her mind is awake but her body is still sleeping. Usually it happens around dawn. It used to frighten her until she asked Mr Keeper about it.

"Get control of your breathing first," he'd said. "When you have that, move a finger. Then the rest of your body will come back into your control and you can wake up properly."

She does this now and gains swift control of her breath, slowing it down, deepening it. Then she moves the little finger of her right hand. It's easy. She wiggles all her fingers on both sides. No problem. She goes for the final push, pressing both palms down on the rough ground to right herself.

She can't move. Something is wrapped around her body, pinning her to the tree. When she tries to push, she feels this thing, like a layer of cheesecloth, resisting her efforts. All she can think is that in her sleep she has knocked the branches of her lean-to and they've collapsed, trapping her.

Her rationality vanishes when she feels something curl around her ankle. Something thin and muscular. Something alive and intelligent. Her mouth dries.

She tries to pull her leg up to her chest, but it is stuck

to the ground as tightly as her body is stuck to the tree. She moves her other leg, already expecting what she discovers: her whole body is bound fast. Other things touch her body, heavy things with too many legs. They crawl onto her hair. Something prickly touches her cheek and she turns away. Her head is free and she shakes it now with all her strength, tossing her hair from side to side to dislodge whatever is on her.

From above, unseen creatures catch hold of her hair, a few strands at a time, and pull it up. She nods her head now, trying to free it from these tiny thieves, but each time she brings her head up, more strands are taken until she can nod no longer. She feels her hair bound tightly to the tree, and this time, when sharp things touch her face, she is unable to shake them off. Tiny determined limbs take hold of her eyelashes, above and below, and these too are secured somehow, leaving her eyes staring, unblinking and blind into the night.

The thing spiralling her ankle has reached her thigh. Another has begun its upward journey along her left leg. Still more of them entwine around her arms. Another, much thicker tendril insinuates itself around her waist, curling and curling more times than she can count. Megan wants to scream now, louder and harder than ever, the loudest sound she can make. But she dare not open her mouth for fear of what might try to invade it. All over her body, things crawl and slide, exploring her landscape. Making themselves comfortable there.

They settle, become quiescent.

From somewhere, there is light. Out of the corner of her left eye she see this light, the deep orange and white of huge forest fires, spilling from the trunk of the tree. She hears a tearing, the sound of a thousand saplings bent until they snap. Beside her is a bulge in the bark of the trunk. The giant tree rips open. Something steps from the heart of it and Megan feels the bark shudder against her back as the dark form passes into the night. In her head the tree is screaming. Light floods the clearing and something takes its place in front of her. She cannot look away, cannot even close her eyes.

Before her stands Black Jack in all his wicked finery. He raises his hands, and behind her Megan hears the tree tearing open in a dozen other places. Firelight spills forth, igniting the clearing, igniting her vision, and she sees all.

61

Some days after he crossed the river, it began to rain so hard that nothing could keep him dry.

When night fell there was no point even unpacking the tent. Gordon found himself in rocky sandstone hills somewhere in Shropshire, and often the best he could do was shelter under an overhang hoping he didn't sicken in the sodden cold. One morning, stiff and sore from lying on bare rock only partially sheltered from the rain, he looked into his rations and discovered what he knew had been coming for several days. He was out of meat.

On this same day, the rain continuous and heavy, he found a track leading into a small sandstone canyon. At the base of the canyon was a flight of carved steps leading up to a round cave entrance. To the right of the steps was a wooden hand rail. Many of the spindles in the rail were rotten, broken or missing. He guessed he'd found some site of historical interest.

He mounted the steps to the cave opening two at a time, only to discover that the hollow in the sandstone was protected by a steel grille. Exhausted and hungry, he squatted in front of the cave mouth, drenched hair hanging in his face, and peered within. It was deep and very sheltered.

Furious, he stood up and kicked at one of the uprights. There was give, where the concrete into which the steel was set met the soft sandstone around it. He kicked it again and red dust sifted down, streaking and darkening in the endless downpour. For a few minutes he set to using the sole of his boot on each of the struts, and soon all of them were loose. He took out his father's lock knife and, careful not to overstrain the blade, he scraped around the concrete housings of the steel grid. More sandstone dust fell, briefly staining his hands rusty before the rain washed the grit away.

An hour later, every housing was weakened and he began to kick again. This time the grille gave, tilting back at an angle. Spurred by this, he kicked harder, the soles of both feet already bruised and his legs shaky with the effort of it. When the grille came free it collapsed back into the mouth of the cave, all the struts breaking off at the same time. Gordon grinned to himself in the pouring rain.

He crouched and stepped through into the darkness. Even though water was cascading down the sandstone rock face of the canyon, inside the cave was dry. Not even a drop of water had entered. There were pieces of litter which people had thrown through the grille, but apart from that the space was empty. Judging by the faded, crumbly paper and plastic, no one had come here for a long time. By the gloom of rain-clogged daylight he could see the cave was compact. Like the steps carved into the rocks outside, the hole had been excavated by human hands.

The solidity of the cave's curving walls was a real

comfort. It was almost homely.

He dragged his pack into the dry and pressed every damp item flat to the sloping sandstone. Once his clothes and sleeping gear were spread all around the inside of the cave, he stepped back into the rain and descended the stone steps. The base of the canyon was well wooded and there were plenty of fallen boughs. He sought out the lightest, driest twigs first, taking an armful back to the cave before returning for larger branches. Back in the cave he used his knife to cut kindling from the smaller branches. He scraped hair-fine curls from beneath the bark of a log until he had a pile of tinder. Using a spark-maker he lit the tinder. It caught first time and he crouched to blow on the spreading red glow. Smoke rose and tiny flames leapt from the tinder. He placed the cave's litter over the flames and built up his kindling a piece at a time until he had a reliable fire. The larger branches spat and crackled but they kept the blaze alive.

Whoever had built the cave had thought carefully about staying warm and dry; the smoke rose up to the curved roof and slowly leaked out through the entrance, which was much higher than the lowest point in the floor. Gordon built the fire as large as he could and went out for more branches, piling them just inside the door to dry. The heat became so intense he was able to strip and add his travelling clothes to the ones already adorning the sloping walls.

Naked, warm and dry, Gordon used his knife to cut his fingernails and toenails. He saved the trimmings and put them in a depression in the rock. After he'd rested up, he intended to scatter these tiny pieces of himself outside as an offering to the land. The maker of the cave had scraped several similar receptacles in the inner walls and Gordon was happy to make use of them. By the light of the fire, which was the cheeriest light he'd seen in some time, he inspected as much of his body as he could.

His palms and fingers were callused and there were a few blisters and cracks in the skin. None of them looked serious. His feet, which had blistered so badly at first, had also hardened over, leathery pads of flesh now protecting his heels and soles from the insides of his boots. There were cuts and scrapes on his shins and knees where he had walked through areas of bramble or caught himself on sharp rocks, but he could see no lasting damage. His belly was flat and there was no spare flesh on him anywhere. He pinched the skin of his stomach and pulled. It was tight, only muscle beneath. His groin had sprouted a mass of dark, brittle curls over the last couple of weeks, and there was no question that his penis and testicles had grown. The cut in his thigh had healed into a shiny pink scar, the one across his palm was still livid and tender. His hair was around his collar now, longer than it had ever been. He knew it smelled but there was little he could do about it. His feet and underarms reeked too, but he had become as used to that as he had to squatting in the bushes to shit and wiping his arse with bunches of leaves or moss.

He was growing. Merging with the land.

62

Megan's lap is the playground of spiders now, many of them as big as her hands. The gauze that traps her against the tree is their web, drawn from a thousand spinnerets, woven and tightened by eight thousand legs. In the night, their tiny eyes reflect white-orange and she knows that every eye is watching her. Snakes have coiled themselves around her limbs and body, nosing their way between the silken fibres, knotting themselves against her. Their heads rest against her in a dozen places, their blind eyes regarding her, their dark forked tongues tasting her terror. Megan stops struggling and sits very still.

"Wise, wise," says Black Jack, his voice the roar of articulate fire.

In the scorching light that pours from the many wounds in the tree, Black Jack shines like polished onyx. This is not the figure she saw in Covey Wood. This thing before her is a mass of evil intent, of spite and unholy mockery. His deranged face has not stopped grinning. He is more animal than man. His breathing is like the breath of the giant bellows in the blacksmith's workshop; he pants and heaves as he paces back and forth. His black feathers flash like blades, his breast feathers ripple and shimmer in anthracitic glory with every breath. The tall, flat-topped hat she remembers from their first encounter is split and broken. Feathers burst up through its torn fabric. He has the bloodthirsty black eyes of the raven. Where his boots were, he now walks on scaly, thin bird feet, the claws of which curve down into the soil of the clearing, tearing it up with every step he takes. All his other clothes are gone. What had seemed to her to be a cloak the first time she saw him is now his folded wings. He still has his human arms, though they are covered with feathers, and his hands are invisible inside cuffs of black down.

His face moves and ripples like the surface of a lake on a summer's midnight, and she sees there many faces: a pale boy with dark hair, a thin adolescent with hunted eyes, a man with the sorrows of the world on his back, the same man's face twisted in wrath and rage, the same man's face white in death. She sees the faces of Mr Keeper and Carrick Rowntree. She sees Bodbran and her hooded helpers. Her amu and apa. The fortune-teller from the market. The stallholder who cooked them the barley bowl. Between each shift of visage return the inscrutable, untrustworthy eyes of the raven, a downturned blade of silky beak, feathery lashes, the wild lust of the corvid for the flesh of the dead. Through all of this Black Jack, the one she believed right up until this very moment to be the Crowman, unleashes his raucous caws into the night like a demented spirit, insane in the loneliness of the forest.

He stops pacing, the mad restlessness departing him

like vapour.

"What are you doing out here, Megan?"

She says nothing. She won't. Until he hurts her, of course, which she knows he will do the moment he doesn't get what he wants. She can't fight a force like this, but she can hold out a little longer if she tries.

The light from within the tree pulses in a slow rhythm, dimming and brightening the creature in front of her. Its face continues to shift form in the changing glow. Or is that her imagination? Perhaps it is only one face she sees there, and the shadows and flickers of light from the tree are playing tricks on her.

"Suddenly you're unwilling to talk to me." His voice has dropped from a roar to a whisper. "How strange." He approaches a few paces. His feathers are so real, gleam so blackly bright in the darkness she has to turn her eyes away. "You used to tell me everything, Megan. And now you can't even look at me."

In spite of the dozens of threads attached to her lashes, she manages to draw her eyes shut. He moves closer. She would turn away if she could but the spiders have pinned her head fast. His face, stinking of rotten meat, comes nearer.

"You know, in some parts of the world, to walk the Black Feathered Path you must surrender your eyes first. Seems a little extreme to me but what do I know? I mean, apart from knowing everything, obviously." His voice is the caw of a crow, jeering and dismissive.

She senses his beak very near her eyes and squeezes them tighter, knowing if he wants them he will merely peck them out.

"They say if you don't seek the Crowman with a

true heart you'll go blind inside, and then you'll never find him."

Megan, her face screwed up tight, weeps. Her bladder releases and then the whimpers escape her mouth. The whimpers become sobs.

"Why are you doing this to me? Why can't you just leave me alone?"

"We both have our obligations, Megan." He withdraws, taking his beak out of her face, but she can hear the smile in his comment. "Your destiny and mine are bound together. We are in each other's bodies, we share the same blood."

"I'm nothing like you," she screams in sudden fury.

He stands a few paces away now, by the sound of it.

"We are the same."

Why is his voice such a gentle whisper now?

"Look," he says.

She can't.

"Open your eyes, Megan. If you have any courage left, you must try to see what is really in front of you."

She allows her eyes to open just a fraction. She sees nothing at first, her vision blurry with tears. She blinks the brine away – something is wrong with Black Jack. He is shrinking, lightening in colour. There is something vast behind him. Megan strains to see now. She recognises this scene. Her focus sharpens. There, just a few steps from her, is a vast tree. In front of it are the white ashes of a dead fire. At the base of the tree is a girl tangled in a poncho and the toppled remains of a shelter. The girl is wrapped in the shelter's thin covering and cannot move. She struggles in her sleep, facing an army of terrors in her own personal night country.

There are no webs holding her against the trunk of

the tree. There are no colonies of spiders creeping over her body. No snakes have coiled around her. Nor does the tree appear harmed or burned. There is no sign of Black Jack, but in a branch not far above the dream-trapped girl sits a raven. Megan could swear the raven is smiling.

She blinks.

On opening her eyes she finds the thin light of morning whitening an insubstantial mist. There is no tree opposite her. Nor is Black Jack there to torment her. She lies amid the collapsed remains of her badly built shelter. Her body is not restrained, other than by a tangle of material.

Above her there is a flurry of wings as a bird leaves the branches just over her head. The raven bursts from the leafless tree and glides out into the fine mist that fills the clearing.

Rarrrk! RRRaaarkk!

His call is laughter.

63

The far end of the tiny canyon proved to be rich with rabbits.

Gordon set his snares daily and daily caught one or more. He roasted them over the fire, drying and saving their pelts. The rain never stopped, but he was never wet for much longer than it took him to hunt or use the latrine he'd dug. Many of his clothes smelled so bad that he took them outside and washed them as best he could in the rain before drying them once more on the walls of the cave. He also used the rain to shower several times a day, and for the first time in weeks he managed to get rid of much of his own stink. He boiled the rainwater and drank it every day.

The luxury of a dry, warm environment with food and water to spare was at odds with the reflective nature of the cave itself. Outside, travelling, he was free and there was a wide sky above him. His problems, though they were weighty and never left him completely alone, did seem to flee occasionally into the beyond of all that space above him. In the cave, every thought he had came back to him multiplied. To counteract this, to release the pressure, he spent much of the

time making entries in his black book, trying to clear
his mind.

November '14
My eyes only

*The rain hasn't stopped for days. I keep thinking this ravine
will fill up and I'll have to swim out, but the water doesn't
seem to collect because of the sandstone.*

*The cave was made by someone who wanted to hide in
these bluffs hundreds of years ago. Maybe a gang of outlaws.
If you didn't know this place existed, you wouldn't find it by
looking. I feel like I was led here.*

*I keep seeing the bad things I've done over and over. And
at night I don't know where I am sometimes. I can't tell if
I'm awake or dreaming. I see the men I've fought – Skelton
and Pike, the raiders who killed Brooke. Most often I see
Grimwold. In my dreams, they all laugh as though they
couldn't be happier. As though the world is a carefree place
and nothing I did to them or they did to me ever happened.*

*Then I wake up and remember how I sliced Skelton's eye
and knifed Pike in the crotch. I remember how I stabbed the
raider in the gut and the look of disbelief on his face. I
remember what Grimwold did, what he would have done if
I hadn't stopped him, and I remember how good it felt to
punish him. But the next time I fall asleep they'll be after
me. All of them. They hunt me across the moors or the hills,
across rivers and through valleys, and there's nowhere I can
go to shake them off. Whenever any of them catch up with
me, and they always do in the end, they ask me why I hurt
them, why I killed them. They ask me to explain. It's only
when I try to explain and find I can't that they get angry.
Whenever that happens, I usually wake up. And then the*

walls of the cave are all around me and their questions stay with me but I still can't answer them.

All I've done is make things worse for the people I meet and worse for my family. Why am I wasting my time searching for the Crowman? Most of the time all I can do is hide. I'm scared to talk to anyone for fear they'll ask too many questions. When I see a village or a town, I go around it. I'll never find him like this.

Somehow, I believe that the land is leading me with signs. It's like reading a language in the shape of the world and the movement of the clouds and the patterns made by flocks of birds or the way they sing in the mornings. I act on all these things, but it feels mad every time. When I question why I've chosen a particular direction or route, the answers worry me. The wind was carrying me that way or the trees in that wood are calling to me or the wren told me to go this way; that's madness, isn't it? What worries me even more is my answer. No, of course it isn't madness. If you don't hear the voice of the land, you're not alive. I can't even be sure it's me answering the question.

The cave makes all that stuff worse, but I know without it I'd probably be too sick to travel or even dead by now. Something must have led me here. Something reliable must be guiding me.

I woke up with all these questions whirling in my mind last night. The fire was down to ash and outside there was the rush and patter of the rain. For just a moment my mind shut up and was totally silent and clear. As clear as anything, from inside and all around me came a voice that said:

"Everything you need will come to hand in the very moment of its requirement."

I know I've heard that before.

Doesn't finding this cave just when I did prove it to be true?

I don't understand what's going on, but I know I have to try and trust what's happening.

64

There is nothing to be done but move on. Packing up takes moments. Megan lets her hand linger on the bark of the tree for a long time before she walks away. The pulse of the tree imparts a kind of strength to her, she thinks, though perhaps she merely regrets having to leave its company.

She sets off in the direction of the opposite side of the clearing. The mist is insubstantial but for several minutes, once she loses sight of the tree, she is surrounded by a nothingness of grey-white. All she can see is the scrubby grassland for several paces in any direction. Above is uniform white. Every point of the compass blurs into indistinct haze. She focusses on a point in the distance where the other side of the clearing will be, in a direct line from where she entered the clearing the day before, but walking a straight line is trickier than she thought.

She stops. Listens into the mist.

The world is silent and still all around her. Not a bird-call or a breath of wind to agitate the branches of the distant trees. She looks behind, trying to penetrate the mist. For long moments she stays this way, not moving.

There is no movement and no sound.

When nothing gives itself away, she moves on, making for the forest as swiftly as she can. The mist begins to break up, and by the time she reaches the embrace of the trees, the clearing behind her is devoid of the merest rag of vapour. She can see the tree in the centre and all the way across to the other side.

There's nothing out there.

The forest yields a few berries and not much more. Megan's stomach growls, but her pace is strong and determined and she moves easily through the woodland terrain, as though in some way it is allowing her passage. It's a bright, cloudless day, and the sun penetrates the canopy through a million tiny breaches. Needles of light illuminate small areas of forest floor, bark, moss, branch, thicket and lichen, painting these tiny patches in bright greens and browns. Megan is amazed at how this small touch of colour is enough to raise her spirits.

But for her footsteps the forest is silent. She turns to look behind less often the farther she goes; there's never anything there, although she catches sight of two wrens on one occasion. To her right the river has returned from the meander which took its course to the far edge of the clearing, but it too flows in silence. The scent of leaf mould and hidden fungi fills her sinuses.

Before the morning is over the forest is thinning, the trees becoming smaller and sparser at its edge. Many of the trees are stunted and unnaturally bent, warped and shrivelled not by age but by disease. She takes out the map for the first time that day. She has reached the area before the map goes blank. Somewhere up ahead is the uncharted place she must enter to find what Bodbran has sent her for. She is more excited now than frightened. Warmth and light radiate all around her, and what could harm her in such golden light, under the watchful eye of the benevolent sun?

The trees shrink to the size of small shrubs, gnarled and twisted, spines broken, limbs bending back on each other. Between them the ground has turned to grey dust. It kicks up around her feet as she walks, finer than sand.

There's nothing out here.

To her right the river has dropped away out of sight. Beyond it runs a ridge, the same ridge she and Mr Kee–

Megan stops dead still, a small storm of dust rolling on ahead of her feet before settling. She is on a plateau which has shielded her from seeing what lies ahead, but she has an idea of how far she has walked and she knows what she and Mr Keeper saw from the ridge. Putting the shape of the land together in her mind, she knows it's more than possible that Bodbran has sent her to a place she hoped only ever to observe from a distance.

No.

I don't know maps. I must be wrong.

She doesn't move. She can't.

Far away, Gordon heard rumbling. He sat up and reached for his knife.

Could the Ward have tracked him down to this place? He listened. The rumble's tone was constant, no strains or gear changes. Not four-wheel drives, then.

The sound had enough power behind it to suggest a squadron of aircraft. Perhaps the wars he'd dreamed of had started and these were the bombers. He moved to the cave entrance but the rumbling didn't seem to come from above. That made it unlikely to be thunder, even though there'd been enough storms to warrant it. He glanced out. The sky was uniformly grey and drab, no flashes of lightning anywhere.

The rumble became a vibration he could feel through his legs and buttocks. He sprang to his feet.

Please. Don't let this be what I think it is.

The rumbling increased in volume. The sound came from all around him. The juddering travelled up his legs and his kneecaps twitched. He threw his arms out for balance but it did no good. The juddering became shaking. The noise in his head was like thunder now, except that it wouldn't stop – one mighty, continuous clap. Unable to keep his footing, he fell against the curve of the cave wall, arms still outstretched, fingers clutching the stone.

The ground bucked beneath him, bumping him into the air as though he was rebounding from a trampoline. The embers of the fire began to scatter. Tumbling coals of burning wood spread out in all directions. Surprised by a sudden kick of movement from the left, Gordon fell onto his face and slid towards the scorching ashes. It was more through luck than skill that Gordon managed to regain his footing.

Before the fire could spread too far across the cave he crouched and hoisted a double handful of coals out of the cave mouth. They hissed in the rain before they even hit the ground and Gordon held his hands in the downpour for a moment to douse the heat. Frantic now, he chased the scattering fire, picking up burning branches and glowing orange embers and tossing them out before they could scald him. A coal lodged between the little and index finger of his left hand long enough to raise smoke from his skin. There wasn't time to lament the pain. As though bailing water from a sinking boat, Gordon emptied the cave of fire. When it was done, he held his hands into the rain for a few moments but falling debris forced him back inside. Rocks were falling into the ravine.

The shaking caused Gordon and all his equipment to slide into a pile at the centre of the cave. All he could do was lie with his arms outstretched, praying the cave wouldn't collapse. Stronger quakes, accompanied by deafening booms from deep below the earth, sent him and everything else in the cave three and sometimes four feet off the ground. His ribs, knees and elbows all took punishment but the knocks to his head were the worst. Twice he came down on his chin, rattling his teeth and knocking himself half stupid. Another tremor flipped him over and rapped his ear against the cave floor.

Roaring and shaking, the land entered a frenzy of rage. It sounded as though the planet was tearing itself apart from inside. Gordon prayed to everything he considered holy; all the elements and the creator spirit that formed them, all the creatures and the land they lived upon:

Don't do this. Give us a chance to prove...

To prove what?

...to prove we care. That we're still listening. To show you we're worthy of your abundance.

The hammering upwards of the ground lessened. The

massive upthrusts that had thrown him into the air ceased. Now there was just rumbling and shaking, more like a shiver than a convulsion. The sound of underground explosions diminished. There was a sense of settling as the ground fell back into place. Tremors became vibrations, anger subsided like the sound of an engine receding into the distance.

Cease.

Silence. The worst silence.

For all Gordon knew the world outside was dead. Every animal, every person gone. The mountains shattered to rubble and the rivers scattered like droplets. Or perhaps the world had broken apart and he now floated through space on a discarded fragment.

After a few moments he noticed a sound all around him. A whine. It was his own eardrums whistling as they recovered from the auditory assault.

His cave had held. There were no cracks in its walls and none of the falling debris had come through the entrance. Once again he had been saved simply by the luck of being in the right place at the right time. But of course, he now knew, that there was no luck in that. Something was guiding him. Something was protecting him.

And something had answered his prayer – almost instantly. Surely this was proof that he was on the road to the Crowman.

Exhausted and bruised. Gordon lay amid the tangle of his belongings. And, though the world all around him was silent and still, his whole body vibrated like live cable.

65

Megan walks down the gentle, rocky slope from the highest point of the plateau, and the city sprawls grey, shattered and scorched before her. The strange line on the map, the only feature crossing the uncharted area, is formed by the giant skeletal structures she saw on the way from Beckby village to Shep Afon.

Nothing grows in the city. Nothing grows around it. Megan approaches across a dusty expanse of what she knows is dead land. Here, even the bright sun can do nothing to raise colour from the drab destruction. Some yards from the first broken structure she halts.

She could still turn back or merely try to escape across the river. She could climb the ridge on the other side and either wait for Mr Keeper or go back to Shep Afon's hub to find him. Or she could just journey home to the warmth of Amu's kitchen and the strong arms of her father. They would protect her. She could forget all this nonsense about the Crowman and walking the Black Feathered Path. She could go back and get on with being what she was before. A village girl who knew nothing about the world except what she'd learned in an ordinary school. No magic, no visions, no weaving of night and day, past and present. No more writing in the book. She would swim in the river and take long walks and…

I can never do any of that again. I've changed, and I can't undo any of this.

But it isn't that which makes her body move forwards into the city. It's the fact that she really wants to know everything there is to know. She wants the full story. She wants to know what happens to the boy. She knows it is important, not just for her but for everyone, that she discovers the rest of his history and record it in the book. It is not the fear that drives her forwards, it is the knowledge that there are two ways of doing things, the right way and the wrong way. One way she can be proud of even if she fails, the other will be a source of shame forever. Yet even that isn't the final reason.

The final reason is that she knows this is what she was born to do.

Everything had changed and Gordon supposed it might be changed forever.

Outside his cave the once-rocky ground was covered by a layer of mud, the fallen soil from above the ravine now a quagmire. Already the water was draining down through this mud, down into the sandstone of the ravine's floor. With the calming of the tremors had come the end of the rain, at least for a while. A soft blackish crust covered the earth.

Gordon stood naked in the cave mouth, a hand on each side. Fear and excitement churned his guts. Outside was a new world, changed by the wrath of the Earth Mother and the sadness of the Great Spirit. He knew both these forces existed because he saw them in everything around him, and always had. It was only now that he could accept the words to name them, knowing those words were correct.

His ears whined – sirens and static. The sound of dead technology, a television with no signal, a radio transmitting nothing but hiss. It was the echo of the explosion that began the universe or the sound which preceded it, the first breath of life or the whisper of command which conjured all from nought. Power hummed in the union between Gordon's palms and the lip of the cave. The air outside sang with potential and destruction. His head ached with the noise, his guts fluttered, his penis thumped to the pulse of his heart, the skin of it so stretched and tight he thought it might split.

He stepped up and out of the cave, his feet sinking into the velvet mud. It forced its way up between his toes. The pull of the earth was so strong he fell to his hands and knees. The world spun and he vomited in one single spasm. His stomach tightened like a mollusc under threat until it felt like a walnut. The contraction lasted for several seconds, during which he couldn't breathe. First came food, entirely undigested lumps of rabbit. Then watery mucus and finally bright green, tangy bile. Finally the contraction ended and he drew breath like a fish released from a fisherman's net.

A second cramp came, this time in his bowel. Every inch of his gut contracted to the fineness of wire. More shit than he believed himself able to contain spewed from his rear and this time he was able to scream as it left him, again in a single, agonising clench.

When it was over he crawled away from the mess,

his hands and knees carving troughs in the mud until
he reached the trees where he'd snared so many rabbits. His penis still burned and beat, more the turgid
throb of a pustule than an organ of sex. His third contraction began as a stuttering twitch in his anus and
testicles, the muscles there poised between tension and
release. The quivering spread down the insides of his
thighs and up into his solar plexus. The urge to thrust
was overwhelming. His hands and knees swamped by
mud, he pumped his hips at the air. The juddering travelled along the centre of his penis in a white heat and
a final tightening passed through him.

Am I dying?

He fell on the earth, his penis sinking deep into it, the
mud welcoming it, cooling it, wrapping his belly, and
again he screamed as he ejected into the grip of the
land. His cry too was swallowed as he pressed his face
into the mud. Pain and pleasure drained from his groin
and thighs and belly, pulled downwards into the muck
of the land. He rolled onto his back and looked down
at himself. Blood and semen welled from him. Spent,
he let his head fall back. He was coated now, a smooth
pale boy made dark and heavy by the mire. Too heavy
to move.

He lay there for many hours, unable to think as the
world drew on him, sucked on him, held him fast. The
sense of drainage was terrifying. He feared the Earth
would continue to consume him long after he was
dead, taking his energy and spirit first, then his flesh
and finally his bones, hauling every part of him down
into darkness and imprisoning him there forever.

Even his thoughts descended, all the light in his existence taken down into Mother Earth's secret midnight.

Before he could recall an image of his mother and father or of Jude, it was sucked away. Even his tears were pulled back from the corners of his eyes, to be devoured by the hungry land.

The layer of mud over his body dried slowly, forming a crust which insulated him from the cold and acted like a poultice. Where his body made contact with this covering of mud, there was a drawing, a taking away. He was too exhausted to resist any of it and yet the earth did not let him sleep. Conscious but thoughtless, he lay on his back and the hours passed.

Night came down into the ravine and still he did not sleep.

A crack in the mud covering each eye was enough to let him see the sky revealed above him. The clouds were gone now and all night he watched the slow turning of the heavens, the staring of the moon, the dying of particles striking the atmosphere and being denied access. The whine of his eardrums was gone. He could not hear his heartbeat or feel his own breathing. No aeroplane lights blinked their way along flight paths. No satellites passed overhead. No animals snuffled in the undergrowth. No foxes barked into the night. Upon the Earth there was no sound. No movement anywhere.

When the first light of morning came, it too was hushed. Gordon's ability to think returned. There was a new day, that much was obvious, but the world itself was quiet. Gordon found the strength to move and when he sat up, his suit of mud cracked and crumbled from him. He stood and in doing so dislodged much of the caked soil. The rest he brushed and picked away until he was clean – but for a layer of dark dust and the soil dried into his matted hair. He stood on the mud-coated ground of the ravine, listening for signs of something – of life there were none.

He climbed back out of the ravine, following the path that had brought him into it. At the top he found the nearest and best vantage point and surveyed the land around him.

The world, at the very least, was altered.

At worst, she was dead.

66

The moment Megan steps over the city's threshold, the sun is swallowed by cloud. The warmth is snatched from the air as dark, malignant clouds spread across the once-bright heavens. Her skin contracts.

At first the ruined structures are well spaced but their sharp edges and flat walls press in on her. The dwellings she is used to are built with easy, natural lines and curves or circles. These houses, if that is what they once were, exude conformity even in ruin. Tumbled walls, collapsed roofs and blind wind-eyes do not rob the city of its order. The basic template is the square, beginning in bricks and blocks, repeated in walls and wind-eyes, echoed in the cubiform structures. The dusty, rubble-strewn ways between these shattered buildings feel like runs, like traps. They give no choice about which direction to take; they seem to lead somewhere specific.

Movement flickers at the limit of her vision. She glances to the right but sees nothing stirring in the dead wreckage where more people than she can count once lived. She thinks she hears the sharp call of a wren but there's nothing to see. Nothing but a long-deserted dwelling, its neat lines unpicked and unmade by some terrible event, grey and silent like everything else around it.

The idea that someone walks in her footsteps, close enough to grab her hair, increases with every step. She turns often to find nothing but space behind her, no second pair of footprints in dust that has been undisturbed for generations. Not wanting to go a single step farther but knowing she can't turn back, Megan walks faster to leave the feelings of pursuit behind. The deeper into the city she goes, the more flickers she sees to left and right, but even when she stops and stares, there's nothing to see but derelict, unoccupied destruction.

Darkness and gloom press down over the city from above, making the surroundings indistinct. Megan sees more shimmers of movement on either side but she hears nothing. All she can do is hurry on.

She begins to come across carriages without horses or oxen to draw them. All of them are furry and flaky with rust. Cars. Inside, their seats are skeletal: springs and frames. Some of the cars contain collapsed piles of bone. She skitters past these, panic rising from her guts to her throat.

The path broadens and the feeling of being trapped eases. But soon the remains of the buildings to either side grow in size until she is hemmed in by towering walls of devastation. As she passes a building that looks mostly untouched by the cataclysm, she hears a clatter and the snap of old timber. She staggers away from the noise. The roof of the building caves in. The walls on which the roof sat sag inwards and fall. The weight of them hitting the upper floor collapses it, and once this pattern is in motion the whole structure implodes.

Rubble spews from the lower windows and doors like dry slurry and dust billows outward. The crash is loud enough to make her cover her ears.

Megan realises she has pressed herself against another wall and she staggers away from it now. No structure in this place can be trusted to stay standing. The ghosts of the razed building, roiling clouds of brick and mortar particles exhaled like a final breath, spread out in every direction. Megan hurries away before she is engulfed in the dust. A gritty hiss accompanies the dust cloud but that hiss soon dies, and with its passing the silence of the dead city returns, louder and more threatening than before.

The womb that had shielded Gordon from rain and wind and cold had also saved him from the bucking and heaving of the furious land. He did not want to leave it. In the short space of time he had made the cave his home, he had fantasised at times about an old man who lived there, a man with a long white beard and thin white hair. The man was always warm and dry in his cave and always ate well on the bounty of the land around him. The man had forgotten everything in the world that was painful and goading. The old man was him.

As he gathered his belongings, packing them with care, he was on the point of tears and couldn't understand why. This time, however, he did not cry. It was an act of will. He shouldered his emotions the way he shouldered his backpack and the responsibility to his kin.

When he stepped out of the cave he left a single black feather at its mouth.

"Thanks for your shelter."

He left the ravine the way he had come in, rising from its protection until he was once again a tiny figure on the vast, changed high country. His minuteness and exposure made a target of him – there was no cover anywhere. In every direction the land, certainly broken and altered, possibly lifeless, was silent. Gordon feared for its green mantle, for its animals and for its people.

He descended from the plateau of hills.

Where once there had been a damp green shimmering skin to the world, now there was upturned earth, vibrated from clumps and clods down to marble-sized baubles of soil, almost perfectly round. Damp from the rain, they stuck to his boots, making every step a trudge.

The landscape below the hills was darkened by the exposure of the earth beneath the vegetation. Areas of green remained, and seeing them was enough to make Gordon's eyes water. He kept the tears in check. The damage was far worse than the preservation. Here and there, parts of hedges and trees emerged, only partially swallowed by the quake, but most features of the land had been taken all the way under leaving no demarcations, only vast tracts of exposed soil. Larger trees and areas of woodland seemed to have survived better, perhaps their networks of roots having worked together to save them from sinking. The largest trees standing alone in the landscape had also managed to avoid sinking completely, though many of these looked stunted now, as though the earth had risen like flood waters.

For a long time he didn't notice the total absence of buildings, farm outhouses and dwellings. He was on level ground, the hills far behind him before it struck him. There were no roads, only occasional parallel ridges of hedge where a road might have been. Everything had sunk, the quake so severe that its vibrations had liquefied the earth.

Clods of soil clinging to his soles, Gordon stumbled over the shaken, reordered land. The only sound was the labouring of his lungs as he fought the weight of his boots. Trying to clear them was useless; within three or four paces they were completely clogged again. As annoying as this was, it didn't tire him. It merely slowed him down. His newfound strength persisted, aiding him through all this. It gave him a sliver of hope; perhaps he belonged in this new landscape. Strong enough to survive, strong enough to navigate the aftermath, perhaps he was meant to be here. The idea kept him walking, made the idea of finding something, someone or even somewhere more believable.

67

What Gordon found that day was a crack in the world.

He didn't see it until the moment before he fell in. The soil in front of him, now featureless for miles to either side, began to rise gradually. The gradient slowed his already laboured progress. Something about the slope seemed unnatural, but so did everything around him now. The earth near the top of the slope began to fall away from him and he slid after it, seeming to defy gravity. Instinct seizing him, he dropped to the ground, turning and crawling back down the slope.

As he scrambled, he felt the earth falling away beneath his legs. He paddled at the earth to get away from the landslide but the weight of his pack pushed his hands deep into the claggy soil, slowing him. He felt his legs sucked down and away behind him, and made one final frog hop, away from the falling ground. He gained the air for barely a moment, not showing the strength he'd hoped for, landing with his face in the mud.

Around him everything had stopped. His feet hung in space, the weight of the mud on them bending his knees unpleasantly against their natural range. He pulled himself forwards through the mud, hauling his feet back onto what he hoped was solid ground, and crawled a few feet farther just to be sure. He stood carefully and turned to face the precipice.

He stood at the very edge of a rift about a hundred yards wide. On its opposite side, the world continued but in between was a black chasm he couldn't measure the depth of without putting himself back in danger. The other side of the rift was lower by a hundred feet or so. Gordon couldn't decide whether his side had been thrust upwards or the other side had sheared off and fallen down. It didn't matter much – crossing the gap was impossible.

One heartening fact was clear. The other side had not been destroyed the way his side had. He could see buildings and roads and people and even animals. The trees were particularly laden with birds. There was damage: buildings leaned or were toppled; some houses had cracked in half; roofs had collapsed; the nearest road was buckled and split, no longer passable by any kind of vehicle; unmoving people lay half covered by rubble; others walked without purpose, wailing at the destruction; some sat with their heads in their hands and rocked on their haunches in shock. Bloodied cows and sheep stood among the damage, skittering away from movement when they were approached, otherwise staring forwards in their own post-traumatic fugues. Wounded people and animals wandered everywhere, their cries mingling.

This must have been the outskirts of a town, Gordon decided. Near enough to the fields that the animals trapped by fences and hedges had broken through in their terror and made for the relative safety of the community.

There was no sign of emergency vehicles. The town extended into the distance, reminding Gordon of old footage from the blitz. Most of the buildings were ruined and grey with dust. Smoke rose in grey and black streamers from a hundred fires, creating dirty smog in the sluggish, windless air above the town.

Gordon tried to gauge how far the rift extended. He could see no end to it. To his right, though, it did appear to narrow. That was the direction he ran in.

68

She knows there's nothing more it can tell her, but Megan stops and checks the map again anyway. She sips some water and is alarmed to discover the skin is almost empty. The lack of food and constant walking have left her hungry and weak. The map shows her nothing except a rough idea of how large the city is – almost as big as the forest she has travelled through to get here.

All she can do is move on.

Her pace slows with the gradual realisation of the size of the task before her. Being in a hurry isn't going to help. The route she has taken widens again, this time joined by another route. Both flow into one and move her onwards. The broadness of the way is a small comfort but it does little to allay the sense of movement in all directions and the feeling of something behind her. Cloud smothers the sky, pressing lower, thickening the air, darkening every smashed doorway and shattered wind-eye.

The city may be long dead, but something within it lives. Something observes every step she takes. Though she can't see it, Megan knows it is there. It watches with more than curiosity. It wants something. It hungers.

Gordon stood amid the devastation in disbelief. Until now he'd only seen this kind of scene on the news, usually in countries so far away as to make no real difference to him. Now the news was real. It was here.

To all of this there was one counterpoint: the Earth was not dead. She had been sick, yes, weakened by an infestation. Now she was ridding herself of it. For those who remained alive the choice was a simple one, whether they realised it yet or not: work with the land – respect it and give back to it – or die.

He had run for at least a mile before finding an end to the rift. It narrowed to a sudden point and stopped at the base of a massive ancient oak tree. Gordon walked around the back of the tree, where the roots appeared to be holding the tear in the Earth together. Such a thing wasn't possible, but it made him feel safer. Hurrying back along the other side of the split in the land, he was able to appreciate how deep it was – the crack extended down beyond sight into blackness. Hundreds of metres at least. Even though he walked on what appeared to be safe ground, having the canyon-deep drop beside made him giddy. Fearing aftershocks, he kept well away from the edge.

It wasn't long before he walked among the wounded and the stunned and the dead. No one had escaped the dust thrown up by the quake. Every face was palled grey. Wet eyes stared from gritty faces, the runnels of tears in livid pink or slick brown below them. Gordon, his clothes darkened by mud, was a brown stranger in a country of ash-people.

Uncertain what to do, he walked in the direction he hoped the centre of the town might lie. The survivors walked in a daze, not sure they were still alive, perhaps not believing the fury of the destruction they'd survived. Since he'd first glimpsed the ruined town, some of the people had begun to band together for comfort or to move debris in their search for friends and family lost beneath the rubble.

The chattering of a magpie snapped his attention to the right. As he watched, the bird hopped up and flew away between two wrecked buildings. Near where it had perched, on a spike of reinforcing steel, sat a woman cradling a child. The woman was rocking but the child was limp in her arms. Seeing Gordon, she became alert and curious and the desperation in her eyes reached out. He knew he didn't look like everyone else. With his pack and his boots, he might have been some kind of rescue worker, albeit a young one. She addressed him from her place in the rubble, thirty feet away:

"She was sleeping when it happened and now I can't wake her up. I think she's just scared."

The woman's smile appeared to say: Everything's normal. Everything's fine. Just this slight problem with my little girl. How embarrassing.

Gordon walked towards them.

"Can you help her? Can you wake her up?"

Gordon didn't answer. What could he say? He was fairly sure what kind of sleep the girl had fallen into – the longest, most dreamless of all.

He knelt beside the woman and looked more closely at the girl. She was probably a redhead under all the dust, maybe six years old. Despite the layer of grime, she was still beautiful. The woman placed the girl in Gordon's arms before he could protest. The weight of the child surprised him.

The woman took his face in her hands and stared into his eyes.

"Please. Wake her up."

She was insane with hope. Gordon closed his eyes for a moment.

Why didn't I just keep walking?

But no. Walking by was all he'd ever done, all he'd ever been able to do. Now he had to do more. He had to try. He had to become involved in the world instead of running from its pain. He put his face beside the girl's. No breath came from her nostrils. He laid his ear against her tiny chest and listened.

All around him he heard the sobs of the bereaved and the cries of the wounded. He heard the shouts of the survivors trying to disinter those still trapped beneath jagged layers of destruction. He heard the distant cawing of crows.

But he heard no heartbeat.

As he'd known from the moment he saw the pair, the girl was dead. He opened his eyes and the woman was smiling at him, smiling and nodding. It was magic she wanted and she was waiting for him to bring it. He broke the eye contact by looking down at the girl again. How could he tell this woman her child was dead?

A single black-winged thing streaked across Gordon's periphery and landed on a cracked, leaning brick wall. He didn't have to look to recognise its form. It gathered itself up and let rip a throaty call.

Where the dead lie come the carrion-eaters.

Across the ruins, on their highest prominences,

crows began to land, wheeling in and dropping from every direction. Against the drab of urban destruction they were clean and sleek.

He shouted at them in his mind: *You mustn't be here now.*

And the crows replied, *We came because of you, Gordon. Your need calls to us and so we answer.*

Gordon shook his head at the ruins, making the woman's smile falter. *You can't let the people see you. They won't understand.*

There seemed to be a smile on every beak: *Those who don't understand will die.*

The woman looked at Gordon, her expression changing – not expectation any more but that other thing, that far more dangerous thing: a question. And if she questioned, Gordon knew beyond any doubt he'd be the one she blamed for the death of this little girl.

It wasn't that fear which moved him to act, though, it was the knowledge that there was no longer anything to be gained through fear or inaction. From now on there was only the pursuit of possibility and the belief that something far greater than Gordon, something wise and benevolent, was marking his path for him. In surrendering to that, he might find strength beyond any he'd yet known. There would be hope too, a real and distinct hope for the future for those who, as the crows would have it, "understood".

Silently, he addressed them again: *Help me, then. Help this woman and this little girl.*

Gordon's fingertips began to itch. He placed the girl on the smashed ground and looked at the palms of his hands. Something was gathering there. At first it was only the very ends of each finger that showed a change. Tiny beads the size of pin-pricks welled and sparkled between the whorls of his finger pads – the dust of black diamonds. He rubbed the fingers and thumb of his right hand against each other. The particles did not come off. Instead they shone, glimmers that might have been his imagination becoming solid points of dark luminescence. And then he realised that the beads growing not only in his fingers but in his palms too were not beads at all but openings in his flesh. Something was bursting through.

He held his hands out to the crows, crushing his eyes shut against it all, and his part in all of it – the devastation, the death – he knew there was so much more of it to come.

Silently he offered his hands. Silently he screamed at them: *What is this? What's happening to me?*

What you hold in your hands is the Black Light, Gordon. The beginning and the end of everything.

He opened his eyes. The crows were agitated now, hopping and flapping, changing places atop the fresh ruins, cawing, showing their sharp tongues. The woman watched him, any question she may have had devoured by a new fervour. The way he knelt there, palms outstretched, eyes clenched shut until now – she knew what this was. This was a moment of faith, of the creator moving through his representative on Earth, the precursor to a miracle.

Elsewhere, distracted by the commotion of the crows, survivors were glancing their way. Those not engaged in the search for the buried drifted towards the woman, Gordon and the little girl.

But what am I supposed to do?

You know what to do.

The Black Light burned upwards from his hands, a transmission from the boundaries of the universe and from its very heart. A hiss accompanied the dark emanation: the echo of the beginning of everything, the oldest sound in the universe. Perhaps it was this noise which stopped the survivors, prevented them from coming any closer. His hands bled raw shadows into the smoky air. Did the others see it? He couldn't tell. All he knew was that if he didn't find somewhere for the Black Light to go, it would destroy him.

69

When Gordon placed his hands on her dusty head, the little red-headed girl, limp with crush-wounds, went rigid. The woman and the small crowd recoiled. Whatever had used his hands as conduits was gone in the same instant. On the ground, the little girl coughed and a puff of dust escaped her lips. Then she retched, her lungs and throat clogged with concrete and brick particles. The woman's hands went to her mouth. Her head cocked to one side as though she now saw the little girl for the first time. Her face creased into a tight mask of weeping and shock. She didn't seem to quite believe what had happened – in much the way she couldn't believe the girl had been dead in the first place. Before she could recover herself, Gordon took water from his pack and offered it to the girl, who sipped and spat the gritty muck from her mouth before sipping and swallowing the rest.

Gordon stood up. Instinct told him he needed to move away fast. The crows rose up as one, hundreds of them calling and flapping, blurring the air. He felt the downdraught from their wings and it pushed him away from the woman and the little girl. He turned and walked through the small clot of onlookers. They parted for him to pass. Some of them watched the woman who now held the little girl so tightly in her arms, the woman who now wept tears of joy and didn't care how or why the little girl had been returned to her, only that she had been restored. Others watched the murder of crows, rising in apparent chaos, their knowing caws a kind of tribute, a kind of celebration.

Gordon was already making progress towards what he hoped was the centre of the town. All along his path were strewn the sleek black feathers of crows – dropped in recognition? Dropped in respect? He didn't know. Every few paces he knelt to gather a few up – soon there were more than he'd ever collected before. He filled his pockets with them.

Somewhere behind, the woman had regained herself enough to stand up and shout, "Thank you... Oh, thank you..." between each fresh spasm of tears.

"You're welcome," he whispered.

Though he was already far away, he still heard her voice when it dropped in volume and she said, in embarrassed tones, to those who stood around her: "I don't even know his name."

What Gordon had done was beginning to sink into the minds of the already traumatised survivors.

"If he helped her, he can help us," one of them said.

They spilled away from the site of the miracle and saw Gordon making good speed along the avenue formed by partially razed houses and shops. One of the men ran after him.

"Hey! Wait!"

Gordon looked back at the small crowd in the street. He broke into a trot.

Someone else shouted: "Come back! Please!"

Gordon looked to the sky for guidance but the crows, wheeling above in such vast numbers only moments before, were gone. The sky was grey with cloud and the smoke pennants raised over a thousand ruins. Behind him, some of the people were running to catch up with him. Most of them were desperate but some of them were angry. His trot became a sprint, dodging cracks in the road and leaping piles of debris.

The trail of feathers disappeared.

Ahead, Megan sees several of the largest buildings the city boasts towering up into the sky – wrists with the hands torn away. Among them other structures large enough to hold most of Beckby village within them have been reduced to jagged, spilled walls and jutting, rusted bones. Between these structures, the wide open spaces beckon to Megan. The farther she can be from the buildings, the better.

The ground underfoot softens. She kneels to touch the earth. Beneath the debris and dust, there is soil. Glancing around she sees stumps, some in rows, some scattered. There were trees here once. And grassland. All dead now. Dead forever. The land here is so damaged, she can sense no life in it at all. It may never regenerate. Yet, to know she has found something beneath all the destruction, something that once lived, is such a comfort that she is finally able to weep much of the fear and tension away.

When she is done, she brushes the dust from her fingers and stands, calmer now. Her eyes are drawn to something at the centre of the broad space, something circular. She approaches the structure cautiously. It is a low wall, about knee-high and, unlike everything else, it appears undamaged. At the centre of the circle is a large block. What once stood upon it, an effigy of some kind, lies smashed within the perimeter of the low wall. She places one foot over the wall, testing the ground on the other side with a gentle prod of her boot. It seems safe enough.

She steps over.

She's so used to it now, Megan almost ignores the movement that once again shudders in the periphery of her vision. When she does take a moment to glance, indistinct shapes are moving towards her from every direction. Grey figures swirling like the dust of the smashed and blasted buildings. They have form, though, these shapes. A form she recognises despite the strangeness of their appearance. They are people. Thousands upon thousands of people.

They make no sound.

70

The mud on Gordon's clothes and boots dried and fell away. With every step he kicked up dust. In many areas of the town, the powder of destruction still hung in the air like mist. He was soon coated with enough of it that people didn't notice him anymore. Those who'd chased him, too exhausted to keep up, had fallen behind and given up. Once again, uncommon strength had come to him from somewhere. Even with his backpack he was faster.

When he'd shaken off his pursuers, he kept away from the main road. It was more difficult and certainly more dangerous tacking back and forth through the side streets towards the town centre, but he felt safer, nonetheless.

There were many dead in the streets and each one he came across shocked him. Many had been dealt their final blow by falling stone, timber or brick, some of them crushed or suffocated by the weight of collapsing buildings.

The Black Light still freeze-burned his fingertips, rising there whenever he passed wounded or unconscious survivors. He tried to ignore it but the more suffering he witnessed, the brighter shone the darkness from his hands.

In one street his path was blocked by two houses collapsed towards each other and now united in ruin. In front of one house, eyes bright with pain and disorientation, a man sat with a concrete lintel in his lap. The man's feet lay pointing away from each other at 9 and 3 o'clock. He saw Gordon and shrugged, looking sheepish.

He nodded to his lap.

"Stuck," he said.

Gordon looked around like a kid about to steal a bicycle. There was no movement, but muffled pleas for help came from many of the buildings. It was easier to ignore them when walking, not so easy standing still. His hands thrummed. He wanted to run. The man on the ground smiled up at him, either delirious or particularly lucid.

"It's ironic when you think about. I'd been meaning to fit new upstairs windows and replace all the concrete lintels with steel. Now the whole house has fallen down and the only thing not broken is the bloody lintels." The man laughed a strange, alien laugh and winced. "Still, at least I didn't fit the new windows. I'd have had to refit them when I rebuilt the house."

Gordon smiled in spite of himself.

He wondered if the man knew his injuries were fatal. No help was coming and the only thing this man would build any time soon was a colony of worms. He knelt at the man's side and took a closer look at the damage. The lintel had hit him just below his hips. Both of his legs had been crushed like straws at the moment of impact. The heavy length of concrete had pinched the

flesh of the man's thighs almost to the point of sever-
ance.

"I need to move this off your legs," said Gordon.

The smile was weak this time. "I do wish you
wouldn't. I'm quite comfortable as I am."

"I'm going to help you."

"That's really not necessary."

"You'll die if I don't."

"Oh, I know," said the man. "I know that. It's fine,
really."

"No. It's not fine."

Obsidian flames leapt from his fingers. The man
didn't seem to notice and for that Gordon was thankful.
He reached under the near end of the concrete lintel.

"I'd much rather you didn't disturb the status quo,
young man."

Gordon locked eyes with the man.

"It's going to be all right. Honestly. I just need you to
promise me one thing first."

Overhead, crows circled and Gordon wished them
away.

The man look amused.

"Me promise you something?"

"Never tell anyone."

"What do you mean?"

"Just don't tell anyone you saw me. Never tell anyone what I did. That's all I ask."

The man, fully engaged in considering the ridiculous
request, screamed in pain and surprise when Gordon
freed his legs from the lintel. It came away bloody and
the moment he lifted it blood pulsed in generous
washes from the trough it had created in the man's
flesh. Below the dust on his face, the man drained pale.

Gordon tossed the lintel away as though it were no more than a heavy branch. The Black Light arced between his palms. His entire body shuddered with the build-up. The man stared at his lap where the speed of leakage signalled his end. His voice was a whisper.

"I can't really see what's that's achieved, young man."

Gordon dropped back to his knees and, to the sound of distant cawing, he grabbed the man's thighs just below the crush point. The man's body stiffened, white suddenly showing all around his irises. Behind his pupils, dark fire burned. The depression in both thighs inflated and his feet turned upwards. His legs shortened slightly, pulling off the heels of his shoes. The torn, blood-wet fabric of his trousers remained, as did the stains of his leaked blood on the dusty ground. But his smashed legs were whole again.

The man looked at Gordon, who now stood, spent and relieved by the discharge of power, studying his palms.

"That was... unexpected," he said.

Experimentally, he moved one foot then the other. He bent both legs towards his chest and put his shoes back on properly.

"This isn't possible. I'm... speechless."

Gordon recovered himself. It was time to move on.

"Stay that way," he said to the man.

"I don't know how to thank you. I mean that literally."

"Just keep your promise."

Gordon turned and moved away through the rubble.

"Who are you?" the man called after him.

Gordon kept moving. He heard the man clambering

over the debris behind him.

"I'm no one," he said. "Please. Don't come after me."

After that the man was silent and made no move to follow.

For the rest of that day, the Black Light rose in his hands like sparkling shadows. Whenever he thought he was unobserved he helped those he could, asking nothing in return but their silence before moving on. Night fell and he knew he could not stay in the town. People were talking about him, looking for him despite their promises.

He left the ruins behind him and walked into the darkness, knowing his only safety lay in putting as much distance between himself and the town as he could.

71

Megan looks around for somewhere to run to but the vast ring of eddying, insubstantial figures is unbroken.

She backs towards the stone block at the centre of the low-walled circle. The throng closes the noose around her swiftly, seeming to drift over the ground. As they approach she notices the strange way they are dressed: more variety than she could ever have imagined. She'd thought Shep Afon was crowded, she'd thought its inhabitants diverse, but the swirling dust-storm of wraiths around her, despite their lack of colour, are greater and more multifarious by far.

Her knapsack touches the stone pedestal and she is trapped. Glancing behind, she sees there's a way up if she can use the many cornices as footholds. She turns her back to the throng and scrambles off the ground. Once atop the block she has an elevated view to all sides. The multitude still arrives from all directions, pouring out of every building and along every pathway. She can't see the far perimeter of the crowd. There is no last row, no stragglers thinning out towards the back. They come from everywhere and they go on for-ever. Those at the front are now constricting the aperture around her as they near Megan's miniature fortification. She removes her knapsack and empties it onto the surface of the plinth. The crowd reaches the low wall and stops.

Megan snatches up the knife and takes the handle with shaking fingers. The lake of grey figures observes her in silence. Now they are this close and no longer moving, she is able to study them. They are forlorn. Every face carries the same expression of sadness and loss, but they are expectant too. They have been waiting for a long time and now someone has come. Sensing no threat from them, Megan puts the knife back into the knapsack, hoping none of them have seen.

As one, the crowd reaches out its hands, every person imploring her for something with their upturned palms. Their faces plead. Megan doesn't know what to do. After a few moments, every expression breaks into silent weeping and the arms are withdrawn to cover their faces. The people rock back and forth with grief.

"I'm so sorry," she says. "I don't know what you want."

Every figure in the crowd falls to its knees. The rocking gets worse. Megan is thankful she cannot hear them – the sound of their wailing would be more than anyone could stand. The only other thing in her knapsack that has any significance now calls to her. She removes the black feather from its leather sheath and rotates it by its quill to inspect it. Even as she touches it the crowd becomes still. She looks out across their hopeful faces. She holds up the feather.

"Is this what you want? You can have it. I'll leave it right here."

The crowd becomes agitated again. Those in the front ranks point down into the circle Megan occupies the centre of.

"You want me to put it down there?"

The pointing becomes frantic and finally Megan leans over the edge of her pedestal and looks down. She sees the broken statue and she sees her footprints. There's nothing else to see. She watches the pointing fingers more carefully. They are gesturing towards a particular area within the squat-walled enclosure. Megan scans the dust at the place where every finger would touch if only the people could enter the circle. Though the day is so gloomy it could be dusk and though the light is as grey as the dust it falls on, Megan sees something. A lump in the grit and grime, not far from one of her own footprints. The rest of the dust around it is uniform and level. It might be her imagination, but something seems to glint through the dirt. The crowd knows she's seen something now and they retreat a little, their hands over their mouths in expectation and anxiety.

Megan looks at the people who make up the crowd. If they'd wanted to harm her, they would have by now. Also, it appears they are unable to come any closer than the ridiculously tiny wall around her, a wall so low a rabbit could leap over it. She puts her feet over the edge of the plinth and slides down into the small sunken amphitheatre the wall defines. She kneels beside the bump in the grime. Something does shine there. The hush of the crowd, already profound, deepens. Megan brushes away the dust. Something clean, black and pristine shines beneath her fingertips.

When she picks it up, the entire population of gauzy

grey figures evaporates. Dust motes drift to the ground in the windless air.

Having retrieved and repacked her knapsack, Megan now sits on the low band of stone turning over the object in her hands.

It is a thing of power, ageless and unchanged since it was created. All about it will be destruction and decay and this alone will shine. You will know it by its purity.

A disc of black crystal the size of her palm. The crystal has been intricately carved by an expert, loving hand. The lower half depicts the roots, trunk and branches of a tree. To either side of the trunk sits a crow. One faces east, the other west. The upper half of the of the disc is entirely taken up by a black crow in flight, the underside of its wings presented to the holder of the crystal, its head looking straight up as though it is soaring to the heavens. Its wings form a protective canopy over the tree and the other two crows.

Merely holding it in her hands is a balm to Megan's tired mind and body. The crystal speaks to her of creation and transformation, of the tendency for spirit to progress upwards. It reinforces her sense of treading the right path.

A voice, clear but distant, startles her: *"It's time to come back, Megan."*

She looks up from the crystal. The open space here at the centre of the city is silent and deserted. She is so tired and hungry that she knows the voice must be her imagination this time. All she wants now is to be with Mr Keeper, once more under his direction and protection, but she knows she must rest before she sets off again. Heedless of the grime, she slides down until she is lying in the dust with her head on the knapsack. She holds the crystal over her heart and places her hands over it.

Just a quick nap and then–

But she is already asleep.

72

Gordon walked until dawn but the smell of smoke on the night air never left him. The road he took from the town had suffered some damage but not enough to deny him passage. Clear of the outskirts, he left the tarmac and walked on the grass between the road and the hedges beside it.

Once it was dark, the horizon became a glowing line, the flames themselves invisible but the light they cast illuminating the canopy of cloud, a dusky orange glow rising and falling in waves to every direction. Sometimes he walked through patches of cold smoke, rolling across the land like mist. Other times his way was clear. The Earth itself was calm and quiet, but at the perimeter of his hearing its people wailed laments of injury and loss and death.

Before dawn he heard rumbling again, felt it in the soles of his feet and braced himself for destruction. It didn't come – at least not in the way he'd expected. The rumbling increased gradually, as did the vibrations in his feet. What approached was not an aftershock but a convoy. His first thought was that help was finally arriving – emergency vehicles, medical supplies and rescue workers. That thought was swiftly overruled; some instinct he couldn't define made him throw himself to the ground in the drainage ditch beneath the dense hedgerow he was following. There was no time to get through the hedge and even if he'd tried he wasn't sure he'd have made it through the tangle of thorns.

Immediately soaked by freezing filthy water, he peeped over the lip of the ditch as the convoy passed. Six grey personnel trucks, two grey Land Rovers and three grey armoured cars. Two long haulage vehicles brought up the rear, each carrying three bulldozers and a digger. Every vehicle bore the insignia of the Ward. The armoured cars had heavy machine guns mounted above their cabs.

After they'd passed he crawled out of the ditch, wet and stinking. As soon as he found a break in the hedge – a gate opening into a field in this case – he climbed over and followed the road from behind cover. The Ward had come of age: government, police force and army merged to become a single unstoppable force and, as theirs were the only vehicles on the road, Gordon had to assume they now had control of all the fuel reserves.

When light began to creep over the eastern horizon, Gordon veered away from the road and looked for shelter. Having crossed a couple of fields, he saw the remains of a building frozen corpselike against the lightening sky. Nearing it, he saw it was an old brick outbuilding with a slate roof. One end of it had collapsed in the quake, but most of it still stood. The building was already old and many of the slates were missing at the "good" end. After testing the walls and

some of the fallen beams for movement, he found a
way in through the broken wall and thrashed his way
through the weeds and nettles to the most secure-look-
ing corner of the structure. There was no floor and the
whole place smelled faintly of manure, but he could
put his tent up inside and it would be out of sight from
every direction.

The ground is uneven and uncomfortable. Megan shifts
to find a better position and knocks her head against
the wall. The wall is ridged and rough; a sharp edge
scratches her face as she turns over. Still exhausted, she
opens her eyes just for a moment.

There is no wall. There is no dust.

She scrambles to sit up and hits her head again, this
time on one of the heavy branches leaning against the
trunk of a vast tree. The branch slides off the trunk and
her shelter collapses around her. She struggles to free
herself from the fine weave of the sheet which presses
her against the gnarly bark. Megan springs away from
both tree and shelter and turns to face it, backing a few
paces towards the clearing. She has one hand on her
forehead as she tries to replay what happened after she
lay down in the centre of the city to sleep.

There are no memories. She was there and now she
is here.

The black crystal!

One thing she remembers very clearly is holding the
crystal to her chest as she fell asleep. She no longer
holds it in either hand. Near the base of the tree, partially covered by the collapsed shelter, something
reflects, concentrating the flat, grey light of the day. As
she approaches to retrieve it, a vibration comes up

through her feet.

She hesitates, glancing around the clearing. The vast space is deserted and silent. The sky beyond the outer branches of the tree is white with uniform, indistinct cloud. The bright gloom mutes every colour, deadening the land in every direction. Nothing stirs.

She takes another step and the vibration comes again, stronger this time: a tremor rising from far below. Above her, Megan senses movement. She glances up.

The branches of the tree bristle with dark crawling shapes. Some of them detach and glide slowly towards the ground on wet gossamer threads. She stifles a cry with her fist. At the centre of the tree, descending in slow spirals and sinuous meanders, legless, muscular forms approach the glint of the crystal. Every creature means to possess the black light which the engraved stone reflects. Every creature means to prevent her from taking it away. This she cannot allow.

With the ground beginning to rumble and roar, she dives for the crystal and her pack just as the first of the spiders reach the level of her head. The snakes, seeing their prize snatched up, dispense with crawling and now begin to fall from the trunk and inner boughs. By the time Megan is scrambling out towards the clearing, her knapsack hastily shouldered, it is raining serpents and eight-legged nightmares. Their intelligence and determination nauseate her. She crawls because she wants to stay below the falling spiders for as long as possible, but it means she can't move fast. She hears slithering behind her, fast and loud. Meanwhile, the first heavy-bodied spiders land on her back. She can feel the tongues of a dozen snakes tasting the soles of her boots, preparing to strike.

Megan lurches to her feet, making contact with a hundred more spiders as she rises up. Ahead of her the space beneath the lowest branches of the tree has become a forest of densely populated web. All she can do is flail her arms ahead of her to shake the spiders out of the way. She doesn't remember her knapsack being this heavy; it's enough to slow her down until she realises that the spiders on her shoulders, head and back are where the extra weight is coming from. And what's slowing her is not their weight but the mass of silk threads she is running into.

This knowledge and the touch of many spiny legs on the bare skin of her neck elicit a scream. A few more paces and she'll be stuck. Risking everything, Megan stops running and shakes her body as hard as she can. With fast fingers, she brushes away as many of the spiders as she is able to reach, careful not to leave her hands near them long enough to let them bite her. Some already have their fangs through the fabric of her clothes and she can feel their venom trickling down the naked skin of her back. She tears off her knapsack, scattering thirty or forty spiders into the arriving cohorts of their kin. Inside the pack is the knife which she unsheathes as she pulls it free. The knapsack is only a hindrance now and she throws it behind her. Thousands of crawlers and slitherers make for the pack, hoping she has relinquished the prize in a bid to escape.

Meanwhile, Megan stops flailing so wildly and begins to sweep the knife through the threads of silk which block her path. Spiders fall to the ground and scrabble towards her legs. Others fall and are caught in their own silk, only to be leapt upon by their brothers and sisters and bitten, paralysed and poisoned. Two snakes have bitten her right boot and one has bitten her left. Their fangs are locked into the leather. As she pulls them with her, other snakes use their bodies as ropes, coiling onto them in an attempt to reach her. Once again, the weight of extra bodies causes Megan's pace to slow.

She is almost out from under the branches of the tree. If she can make it that far, there will be no more cloying strands of silk to contend with. She turns and slashes down at her feet mid-stride, lifting her right ankle to meet the blade. It severs the head of one snake. As its body falls away, several other snakes are left behind with it. With a cry of determination, Megan pushes the pace. Her arms are sleeved with spiders that have latched on as she cut their drop-lines. She uses the blade to scrape them off, scattering their broken body parts left and right.

She breaks free of the tree and slashes the knife down at her other ankle. This time she misses. It takes three more attempts, each one slowing her almost to a stop before she has rid her left leg of snakes. She breaks across the clearing, making for the exact place where she entered it.

Looking back as she sprints, she sees a black sea of spiders pour out from under the tree. This sea is shot through with green and brown veins – the snakes riding over their backs. Some of the snakes are three times the length of her body. But she is free of them, she is clear of the tree.

Something sidles over her left shoulder, and out of the corner of her eye Megan sees a spider twice the size of her own hand. It lifts its front legs, exposing two

gleaming black fangs with red, needle-sharp tips. The
fangs unfold forwards and Megan sees the ugly, machi-
nating mouthparts behind them. If she uses the knife
now, she'll stab herself to kill the spider. All she can do
is swap the knife into her left hand and reach up with
her right. She grabs the spider, trying to keep her fingers away from its fangs, and pulls it off her shoulder.
Its grip is terrifyingly strong and the spider loses two
legs before she is able to tear it away. She crushes its
body in her fist until its insides burst out through its
mouth and spinnerets. Disgusted almost to the point of
vomiting, she throws its carcass away and wipes the
sticky filth of its innards on her leg.

She glances behind.

The tide of spiders and the snakes that ride them is
flowing fast, closing the space between them.

The trembling of the earth increases, causing her to
stumble. She puts out her hands to save herself from a
fall, staggering but managing to keep her balance. The
stumble costs her time, though, and her pursuers gain
ground. From behind her comes a terrible noise, something like a splintering rip in one moment, in the next,
a howl. She hazards a look over her shoulder in time to
see the tree being forced open from within. Sparks and
prongs of flame dart out of the rend in the tree's bark.
The tear extends down into the earth, which also parts
in that instant. A black-winged creature steps forth.

Megan knows she risks a fall by running forwards
and looking back but she cannot take her eyes from the
dark angel who now stands beneath the tree's spread
of branches. The tearing of its trunk is so severe, the
tree has begun to list backwards. There's a deeper tearing sound now, accompanied by the sound of roots

snapping below ground. The tree cants away from her and begins to fall, shattering branches and sending up a spray of earth and splinters. An explosion of burning heartwood bursts from the place where the tree has broken, rebounding harmlessly from the creature's black feathers but setting alight the scrubby grassland. The Crowman ignores the death of the tree.

He steps away from the destruction and upon his black-taloned feet gives chase.

73

The shade of the building and the covering of Gordon's tent weren't enough to keep out the light of day, and sleep, though he was exhausted, would not come.

He took out the letters from his mother and father and the scrapbook given to him by Knowles. He placed the black notebook in his lap and began to reread everything. The times he'd read the words of his parents had not faded the emotions they brought up for him, but he knew he had to look at them in a different way now, as if they were merely another few pages of the scrapbook. He had to find clues. He had to find names or places. He needed a method, a way of searching for the Crowman that was both safe and efficient.

He read the letters to begin with. They made more sense now. In his bleaker moments, Gordon couldn't help thinking his parents had shared some kind of delusion. Now he'd experienced for himself some of the things they'd mentioned, he knew they were sane: beautifully, naturally in tune with the land and all its creatures, open to the messages of the Earth and the Great Spirit. It had been Gordon who was deluded. Deluded and ignorant. Now he knew the power they'd

talked about. It had flowed through him. And sometimes, when he prayed, those prayers were answered
as though the Great Spirit and the Earth Mother were
standing right in front of him doing as he asked.

But his power was dark too, and he had used it both
to protect himself and to punish. In his heart he knew
that to fight evil with evil was wrong, that it didn't
work. Yet his rage, his offended soul, demanded retri-
bution and the ending of evil men.

The Ward were the hands of evil on Earth, control-
ling people, using up every resource in their pursuit of
dominion. They said their mission was to destroy the
Crowman and thereby save the world, but all they
really wanted to preserve was their hold on everything.
They had become the right arm of a vast, globally active
corporate mind which saw only profit and loss in all
things, which understood and lived only for the sake of
self-perpetuation and growth at any and all costs. To
serve the self at the expense of the lives of others and
the life of the world itself, this was the greatest evil
Gordon could imagine. From such thinking was all
malevolence born.

To oppose that would take a strength, perhaps
unimaginable. Gordon knew he did not possess it. No
single creature in existence did. But together, perhaps,
united in some way by spirit, the creatures of the land
and its people and the very land itself might work
against the Ward and remove their grey-gloved fingers
from around the world's throat.

The Ward were an outward manifestation of the
greed and terror in every heart. For too long people had
been encouraged to care only for themselves and to
take what they could whenever they could get it. They

had become ignorant and blind. Yet the seed of reversal existed in every heart. This seed was an idea that had to spread, a way of thinking that had always existed within every human but one which had been drowned by the lure of technology. The Green Men understood this and were mounting their resistance.

One thing Gordon knew about the Crowman without having ever met him: he was the figurehead of this seed of reversal, this old idea, he was the symbol by which people would remember what an existence on this Earth, what a simple life played out upon the land, was all about.

The scrapbook was less useful in defining these things.

Too often the Crowman was portrayed as evil or, at the very least, terrifying. Yet the fact that he had visited so many people in dreams and visions was a sign that the ideas he represented, the things he stood for were alive and well all over the country. Gordon was sure this scrapbook was only one of many that the Ward had gathered, stolen or collected along with their owners, people who had died revealing what little they knew about the dark phantom who'd haunted their nightmares and daydreams.

Gordon resolved in that moment that even if the Crowman was nothing more than an idea or a spirit, he would still seek him out and reveal him to the world. It was what his parents wanted him to do. More than that, since the gift of the Black Light he knew beyond any doubt that this was his purpose. He would use his life to make up for all those which had been destroyed by the Ward and everything they represented.

Inspired but no wiser, Gordon scanned the leaves of

the scrapbook for signs: any evidence, any kind of
pointer that might lead physically and directly to the
Crowman. There was passion on every page, so much
the book almost hummed with emotion. People had
written poetry in rage or fear or fervour. They had told
allegorical stories, embellishing their handwriting with
scrolls and flowers and animals of the hedgerow like
devout monks. These flashes of creativity must have
come suddenly and unexpectedly to their seers. They
had used whatever was nearby to capture the assault of
inspiration upon them. With furious strokes they had
inked their visions in biro onto lined A4 paper, pen-
cilled their hallucinations in verse on paper napkins
and hotel notepaper. Gordon believed that some of the
sketches and lines, a rusty brown in the scrapbook,
were written in blood. Until now he'd wondered how
or why anyone would choose to record their phan-
tasms in that way. Today it made more sense. What the
many creators of the scrapbook were really communi-
cating was that their message was more important than
their own lives, that their message must survive even
though they might not. The place in each person where
such intensity arose was the place where love and
death acknowledged each other: in the heart. When
everything else was taken away only this remained, the
dark fire of the heart, here spilled and thrust onto mis-
cellaneous pages and collected in the scrapbook.

Whether he found in it the directions he so dearly
sought had less significance now than preserving the
scrapbook's revelation of what lay at people's core. The
spirit of the Crowman was alive in this book, and Gordon meant to keep it that way.

His skimming and scanning of the pages brought him

to an enraged representation of the twisted tree he was so familiar with. At the crest of a windswept, barren-looking hill stood this tree and above it circled a vast black bird – something like a giant raven. Crows sat among the dead branches of the tree, and at the base of the hill, great lines of people passed by looking upwards. What interested Gordon was not so much the subject matter; he'd seen it in his dreams and in the scrapbook more times now than he could count, and he knew beyond doubt it was important. But this particular representation was drawn from a different viewpoint. In the far distance there was a skyline not shown in any other drawing. It showed vast, squat buildings, many of them ruined by some unknown cataclysm but still standing. The structures were industrial, not a container port exactly but something similar. Warehouses? Storage units? Whatever the case, Gordon was pretty certain he could memorise the low, broken form of this skyline and the two enormous wind turbines that marked each end of the buildings. This was more solid intelligence than he'd been able to glean in all the time he'd had the scrapbook. If he came across the location, he was sure he'd be able to recognise it. Delighted, he scanned every sketch, story and poem again and again, searching for common themes.

The Crowman, Black Jack, Scarecrow: these were the names people gave him. Some saw him as supremely evil, others as selflessly good. No one seemed certain if he was a man, or part man and part animal. Like the Ward, many seemed to believe his arrival on Earth would trigger the end of the world. Just as many believed he had come with a message of hope for the future. Gordon wondered if there was a way that both these things could be true. Maybe none of the authors of the scrapbook were completely right, yet perhaps all of them were right in certain aspects.

The sun arced over the half-collapsed barn, brightening the tent, and Gordon put aside his studies for a moment. He needed a break and the touch of the open air. Unzipping the tent, he slipped out and stood in the shelter of the ruined brick walls. He crossed to one glassless window and looked out.

Far across the fields he could see the road along which the Ward had arrived at the ruined town in their military convoy. How long would it be before the people he'd helped told them what he'd done and pointed in the direction he'd taken when he left? Wardsmen might already be coming back up that road by car or on foot to look for him. Something about being pursued in this way was tiring to his very soul. He knew they'd never stop searching; no matter what he did, he would always be on the run.

From the very beginning, a small voice within him had whispered that he should give himself up to the Ward or, at the very least, let them catch him. Then it would be over and he could rest. Stronger by far, however, were the voices that pushed him onwards, those of his mother and father and Judith, the voices of the animals and the call of the land. Most profound, most resonant of all was a voice from within, the source of which he could not define. This was a voice that called him onwards and commanded that he never lose faith. He had come to think of it as the voice of the Crowman. He believed that not only was he destined to find the Crowman, but that the Crowman wanted to be found – specifically by Gordon.

As he looked across the fields, smoke rose from the devastated town and Gordon considered, not for the first time and knowing that it would not be the last, that he might simply be mad. Only an insane person would allow themselves to be led across the country by disembodied voices. Maybe the intervention of the Ward in his life had been too much for his rational mind to bear. Unable to deal with the collection of his family, he had simply created a fantasy in which he could exist, not safely perhaps, but without ever having to face the reality that everyone he cared about and everything he loved might be dead, gone forever without hope of retrieval.

His eyes filled and tears overflowed without a hitch in his breathing. There were no sobs or whimpers. If he could think these things, he knew he could not be insane. This mission of his, this destiny his parents had told him was his to fulfil, it was not something that thrived on being thought about or pondered. It was not the conjuration of a sick mind. It was, just like every seemingly mad but incredibly sane piece of art in the scrapbook, the commanding of a true and honest heart that pushed him forwards and kept him moving. This was not some clever idea about the way life should be. It was about the survival of right living, it was about the survival of the spirit in a world where spirit had been superseded by technology and greed.

He collapsed to his knees in the barn and thrust his fingers through the cracks to touch the earth below. Its coolness welcomed his fingertips.

"Give me strength," he whispered. "Send me every helper you can and all the luck you have. And even if you can't do that, I swear I'll give you everything I

have. I'll keep searching. I'll keep fighting. And I'll
never give up until I find him. If I die trying, I know my
life will have been well spent."

The sky darkened overhead and Gordon smiled, eyes
closed, tears coursing down his face and dripping
through the barn's broken floor to touch the cold black
earth below. Distant thunder unrolled, approaching
across the landscape. The earth shuddered and then all
was silent and still.

His very blood alive with energy for the search, he
packed everything up. He felt no need for rest. He
pulled on his pack and strode from the barn. Outside a
gloom had fallen across the land, so deep and sullen it
might have been twilight. Gordon thanked the life in
everything for these midday shadows, knowing they
would conceal him as he continued on his journey.

74

Megan has nothing left but her will to protect herself and the crystal. She draws it out now from her pocket, holds it tight and prays for help in the name of the land and every sacred thing that lives upon it. There is no doubt that strength comes to her in response, rising up from the earth and filling her legs with the resilience and agility of a deer. She speeds towards the trees, opening up a little distance between her and the black and green spill of snakes and spiders.

The Crowman has already cleared his tide of familiars. He is fleet of foot in a way Megan will never match. In the open she cannot outrun him. Her only chance is the trees. There's a small chance she'll be more nimble through the forest and its obstacles. The world turns several shades darker as she breaks into the woodland. Her feet skip light and quick over fallen branches, and she dodges between closely spaced trees and through small breaks in thickets, knowing he will have to go around.

Another rearward glance.

No sign of the Crowman.

Triumphant but not yet daring to slow the pace,

Megan sprints onwards through the forest, covering ground in minutes which took hours to pass through on her way in. She is inspired and powerful. Her legs could carry her like this for miles. The terrain will have slowed the spiders and snakes. Looking behind her, there's no sign of them. Like their master, they may not even have followed her into the wood. None of this is enough to slow her. She must make all the ground she can.

When she can maintain the sprint no longer she slows to a good run, knowing that if she can maintain it, she'll be back in Bodbran's hovel before the day is done.

At first the shadow catches her eye and she assumes it is nothing more than the flashing past of tree trunks. The shadow passes over the ground moving faster than her, sometimes across her path, sometimes in the direction she runs in and sometimes against it. A dark silhouette flits through the already shaded world of the forest. She fears he has sent the ghost of himself to claim her; she knows he must have that kind of power. And then something causes her to look up and she sees vast black wings spread wide overhead. The Crowman tracks her from above, gliding silent and without effort while she pounds her legs and wracks her chest for air.

She falters.

If he can do this, he can take her anytime he wants to. What is the point in trying to flee? He will descend on her the way a falcon takes a dove. He will take her and he will take the crystal too. As she is about to give up, she hears a clear, strong voice. It comes from all around her.

"Come back, Megan. You're almost home."

This voice, though it has no owner and may be nothing more than her imagination trying to keep her spirit aflame, is enough to keep her running.

The open ground on the other side of the forest is dangerous and if he is going to fall upon her, that is where he will do it, but at least she will see the sky again before the end comes, and if she can find the strength to sprint again, there are places where she can take cover when he dives. If she is going to die, it will not be with a curse upon her soul: she will die trying to return the crystal to Bodbran and trying to reach Mr Keeper. She will die trying to return home. She races for the edge of the forest.

It is nearer than she remembers.

She runs from heavy cover into sparsely spaced, smaller trees and in swift order she is covering open ground. In the far distance she can see the smoke which rises over Shep Afon. High above she hears the triumphant, jeering call of a crow.

She ignores it.

Ahead is a bank of hawthorn that will give good cover. She looks up to check his position and he is in stoop, falling fast, wings pulled tight and short, neck outstretched, claws drawn back but ready to strike. As she nears the hawthorn and looks for a place to duck into, four black-hooded figures step forwards from between the thorny branches. Each carries a catapult. They aim into the sky and fire.

Megan makes it to the hawthorn and dives behind Bodbran's girls. She looks back to see the Crowman has veered away, flapping hard to gain altitude.

"Thank you," she pants. "Thank you. Thank you."

The figures ignore her, keeping their eyes skyward

and taking more projectiles from small sacks which hang at their waists. They release another volley of shots high into the air. Megan, who has landed on her front in the dirt, doesn't see if the missiles make contact. She crawls deeper into cover, labouring for breath, suddenly drained.

A voice comes from within the hawthorn, not from the figures who protect her:

"Don't give up yet."

Rallied, she crawls on through the hawthorn, catching her face and shoulders on its woody barbs. Thorns which have dropped to the ground now penetrate her palms and fingers, but she ignores the pain. She comes to the other side of the trees, stands up and begins to run again. It is a fast trudge now.

She runs like an old man wearing lead shoes, but she runs. From far above she hears the frustrated cry of the Crowman and from behind the thump of booted feet as Bodbran's hooded assistants run to follow and protect her. She doesn't look back. Ignoring the ache and weight in her legs, Megan keeps running.

She can't feel her legs any more.

All around her the colour bleeds from the land. She spares a glance for this and sees the sky has darkened to twilight in a matter of moments. Darkness falls but not because the night has come; the Crowman has drawn his black wings across the sun. He means to hunt her in darkness so Bodbran's helpers can help no more.

Down comes the blackness and the stars shine from ill-dignified positions in the sky. But for the faint starlight it is full dark. Megan's eyes don't have a chance to adjust. She runs blind now and soon she begins to stumble, unable to see where she is putting her feet. One boot half slips into a small rut, something that by day she would have stepped into or around without any trouble, and Megan falls.

She waits for the impact, expecting the ground to thrust what little wind she has left from her lungs and knock her half senseless in the process. She never makes contact. The fall lengthens into a dive, into a plummet. Through the Crowman's woeful night she plunges into an abyss and, she expects, into the embrace of his black wings.

The fall slows; the liquid rush of darkness all around solidifies and she floats. She has a sense of looking upwards from a supine posture. The floating sensation quickly leaves her, to be replaced by the ponderous drag of incorporation. She sinks into her exhausted body, not wanting to return to it but having no way to resist the process. She feels the pressure and discomfort of uneven ground pressing up into her back, smells burning tallow and smoky spice. A wheezing, phlegm-speckled voice breathes:

"Do you have it, girl? Did you bring me the Crowspar?"

Megan tries to speak but her throat is dry and closed.

The Crowspar.

She pats her pocket with her hand and feels the carved crystal disk safely within. Unable to utter a word, she nods instead. Bony hands are upon her immediately, invading her pocket and removing the crystal before she can resist or even raise a word of protest.

There's an admiring sigh followed by a long spasm of coughing, and Megan knows without opening her eyes that Bodbran has what she wants. Finally, she is able to part her leaden eyelids. Her body won't respond to her commands. Through the crack she has created, she sees Bodbran turning over the Crowspar in her ancient hands, admiring it by the light of the candles. Black auras and sparks of black light jump from the crystal wherever the old woman's fingers touch it. She chuckles, presses the carved disk between her fingers and kisses it. When she takes her hands away from each other, the Crowspar is gone.

Megan tries to sit up but she's paralysed. A grunt escapes her lips and her eyes widen. Other than that she is utterly immobile. The thing she has risked everything to find has vanished. Bodbran chuckles again, patting Megan's thigh.

"Not to worry, Megan Maurice. Not to worry. You've done a fine job. You've done as we asked and no one could ask for more." Bodbran stands up – this shocks Megan, who has supposed the old woman was crippled because she never moved her legs. The blanket falls away and she is naked. Her pierced breasts swing like empty sacks, her folds of belly-flesh hang over her crotch, hiding her womanhood from Megan's sight. Her dirty legs are like sticks wrapped in loose brown leather. From her lips hangs a half-smoked cone. Her face sags like that of a bloodhound but she is smiling. "You've done all right, girl. Time to go home now, eh?"

Bodbran begins to unwrap the reeds from her hovel, exposing Megan to the sky. It is not night time. Instead the sky is bright with mid-morning sun. Bodbran peels away the coverings of her home and sounds rush in – the swoosh of the river, the clank and creak of the waterwheels, the chatter of buyers and traders in the market. When she has finished unwrapping the reeds, Bodbran squats beside Megan and places a gentle palm on her chest.

Megan opens her eyes wider and sees not Bodbran but Mr Keeper kneeling beside her on the sandy bank of the river. He is smiling. On her other side sits Carrick Rowntree, smoking a pipe and nodding to her.

"Well done, Megan," he says between puffs. "Well done indeed."

The immobility of her body seeps away and she regains control of her limbs. Blinking and swallowing, she pushes herself up onto her elbows and then sits up. The effort makes her queasy and she sways a little. Mr Keeper steadies her and holds up a water skin. She drinks a few sips and the water is like medicine; her mind reawakens and her body revitalises. She rubs her face with her hands and sits up straight to look around.

They are sitting in the makeshift camp they made after their meal in the hub.

"How long have I been…"

"Just for the afternoon, Megan," says Mr Keeper.

"But I was away for two days and nights."

"That's how the Weave works," says the old man.

She considers this but it only creates more questions.

"You said 'well done'. How do you even know what I did?"

"Because we journeyed with you," says Mr Keeper. "Don't you remember?"

Megan thinks back to the times she looked behind her in the forest, certain someone was following her. She remembers the wrens.

"That was you?"

Both Mr Keeper and the old man nod. Their grins are

touched with mischievous embarrassment.

"Why did you do this?" asks Megan. "What did you do?"

"We took a sacrament, Megan. We ate it together in the market and then we returned here so you could make your journey."

"What was the sacrament?"

"It's a kind of fungus," says Mr Keeper. "You and I have collected and dried it on many occasions. It belongs to the sacred family of teacher plants, left on earth by the Great Spirit to help us pursue wisdom. Even if we lost all our knowledge, the teacher plants would be there to help us rediscover it."

Megan stands up and stretches. Her body aches exactly as though she has been on the journey she remembers. She takes a few steps towards the river and then turns back, every question that arises in her mind giving birth to two more.

"Is Bodbran real?"

"Everything is real," says the old man.

Suddenly, Megan remembers the spiders and snakes and the tearing open of the vast tree in the clearing. She falls to her knees on the damp sand, crying.

"Why?" she asks. "Why is the Crowman so cruel?"

Mr Keeper rushes to her side and squats next to her in the sand.

"Everything has two sides. You've seen the side of the Crowman that is Black Jack. But he didn't harm you – other than to give you a scare. He introduced you to your fears and caused you to confront them. He made you discover more strength within yourself, Megan." Mr Keeper puts an arm around her shoulder and holds her to him. It's an unusual display of closeness, but she welcomes it. Mr Keeper is all the family she's got now. "And, what's more, he led you to the source of the Black Light. Even among the Keepers there are very few who ever set eyes upon the Crowspar, let alone hold it in their hands. You must understand how blessed you are."

Megan's weeping worsens. She is disorientated by the concertinaing of time and the contradictions of her journey. She is exhausted and sore. Softly, Mr Keeper leads her back to the shelter on the sand and lays her down. He covers her and soothes her as though she is an infant, and like an infant she is soon asleep, tears drying on her hot red cheeks.

After a time, Carrick Rowntree speaks.

"She could be the one."

And, after a time, Mr Keeper nods.

"She is," he says. "She is the one."

75

"Unfortunately, it has taken our ex-colleague, Wardsman Knowles, several days to share his knowledge with us."

Skelton addressed the assembled Wardsmen he'd brought with him from London and those from the Monmouth substation.

"More unfortunate even than this, it transpires that the man had little more information for us than the boy's family. We can now be fairly sure that Gordon Black did enter the disused railway tunnel and that he did find a way through the blockage. Knowles told us that the boy was in receipt of letters written by both his parents and that these letters, given to the boy by Knowles when they met at the mouth of the tunnel, instructed the boy to run and not turn himself in. Knowles also gave him one of the more telling scrapbooks from the prophetic archive."

Pike stood to Skelton's left, waxwork-still with his slab-like hands clasped in front of him. The only clue he was alive; an occasional blink of his sunken eyes.

"We can therefore reasonably assume a couple of things. First, Gordon Black has run as far away from

here as he can. We now have to make this a nation-
wide search and ask for assistance from other
substations around the country. Second, if he wasn't
aware of the Crowman prophecies before meeting
Knowles, he certainly is now. How the knowledge will
affect him is impossible to predict. If we're lucky it may
make him unstable and he may be easier to bring in. In
the worst-case scenario, the stories of the Crowman
will boost his confidence, perhaps give him some kind
of goal to work towards.

"We can take nothing for granted now, in any case.
The boy is dangerous and determined. The days of a
simple capture and swift conclusion to this problem
have passed. We're into a long phase now. What works
in our favour is that Gordon Black doesn't have anything like the amount of data that we have – we know
his family, much of his personal history and possibly
some of his future. He, on the other hand, is travelling
blind. He is but one against many. What works against
us is that he may be just another boy on the run. We've
caught enough of those already to know that red her-
rings are everywhere. But the more we've watched
Gordon Black and the more… dealings we've had with
him, the more certain I've become that he is the one
whose capture may mean an end to the cataclysm the
prophecies predict.

"From now on, most of you will take alter egos and
work under cover. If that boy sees a speck of grey he's
going to run. Pike here is going to hand out reports and
instructions. Each pair of you going out will take
different directions and link with different operatives
dependent on the counties you pass through. You'll go
on foot as we can no longer afford the number of

vehicles necessary to do this the easy way. In addition, as you all know, all mobile phone networks are suffering interference at the moment. Should it become necessary, I will expect you to write your reports and deliver them by hand. According to the Met Office, the sunspot activity is set to worsen.

"One final thing. The ideal scenario will be to find him before he hits puberty. A high proportion of the prophetic texts we've gathered point to the child's boyhood as a crucial and therefore vulnerable time. The quicker we do this, the better. I only hope we're not too late." Skelton appraised the silent faces. "Any questions?"

One hand went up.

"Yes, Jones."

"If we find the boy and he puts up a fight, what lengths can we go to bring him in?"

"You may use any means at your disposal. But he must be brought in alive or you'll join him in Hades. Understood?"

"Yes, sir."

"Good. Anything else?"

There were no other raised hands.

"In that case, I wish you all the luck in the world. After all, the world now depends on you apprehending Gordon Black."

EPILOGUE

And so it was that the boy began his journey, torn from family and stained by the blood of those who stood in his way. An innocent, transformed by hardship and the demands of a sickened Earth. Guided by the mother and father of us all, he took his first steps into manhood.

His search for the Crowman was far from over, but his faith in the land had been rewarded. He stepped into power, into the mighty shadow of the Black Light. Under cover of that sacred dusk he sought out the dark force which would reunite us with the Earth, healing all rifts.

And yet, whether he was to succeed in this or not, the boy's every effort would have been as naught had it not been for another. A girl of whom he knew nothing. A girl as yet unborn. A girl of whom he could, at best, only dream. Without her, triumphant or defeated, his travails would be utterly wasted.

For, without the teller, there can be no tale.

AND IT WILL COME TO PASS

THE BOOK
OF THE
CROWMAN

THE BLACK DAWN VOL II